ABOUT THE

Meredith Appleyard lives in the Clare Valley wine-growing region of South Australia. When a friend challenged Meredith to do what she'd always wanted to do – write a novel – she saved up, took time off work, sat down at the computer and wrote her first novel. Realising after the first rejection letter she needed to learn more about the craft of writing, she attended workshops, joined a writers' group and successfully completed an Advanced Diploma of Arts in Professional Writing with the Adelaide Centre for Arts. Meredith lives with her husband and border collie Lily, and when she's not writing she's reading!

meredithappleyard.com.au

Also by Meredith Appleyard

Home at Last
When Grace Went Away
All About Ella
Becoming Beth
Daisy and Kate

The SEACHANGERS

MEREDITH APPLEYARD

The Seachangers
© 2024 by Meredith Appleyard
ISBN 9781867271208

First published on Gadigal Country in Australia in 2024
by HQ Fiction
an imprint of HQBooks (ABN 47 001 180 918), a subsidiary of HarperCollins Publishers
Australia Pty Limited (ABN 36 009 913 517).

HarperCollins acknowledges the Traditional Custodians of the lands upon which we live
and work, and pays respect to Elders past and present.

A catalogue record for this book is available from the National Library of Australia
www.librariesaustralia.nla.gov.au

Printed and bound in Australia by McPherson's Printing Group

MIX
Paper | Supporting
responsible forestry
FSC
www.fsc.org   FSC® C001695

Be yourself; everyone else is already taken.

1

Ruth

I flipped the sign on the door of Rosie's Cafe from closed to open and caught a glimpse of my tired self reflected in the glass. It was eight o'clock Tuesday morning. Again. Where had the past week gone? There were tentative signs of life on the main street and the visible line of sky was an uninspiring gunmetal grey. Parked along the kerb opposite the cafe stood the usual line-up of tradies' vehicles; the hardware opened at seven thirty. So did the bakery, with their menu of iced coffees, meat pies and sticky buns. I yawned and polished away a smudge of fingerprints with the corner of my apron. A delivery truck lumbered past. Litter skittered in its wake. Good morning, Cutlers Bay.

Rosie's Cafe was closed Sundays, Mondays and public holidays. Over the years, I'd lost count of how many well-meaning customers had advised me that I was crazy for not opening every day, but Mondays and public holidays were non-negotiable. Not even during the summer break, when folk flocked to the seaside towns on the Yorke Peninsula. But the Sundays? I'd reluctantly put aside my own needs and bowed to local pressure to open the cafe, but only over the holiday season. Rosie's only opened from nine until two on the weekends, but the summer days were long and the cafe was at its busiest. I needed my Mondays off, because when was I supposed to go to the dentist or the doctor, do my own shopping, visit a friend and have them make me a coffee, or heaven forbid, leave town for a few hours?

Now, with December a mere month away, an insidious dread curled its way into my stomach every time I thought about giving up one of my precious days off. My days off didn't come around quickly enough, or last long enough as it was. Often there'd be baking to do, tea towels and aprons to wash and supplies to be ordered for the coming week. And the banking and any extraneous paperwork. But at least I could lie in; get up at eight not six, or five, depending on how much catching up there was to do. I could sit down and eat a leisurely lunch, instead of quick bites grabbed on the run.

On the way back to the counter, I straightened chairs and tidied condiment sets on the tables, my actions rote. Once upon a time these simple tasks had filled me with joy and pride. My own cafe. I was the boss. What an achievement.

Taking a deep breath, I squared my shoulders and mentally ran through the daily checklist: coffee machine on and seasoned; grill heating; fryer ready; chairs down and tables clean; dishwasher on; drinks fridge and undercounter milk fridge restocked … a quick double-check of the cake cabinet and muffin basket—loaded and ready to go. With a pang of something akin to disappointment, I realised that less than half of the cakes and slices on display were homemade. At the beginning of this venture, I had prepared and baked everything on the premises. Homemade food with healthy choices available, all served in a homely environment, had been my vision for the cafe. I'd firmly resisted commercially produced fare. I'd worked around the clock to avoid it. But the years had taken their toll on my energy and enthusiasm and if I thought I could get away with it, the current menu would shrink and even more of the choices on display would be commercially produced.

The front door squealed and, regular as clockwork, Audrey Franco came in clutching her pink to-go mug. Audrey was a volunteer at the op shop around the corner and my first customer every Tuesday morning.

'Good heavens, Ruth, why on earth don't you put a few drops of oil on those hinges. The door wouldn't make such a dreadful racket.'

'Good morning, Audrey! With luck we might see some sunshine this afternoon. The usual?'

'Yes, please.' She handed over the insulated cup, her gaze firmly fixed on the basket of muffins under the mesh cover. 'Are they chocolate-chip muffins?'

'Blueberry, with fresh blueberries.'

'Oh, lovely. I can convince myself I'm being halfway healthy if it's fruit rather than chocolate. Have you heard the news?'

'I hear a lot of news, Audrey. What specifically?'

'Cutlers Bay Financial Services is closing its doors. Graham Wurst is retiring at the end of the year,' she said with a self-satisfied smirk.

'Is that so? I hadn't heard. I wouldn't have thought he was old enough to retire. He's not sick, is he?'

'Not to my knowledge.' She sniffed. 'Besides, how old is old enough to retire? My Reggie was seventy-two when he eventually downed tools. Now look at him—all he does is sit in front of the telly and watch Netflix and that Tube thing.'

Seventy-two. The thought of doing what I was doing for another decade was enough to make my skin prickle. With the lid firmly fixed onto Audrey's flat white with one, I bagged up a blueberry muffin, still warm from the oven. 'There you go. Do you think Graham and Marcia will stay put in Cutlers Bay?'

'Unlikely,' Audrey said with confidence. 'Marcia's never made a secret of the fact she thinks we're all a bit *rural*. And their children and grandchildren live in Adelaide.'

'What about Graham's clients? What will they do?'

'Apparently,' Audrey said, leaning in and giving me a close-up of what you did with lipstick when you had no lips, 'his son has a similar business in the city and he'll take on the clients, those who choose not to move elsewhere.'

'I see. Just how old do you reckon Graham is?' I'd always put him at around my age: early sixties. Too young to retire.

'He's fifty-seven. But in my opinion, he looks older. And before you ask, Marcia's sixty. Or so Peg says.'

'Really,' I said and tried not to sound as disgruntled as I felt because Graham was half a decade younger than me and he was retiring. 'Peg would know.'

Peg and her husband owned the fish and chip shop and Peg's vast and real-time knowledge of local goings-on was legend. Basically, if it'd happened in Cutlers Bay or surrounds, Peg knew about it. But I'd never thought of her as a gossip. She dispensed information prudently, without elaboration or exaggeration, and by all accounts, if the situation required, she could be stubbornly tight-lipped.

'I'd better be on my way,' Audrey said after I'd passed over her change and initialled her loyalty card. 'I'm opening up this morning and Tuesdays are always frantic.'

She held the door for the next customers: two women who worked in the hospital's administration office. They walked to work and stopped in for coffee on their way.

'What'll it be this morning?' I said and accompanied it with as genuine a smile as I could muster. Only fifty-seven and retiring … How dare he?

And so went my morning. The same routine as every other. Mostly takeaway coffees and snacks until mid-morning when the 'have heres' out for coffee and a chat trickled in, along with the usual regulars. Theo Adams was one such regular: Tuesday and Thursday mornings on the dot of nine thirty he shuffled in for a milky cappuccino and two thickly buttered slices of toasted raisin bread. Another menu choice I used to bake myself. Now it came pre-sliced in a plastic bag.

'You're looking bright and chipper, Theo, for an overcast Tuesday morning.'

'Ruth,' he replied, nodding and doffing an imaginary hat. He moved across to his usual table by the window—table three. I watched and wondered briefly if his gait had worsened. For a moment I thought he might topple over. Then his face relaxed into a rare smile when he spied today's *Advertiser* waiting on the table. I dropped two slices of raisin bread into the toaster and made his coffee. Theo was well into his eighties and had been a regular at the cafe since his wife had died several years ago. It was plain to see that his health was failing. How much longer he'd be able to navigate his way to the cafe two mornings a week was anyone's guess.

While I frothed milk, I contemplated how easy it was to identify the day of the week just by who sat at which table. Tuesday and Thursday were Theo's; Wednesday mornings brought the Cutlers Bay version of the yummy mummies, with their designer pushers and destructive toddlers, and occasionally a group of women golfers red-cheeked and gloating. Or the bowlers out for a bite of lunch. Third Thursday of the month brought the book club ladies. They'd laugh and talk loudly; every now and then they'd discuss books. Their appetite for cake and coffee was vast so I did nothing to discourage them. And on it went.

Allie Thomas breezed in at ten, blonde ponytail bouncing, all set to go in navy blue polo shirt with *Rosie's Cafe* embroidered in gold above the pocket. Allie worked Tuesday to Friday from ten until two thirty; later if needed, but only ever until school was out. She was a single mum and adamant her children, now teenagers, wouldn't come home to an empty house. I valued her intelligence and quick-wittedness and that she was not afraid of work. I didn't know what

I'd do without her. After three years, we worked together like a well-oiled machine and my only regret was that she hadn't been with me since I'd first opened.

Over the course of time, I'd learned that Allie's husband and the father of her children had made a hasty and unexpected exit only weeks after their second child was born. 'Brett decided he didn't want to be tied down with a family after all,' was how Allie had put it. She'd never elaborated and I would never ask. What role Allie's ex played in the ongoing parenting of their children was unknown to me. Except for that one time, she'd never mentioned him again. Or his parents, Mia and Cody's other set of grandparents. The split had happened long before we'd met and from what I'd observed, she'd done an amazing job as a single parent. Cody, her youngest, had recently turned thirteen and Mia was seventeen. I'd had little to do with Cody or Mia until about six months ago when Mia started working at Rosie's on Saturday mornings. She'd picked up the routine in no time and was proving to be a quick and efficient worker. She didn't have much to say, unlike Suzie, another of the young casuals who never shut up, but Mia didn't miss much of what went on around her.

'Are you okay, Ruth?' Allie said in a brief lull between the morning crowd and lunch. 'You seem a bit flat today.'

'Graham Wurst is retiring,' I said as I stacked clean cups and mugs onto the top of the espresso machine. 'He's five years younger than I am.'

'Ruth! You sound as if you're jealous.'

I paused for a moment and stared into space. 'You know, I think I might be,' I said, as much to my own amazement as hers. 'But goodness knows what I'd do to fill in the time without the cafe. I've always worked at one job or another.'

'Ha! Mum said that until she retired a couple of years ago. Dad grumbles because he sees less of her now than he did when she worked full time. She volunteers, belongs to a quilting group, plays mahjong—' Allie raised her eyebrows, '—and has no time for an extended visit to give me a break from the kids. But good luck to her, I say. She's already raised one family.'

The cafe started to fill with the lunchtime crowd, about average for a Tuesday, and any conversation with Allie was limited to clarifying orders and brief instructions. Another pair of hands would have been helpful at this time of the day, but the busy spurt only lasted a couple of hours at the most and Tuesday afternoons were traditionally dead, so we managed. If there were groups booked on a Tuesday or Wednesday, I'd call in an extra casual to cover the rush and the clean-up afterwards. Thursdays, Fridays and Saturdays were busier and there was always three of us.

By two thirty, only two tables remained occupied. I was at the kitchen sink, washing up dishes that didn't fit into the dishwasher. The kitchen was partitioned off from the main counter and cafe proper by a wall with a servery window. With the ovens, grill, fryer, fridge and freezer, it was hot and the hissing and gurgling dishwasher added to the mugginess.

'You go home,' I said when Allie bustled in carrying several stray pieces of crockery and cutlery.

'Table seven want more drinks,' she said, scraping food scraps into the bin. 'I can stay a bit longer if you like.'

I shook my head. 'Go. I'll be fine, thanks.' I washed and dried my hands. 'Laurie'll be here later to put up the chairs and do the floors.'

Laurie Randall was a gentle giant of a man, a retired farmer and another, more recent, widower. Unlike Theo Adams, I'd never thought of Laurie as a regular—he'd appear every now and then for scones with jam and cream and a pot of tea. Then one afternoon several months ago, we'd started chatting while he'd lingered over his second cup of English Breakfast. He'd been the only customer in the cafe and was telling me how much he missed his wife; that he had no idea how to fill in his days.

'The house is so empty,' he'd said. 'And although he'd never say it to my face, the lad doesn't want me out at the farm poking my nose into whatever he's up to.'

'What about the men's shed? I've heard they do all manner of things there. Audrey Franco said they made a bookshelf for the op shop.'

He'd scoffed. 'A team of horses couldn't drag me there, nothing but a mob of old gossips.'

Closing time had come and I'd begun stacking the chairs onto the tables ready to sweep before I mopped the floor. Wordlessly, Laurie had pushed himself to his feet, taken his empty cup and teapot to the counter and then helped me lift chairs. The following afternoon he'd reappeared minutes before four and the moment I'd spun the sign on the front door he'd started lifting chairs onto the tables. By the end of the week we'd come to an arrangement: for a few home-cooked meals and the occasional fruit cake, he'd do the chairs and the floors and any other jobs I asked him to do from Tuesday to Friday. So far he'd only missed one afternoon—he'd had a doctor's appointment. He did a more thorough job of the floor than I did.

'I'll be off then,' Allie said and collected her belongings from the cupboard shelf set aside for that purpose. With a wave and a flip of her ponytail, she let herself out the kitchen door. It opened into a narrow service lane where the gas bottles stood and the rubbish bins were stowed. The mop and bucket lived beside the tap and outdoor sink. I washed my hands and went to make more coffee for table seven.

Three hours later, I was still at it. Motivated by my earlier self-reproach, an orange and poppyseed cake cooled on a rack and two trays of muesli slice were turning golden brown in the oven. The slice was a favourite, another recipe of Mum's. All the recipes I used were Mum's, rejigged to suit the circumstances. Many of her recipes worked just as well if you doubled or even tripled the ingredients. Others, I'd discovered, required tweaking.

While the cake and then the slices were in the oven I'd restocked the fridges and finished unpacking and putting away the morning's wholesale order. In the early days of the business, I'd sourced as much local produce and groceries as I could. But then the fruit and veg shop had gone bust during Covid and I'd been forced to procure fresh produce from a supplier out of Adelaide. Then it became easier to get everything from the one place. Deliveries came twice a week. On the odd occasion I ran out of an item or I missed it on the order, I'd shoot up the street to the IGA supermarket. Bread and bread rolls were the only items I bought locally.

Laurie had been and gone, and the floors were squeaky clean and the bins out on the kerb for collection the following morning. He'd left with a spring in his step and a green supermarket bag weighed down with six frozen single-serve meals and a sultana cake. While I waited for the muesli slices to cool enough to store, I shredded lettuce and sliced tomatoes and cucumbers ready for the next day's sandwiches.

On a positive note, when it finally came time to go home, I didn't have far to go, because I lived in the residence at the rear of the cafe. About twenty steps took me through the office, past the storeroom door and into the compact and comfortable living space. Home. A two-bedroomed flat. It hadn't taken me long to discover what a mixed blessing those twenty steps were. Even after I'd closed the doors between the cafe and the office and then the office and my living room, some days I felt as if I'd never actually left work.

★ ★ ★

That night after I'd showered and stumbled into bed, I didn't immediately drop off into the customary coma. I was exhausted but for some reason my mind refused to acquiesce to the relentless pleas from my aching limbs. I blamed Graham Wurst and his pending retirement. How dare he retire and at fifty-seven. Here I was at sixty-two without so much as a plan for when I might retire.

Life had panned out far differently than I'd ever envisaged. But then, whose life doesn't? When it all boils down, we have far less control over what happens to us than we think we do. If I hadn't become increasingly dissatisfied and disillusioned with my job in the months after Mum died, would I have made the seachange to Cutlers Bay? Probably not. If the job had fulfilled me, it would have provided a refuge of sorts and a distraction from the grief in the wake of Mum's death. Alternatively, if Mum hadn't suddenly taken ill and died, she would have been there, ready and willing to support me in whatever way she could when the job became untenable and my only choice was to resign.

Then I'd done what intelligent and qualified people the world over advise you not to: I'd made life-changing decisions when I'd been unhappy, dissatisfied and grieving. Mum had been dead mere months when I'd handed in my resignation and pooled my savings and my share of the inheritance to buy a vacant, rundown shop in a small country town that hadn't had a lot going for it even before Covid.

Why Cutlers Bay? And why a cafe? Being a cafe owner and operator had *never* been on my list of life aspirations. Sure, I'd waitressed and done bar work in my youth and hospitality work had helped fund my years of overseas travel. But running a cafe had been Mum's dream, or rather our dream for Mum, because she'd always been such a fabulous cook. Ask anyone who'd ever eaten at her table.

In my defence, said decisions hadn't been made without *any* consideration. Along with a then family connection, there'd been something about Cutlers Bay that had appealed to me. The first time I'd ambled along the main street and spotted the vacant premises, I'd glimpsed its potential, primarily because of its location slap-bang in the centre of the small shopping precinct. When I'd pressed my nose to the grimy window panes and peered inside, my imagination had run wild. According to Bryan Chalmers, the local real estate agent, in days gone by the premises had been a Four Square grocery shop and later a delicatessen. Along the way, a home-grown entrepreneur had added a few chairs and tables, allowing customers to sit and eat their pies and pasties out of paper bags, washed down with milkshakes and cups of tea, way before the cappuccino boom.

'Why did the deli close?' I'd asked Bryan.

'Like every other place in the country,' he'd said, 'supermarkets took over. They stayed open all hours and sold everything but the kitchen sink, far cheaper than a corner shop ever could. But a town this size, with the influx of tourists we get in the summer, needs a place where you can sit and enjoy a light meal and a decent espresso. Cutlers Bay is crying out for the enterprise you have in mind, Ruth. I'd be your first customer.'

At the time, I'd been too caught up in my vision for the place to notice if his enthusiasm for my proposed business venture was genuine or if it was more about the commission he'd *finally* make from the sale of the shop and attached flat.

No-one could argue that Rosie's Cafe, so called in memory of my dear mum, hadn't been an unmitigated success, though there'd been plenty of ups and downs on the road to that success. Nevertheless, five years on, I wasn't the same Ruth Clancy as the person who'd peered through the vacant shop's filthy windows and imagined all sorts of wonderful things. My biggest mistake, clear now even in the pitch black of the wee hours, was underestimating how tired and worn down I would become. I did not have an exit strategy. To my way of thinking, retirement was something other people did when they were old. And here I was, thinking about retirement.

2

Hamish

'Natalie, when did you last talk to Dad? I've rung a couple of times and he hasn't answered.' Hamish stared mindlessly at the muted flat-screen TV. It took up half a wall. Ostentatious, to say the least. He shifted the phone to the other ear and waited for his sister's reply.

Nat huffed out a long breath. 'I dunno. A week, maybe ten days. Whenever I think to ring it's usually too late in the evening. He goes to bed at some ridiculous hour.'

'Then I'll keep trying.'

Natalie tutted. 'Not like you to stress over Dad not answering his phone. Even though he is eighty-eight, going on eighty-nine—'

'Get stuffed, Natalie. I know how old he is.'

'If you are so worried, why don't you jump in that fancy car of yours and take a drive out and visit him? You're the one who's retired and has time on your hands. That's if you remember the way, of course.'

'How long since you've driven across to see him?' he snapped, and when there was no ready reply, he smirked. 'I thought so. That long ago you can't remember.' When he'd dialled Nat's number, he'd expected the conversation to go something like this. It always did. His sister was younger than him by six years and his only remaining sibling, but that didn't mean he had to like her. 'Let me know if you hear from him. A text message will suffice.'

'Ditto,' she said and hung up before he could.

'Happy families,' he muttered and dropped the phone onto the couch beside him. It bounced and slid between the cushions.

He scanned the tastefully decorated fifth-floor inner-city apartment. It was everything he'd ever dreamed of: luxurious, close to every conceivable amenity, his own undercover car space, a view of the parklands and within walking distance of the city's night-life. He'd worked damned hard to salvage and build on what little he'd had left after his divorce from Andrea. He'd regrouped, saved for a deposit and bought the apartment. Because his work took him away for long periods, he'd leased it out and worked his backside off to pay for it. The thought of being older and homeless had terrified him.

Now, after living in the apartment permanently for a year, he'd finally drummed up enough courage to admit to himself that he hated it. He'd never felt more hemmed in than he did now, verging on claustrophobic. Why hadn't he had more insight after years spent working in the wide-open spaces? And would he feel differently if there was someone special sharing the space? Except for a miracle, that situation was unlikely to change any time soon. A substantial part of it was him and his reluctance to open up to another person. Although he knew that about himself it didn't mean that he didn't yearn for things to be different. But with one failed marriage under his belt, he had no desire to repeat the same mistakes again. But if he did want to meet someone he needed to get out and about more, because hell would freeze over before he'd resort to the internet or dating apps to find a partner.

He scooped up his phone and swore, loud and explicitly. The curse bounced around the walls, absorbed by the plush furnishings, which only added further to his disquiet.

* * *

The next morning, after a night spent tossing and turning, Hamish made several phone calls. He sat in dappled shade outside a Melbourne Street cafe and sipped his second espresso for the morning while he waited for his enquiries to be addressed. The wait wasn't a long one and by midday the following day, his luxury apartment was on its way to being listed for sale. It had occurred to him that he'd have nowhere to live if it sold quickly. But he'd have means and he'd be able to take his time deciding where to settle. Wherever that might be, it would have a yard and a shed and he'd be able to see and occasionally chat to his neighbours over the fence. In the meantime, going back to work was always an option because accommodation was generally part of the deal and his previous boss would have him back on the payroll in a flash.

What Hamish did know for certain was that after he'd made the decision to sell the apartment, he felt easier than he had in a long time. What ridiculous flight of fancy had had him believing a retired diesel mechanic who'd worked in the outback for decades would feel at home in a multistorey inner-city apartment? Granted, he had been city born and raised and he'd expected to slot back easily into urban living, and he had mates who lived nearby and there was the golf course. Not forgetting the purchase had been a sound investment in a prime location. But in the end, none of it had been right for him, except perhaps the last point, given the asking price suggested by the agent.

As well as listing his apartment, Hamish made several more attempts to raise his father. There had been no news from Nat and he had a nagging feeling he should be doing more. As fathers and sons went, they weren't close, but they spoke regularly, at least every month or so, if only for a few minutes. By mid-afternoon Friday, Hamish felt he could deliberate no longer. His father was old and increasingly frail, so he rang the Cutlers Bay police station to ask the local copper to make a welfare check on his father.

'That's right, Theo Adams,' he said to the policemen who'd identified himself as Sergeant Cooper. 'Thirty-four East Terrace. He lives alone since my mother died and he isn't answering his phone, which is unusual. He's nudging ninety.'

'Maybe he lost his phone?'

'He doesn't have a mobile phone, only a landline.'

'Neighbours?'

'I'm sorry, sergeant, I don't know his neighbours.'

'Have you tried the local hospital?'

'They would have contacted my sister if he'd been admitted. She's listed as his next of kin. The last time we spoke, she hadn't heard anything.'

Sergeant Cooper confirmed the address and Hamish's contact details. 'I'll get back to you as soon as I can,' he said.

The policeman's voice held no hint of judgement or censure and for that, Hamish was grateful. The stone that settled in the pit of his stomach whenever he thought about his father and the frayed state of their family ties was recrimination enough.

After he'd hung up, Hamish paced and tried not to dwell on the likely reasons for his father not to be answering the phone.

★ ★ ★

At seventeen minutes past five that same afternoon, Hamish's phone rang. He snatched it up, surprised to see the call was from his sister. He was expecting it to be Sergeant Cooper.

'Dad's been taken to the hospital,' Nat said breathlessly and without preamble. 'They said you'd called the police to check on him. He was unconscious when the policeman found him.'

Hamish's heart raced; he felt the pulse of it through his entire body. The saliva in his mouth dried up. He licked his lips. 'Unconscious? Did they say what had happened? Is he going to be okay?'

'The nurse didn't say much, just that we should come as soon as possible. Dad's GP has a copy of his advanced care directive, so let's hope there're no unnecessary heroics.'

Said with Nat's characteristic bluntness, the words gave Hamish a jolt. He hadn't known his father had an advanced care directive. 'I'll go,' he said. 'It'll take me ten to throw a few things in a bag.'

'I can't leave until Robyn finishes her shift at the servo and picks up the kids. She works until nine. Pete's away.'

Robyn was the youngest of Natalie and Pete's four children, and her partner was a fly-in fly-out worker so Nat often had their two children in tow. Hamish shook his head. He didn't begrudge anyone wanting to have a family, but *four* children? Was it any wonder that Nat and Pete were endlessly broke and always complaining about not having enough of anything? Now his sister had a horde of grandkids and he sometimes wondered how much she enjoyed the perpetual babysitting and out-of-school care she provided at no cost.

'I said I'd go,' he said.

'Good,' Nat said. 'I'll come as soon as I can.'

Hamish dragged a canvas duffel bag off the shelf in the walk-in robe and started shoving in jocks and socks.

'Take you a good two and half hours, maybe longer,' Nat said. 'Peak-hour traffic and all the weekenders heading to the peninsula. Main North Road to Port Wakefield Road would be your best bet.'

'I do know how to get there, Natalie, believe it not.'

'Of course you do. I suppose your fancy ute has GPS.' She inhaled deeply. 'I'll let you get on with it,' she said but didn't disconnect.

Hamish paused. 'Was there something else?' He went into the ensuite and hunted out his toiletry bag.

'No, I suppose not.' She swallowed hard. 'I'll ring the hospital and tell them you're on your way. See if there's been any update on Dad's condition.'

'Right. Let me know if you find out anything new.' One-handedly, Hamish shoved his shaving gear, toothbrush and toothpaste into the bag, impatient now to get on the road. Why hadn't he asked the police to do a welfare check earlier in the week?

'Travel safely,' Nat said and was gone before he could reply. She'd sounded shaken, although still her usual snarky self.

Hamish slipped the phone into the pocket of his jeans and went back to the task at hand.

Twenty minutes later, he was accelerating onto Main North Road and trying not to speculate too much about what he might find when he reached his destination.

3

Ruth

When Allie showed up unannounced on my doorstep early-ish Sunday morning, I knew something was up. We didn't make social calls on one another, and I was still in my dressing gown.

Her words came at me like a gut-punch. I frowned at her, conscious my mouth was opening and closing as if I was struggling to get enough air.

'Come again?' I said when I caught my breath.

'Theo Adams is dead. Zach Cooper found him.'

'That's what I thought you said, but Theo was here, Thursday morning. I toasted his fruit loaf. He only wanted one slice. He didn't finish his cappuccino. I wondered if his shuffle had gotten worse, but not bad enough to kill him.'

'Zach found him Friday afternoon.'

'Where?'

'At his house. In his garage.'

'How do you know all this? Let me guess: Peg told you.'

Allie shook her head. 'Theo lives—lived—a few doors down from me, on the opposite side of the street. When I went home Friday afternoon the ambulance was parked in his driveway. It'd gone by the time the kids came home from school and I didn't give it a second thought. It was often there when Mrs Adams was alive. But then this morning, just now, I nipped into the supermarket for milk and ran into Leslie Giles, who just happens to be one of Theo's neighbours. They share a back fence.'

'Leslie's home already?'

'Yesterday.'

'That fortnight went quickly.'

'Didn't it. She said they thoroughly enjoyed the cruise but wouldn't do it again. Merv ate and drank too much and she caught a cold on the third day. Luckily it wasn't Covid or they would have had to spend the rest of the trip in their cabin.'

'Oh. Do you want come inside? I'm having coffee. I'll make you one.'

Allie glanced over her shoulder. 'All right. A quick one,' she said. 'There's groceries and milk in the car. The kids'll want their breakfast.'

She came in through the flat's sliding door and I waved a hand in the direction of the table and chairs. She wore faded cut-off jeans and an oversized T-shirt. Thongs on her feet and her hair in its usual ponytail. My unfinished coffee waited on the table beside the spread-out *Sunday Mail*.

I took down another mug and dropped a pod into the coffee machine. 'So tell me, was he dead when Zach found him?'

'Unconscious. He didn't regain consciousness.'

I made the coffee how she liked it and put the mug in front of her. She was pale, fidgeting with the hem of her T-shirt.

'Allie?'

'He took his own life, Ruth,' she blurted. 'Gassed himself in his car.' Her eyes widened and turned glassy and I thought she was going to cry.

'Shit,' I said and sat down, heavily. 'That's awful. Poor Zach. Poor Theo. My god.'

We stared at each other, mouths open.

'There are two loaves of raisin bread in the freezer,' I said. 'No-one else orders it, not since I stopped baking it. I buy it in especially for him.' Banal, I know. But don't we often retreat to the banal when we're hit with something we can't quite get our heads around?

Allie nodded as if she understood completely. She picked up her drink, blew on it and then took a sip. 'What shall I tell the kids?' Her voice came out as a hoarse whisper. 'That's if they don't know already. You know how the grapevine works in a country town.'

'Tell them the truth, I suppose. Better they hear the details from you rather than embellished by someone on social media.'

She nodded again. Cradled the coffee mug in both hands as if she was cold. I shivered, took a sip of my lukewarm brew and relished its bitterness.

'You know he has children,' I said. 'He wasn't big on conversation, quite dour in a way—miserable, you could say—but he did mention family from time to time ... grandchildren and even great-grandchildren. I know there's a daughter and that she visited him every now and then.'

'I didn't know that,' Allie said. 'Funny how we see these people all the time, think we know them but we don't really have a clue what's going on in their lives.'

'That's not a bad thing, either,' I said. 'Keeping it all in context.'

'Yes, I know, but maybe if we'd picked up on Theo's distress ...' She shrugged, her expression sad.

'That's the thing, Allie, when he came into the cafe on Thursday he was chatty, for Theo. I remember wondering if he'd had some good news. Or maybe his grandchildren were visiting on the weekend.'

'They say that, don't they, that the person might appear unusually cheerful, if the suicide's premeditated and the time is getting close.'

I glanced at her, eyebrows raised.

'Last year the high school ran information sessions on suicide, after one of their students took his own life,' she said matter-of-factly.

'I remember when that happened. Tragic.' I contemplated the dregs at the bottom of my coffee mug. 'I always thought Theo was a lonely old soul. Unhappy.'

'Yeah. A few of them about. Leslie said he rarely spoke to her or Merv. The wife was the chatty one. She had dementia and he was her carer, so Leslie said.'

'I wonder if he left a note?'

'Dunno.' Allie said finished her drink and stood. 'I'd best get home with the groceries. Thanks for the coffee.'

I walked her out to her car, pulled in behind my station wagon. The flat had a separate back entrance. A glory vine wound its way over a tiny pergola, lush and green. It whispered in a waft of breeze.

Allie opened the car door. She appeared as reluctant to leave as I was to see her go.

'Let's hope for the family's sake he did leave a note,' she said. 'And it gives them some kind of closure.'

'Wouldn't that depend on what he wrote?' I said, but I don't think she heard me.

She slammed the door and started the car. I waved and she was gone. I went inside. The news had left me feeling hollow and acutely aware of my own aloneness.

It's not as if I'd actually *known* Theo Adams. He'd only become a regular in the years since his wife died. He'd sit in Rosie's twice a week, for an hour each time. Almost every week, say fifty out of the fifty-two weeks of each year. That was one hundred hours a year. 'Gee,' I said out loud. I had friends I saw a lot less often than that.

My stomach rumbled. It was after nine and here I was still in my dressing gown and without breakfast. Okay for a Sunday morning. Without conscious thought I then did something I purposefully tried never to do on a day off: I went through to the cafe and rummaged in the freezer for the loaf of raisin bread. Somehow it seemed fitting that I toast two slices for my breakfast.

★ ★ ★

There was an unknown customer waiting at the door at eight on Tuesday morning when I flipped the sign around. I held the door open for him to enter. He was of average height, fit looking, with thick chestnut-brown hair threaded with grey pushed back from a high forehead.

'Tell me you know how to make a decent cup of coffee,' he said, not nastily but grumpily. He followed me to the counter.

'Well, they keep coming back and I'm sure it's not just because of my good looks,' I replied—flippantly, I hoped.

He gave me a brief once-over; the perfect poker face. The fan of squint lines at the corners of his eyes and the deep furrows etched into his cheeks told of a life lived outdoors. He was older than I'd first thought, possibly around my own age, and I wondered how long it had been since he'd smiled. A while would be my guess.

'What'll you have?'

'Macchiato,' he said, eyes narrowing as if he expected me to stutter and ask what that was.

My hackles rose. 'Have here or take away?' I didn't snap, but I had to work hard not to.

He glanced over his shoulder. 'Here. And one of those muffins.'

We made brief eye contact. He must have read something in mine, because he said, 'Thanks,' as an afterthought. His eyes were dark brown, like Haigh's dark chocolate.

Now why had I noticed that?

'Have a seat and I'll bring it over,' I said, with forced politeness. By then I was talking to his back. I started on the coffee.

The door squealed and in trotted Audrey.

'For goodness' sake, Ruth, will you *please* oil those hinges. I can't stand it. Shall I send Reggie over to do it?'

'No, thanks all the same. The usual?'

'Please, and a soy latte for Bryony.' She pronounced it Bry-ony, as if it were two words. Her gaze was fixed on the cake cabinet so I took the macchiato and muffin to the man at table three. He didn't look my way when I put them down, didn't even grunt in acknowledgement. His arms were folded, his jaw tense. He stared out the window, his glazed look suggesting he wasn't seeing anything other than what was going on in his head. I opened my mouth to ask if he was all right, but the front door opened and the hospital admin girls bowled in. I doubted my concern would have been received with grace.

Everyone was early this morning and I felt as if I had lead in my limbs. Awake half the night only to sleep through the alarm. No time for coffee or breakfast and the customers didn't let up long enough for me to grab something. Macchiato Man had a refill, picked at his muffin and left. When Allie arrived at ten, I was famished.

'Apparently, there's not going to be a funeral,' she said. She stowed her gear in the cupboard. Now she was here I took a minute to make myself a toasted cheese sandwich out of crusts. Luckily, the crusts from the ends of the loaves were a favourite.

'Understandable in the circumstances, I guess. But I wonder if that's what he wanted? It all sounds a bit odd,' I said.

'My thoughts exactly. Leslie Giles has been talking to the daughter. She drove up from Adelaide on the weekend. Les said that, about a year ago, Theo's GP diagnosed him with Parkinson's disease. I hadn't noticed anything different about him. Had you?'

Before I had a chance to answer her—because yes, I had noticed—there was a loud clearing of a throat from the direction of the front counter.

Allie rolled her eyes and peeked through the servery window. 'I'll see to them. You eat your sandwich,' she said and scuttled off.

I perched on the only stool and gobbled the food, careful not to burn my tongue on the melted cheese. I had noticed Theo's shuffle had become a bit more … shuffly. That his hand would shake and he'd fumble with the newspaper and slop coffee into the saucer. And every now and then when I'd glance his way, he'd be staring into space, glassy-eyed, not moving at all. Just when I'd decide to go over and see if he was okay, the moment would pass and he'd be the same as he always was.

Allie was back in a flash with food orders. I downed what was left of my coffee, washed my hands and set about preparing the sandwiches, which were my least favourite because everyone wanted something different. I don't know how many times I had to look at the slip of paper to remind myself what I was preparing.

'It does seem weird that they won't have a funeral for Theo,' I said to Allie when she was collecting her things. The intervening hours had flown by; it felt as if she'd only just arrived and here it was, close to three.

'Like you said earlier, understandable in the circumstances, I guess. And maybe it is what he wanted.' She paused. 'You know, I only ever saw him when he came here. Not once have I ever so much as glimpsed him in the garden or putting out his wheelie bin. I used to see her a bit, out in the garden. She'd always wave or pass the time of day. She seemed nice. Les said they'd always kept to themselves.'

'Did they always live in Cutlers Bay?'

'Don't think so. But they were there when I bought my house over a decade ago.'

I opened the dishwasher and was enveloped in a cloud of steam. 'It's a known fact that men don't cope as well with widowhood as women do.'

'And not just widowhood,' Allie said. 'See you tomorrow, Ruth.'

'Bye.'

While I unloaded and then reloaded the dishwasher, I kept an ear out for customers and thought about Theo. What a sad ending to a life. How lonely and unhappy he must have been. Had he not wanted to be a burden to his family when the Parkinson's disease progressed to the point where he couldn't care for himself any longer? He would have known what an undertaking it was to care for someone unable to care for themselves.

Then I thought about my own parents, both dead. Dad had died years before Mum. She'd grieved deeply for him but hadn't let that grief stop her living life to the fullest, in her own quiet way. Would Dad have managed if Mum had gone before him? It was something I'd never contemplated until now. I liked to think that he would have, with the support of me and my two brothers.

4

Ruth

Macchiato Man was waiting at the front door again Wednesday morning. I took it as confirmation the coffee had been up to his standard. He looked fresh out of the shower, his hair damp.

He sidled past me. A gentle waft of a subtle—and therefore expensive—cologne drifted in with him.

'Good morning,' I said.

He grunted.

I leaned out the front door. Beyond the verandah the footpath was wet, the air choked with moisture. 'We haven't had much of a spring, that's for sure. Farmers are mumbling about *too* much rain.'

'Farmers are known for being impossible to please,' he said and I blinked with surprise. 'But then, they are up against it most of the time.'

'True. Same as yesterday?'

'Please,' he said, sounding almost affable. He must have slept better. 'Do you serve anything as simple as toast and Vegemite?'

'Sure do,' I said and jerked a thumb in the direction of the menu board on the wall behind the counter, above the servery window. He scanned it while I ground the coffee beans.

'Just the toast, with Vegemite, thanks.'

Wow, I thought, a please *and* a thank you. Nothing pressed my buttons more than an ungracious customer who treated me like the help. He took the coffee and sat at the same table as the day before.

When I put a plate bearing two slices of perfectly toasted multigrain down in front of him five minutes later, he said, 'I'd like to apologise for being rude yesterday. Totally uncalled for. I'm sure it's the coffee *and* your good looks that keep bringing 'em back.'

He made eye contact and although he didn't smile, his eyes hinted at humour. For a second I was stupidly tongue-tied. Then the front door squealed and the sound loosened my tongue. No way I was going to oil those damned hinges.

'We're all entitled to a grumpy day every now and then,' I said and breezed off to serve the woman who'd come in.

She made a beeline for Macchiato Man's table. 'There you are,' she said stridently. His wife? Oh, dear. She looked to be a similar vintage. Same colour hair. There was something vaguely familiar about her. Had she been into the cafe before? She slung a ridiculously large handbag over the back of a chair at his table and made her way over to the counter.

'I'll have a large cappuccino with two shots and he's paying,' she said, her chin jutting in Macchiato Man's direction.

'Something to eat?'

She shook her head. Her face was devoid of makeup, her eyes red and puffy with purplish-coloured bags underneath. It'd been a while since her eyebrows had seen a pair of tweezers, but then, I was no-one to talk.

'I'll bring it over,' I said, but she loitered. She watched as I loaded the basket, locked it into place and set the machine going.

'You must be Ruth,' she said, startling me. 'Dad told me how he used to come here for a cappuccino twice a week, Tuesday and

Thursday mornings.' She had to raise her voice to be heard while I frothed the milk.

'Oh,' I said, as realisation struck. I tapped the metal jug on the counter and then poured the milk. 'You're Theo Adams's daughter. I was sorry to hear that he'd passed away. Please accept my sincere condolences.'

She glanced away. I saw her pallor and red-rimmed eyes for what they were: the mien of the freshly bereaved.

'I didn't get to visit Dad as often as I should have,' she said. 'I, for one, didn't appreciate fully how lonely he was after Mum died.' She took a deep breath, exhaling slowly. Her shoulders slumped with it. 'It has been a horrendous few days, as you can imagine. I don't know how anyone ever comes to grips with something like this.' She blinked rapidly. 'I can't even put all the pieces together yet.'

Crikey, I thought. What response goes with something like that? To my immense relief, the hospital admin girls chose that moment to burst in through the door, chatting animatedly. I really needed to thank those girls for showing up the way they did.

'Why don't you sit down with your husband and I'll bring your coffee over,' I said.

The woman's eyes widened and she snorted, of all things, disconcerting me completely. My hand jerked and the chocolate sprinkle went everywhere except where it should have landed.

'He's not my husband,' she said with a grating laugh.

'Sorry,' I said, conscious the admin girls had stopped chatting to listen in. 'I shouldn't have assumed.'

'No,' she said, 'you shouldn't have.'

Just like that, any compassion I'd felt for her moments before evaporated. Confide in me one second and then rebuke me the next? I came around the counter with her coffee and followed her to the table where the man who wasn't her husband sat.

'I haven't paid,' she said and sat down. I placed the cappuccino in front of her. He threw a dark look her way before extracting a note from his wallet. She didn't so much as say thank you to either of us.

The front door opened and several more folk came in for their morning caffeine fix. I hurried back to the counter. The admin girls rolled their eyes as I passed. I winked.

Macchiato Man and his sidekick drifted out about fifteen minutes later. I didn't think they'd said one word to each other the whole time they'd been there. Was she sure they weren't married? Thank goodness they were out-of-towners and it was unlikely I'd ever see them again. Sure, the customer was always right but that didn't mean they couldn't be nuts along with it.

★ ★ ★

No-one was more surprised than me to find Macchiato Man loitering outside the front door when I opened the cafe on Thursday morning. It was a few minutes before eight and I was tired and irritable.

'You're still here,' I said. 'I thought by now you'd have gone back to wherever it was you came from.'

'Now who's being rude,' he said with a lift of an eyebrow. He held open the door while I took an ice-cream container full of water outside to top up the dogs' water bowl I left on footpath. It was for customers' dogs to drink. Or any passing dog really. Dogs didn't discriminate.

'Sorry about that, but I did think you'd have gone by now, given there's not going to be a funeral.' We went inside.

'Apology accepted, besides I have a remarkably thick skin,' he said. 'Or so I've been told. And, I'll be honest I'm conflicted about the whole no-funeral thing. It might have been what Dad wanted in the … circumstances … but it doesn't sit right with me.'

'Dad? Are you Theo's son? The woman you were with yesterday, she's your sister?'

'Good coffee, good looks *and* intelligent,' he said. 'And please don't hold Natalie against me. She doesn't like anyone, especially not me.'

'She's grieving. We're not ourselves when we grieve. If the loss is great enough, we're never that same person ever again.'

'No, I suppose not,' he said, eyeing me with something akin to respect. 'I don't think it's sunk in yet. I'm trying to make sense of what he did, but it's as if it's all too much. That I don't have what I need to process it. And the policeman's taking me to Kadina today so I can bring Dad's car back. I'm not sure how I feel about doing that.'

'Couldn't you get someone else to drive it back?'

'Who?' he said. 'The police took it away Friday evening but now they want rid of it, because they've done what they needed to do with it.'

I began making his coffee, trying not to dwell on what he must be feeling about the task he had in front of him. My long black was cooling on the counter beside the machine. 'Breakfast?' I said, for want of anything else.

'I'm Hamish, by the way.' He glanced up at the menu board. 'And are you Rosie?'

'Ruth. Rosie was my mother. She loved to bake and we always told her she should have had her own cafe.'

'Ah,' he said, the single syllable loaded with meaning.

I looked up to find him watching me. 'I'm not living my mother's dream, if that's what you're thinking. It never was her dream, more our dream for her because we thought she'd be good at it.'

'We?'

'Me and my two older brothers. Breakfast?'

'Same as yesterday, thank you, Ruth,' he said. I slid his coffee across the counter. 'And in answer to your earlier question, after I've collected the car, I'll head back to where I came from. Which is Adelaide. North Adelaide, to be precise. Nat went home yesterday.'

He paid and took the coffee to table three. Did he know that's the table his dad always chose? I made his toast and tried to ignore how unsettling I found his situation, and this conversation. I'd become so used to a diet of superficial chit-chat; the most in-depth discussions I had were the ones I had with myself. The ones that kept me awake in the middle of the night.

When I delivered his toast, I said, 'I am sorry about your dad. Hard enough to lose a parent without adding any of the other, er, complications. I imagine after experiencing something like this there'd be a certain amount of … soul-searching?'

He lifted his shoulders and then let them drop as he gave a resigned sigh. 'That's a very tactful way of describing what I call a guilt trip. Does everyone in this town know the poor old bugger topped himself?'

'That's not the impression I get and I hear a lot of what's going on around the place because, believe me, people can't wait to share,' I said. 'But I understand your father kept to himself, more so since your mother died.'

'And how did *you* find out?'

'One of my staff lives a few doors down and she saw the ambulance and of course she knew Theo because he was a regular here. Twice a week. A milky cappuccino, raisin toast and the *Advertiser*. Only ever stayed an hour. You could set your clock by him.'

Hamish took that in, his expression grim. He waited a bit and then said, 'You would have seen more of him than I did.'

'Perhaps. However, let's keep it in context. I'm not a gossip and neither is my staff member, but this is a small country town.' I didn't let the defensive edge creep into my tone, even though it was how I felt. This man had enough to deal with.

'Fair enough. I'd better eat the toast before it goes cold. And thanks for being upfront with me.'

'My condolences to you and your family and travel safely, both trips,' I said, thinking how strange this conversation and the whole situation was. I suppose some things are easier to say to a stranger, a person you'll probably never see again.

When I returned to the counter I was surprised to find the admin girls and two others were waiting for me. I hadn't heard the door.

5

Hamish

His dad's house smelled stale and sour. Old man smell, Hamish thought. Clothes that weren't laundered often enough along with sketchy housekeeping practices. When his mother had been alive and with it, the place had been spotless—the few times Hamish had visited. He locked the door and returned the key to its hiding place under the plant pot; the plant was long dead. The mains power was off. What few things that had been left in the fridge had been dumped into the rubbish bin, although he'd missed this week's collection. The neighbour over the back fence had offered to put the bin away after next week's pick-up.

What would happen to the house and everything inside would be resolved in due course. And the car. It was back in the garage, behind padlocked doors. Remnants of police tape wrapped around the garage door handles flapped in the breeze. Hamish couldn't think clearly about any of it yet, he couldn't bear to. Not thinking was how he'd managed to drive his father's car all the way home and not abandon it on the side of the road to be stripped and torched. Before she'd left, Nat had refused point blank to discuss any of it: not the car, the house, their parents' possessions or the suicide note addressed to both of them. All she did say was that the car was worth money and part of the estate. And what a failure Hamish had been as a son and a brother and what a model of virtue she was. If he'd had to spend another day under the same roof with her he couldn't have been held responsible for his actions.

Hamish loaded his duffel bag onto the dual cab's back seat. He climbed into the driver's seat and buckled himself in but couldn't bring himself to start the engine. The thought of returning to an empty and soulless apartment held about as much appeal as staying here did. No-one other than himself for company. He'd had more real conversation with Theo's neighbour and Ruth, the woman in the cafe, than he'd ever had with his own neighbours or the baristas at the trendy coffee shops on Melbourne Street. He imagined that, to them, he just looked like an older man attempting to be cool and missing the mark by a mile.

He reached for the ignition. There was nothing to hold him in Cutlers Bay any longer. But that didn't mean he could casually cast off the conflicted and unsettled feelings tying his gut in a knot. The single-fronted stone cottage with the bull-nosed verandah was his parents' house, but it no longer housed his parents. They were both dead. He couldn't look at the garage.

As he reversed out of the driveway, he wondered—and not for the first time—how differently life might have played out if Jonathon hadn't died.

★ ★ ★

When Cutlers Bay was far behind him, the knot in Hamish's gut loosened slightly. He hadn't experienced the same inner turmoil when his mother had died. But then, she'd died in her sleep. He'd rushed home for the funeral, and returned the day after to the refuge of the outback and his job, giving himself no time to think and ruminate on how it might have been for his father. Hamish had never had any doubts that his mother had loved him, even as dementia had cruelly eroded away the woman she'd once been; they'd always said whatever it was they'd needed to say to each other. But he had never been sure of his father's affection. More so after Jonathon's tragic death at age eleven.

Awash in memories, regrets and remorse, the countryside flew past unnoticed and the outskirts of Adelaide were upon him before he knew it. He'd sped past new and unsightly housing developments as far out as Two Wells. Dwelling after dwelling, tucked in side by side, sprawling across fertile paddocks that had once been market gardens and farmland. Towns that had previously been firmly established in the country were being subsumed by urbanisation. *Everything is changing*, he thought. Out of control.

He gripped the wheel tightly as he experienced a potent and visceral urge to head for the wide open spaces of the outback, away from this rat race. Similarly out of his control, but in a different way. Out there, he'd learned it was predominantly Mother Nature who pulled the strings and somehow that made the lack of control easier to accept.

He was home by late afternoon, well after school was out, the traffic relatively light. Nat rang when he was loading the washing machine with clothes from his days away.

'You know Dad wanted to be cremated,' she said, without so much as a hello. 'And we can't do that until the coroner's sign-off.'

'I did know that,' Hamish replied. 'I *was* there when Sergeant Cooper explained the process. He didn't think we'd have to wait too long.'

'What's all the noise?'

'The washing machine.'

'You're home then. Have you seen Dad's will? Did he ever talk to you about it?'

'No and no,' he said. Why would he have? Hamish closed his eyes, not in the mood for this conversation. He was tired. Heartsick. Four days they'd been together in Cutlers Bay and when he'd wanted to talk, Natalie hadn't.

'Me either. I rang the solicitors. They said probate could take weeks, maybe months.'

'There's no rush, is there?'

Nat didn't answer immediately and that in itself was an answer. When she did speak, she snapped. 'It's all right for some. You haven't struggled financially your whole life, not like we have. A bit of extra cash before Christmas would be a godsend.'

Their father was dead by his own hand and all she could think about was the money. 'We each made our own choices, Nat,' he said, as evenly as his rigid jaw allowed. 'No-one forced you and Pete to have four children.'

'At least we had children and they all have jobs and pay tax. What's your contribution?'

Was she for real? Hamish pinched the bridge of his nose. 'Not having this conversation, Natalie. Was there something you wanted?' Apart from the obvious.

'One of us will have to go across and check on the house, pay any bills, all that stuff. You know what they say about empty houses. And I still have a job and my own bills to pay.'

'You realise that whoever pays the bills will be reimbursed when the estate is settled? But don't worry, given how busy and financially strapped you are, I'll do it,' he said.

'It's all a bit sad, isn't it,' Natalie said and he almost heard the wind whoosh out of her sails. 'You know, Hamish, we're orphans now. Feels weird. Like I'm closer to my end now that Mum and Dad have both gone.'

'I suppose so.'

'Should we have visited him more often? Especially after Mum died.'

'In case you've forgotten, until I retired a year ago, I was working out bush most of the time.'

'Yeah, well, for the first two or three months after Mum died, I went every couple of weeks, but Dad said he was doing okay so I stopped going as often. Travelling up and down to see him, working, looking after grandkids, along with everything else. And you haven't been out bush for a year.'

'And I visited him. And phoned him regularly.'

'You've visited him once since you retired.'

'What are you trying to say, Nat? That *I* didn't do enough? Did you?'

She sucked in a lungful of air and he braced himself for what might be coming.

'So, Hamish, don't you feel just a *tad* responsible for what's happened? For Dad to do what he did, he must have felt like he had no other options. Had you thought that if either of us had visited more often we might have noticed something was not quite right and we could have stepped in? After all, you can't tell much just by a phone call.'

'You read the letter he left, Nat. He was quite clear about not wanting either of us to have to look after him twenty-four seven, and he did not want to go into care and he would have had to—soon, according to the doctor.'

'But we'll never know, will we.' The brittle edge was back in her voice. 'He should have told us how sick he was. He should have given us the opportunity to at least offer help.'

'Easy to say in hindsight. But you're right, we will never know.'

While they'd talked, Hamish had gone into the kitchen and grabbed a beer out of the fridge. He walked through to the living area and sat down; flicked on the TV without the sound. If she wanted to talk he might as well be comfortable.

'Whatever happened between you and Dad that made you both

so stand-offish with each other?' she said. 'Mum never would say anything when I asked her.'

'What makes you think something happened? We were just different. Never that close.'

'Sure, and I know I was only nine when Jonathon was killed, but I was old enough to notice that Dad changed after that. He sort of closed himself off and I don't think he was ever the same again. Did he blame you?'

Hamish's mouth turned sour and his stomach roiled. He carefully put his drink onto the glass-topped coffee table. 'Why would he blame me?' he said slowly. He gripped the edge of the sofa, knuckles whitening as he waited for her answer.

6

Ruth

Officially, summer was only weeks away, although the weather suggested otherwise. It was unseasonably cold and when it wasn't raining it was trying to. Usually by November, soup had disappeared from the menu. Not so this year—today's potato and leek had already sold out.

Along with—or because of—the protracted start to the warmer weather, I'd decided that this summer I wouldn't open Sundays; people could stay at home and make their own coffees and cooked breakfasts. I needed two full days off each week to recharge my batteries. Alas, I was becoming more like my mobile phone: never fully charged because the battery was on the blink. I would not be coerced by anyone or anything to renege.

When I informed Allie of my decision, she frowned.

'Mia's Saturdays won't change and there'll be other casual shifts over the holidays,' I said, assuming that was the reason for the puckered brow. I had promised her daughter Saturday *and* Sunday work when the summer season began.

'You could always have Tuesdays off,' Allie said, throwing me completely. 'I could work the long shift that day. One of the other casuals might be interested in my shift. Liz or Gayle, or even Lorna. Then you could open Sundays and still have two days off.'

Why hadn't I thought of that? Truthfully, of late I was struggling to think of everything I already had to think about, never mind coming up with new and innovative ideas.

Then Allie shrugged. 'Locals look forward to the cafe being open on a Sunday over the summer,' she said. 'Your cooked breakfasts are a treat. When Mum and Dad come up over the holidays they make sure they include a Sunday.'

'Do they?'

'Absolutely. They only get instant coffee and toast at my place.'

I chewed over what she'd said. 'You'd have to start early on Tuesday mornings to open by eight. There're the muffins to bake so they're fresh and still warm for the early birds. And the wholesaler's delivery can arrive at any time. The perishables need to be unpacked and put away. And what about your school run?'

'The kids are old enough to get themselves to school on their own one morning a week. Cody's thirteen, for goodness' sake.'

'I'll give your idea some thought,' I said. If I was considering rolling over on a decision I'd told myself I definitely wouldn't, I had to at least given it some thought beforehand.

Later that afternoon, just as Allie was about to leave, she turned to me with a serious expression. 'What I'm about to say isn't meant to put pressure on you, Ruth, and it's totally up to you because it's your business, but any extra hours of work would be extremely helpful. Things are a bit tight in the Thomas household.'

My surprise must have been obvious. Not because things were tight in her household, rather that she'd shared the information with me. We'd worked together for years and Allie rarely disclosed anything personal.

'Mia and Cody's dad was retrenched a while ago,' she continued in the same serious tone. 'He hasn't found another job. Hence, his contribution has dwindled significantly. Teenagers are expensive to run.'

'I imagine they are,' I said. 'And your idea has merit and I've almost made up my mind. Just let me think on it a while longer. Do a few sums.'

'All right and thank you, Ruth. I'll see you tomorrow.'

The kitchen door clicked shut behind her. I went back to wiping down the counter and unloading the tray of clean mugs.

Did Allie need more hours than the extras she'd get if she worked on Tuesdays? Would she look for other casual or part-time work if I couldn't give her those hours? If she took on another position, would she be less available for me?

Lost in those thoughts, I jumped when a familiar voice said, 'Earth to Ruth. Any chance of a coffee and that last chocolate muffin?'

'Henry Cooper! Long time, no see. How are you? Do you want the muffin warmed, with ice cream on the side?'

'Ah, you dear woman, you read my mind. As to your first question, I'm very well. And how are you?'

I paused, tongs grasping the muffin in mid-air while I gaped at him. People always asked how you were without really wanting to know, but Henry's probing gaze didn't falter.

'It's Tuesday,' I said. 'It's the first day of my working week and I feel as if it should be Saturday, the last day of my working week.' My personal rule was to never share my gripes with the customers; as far as I was concerned, nothing was more of a turn-off for paying patrons. All they wanted was to sit and relax over a cappuccino and a slice of pecan pie, without a side serve of my woes.

But Henry had asked with genuine interest, which was nice. Henry Cooper was a gentleman, as was his son Zach, the local policeman. Henry didn't live in Cutlers Bay but he visited often.

'You'd put in a helluva lot of hours,' he said, glancing around the cafe, 'to keep this place ticking over the way it does. It's a credit to you and I imagine it's hard to get away, to have a break. You're never not here.'

'What's a break?' I said. 'But thanks, Henry, and please don't mind me. I'll get over myself.'

He watched while I finished making his flat white. The microwave pinged and a group of women who'd lingered over lunch and dessert waved and called out their thanks as they left. The noise level in the cafe dropped considerably.

'I can take the coffee,' he said. 'And I'll come back for the muffin. Save your legs.'

'You are a kind man, Henry.'

I dolloped a generous scoop of vanilla ice cream onto the plate beside the muffin and handed it to him when he came back. He practically salivated.

'Don't tell Zach or Angie. They've gone even more health conscious now they have a toddler and I'd be in strife if they knew I came in here for a fat and sugar fix. But I've been working bloody hard.' He scrutinised the paint-clogged fingernails of his free hand. 'Antique white,' he said and I noticed his paint-splattered clothes. 'I'm helping Zach paint the new house.'

'They're moving?'

'Yep. Into the other police residence, the one next to the station. It's bigger and has a real garden. Much more suitable for a family. Only downside is that it's right next to the police station.'

'Yeah, I can imagine,' I said. I knew what it was like to live on the doorstep of where you worked.

Henry wandered off to eat his muffin and drink his coffee. He waved when he left twenty minutes later.

I kept up with the steady stream of customers wanting coffee and teas and cakes, along with the school kids after soft drinks and ice creams, until it was four pm and closing time. Laurie came at four thirty. We'd renegotiated, because the extra half an hour gave me time to clear and wipe the tables before he came along to put up the chairs.

'How goes it?' I said when he came in through the kitchen door.

He lifted a hand in greeting and immediately set to work. Never what you'd call a chatterbox, some days he was more taciturn than others. The previous week we'd touched briefly on Theo Adams's death. It was Laurie who'd brought up the subject of Theo's suicide.

'The poor old bugger,' he'd said. 'Awful way to go, to think you have no other choice. His family, that's who I feel for. That said, life can be lonely when you're old and on your own.'

'Life can be lonely when you're not so old and on your own,' I'd said, more to myself than to him.

He'd stared at me for a good ten seconds, given me a nod of acknowledgement and carried on mopping the floor, leaving me to wonder what on earth was wrong with me. I wasn't lonely, was I? Not with people around me all day. And I *never* shared my discontent with others. Probably because I'd rarely been discontented. But I'd been brooding ever since Audrey Franco had told me that Graham Wurst was retiring, and I didn't consider myself a brooder. Here I was, the wrong side of sixty, working full time and without a satisfactory buffer between me and poverty if I decided to stop working and retire. And with no-one to go home to. The last part had never bothered me before. Why did it bother me now?

You're getting old, Ruth, a voice whispered in my ear. *Who'll be there to care for you if and when you can no longer care for yourself?*

'Ruth?'

I blinked.

Laurie loomed in front of me, a worried expression on his craggy face. 'Are you all right?' he said.

'Yes, yes … I'm fine.' I felt flushed and foolish.

'You don't look it.'

I flapped my hands about in an attempt to cool my face.

He nodded knowingly. 'The wife used to get those hot flashes. Went on for years. Always said she was fine, but I could see she wasn't.'

'It'll pass,' I said and patted his arm.

'Right-o. I'm done here. Unless you have other jobs need doing.'

I pushed a hand through my hair. There was something … 'Yes! The drum of used oil from the deep fryer. Could you please carry it out into the service lane? The recycle bloke's picking it up in the morning, early.'

While he did that I wrapped up the few leftover scones for him to take home. I could have put them in the freezer but Laurie would enjoy them. I bundled them into the green supermarket bag, along with the usual frozen meals and a date and walnut roll.

When I handed him the bag, he looked inside.

'There's too much here, Ruth. You need to give me more jobs or less food.'

That made me laugh. I locked the kitchen door behind him. Instead of baking like I'd planned, I went home with the leftover lasagne and salad and opened a bottle of wine.

Two generous glasses later, I was nowhere closer to having a clue who'd care for me if I ever needed caring for. Who'd be there for the long haul, if it ever became a long haul? It was a sobering thought. I poured myself another, smaller, glass and pretended I had nothing better to do than sit and cogitate about who I could call on, if in my dotage I ever needed someone.

Don't get me wrong, I wasn't completely alone in this world. There were people I could, and did occasionally rely on. Friends. Family. Robert and Elliot, my two brothers, were older by a decade. Twins. Both had married and then unmarried and Robert had married again. Both had produced progeny somewhere along the line. As a result, I had two nieces and a nephew, who now had offspring of their own. It was because of one such niece that I'd wound up in Cutlers Bay in the first place: Stacey, Elliot's only child, had been living here with her husband, Chris, and their two children, when, in the days following Mum's death, I'd experienced an urgent need to reconnect with family. Interestingly, Stacey and her family had moved on and were living in Far North Queensland, closer to her in-laws. I couldn't see myself visiting them up there any time soon. Or them rushing down to help if I was in strife.

My brothers? They were in their early seventies and polar opposites despite being twins, though not identical. But they were close and looked out for each other in the way that twins often do. Being a decade younger, I wondered if they sometimes forgot who I was. It'd always been that way and I'd learned to never take it personally. Besides, although we kept in touch regularly, I didn't go out of my way to remind them of my existence.

And friends? Well, that's the thing about seachanges. Initially, curiosity wins and they flock in for a stickybeak. The more faithful follow through for a while but gradually the novelty and the visits peter out completely. Sad, but true. And understandable. Only the very committed hang on. And I'd had other priorities to consider rather than driving south to visit them.

Since I'd moved to Cutlers Bay, my whole focus had been on making the business a success. Along the way I'd met a lot of people, acquaintances, knew many of them by name, but the long hours I worked had prevented the pursuit of meaningful friendships.

Thinking about it now, it was all a bit depressing. Bloody Graham Wurst. I hadn't considered any of this until he'd decided to retire.

Resisting another top-up, I put the wine back into the fridge and set about doing what I'd promised Allie: working out if the business could afford to pay her for another five hours a week so that I could continue opening Sundays and still have two full days off a week over summer.

I glanced at the time. It was almost eight thirty and despite the wine, I felt remarkably clear-headed. Without a second thought, I picked up the phone and called Selina. Her kids would be in bed, her partner glued to the television and she'd be settling down to her paying job: bookkeeping for various farms and small businesses around the district. She'd been doing Rosie's Cafe's books for several years now, after I'd almost crashed and burned trying to do it all.

'Ruth, hello,' she said after several rings. 'How did you know I'd have Rosie's file open?'

'Pure luck. I was hoping you'd have a minute for me to run something past you, then I can make a decision.'

'Fire away,' she said and I quickly outlined Allie's suggestion, finishing with, 'Can the business afford it?'

'And it's just for the three months over summer?' I could hear her computer keys clacking.

'To begin with, but if it works and it's affordable—'

'You might keep it going.'

'Yes, and not just for me. Allie's financial circumstances have changed and I'd hate to lose her because I couldn't give her the hours she needs. And honestly, Selina, I'd already made the decision not to open on Sundays over summer because I desperately need two full days off a week.'

'Hmm,' she said and then quoted what the extra hours would cost the business. 'Easily doable. In fact, if you wanted to, you could comfortably give her more hours than that … say, double the amount?'

'I could have her start at nine or nine thirty on the other three days …' I could hear excitement creeping into my voice as I warmed to the idea. 'And finish at three instead of two thirty. That would be wonderful. I could do more baking.' Or not.

'Or take time for yourself,' Selina said, with her usual candour. 'When I came into the cafe last week for lunch, you looked exhausted, Ruth. Similar owner/operator businesses tend to change hands every three or four years. Sometimes even sooner than that. You've been going at it for five years. There's more to life than work.'

'Funny you should mention that … Thanks for your help, Selina. I'll let you know what Allie and I agree on.'

I wanted to call Allie with the good news but it was almost nine and it could wait until the morning. Thinking this deserved a celebration, I went to the fridge for the bottle of wine. It was a wine I'd been gifted. I lifted the bottle to read the label and then laughed when I saw it was low alcohol. That explained my clear head.

But not the dreadful headache I woke with the following morning.

★ ★ ★

'You look awful,' was Allie's greeting when she came in at five minutes before ten. I was in the kitchen leaning heavily on the sink.

'I feel as if I can barely drag myself around.' The usual two-shot long black earlier had done nothing other than make me feel as if I was going to be sick. I swallowed hard to stave off another wave of nausea.

'Do you get migraines?' Allie said, her brow wrinkled with concern.

'Never have before,' I croaked.

She stowed her bag. 'Why don't you go and lie down? I'll manage here.' She peered through the servery window into the cafe. 'There's no-one waiting.'

'Should I test for Covid?' I said. 'I've never had a migraine. In fact, I'm rarely ever sick at all.'

'Do you have a fever? A sore throat? Sneezing?'

I shook my head and then wished I hadn't. 'Just a headache and I feel like throwing up. I suppose it could be a virus.'

'Sounds more like a migraine to me. Mia gets them occasionally. But do a test if it'd put your mind at rest. Now go,' she said. 'Lorna's home and I'm sure she'll come and do a few hours. I'll call her now.' She whipped out her phone.

Feeling too unwell to do anything other than put myself to bed, I sidled past her to the cool, quiet comfort of home. Not even bothering to get undressed, I closed the blinds and fell onto the bed, dragging a blanket over me. I was asleep in minutes.

I slept for eight hours. When I woke, my head was fuzzy but nothing like the pounding pain I'd had that morning. Allie had returned my mobile phone, which I'd left in the cafe kitchen, along with a note. I found both on the dining room table beside the day's takings. Allie had written:

Wanted to check you were okay before I went home. You were sound asleep so didn't wake you. We had a good day. Hope you're feeling much better. Drink plenty of water. Lorna brought soup and it's in the fridge if you feel like eating. Ring me if you need anything. I'll open up in the morning, so don't stress if you're not feeling up to it. Allie.

Bless her heart. She was a good soul. Sure enough, there was a Tupperware container of chicken and vegetable soup in the fridge. After drinking a tall glass of water, I took a hot shower and changed into my pyjamas before I heated a bowl of soup. Two toasted crusts of bread made the meal. I was hungry and it was delicious.

The food had me feeling even better. At this rate, I'd be okay to open the cafe in the morning. But after an hour spent doing a few light chores, I was yawning widely and not so certain I'd be up to tomorrow's early start. Before I went back to bed, I attended to the day's takings and then flicked a quick message to Allie to confirm I was much better, the RAT was negative and yes, I would appreciate her opening up in the morning. I'd be there later.

I did hesitate before I tapped send. It was a rare thing for me to be relying on someone else. I could not remember a morning I hadn't opened up in all the years I'd been working the cafe.

It's one day, I remonstrated with myself and sent the message.

Allie responded immediately with a smiley face and a thumbs-up emoji.

★ ★ ★

'You're all better?' Allie said when I went through to the cafe just before ten the next morning. She was at the coffee machine. It was busy, the orders piling up.

'Feel a bit fragile, but otherwise I'm good to go.'

'Hope you've had breakfast.'

I laughed. 'Yes, Mum.' When I'd woken, I'd been ravenously hungry and had eaten three slices of toast with Vegemite. But no coffee yet and the smell of it as I'd come into the cafe had been enough to make me feel queasy. I went to the kitchen, tied on a clean apron and read the next food order: a bacon, lettuce and tomato sandwich. Peeling off two slices of bacon, I slapped them onto the grill. *This will be the test*, I thought, as they started to sizzle. I took a deep breath and was fine.

When the place had emptied out after lunch, I said to Allie, 'When can you start opening on Tuesdays?'

She grinned. 'Whenever you want me to.'

'Sunday trading will begin on the first Sunday in December. What about the Tuesday after that?'

'Done!' She high-fived me after she'd put down a pile of dirty crockery.

'And,' I said, drawing the word out. Her eyes narrowed. 'Would you be interested in extending your hours on the other days? Say, start at nine thirty and finish at three?'

She took half a second to process the offer. 'Yes! I can do that, and thank you, Ruth. I'd offer to fill in on weekends as well, but Mia would be horrified. Bad enough me telling her what to do at home. Plus, there's the cost ... I understand having the casual juniors working weekends makes it easier.'

'You're after even more work than that?' I said, half-dreading the answer. But any further discussion was put on hold when a group of golfers, older women, blew in wanting cakes and cappuccinos. And one hot chocolate. It was that kind of weather.

'I'm not doing anything about more work until the new year,' Allie said after we'd delivered all the food and drinks. 'Get Christmas and the holidays out of the way.' She sighed. It came from deep down.

I squeezed her shoulder. 'Life throws up all sorts of challenges and somehow we manage,' I said.

We cleared tables, washed dishes and replenished the milk fridge. The golf ladies scattered in a whirlwind of laughter and good cheer. For a moment I hated them, their easy camaraderie and the free time they had to play golf. How dare they? I'd played golf, once, par three. I'd been at uni, making it about forty-five years ago.

Allie cleared and wiped the recently vacated tables, chatting to the few remaining customers as she went. Today her boundless energy was enough to wear me out. I refilled the cake cabinet and added a few things to the list on the whiteboard where we wrote reminders to restock, order, etc. My head began to pound. Nothing major, just a dull thud, a bit like distant drums. I had a drink of water and reminded myself that if I did need more time off because I was sick there was money put aside to cover costs. But not for long. The cafe needed me fit and healthy to keep it afloat and vice versa.

7

Hamish

Hamish felt antsy. No other way to describe it. He couldn't settle to anything. The real estate agent had been back again to take more photos and videos of the apartment. For their website, she said, a virtual tour or some such nonsense. That was part of the reason for his mood, but not wholly. When he considered what else might be the cause of his restlessness he settled on the uncomfortable fact that they hadn't had a funeral or formal farewell for his father. Even though the old man's instructions had been explicit: he was to be interred next to his wife in the niche wall of the Cutlers Bay Cemetery and there was to be no funeral or memorial service.

Fed up with feeling out of sorts, Hamish braced himself and broached the subject with his sister.

'The kids have been at me about that very thing,' she said when he rang her. 'They don't feel as if they've been given the opportunity to say goodbye to their grandpa. We've decided we'll drive over one day and have our own family thing.'

'And am I included in this ... family thing?'

'Of course,' she said, but Hamish hadn't missed the beat of her hesitation. 'If you want to be.'

Did he want to be? If he had his own family thing there'd be him, all on his lonesome. He had let his ex-wife Andrea know that his father had passed away. She'd murmured the appropriate condolences, but hadn't asked about a funeral. They had no children.

'Why don't we all go together when the plaque's done and Dad's ashes have been interred next to Mum?' Nat said—grudgingly, he thought. 'We can set a date when you hear from the funeral home. Sooner rather than later.'

'I suppose we could make that work,' he replied. 'I'll be in touch.' Hamish put away his phone with a vague sense of relief.

★ ★ ★

So it came about that on the Wednesday of the first week in December, Hamish, his sister and her husband and whoever of their children and grandchildren could get away, made the trip from Adelaide to Cutlers Bay to make their last goodbyes to Theo.

They left early, the three cars travelling in convoy. Hamish had Natalie and Pete with him. None of them were overly chatty. Nat had climbed into the back seat of the dual cab without complaint. The few times Hamish had glanced in the rear-view mirror, she'd appeared preoccupied, mindlessly staring out at the passing scenery.

'All right there, Nat?' he said one of those times.

'Yep, all good,' she replied in a flat voice.

Pete swivelled around to look at his wife. 'Day'll be over before you know it, love,' he said.

She half-heartedly returned his smile.

There were a dozen things Hamish could have said, some nice and some not. Prudently, he concentrated on the road. After all, it was his choice to be doing this with them.

The plan had been to go directly to the cemetery when they

arrived in Cutlers Bay. They'd stopped en masse at Port Wakefield to use the restrooms and then the others had insisted on coffees, bacon sandwiches and the likes. Hamish had wanted to press on to their destination. He didn't want the day to go on forever.

'I wonder where the others have got to?' Pete said, after another anxious glance over his shoulder. They were roughly ten kilometres out of Cutlers Bay and there were no other vehicles in view.

'They are behind us,' Hamish said. 'Although I haven't seen them for a bit.'

'One of the kids probably needed another toilet break,' Nat said.

'That's true.' Pete settled back into his seat. 'It's not as if we have to be there at a certain time.'

Too bad if they had. Hamish eased his foot off the accelerator. No point getting there long before the rest of the family and who knew when that would be? In Hamish's experience, the younger generations tended to be careless of the plans of others, especially older others; they did whatever suited them when it suited them. Come to think of it, hadn't he been a bit like that when he was younger? Was it the hubris of youth? To believe you had all the time in the world and, as a consequence, you squandered the precious time of those who had a lot less of it to waste? How thoughtless and selfish. Was it the destiny of the human species to make the same mistakes over and over, one generation after the next? To never learn? *Whoa*, he thought. *Bit deep.*

It was a few minutes before eleven when they reached the outskirts of Cutlers Bay. Nat had asked if Hamish would stop on the side of the road and wait for the others. He'd refused.

'They'll be able to find the cemetery, love,' Pete said. 'It's well sign-posted and remember, Robyn was there for your mum's funeral.'

'Whatever,' she said and didn't speak again for the remainder of the trip.

At the cemetery, Hamish parked in the shade of a clump of straggly she-oaks. They sat in silence for several minutes, the only sounds the wail of distant corellas and the gentle sigh of the wind through the trees.

'Do we just wait here for the others?' Pete said and craned around to look at his wife.

'You can, mate, but I need to stretch my legs,' Hamish said.

Leaving his sunglasses on, he climbed out and closed the door. The air was fresh and smelled of the sea. He stretched and then began the walk up the rutted pathway that led to the niche wall. Stones crunched underfoot and sparrows flitted among the headstones. Now he was here he felt empty; devoid of emotion. Why had he felt so compelled to do this?

Nat fell into step beside him and he found her presence oddly comforting. They reached the wall without speaking and went straight to the spot. The brass plaque gleamed in the sunlight, new and untarnished. Pete wandered up, all the time looking over his shoulder for the stragglers. It wasn't hot but he mopped his brow with a snowy-white handkerchief.

'It's nice,' Nat said. 'But then it'd want to be, the amount they charged. Bloody robbers.' She turned and took in the country cemetery. Headstones ranged from glossy new to old and decrepit and falling over; dead and dying bouquets abounded. The paths between the graves were uneven and needed resurfacing. Weeds flourished. 'And it's not as if the place is anything to die for.'

Pete smirked at his wife's unintended pun.

Behind the screen of his sunglasses, Hamish rolled his eyes. 'Don't worry, the plaque is all paid for. You can reimburse me for your share when you have the cash.'

'Our share? Shouldn't it come out of the estate?' Nat demanded, squinting at her brother, hands on hips. Pete threw Hamish a nervous glance then jammed his hands into his trouser pockets and stepped away.

'Yes, but in the interim, I've paid for it.'

'Yeah, well, you're the one with the all the money,' Nat hissed, before directing her attention towards the car park. Two cars had stopped and disgorged the remaining family. The motley group eventually made their way along the path towards Hamish, Nat and Pete.

'Where the hell have you lot been?' Nat said, her ear-piercing tone carrying clearly across the distance.

Pete edged up next to Hamish. 'She's upset,' he said in a confiding whisper. 'Taken her dad's death really hard.'

'Has she?' Hamish said. He raised his eyes heavenward, hoping for an alien abduction or the likes, anything to get him out of here. Now. *But you wanted to be included*, he reminded himself.

'I know he was your dad too, but the two of you weren't close.'

Hamish took off his sunglasses and stared at his brother-in-law. He didn't speak. He couldn't. No words would come. He slid the sunglasses back into place and pretended to read the other memorial plaques on the wall.

Next thing, Nat was ordering him to come and stand beside her.

'Robyn's going to say a few words. Bridie wrote a poem and she'll read it out.'

Oh, goodie. Eight-year-old Bridie belonged to Robyn and was Nat and Pete's youngest grandchild. Hamish had always thought her precocious. The child had a way of staring at him with her pale blue eyes as if she could see right through him. Creepy.

Nat fossicked in her handbag and pulled out a folded A4 sheet of paper along with her reading glasses. 'I've written down a few things I want to say. Have you got anything to contribute, Hamish?'

'No,' he said. *Except my capacity to pay for things.*

A cloud of smoke drifted over from where Carmel's partner sucked hungrily on a cigarette. Carmel was Nat and Pete's eldest. She was a registered nurse. The partner hadn't been in the picture long and as hard as Hamish tried, he couldn't remember the bloke's name—that's if he'd ever known it. Probably no point asking, given Carmel's history with men. At least she had the smarts not to marry them or have them father any brats.

Cate was next in line after Carmel. She was a freelance editor. Hamish liked her; out of all his nieces, he found her the easiest to be with. She was quietly intelligent and had a wry sense of humour. She reminded Hamish of his mum. Her husband Nigel was a lawyer and he hadn't been able to get away. Their two gangly teenage sons stood next to Cate, one on either side, a bit like bodyguards. They were handsome boys and both taller than her.

Sally, the second youngest, was trekking in South America. She was always trekking somewhere in or outside of Australia. Probably to get away from her mother, because when they were together all they did was fight. Hamish hadn't seen Sally for at least a decade. He didn't think any of the others had either, except perhaps Carmel.

Robyn cleared her throat. 'Let's get this show on the road, people,' she said, a facsimile of her mother in both looks and voice. And personality. Hamish always kept his distance from his youngest niece.

Without the aid of notes, Robyn gave a simple but eloquent tribute to her grandpa. After that she read out an email Sally had sent. Neither Cate nor Carmel had anything to add. When it was Nat's turn, she made a show of unfolding the sheet of paper and sliding on her glasses. 'Dearest Daddy,' she started.

Hamish gritted his teeth and asked himself again why he'd felt the need to do this. He fought hard against the urge to tune out completely. To just walk away.

His sister droned on. The man she eulogised wasn't the man Hamish remembered. He understood that siblings growing up together in the same household with the same parents recalled childhood events and experiences differently. Nat remembered her father's sadness in the months after their brother Jonathon died; he remembered the slow burn of Theo's bitterness and anger. In the immediate aftermath of the tragedy, Hamish would have left home if he'd been a year older. But he'd been barely fifteen and his mother had begged him to stay on at school for another year. She'd told him countless times that his brother's death hadn't been his fault, that he was blameless. It had been a horrific accident and his father would have to eventually accept it for what it was.

But Hamish didn't think his father ever had. He'd never stopped holding Hamish accountable in some way, just for the fact that he'd been the oldest and nearby when Jonathon had been knocked off his bike and killed by a drunk driver.

Hamish thought of his life as having two parts: the years that came before his brother was killed and the decades that came after.

No-one was more relieved than Hamish when Bridie admitted to her mum that she'd left her poem at home. 'And I didn't learn it off by heart,' she said in a loud whisper, her cheeks pink with uncharacteristic embarrassment.

'Never mind,' Nat said and hugged her. 'It's the thought that counts.'

'I could murder a beer,' Carmel's partner said loudly. Carmel nodded and Pete grunted in agreement. Nat glared at them.

'We'll go to that cafe, the one in the main street, and have lunch,' his sister declared as if she was in charge. She sailed off down the pathway towards the parked cars. Everyone traipsed after her.

'How are you doing, Uncle Hamish?' Cate said as she came up beside him. She linked her arm with his.

'All the better for that being over,' he muttered. But he knew in his heart that it wasn't over. He'd tried to say his own silent goodbye to his father while Nat had droned on, but the words wouldn't come. He hadn't been able to farewell Theo here, or anywhere. He didn't know why he'd even considered it possible. First he needed to forgive: his father and himself.

Cate leaned into him, her head resting briefly against his shoulder. 'Mmm,' she said, 'Mum does like to think she's always the one in charge. Dad never contests. Who am I to dissuade them of the notion?'

Hamish laughed.

8

Ruth

A person can look at themselves in the mirror every day and not really see what's there, staring them in the face. I did it every morning. I cleaned my teeth, moisturised, applied tinted sunblock—heaven knows why, because I rarely got outside when the sun was shining—brushed my hair and pulled it into its usual twist then swiped on lipstick. Always bright-coloured lipstick. All without actually *looking* at myself. If I had, I might have noticed how worn out I was; how this endless work was leaching the colour and vitality from my very being.

Since the first headache, I'd had two more. Obviously not a virus. The second wasn't as severe; the third on a par with the first. Luckily, that one had come on the afternoon of our first Sunday opening for summer and I'd had all of Monday and Tuesday to recover. When I'd started to feel better on Monday afternoon, I'd googled migraine headaches and almost convinced myself it wasn't that. I made a promise there and then that if I had another headache as severe I'd make a doctor's appointment. Much to my shame, I hadn't had a serious check-up since I'd left Adelaide half a decade ago.

By mid-week the weather had warmed up and folk were on the move. I couldn't remember having a busier Wednesday morning. Allie and I didn't stop. Lorna was in Kadina visiting her elderly mother and although I'd tried, I hadn't been able to raise any of the other weekday casuals. Of course the juniors were at school and that didn't break up for the summer holidays until the end of the following week.

By half-past midday, the lunch orders were piling up and I was sweating over the hot plate. When I leaned down to place more loaded plates onto the servery shelf for Allie to deliver, the front door opened and Hamish Adams, aka Macchiato Man, came inside, accompanied by the surly woman he'd said was his sister. What was her name? A younger woman and a girl of about eight or nine, who, by the looks of them, had to all be related, followed them in. Allie directed them to the recently vacated table six and the menu board on the wall above the servery window.

What on earth were they were doing in Cutlers Bay in the middle of the week? Or any other day of the week, for that matter. While the four of them clustered together at the counter and read the menu, not a smile between them, Allie whipped around clearing and wiping their table.

'I want fries,' I heard the girl demand.

Allie dumped the dirties, washed her hands and went around to grab the plated food orders from the servery. Our eyes met across the salad sandwiches and chips. No fries in this establishment. She raised her eyebrows expressively. 'Table five,' she confirmed, glancing at the docket and then back at me. She swept up the meals and as she passed the counter, I heard her say, 'Be with you in a minute, folks.'

Steak was sizzling on the grill for two steak sandwiches with the lot plus side serves of chips. A slice of quiche heated in the microwave while I plated the salad and there were more sandwiches to prepare. Otherwise, I would have gone out and served Hamish myself. If only to ask what he was doing in Cutlers Bay again.

The dishes were piling up, along with the food orders. When the steak sandwiches and chips were ready, Allie was busy at the coffee machine, so I delivered them to table eight. 'Bon appetit,' I said, recognising the two hirsute workers in hi-vis who'd become regulars. They grinned and tucked in. My steak sandwiches were obviously better than a meat pie from the bakery.

I just happened to glance towards table six as I returned to the kitchen. Another woman with two teenage boys had joined the party, crammed at the same table. Natalie! That was his sister's name. They were all dressed semi-formally, making me wonder again what they were doing in town. A reading of the will? Nah. There was no legal practice within cooee, so why would they be here to do that? If they were cleaning out Theo's house they wouldn't be dressed in their best clothes.

When it was ready, I helped Allie ferry out their food, the table groaning under the weight of it all.

Hamish smiled widely and said, 'Hello, Ruth.'

I beamed back in return. His sister acknowledged me with a curt nod.

Things calmed down somewhat after that. It never ceased to amaze me the way that happened. One minute I was being overwhelmed by orders and an hour or so later the place was all but empty, the pile of dishes the only evidence customers had been there at all. The stayers had moved on to cake and coffees.

The dishwasher gurgled away and I was at the sink up to my elbows in hot soapy water and dirty pots and pans and utensils when Hamish appeared in the kitchen doorway.

'Thanks, Ruth,' he said. 'Great food and your sidekick makes coffee almost as good as yours. It sure is a busy little place. You need more staff.'

'Are you volunteering to wash dishes?' I held up my pink rubber glove-encased hands.

He laughed and it did all kinds of lovely things to his face. Captivated, I stopped what I was doing to stare.

'It wouldn't be the first time I've washed dishes,' he said.

'Wednesdays aren't usually this busy and none of my casuals were available at short notice. Anyway, what are you doing in Cutlers Bay?'

'Dad's ashes have been interred next to Mum's and we had a bit of a family thing to say goodbye.'

'Oh, that was a decent thing to do. I remember you saying it didn't feel right not having a funeral.'

'Yeah,' he said and seemed to withdraw. 'I'd better go. Just wanted to say thanks.'

'You're welcome,' I said. 'Safe trip home.'

He nodded, a brief incline of his head, and was gone.

Allie returned with more dirty crockery and cutlery. 'Who was that?' she said.

'Theo Adams's son and daughter. Not sure who the others were. Obviously related.'

'The younger women were calling the older one mum.'

'There you go,' I said.

She took off to serve customers.

Just after three there was a ruckus out front, punctuated by a burst of raucous laughter. Allie had left for the day so I hurried out of the kitchen to find Ella Sinclair wrangling Claire Cross and her walking frame across the threshold. They were both giggling.

'It's you two,' I said, feigning exasperation. 'I should have known.'

'Damn thing,' Claire said and gave the offending walker a hefty shove. 'Gets hooked up on just about every damn thing.'

'Never mind, we're in now. Will you have tea, Claire?' Ella said. The pair made their way to table two, their usual.

'Please, and a piece of the richest, most unhealthy cake you have.'

Ella settled Claire at the table and came up to the counter. 'Claire's been unwell. Nothing serious, but she's almost ninety and really shouldn't be living on her own in that old house. But of course she won't agree to the old folks' home. Not that I blame her.'

That explained why I hadn't seen them for the last few weeks.

'If you're going to talk about me rather than to me, keep your voices down,' Claire called and cackled with laughter.

'How is she now?' I said and loaded a generous slice of hazelnut gateau onto a plate. I added a squirt of whipped cream.

'Frail, but feisty, as you can hear. Between me, Angie and the community nurse, we're managing to keep her at home, which is what she wants.'

'Is there anything I can do to help? I have Mondays and Tuesdays off over summer,' I found myself offering without thought.

'Ruth,' Ella said in a kind but firm voice, 'pardon me for saying this, but you look as if you need a month at a tropical resort, not more things to do.'

'I don't mind helping, not one little bit,' I said. I could be feisty too. 'And I like Claire. She brings me lemons to make lemon curd. Now, will you have your usual?'

'Thank you.' Ella studied me some more, almost to the point of discomfort, while I made Claire's pot of tea and her cappuccino. 'Tell me, Ruth, for interest's sake, when did you last have a holiday?'

'I don't remember,' I said.

She tutted and then carried the cake across to Claire. I followed with the drinks.

Ella was in her seventies. She'd been visiting friends in Cutlers Bay several years ago and at a crossroads in her life when she'd ended up buying a house and staying. She'd been a regular at the cafe ever since. I remembered vividly the first time she'd come into Rosie's. She'd looked sad and lost and I'd later discovered she'd had every reason to be that way: recently widowed, she had been forced into a sudden and unexpected seachange that she'd turned into an opportunity to make a new life for herself. Claire was her elderly neighbour and the two women had forged a firm friendship, right from the get-go.

'Why don't you get a drink and join us? Sit down for a bit,' Ella said. 'My treat.' She scanned the near-empty cafe as if to emphasise I had no pressing business.

'All right, I will. Thanks.' I usually didn't dare stop at this time of the day because, as lovely as it was to sit down, if a customer came in I didn't bounce up as quickly as I used to. I grabbed a glass and a cold drink from the fridge.

'I heard from Henry that Zach and Angie are moving into the bigger police residence,' I said. I half filled the glass with sparkling water. It was deliciously cold.

'Lily's two and a half now and desperately needs a yard to play in. The bigger house had a lawn that Henry and I are slowly coaxing back to life. And there's even room for Angie to plant a veggie patch.'

'Lily's a gorgeous little thing,' Claire said. 'Bursting with energy. Exhausts me just watching her.'

'When are they moving house?'

'In the new year. Zach's requested a few days off,' Ella said. 'Angie can't believe how much stuff she's accumulated in a relatively short time.' Angie had been travelling and living in her car or a tent when she'd first passed through town and met Zach and Ella.

'That was to die for,' Claire said, scraping her plate clean. She slurped her tea and smacked her lips in appreciation.

I laughed. 'Good to see you haven't lost your appetite for tea and cake.'

'When I do, I'll know my time's well and truly come,' Claire said, suddenly serious.

'Get away with you,' Ella said. 'You'll probably outlive us all.'

The door opened and a group of schoolkids tumbled inside, Allie's Cody among them. He threw a tentative glance my way.

I stood slowly, easing the kinks out of my back. 'Thanks for the drink, Ella. Good to see you both.'

Ella touched my hand when I reached for Claire's empty plate. 'Are you taking a break over Christmas, Ruth?'

'Three. Glorious. Days.'

'Why don't you close for the whole week? Give yourself a decent break.'

'Tempting, but I have a few bookings already.'

'I don't know how you keep up with it,' Claire said. 'Be careful, girl, or you'll run yourself into the ground.'

First Henry and now Ella and Claire. I must've looked as worn out as I felt. Instead of going to Robert's on Christmas Day, perhaps I should stay home and sleep. No, I needed to get away from Cutlers Bay for a few days as much as I needed sleep. I hadn't seen either of my brothers since Easter.

That night, when I should have been ordering supplies and planning next week's specials, I googled tropical resorts and let myself dream.

9

Hamish

The festive season was more ho-hum than ho ho for Hamish. All Christmas did this year was provide another reminder of how dysfunctional his relationship with his only sibling had become and how alone he was in the world, even more so now both his parents were dead. Loneliness wasn't something he'd ever given much thought until recently; he'd always had his work. Ruminating on the way his father had died could account for why he was contemplating his own situation. The more he thought about Theo's suicide, the less he understood. And the remorse for any part he'd unwittingly or otherwise played in his father's demise snowballed. He'd read and reread a copy of the suicide letter, searching for what might be hidden between the lines. He'd found nothing.

In the days leading up to Christmas he'd lunched and had a few drinks with a couple of mates after they'd played eighteen holes of golf. It'd been a welcome distraction. His mates had both returned home to wives and families and Christmas festivities and Hamish had experienced a feeling of what he suspected was genuine loneliness. It frightened him, so, on Christmas Eve, he'd made himself go out on his own for a drink and dinner, and listened to live music afterwards. He came home feeling lonelier than ever.

From his sister, he'd heard nothing since their trip to Cutlers Bay. The day hadn't ended in total disaster, but it very nearly could have. Pete and Carmel's bloke had got themselves nicely mellow at the Cutlers Arms hotel while the others had had lunch at Rosie's Cafe. Not only that, they'd kept everyone waiting back at Theo's place while they drank their fill and then some. It was almost five when they'd finally tumbled out of Carmel's car and staggered up Theo's driveway. Nat had been incandescent with rage. Robyn and Bridie had left at three with Cate and her boys. Carmel had had the foresight to switch to lemonade or they would have been spending the night at Theo's.

To make matters worse, Pete, not being the seasoned drinker Carmel's boyfriend was, had been sick twice on the way home. It'd only been Hamish's rapid response to Pete's distress that had prevented his brother-in-law throwing up in the ute. That would have stretched even the firmest of friendships and theirs was hardly that. Not Pete's proudest moment. Nat had been monosyllabic with fury. When Pete wasn't being sick he'd slept and Hamish had borne the brunt of her anger. When he'd dropped them home after nine, he'd never been more pleased to see the back of them. He wouldn't have wanted to be in Pete's shoes when the poor bloke sobered up.

Needless to say, there'd been no invitation to spend Christmas Day in their company. Cate and Nigel were the only family who'd thought to include Hamish: he had a meal with them Christmas night; the usual Christmas fare served outside on their leafy deck with a view out over the twinkling city lights. It was a balmy evening. Very pleasant. After they'd eaten, the boys went inside to do whatever it was they did on their devices.

'Mum's still not talking to Dad,' Cate said. 'Not since the Cutlers Bay incident. Dad comes across as a real pushover and most of the time he is, but even he has his limit.' She picked at the bowl of cherries on the table and popped a couple into her mouth.

'More wine, Hamish? Cate?'

'No thanks, mate,' Hamish said.

Cate held out her glass and Nigel topped it up before emptying the bottle into his own glass.

'Mum forgets that Dad was very fond of Grandpa Theo and he has every right to grieve in his own way.'

Nigel murmured his agreement. Hamish swatted at mozzies. The coils weren't doing their job.

'Besides, I've never known Dad to get as drunk as Mum reckons he was. Was he that drunk?'

'He was,' Hamish said. 'Could barely scratch himself. That bloke of Carmel's thought it was a huge joke.'

'Barry. He's a thing of the past. Carmel gave him the flick after that. One positive thing to come out of the whole fiasco.'

'Poor old Pete. A couple of days after the event, he rang and apologised for almost throwing up in my car. Said he still felt crook.'

Nigel laughed, a low rumble. 'It was bound to happen sooner or later. Cate's mother would be enough to drive the staunchest teetotaller to drink.'

Cate snorted and threw a cherry at him. He ducked and they both laughed.

Hamish left for home not long afterwards. On the drive, he tried not to think about anything except how enjoyable the evening had been.

★ ★ ★

Pete showed up on Hamish's doorstep totally out of the blue early on Boxing Day morning. Hamish invited him in.

'Tea? Coffee?'

'Nothing, thanks, mate. I thought I'd head off to Cutlers Bay for a few days, until I go back to work. Hole up at Theo's. Things at home are—' He shrugged, his attention focussed forensically on his feet. 'I wondered if you had a key. I wasn't game to ask Nat.'

'There's a key under the pot by the front door. The one with the dead geranium in it.'

'Right. As simple as that.'

'Yep. Sure you won't have a coffee?' Hamish filled the kettle and switched it on. 'You look as if you could use one.'

'And you don't mind if I go there for a few days?'

'Course not. Why would I mind?' He held up a second mug and Pete shook his head. He returned the mug to the cupboard. 'Have you told Nat your plans?'

'Nope.'

Hamish studied his brother-in-law. 'So when do you go back to work?'

'In the new year.'

'Anything I can do?'

Pete's gaze flicked to Hamish's and then back to his sneaker-clad feet. He hissed out a breath. 'Nah. Thanks, mate.'

'You'll need to turn on the power at the meter box. Hot water service heats overnight so no hot showers until tomorrow. There isn't anything much in the way of food. Tea, coffee, a few tins of beans and the likes. A couple of cartons of long-life milk. Nothing the mice can get at.'

Pete nodded.

'The supermarket's open every day. Closes earlier on weekends and public holidays. And there's the cafe. Excellent coffee. Food's pretty good too, if you don't want to cook. It's closed on Mondays.'

Pete cleared his throat and looked up. 'Thought I might do a spot of fishing on the beach at Rocky Point. That's if the gear's still in Theo's shed. We used to chuck a line in every now and then. Catch a couple of whiting if we were lucky.'

Hamish raised his eyebrows. Something else he didn't know about his father. The kettle boiled and he made instant coffee. Two teaspoons full, no milk or sugar.

'What do I say if Nat asks me where you are? Unlikely, but you never know with her.'

Pete scoffed. 'I doubt she'll even notice I'm not there.' He folded his arms. He was brawny. Balding. Not short, but not tall either. 'Do what ya gotta do, mate, she's your sister. Just don't get on the wrong side of her, not on my behalf.'

'I reckon that ship sailed a long while ago.'

Pete's mouth tilted into a wry smile. 'Yeah. Well, I'll leave you to it.' He backed away, towards the front door.

Hamish followed. 'Take care, Pete. Give us a hoy if there's anything I can do.'

'Cheers, mate,' Pete said and lifted his hand in a waist-high wave.

Hamish closed the door after him. He fetched his coffee from the kitchen and took it out onto the balcony that overlooked the parklands. He'd always assumed his sister's marriage was solid. Maybe it was and this was only a minor blip. Hamish knew from his own marriage there were plenty of those. But regardless of Pete's casual remarks, underneath it all he'd looked lost and a trifle sad. When he finished his coffee, he realised with a start that he hadn't even tasted it, so caught up had he been in his musings.

Should Hamish call his sister? Visit her? Give her a metaphorical shake and hope it was enough to bring her to her senses? Maybe if they'd had a closer sibling relationship he'd feel comfortable doing that. But in the interests of self-preservation, he decided not to poke his nose into something that wasn't his business. If that meant he was a coward, then so be it.

When his own marriage had been floundering he hadn't confided in Nat nor his parents, not until he'd moved out. His mother had been the only one to show him any sympathy. Nat's comment was 'I'm surprised you stayed together as long as you did. There's only room in a relationship for one selfish person.' *She'd know*, is what Hamish had thought at the time. How she was treating Pete now only reinforced that belief.

Although, he would never have called Andrea selfish. He'd always considered her as being *driven*. Focussed. She'd always known what she wanted out of life and God help anyone who stood in her way. But that didn't make her selfish. She could be extremely thoughtful and generous. And fun. That left him as the selfish one in the marriage. There was a novel idea. Was refusing to compromise when it counted selfish? If so, then he was guilty as charged. But only ever when it came to his job, or so he liked to think.

It was when Andrea took a promotion in her job and her salary ended up much higher than his that things got dicey. She wanted him home more to support her. The more she asked for him to find a job back in the city, one that didn't require long stretches away, the more he'd dug his heels in and stayed out bush. In the end, without children, there was nothing to keep them together. Not when all they did when they were together was bicker.

Back then, Hamish had wondered if she'd found another bloke and that's what had propelled her into finally asking him to leave for good. But there'd never been anything to suggest that. As far as he knew, she'd remained single to this day. Maybe some people just weren't meant to partner up, were better off on their own. His stomach rumbled. Breakfast and then another game of golf with his mates. The thought of either activity did little to lift his mood. He shook his head in an attempt to shift the melancholy that had moved in along with the memories. No point trying to make sense of any of it, he thought. It'd only ever do his head in if he did.

10

Ruth

'How was your Christmas?' Allie asked when we came back after the break.

'It was pretty good. Ate too much and drank too much. Same as usual. Yours?' I asked. I was down on all fours, defrosting the milk fridge underneath the bench with the coffee machine.

'So-so,' she said.

The tone of her voice was such that it had me sitting back on my haunches to look up at her. 'What happened?'

'Cody and Mia's dad showed up Christmas morning. No warning. I opened the door and there he was. I was expecting my neighbour. We have coffee and fruit mince pies together every Christmas morning.'

'Were the kids excited to see him?'

'Sort of,' she said and her mouth thinned into a firm line.

I waited but when she didn't elaborate I went back to the fridge. I'd opened this morning as usual at eight. When I'd first let myself in, the cafe had been overly warm and stuffy. We'd had a burst of hot weather through Christmas and that had combined with the heat generated by the refrigerators and freezers to make the place uncomfortably warm. It was when I'd checked the fridge temperatures that I'd discovered the small fridge under the counter wasn't as cold as it should have been. Serendipitously, restocking it from the storeroom fridge was one of the tasks I'd put off when I closed up Saturday and there wasn't much that needed throwing out.

Street traffic was at a minimum between Christmas and New Year and so far there'd only been a couple of early-morning caffeine seekers. Some of the shops were still closed and the hospital admin girls were both on leave. Business would pick up around lunchtime when the holiday-makers got moving. And there were bookings, one for a group of eight. I'd already pushed together two tables and arranged the chairs and the reserved sign was ready to be placed in the middle of the tables.

'There,' I said, the defrosting of the fridge complete. I closed the door and turned on the power. The motor rattled to life. 'Let's hope de-icing was all it needed.' I smiled at Allie. She looked miserable. 'Does he usually see the kids at Christmastime?'

'Other Christmases he's phoned or FaceTimed and posted them ridiculously expensive presents. No money for that this year, so I suppose he thought he'd grace us with his presence instead and eat me out of house and home while he did.'

'He's not still there, is he?'

She nodded and her expression darkened even further. 'But he'd better be gone when I get home today.'

'You told him he had to go?'

'In no uncertain terms.'

She continued wrapping the knives and forks together with paper serviettes. Transfixed by her nimble fingers and the practised way she went about the task, I tried to imagine what it'd be like to have your ex-husband show up out of the blue. Awkward.

Without slowing or even breaking her rhythm, Allie said, 'When Cody was four, Brett showed up unannounced. He wanted to make a go of it again. I don't know why he came back. He could have been between jobs—or girlfriends. I tried my best to make it work because kids need both their parents. We stuck it out for about a year. The last few months were a struggle for me and of course it all ended in tears when he left again. Cody was inconsolable. Mia didn't speak to me for a month. They both blamed me for their father leaving.' Her fingers stilled and she stood motionless at the bench, a knife and fork in one hand, a paper serviette in the other.

Where had my bright and bubbly employee gone? This woman who stood before me was unrecognisable as the Allie Thomas I knew.

'Allie? Is there something I can do for you? Do you need to go home? I can manage if you do. Maybe Lorna could come in.'

Spell broken, she shook her head and returned to the task. 'If I went home and he was still there, I'd probably kill him,' she hissed.

Before I could gather my wits—and with them, an appropriate response—the front door squealed and heralded two customers. I didn't know whether to be irritated or relieved.

What I ended up feeling was surprised when I recognised Hamish Adams. The man with him was unfamiliar, although of a similar vintage.

'Can't keep away from the place, I see,' I said.

'Who would have thought?' Hamish responded with a flicker of a smile. 'And this bloke here is Pete, my brother-in-law. He needed a break from my sister and I needed to get out of my apartment.' Hamish nudged his bemused companion with a shoulder. 'Don't worry, mate, Ruth has had the pleasure of meeting our dear Natalie.'

Pete relaxed slightly and threw me a hesitant—or was that an apologetic?—smile.

'What can we get you? Coffee to begin with?'

'Yep, thanks. Macchiato for me and a flat white for Pete.'

The men moved their attention to the menu board. Like an automaton, Allie started on the coffees. When they both ordered big breakfasts, I headed to the kitchen.

Things didn't let up from then until closing time.

★ ★ ★

The next morning Allie showed up for her shift an hour early. 'I don't want to be paid, I just had to get out of the house,' she said. She was pale, her still-wet hair pulled back into a tight ponytail. No makeup, not even a smear of lipgloss. So unlike her.

'I take it he was still there when you went home yesterday.'

She swallowed, her nod barely there.

'Should I expect Sergeant Cooper any moment?'

She frowned.

'To come and cart you off in handcuffs … lock you up and throw away the key.'

She rolled her eyes. 'Don't worry, he's still alive. You won't have to advertise for staff. Coffee?'

'Please.'

There were no customers yet so we sat by the window at table eight, sharing a chocolate chip muffin and drinking coffee. It was pleasant to do such a thing and to see colour creep back into Allie's cheeks.

'He has nowhere else to go, or so he says,' she said, halfway through her cappuccino. 'He couldn't pay the rent on his flat so he was evicted. That's what he told me last night. No job, no money, no home.'

'Parents? Friends?'

'His parents live in Queensland and I reckon he might have worn out his welcome with any friends. He was evicted six weeks ago and has been couch-surfing ever since.' She closed her eyes briefly and pinched the bridge of her nose. 'I couldn't face him this morning so I left before he emerged.'

'Where's he been sleeping?' Not that it was any of my business.

'On a camp stretcher in the sleep-out. He cannot stay there, for multiple reasons. The main one being how it's affecting the kids. Mia's ignoring him and me and Cody's mooching around like a bear with a sore head.' She sighed. 'I am so sorry to be dumping all this on you, Ruth. Not when you're struggling with your own issues.'

'I have issues?' I said.

'You know, the headaches, always tired and your being peed off with having to be here all the time, working. No life, so to speak.'

'Oh, *those* issues. Have I been that obvious?'

'Don't forget, we've worked together for several years, Ruth. We spend as many of our waking hours together as some married couples. And I can see you're losing steam and I don't blame you for that. What you do is nothing short of amazing. To have built up this business out of nothing and kept it going the way you have through Covid and everything.'

'Do you think other people have noticed? That I'm losing steam? Has Lorna or any of the other girls mentioned anything to you? Perhaps I should make a doctor's appointment and have a check-up in the new year.'

'That would be a sensible thing to do, Ruth, and no-one's said anything. But don't go to the local GP. He's all right for coughs and colds and he was okay when Cody broke his arm, but I haven't found him very user-friendly when it comes to women's issues. In fact, quite the opposite.'

'I have a GP in Adelaide. I can't remember the last time I went to her, but it's since I moved up here.'

'Sounds like you're long overdue for a check-up,' Allie said. I was old enough to be her mother but I often felt she had a better handle on life matters than I did. But then, she *was* an actual mother.

Two women walked past the window and for a moment I expected them to come in. I readied myself to stand up, but they kept walking. I shouldn't have felt relieved, but I did.

'What about the hotel?' I said.

'For what? A drink?'

'No! Accommodation for your ex, if he's sticking around. It's probably the cheapest alternative in town and he could stay there until a better solution presents itself.'

'What, like crowdfunding the airfare to send him home to his parents? They'd send him straight back, believe me. I think there was a reason they moved to Queensland.'

'Then crowdfunding an airfare is out,' I said, arching an eyebrow.

'Not necessarily,' she said, picking up on my banter. 'There are places much further away than Queensland.'

Several more people walked past the window and this time they did stop and come in and we unfortunately had to wind up our tete-a-tete and get to work. But that didn't stop me reflecting on Allie's situation while I toasted sandwiches and stacked pancakes. It would have been helpful to have come up with a workable option for her. While the hotel rooms were cheap, the cost would escalate if he didn't move on in the shortest time. Which, by her account, he had no intention of doing. And if he was staying around he'd need a job so he wouldn't have to sponge off her for too long. They were all practical issues. Solvable. It was the emotional side of the situation that flummoxed me. Hats off to Allie for letting her ex-husband camp in the sleep-out, but then he was the father of her children, so what choices did she genuinely have?

Allie reluctantly left at three. I'm sure she would have stayed the night if I'd offered. I sent her home with a few leftovers. Normally I would have given them to Laurie but he was staying with his daughter in Port Pirie until the new year. When the cafe had emptied out by three thirty, I wiped down tables and started stacking chairs ready to do the floors. At ten minutes to four I was on my way to flip the sign from open to closed when Hamish appeared on the other side of the glass.

'Am I in time for a coffee?'

I glanced over my shoulder at the machine. 'Just. My next job was to clean it.'

'Make it a long black, thanks. Two shots. I can take it away.'

'No need, if you don't mind me cleaning up around you. Has your brother-in-law gone home?' I spun the sign around and locked the door.

'No, he's out at Rocky Point, fishing.'

'Dare I ask why you're not out there with him?'

'Rather watch paint dry, if you must know.'

'I'm with you. While I enjoy eating fish, I'm quite happy for others to catch it. How was your Christmas?' Back behind the counter, I tamped coffee grounds into the basket, locked it in place and set the machine going. Rich, black espresso oozed into the cup.

'Unremarkable. Yours?'

'Completely over the top food and drink-wise, but that's my brothers for you. They have unlimited means, never want you to forget that and never give up trying to outdo each other. There's always too much of everything. I could live for a fortnight on what they throw away. But it was nice to spend time with family. Without Christmas and Easter, we'd probably never get together.'

'They say Christmas is all about children but as far as I'm concerned, it's become nothing other than a consumption ritual.'

'My, don't we sound like the Grinch,' I said and slid his coffee across the counter. He paid. I discarded the used coffee grounds and wiped out the basket.

'Don't I? But then I could easily do without Christmas. There's only so many times one needs to be reminded of the dysfunctional state of one's family.'

'No grandchildren? Children?'

'Nope. What about you?'

'No, only ever nieces and a nephew and now their kids. Makes me feel older than ever.'

He took a sip of coffee and briefly closed his eyes in bliss, if the expression on his face was anything to go by. 'On a lighter note,' he said, 'do you have any plans for seeing in the New Year?'

'Only to be home in bed and sound asleep well before midnight arrives.'

Hamish laughed, the sound deep and surprisingly melodious. It sent a tingle down my spine. 'We could be twins,' he said.

He drank his coffee while I kept on with the closing routine. Then he took his dirty cup through to the kitchen and stacked the remaining chairs onto the tables for me.

'If Pete catches any fish you must come around and have a meal with us. Fish is best eaten freshly caught.'

With that, he said goodbye and let himself out of the kitchen, leaving me wondering what all that had been about.

11

Hamish

Pete and Hamish had never been the back-slapping, have-a-few-beers-together type of brothers-in-law who shared confidences—or anything else, for that matter. There was a mutual respect there, but basically they didn't know each other well at all. Natalie was about all they had in common.

So when Hamish had arrived unannounced at Theo's place the day after Boxing Day, Pete had folded his arms and gaped at him. Much the same way Hamish had responded when Pete had shown up on his doorstep the day before.

Hamish had grabbed his duffel bag out of the ute and explained that his apartment was on the market. 'The agent has arranged several private inspections over the next few days and she wanted me out when they were there,' he said. 'Easier for me to pack up and leave altogether and then she can come and go with the clients as needs be. And I only had to clean up the place once.'

Astonished by the news, Pete said, 'What are you gonna do when it sells? Go out bush again?'

'What I end up doing in the long run is anybody's guess. Might even buy a campervan and take off.'

'I thought you liked the apartment, that it was what you'd always wanted. Flash bachelor pad, close to the city and the night-life.'

Hamish shrugged. 'You know how things often turn out—reality rarely lives up to the dream.'

'You're telling me,' Pete said.

Pete hadn't asked any more questions, accepting Hamish's explanation at face value, and had kept to himself for the remainder of the week. They'd shared a beer and their evening meal, but Pete had spent most of the daylight hours out at Rocky Point dangling a fishing line in the water. Not that Hamish had envisaged end-to-end brotherly bonding sessions when he'd decided to gatecrash Pete's getaway, but he had looked forward to company other than his own.

Pete ended up going home on New Year's Eve. Prior to his departure, there'd been several long after-dinner telephone conversations that he'd always taken outside. He hadn't said much to Hamish about the calls, but reading between the lines, Hamish had surmised that Pete had been talking to his wife. Given he was going home, Hamish assumed they'd finally sorted out whatever it was that had driven Pete to seek refuge in Cutlers Bay in the first place.

Lunchtime Saturday, after he'd helped Pete pack his bags into the car for the trip home, Hamish said, 'I take it everything worked out with Nat?'

'As well as it ever will. I'm getting too old to take her crap anymore and I told her that. Theo's death reminded me how short life is and you want what's left of it to be the best it can be. And if the best thing for me ends up me being on my own, so be it. I know the girls would never hold it against me. Let's hope Nat got the message this time.'

'Bloody hell, as bad as that. I had no idea. I'm sorry.'

'Don't be. It's been brewing for a long while. And you've had your share to deal with over the years.'

'Did Nat know you came here?'

'I didn't say where I was. We didn't discuss it but she might have guessed.'

Hamish stood by the kerb and watched until Pete's car turned the corner and was out of sight. He glanced up and down the tree-lined street and idly wondered where the woman who worked for Ruth lived. Further up the street, two young lads were tooling about on their pushbikes. A maroon middle-of-the-range SUV drove past and the driver waved. Hamish waved back, but had no idea who was behind the wheel. A surly-looking man slumped in the passenger seat and the driver was too young to be the woman who worked at the cafe. An L-plate was on display in the back window. The car eased into the driveway of a tidy stone bungalow a few doors up on the opposite side of the road. A slim teenager with dark hair climbed out from behind the wheel and car doors slammed. She collected a bulging bag of groceries off the back seat and carried them to the front door. The man had already disappeared down the side of the house. Hamish went inside.

At first it'd felt strange staying at his parents' place without either of them being there. Even when his mother had been alive, he'd never felt overly welcome the few times he'd visited, but he'd always liked the old stone cottage. Now it was shabby, paint peeling on the woodwork, and the garden his mother had once tended so lovingly was a tangled and dying mess.

When his father had retired, his parents had moved to Cutlers Bay, much to the bewilderment of their two children. While Hamish had fully understood the lure of country living, Nat never had. City born and bred and happy to remain that way, she'd never missed an opportunity to castigate her parents for their retirement choice and the fact it was two-and-a-half hours' drive from her home. It had occurred to Hamish that they might have desired, consciously or not, to put as much physical distance as was acceptable between themselves and their daughter and her brood.

One afternoon, not comfortable just to sit and twiddle his thumbs while Pete fished at Rocky Point, Hamish had sorted through and bagged up all his father's clothes and shoes ready for the op shop or the rubbish bin. He messaged Nat to tell her what he was doing. When she didn't respond, he carried on. There was little left of their mother's clothes and personal possessions and he left them for Nat to deal with. In a million years, he'd never have imagined it'd be him clearing out his father's wardrobe. There was nothing he wanted to keep for himself. He wouldn't dream of it. Besides, he was taller and leaner than his father had ever been. Pete was more Theo's build, or what he had been before old age had shrunk him several sizes. He'd gratefully accepted a couple of newish woollen jumpers and three shirts still in their packets, along with a selection of unworn socks and jocks. Hamish recalled the clothes the hospital had returned to him and Nat in a black garbage bag with a yellow tie: a pair of ratty old trousers; the threadbare collar of the faded flannelette shirt; underpants with perished elastic at the waist; socks with holes in the heels and a pair of scuffed leather shoes. The clothes his father had been wearing when he'd gassed himself in his car. And here in the chest of drawers smelling of mothballs were so many clothes that had never been worn.

After Pete had gone home, Hamish loaded the bags into the back of the dual cab. He drove downtown and dumped them into the metal bins he'd noticed in the lane adjacent to the op shop. The bins were full to overflowing after his contribution. Clearly sorting out stuff at home was something people did during the Christmas–New Year holiday break. How many unwanted Christmas gifts had already found their way into the op-shop bins or the rubbish tip? What a waste.

He drove home via the main street. Rosie's Cafe was closed. He wasn't after coffee, rather company—anything to distract him from the thoughts spinning endlessly in his head. He passed the hotel, the only business showing signs of life. Without second-guessing himself, he eased the vehicle into the first vacant parking space. Five minutes later he was perched on a stool at the front bar with a cold beer in front of him.

'Cheers,' Hamish said. He raised his glass to the barman, an older bloke with slick-backed hair and a sizeable beer gut, his face beetroot-red. He looked as if he could expire at any moment.

'Leon!' yelled a grizzled old bloke propping up the bar a few stools down from Hamish. He held aloft an empty glass. His eyes were red-rimmed and rheumy, his slouch that of a front-bar fixture. Every pub had them.

'Hold your horses,' the barman, Leon, snapped. 'I can only see to one person at a time.' He didn't hurry with Hamish's change before wheezing off to serve the restive regular.

Hamish was halfway through his pint when a man walked into the front bar. He was tall and solid, at least a decade or more younger than Hamish and vaguely familiar.

Hamish eyed him as he came up to the bar.

'It's Zach—Cooper,' the man said and they shook hands. 'Are you here sorting out your parents' place?'

'Ah, Sergeant Cooper. Didn't recognise you out of uniform. Yeah, making a half-hearted start. Plenty to do to keep me occupied.'

'Are you going to sell up?' Zach asked. Leon placed a can of diet cola and a glass of ice on the bar in front of Zach, who paid the man. 'Thanks, mate.' He poured the drink, took a long pull, licked his lips and said, 'Expecting a big turnout tonight, Leon? New Year's Eve and all.'

'Nah. There's a shindig out at the sports club and a few private get-togethers around town, or so I've heard. My guess is it'll be pretty quiet here. Just the regulars. Usual crowd in the dining room.'

'Well, I'll be around and I'll check in from time to time,' Zach said.

'Cheers,' Leon said and nodded. He glanced at Hamish's glass. 'Go again?'

'No, I'm good, thanks.'

Leon huffed and trudged off.

'So the house?' Zach said. He leaned against the bar, angling himself towards Hamish.

'Yeah, the plan is to sell it in due course. It's the car I don't know what do with.'

'A 2017 Holden Commodore, VF, if my memory serves me correctly. Some of the last Holdens to be manufactured in Australia.'

'Spot on. He bought it new, believe it or not. Mum tried to talk him out of it. A V6 for a man in his eighties was completely over the top. But he wouldn't budge. Said he'd never had a new car and wanted one that had been made in Australia. He'd only clocked up thirty-three thousand clicks … barely run-in. It's just sitting in the garage collecting dust and it would be a shame to wreck it.'

'I'd almost guarantee there'd be someone around town who'd snap it up, if the price was right. There are those who can't help themselves when it comes to a bargain and they don't ask, or even care, why it's a bargain.'

'True,' Hamish said and stared into what was left of his beer. 'In the end, it'll be up to the executors of Dad's will. Just the same, I'd feel uncomfortable if it was sold without mentioning what happened.'

'I can understand that,' Zach said, after a thoughtful pause. 'But if it was me wanting to sell it, I'd let it slip to the likes of Leon and he'd put the word around. I can think of a few blokes in the vicinity who would be tripping over themselves to get at it.'

'You think so?' Hamish said. He looked sideways at Zach. 'I reckon this is one of the strangest conversations I've ever had.'

The policeman grinned.

'But I'll have a word with the solicitors. They might be happy for it to be disposed of locally.'

'Save them a job,' Zach said, with a lift of his wide shoulders. He tipped up his glass and drained it then crunched on a mouthful of ice.

Hamish finished his beer and stood, pushing the stool into the bar.

'Catch ya later, mate,' Zach called to Leon.

The publican acknowledged it with a nod that made his jowls wobble. Hamish and Zach walked out together.

'Are you staying around town for a while or heading back to the big smoke?'

'Might go home tomorrow or Monday,' Hamish said. 'I'll be back and forward for a while, getting the place ready for sale.'

'You know there's a local real estate agent? Bryan Chalmers. He's a straight-up-and-down sort of a bloke. Been around the area for decades.'

'I've seen where he is. When the time comes, I'll point the solicitors in his direction.'

'Good luck with it,' Zach said and clapped Hamish on the back. 'I don't envy you. Helluva lot for you to deal with, you and your sister. Yell out if there's anything I can do.'

After Zach had driven off, Hamish glanced up and down the near-deserted main street. Should he pack up and drive home to Adelaide now? He could be home before dark. Then he could wander down to Elder Park or into the city. Grab a bite to eat, have a beer or two. There'd be something happening, somewhere. Bring in the new year with all the other revellers. Or he could retrace his steps into the bar here and have another beer—or three. When he'd had his fill all he'd need to do was stumble back to his parents' place and crash.

But it was hot and booze would only make him feel more melancholy. Before he could talk himself out of it, he returned to the house, packed up and drove back to Adelaide and his empty apartment and his empty life.

12

Ruth

Although I hadn't stayed up to formally see in the next year, I woke early on New Year's Day with a sense of anticipation. For what, I had no clue. I'd tossed up whether to open at all on New Year's Day, but decided I would. The cafe had closed for Christmas Day and I was reluctant to lose another summer Sunday's trading, and there were a few lunch bookings. The New Year's special was ham and cheese croissants. And I'd decided on apricot and almond muffins, plus the usual breakfast fare.

Mia and George were rostered to work. George was the eldest son of a local farming family home from uni on his summer break. He'd worked for me over the previous summer and I was thrilled when he'd approached me to say he was available again this year. He was an enthusiastic barista and the customers liked him.

Mia arrived early. In looks and expression, she was a lot like her mum, except her hair was dark brown and she was slimmer and already several inches taller. When she'd worked yesterday she'd had even less to say than usual. I don't think I noticed her crack a smile the whole five hours she was here. I wanted to say something to her about the need to put on a smile for the customers even when you didn't feel like it, but I was privy to what was happening at home and didn't have the heart to put more pressure on her.

'Happy New Year,' I said when she came in. 'Did you stay up until midnight?'

She shook her head. 'I wanted to, but I was knackered.'

I lifted the two trays of croissants out of the oven in a blast of buttery-scented air. The muffins went in. I glanced at the clock. The muffins wouldn't be quite ready by opening time. Never mind.

Mia washed her hands and helped me lift the croissants off the oven slides and onto cooling racks.

'Make any New Year's resolutions?' I said.

'Same as last year: Get out of Cutlers Bay as soon as I can,' she said. 'I am so over this place. I'm saving every cent I earn and as soon as I turn eighteen, I am out of here.' Her jaw was set, her expression fierce.

I was taken aback by her vehemence. Never before had I seen such a display of emotion from her. Any emotion actually.

'And what are your plans for when you do get out of Cutlers Bay?'

'I'm going to travel.'

'Oh! Good for you. Where?'

'Everywhere. But especially Italy. I want to go to Florence and to Venice. And France. Paris, the Louvre. Morocco. Spain.'

'Great choices, lots of wonderful things to see. So much history.'

'Have you *been* to those places?'

'Sure have. And I lived in Paris for a year when I was about twenty-five. Had the most amazing time. Shared this poky studio apartment with another Aussie. Camille. Her mother was French and Camille could speak the language like a native. We worked at the same bar.'

Mia was staring at me her mouth open, her eyes like saucers.

'What?' I said.

'I didn't know that,' she said when she'd found her tongue. 'Mum never told me.'

'Probably because I've never told your mum.'

'Why not?'

'No particular reason. It was a lifetime time ago. Sometimes I wonder if it was even me who went to all those places, had all those experiences. But I travelled quite a bit when I was in my twenties and thirties. When I ran out of money, I'd come home for a spell, save up and travel some more.'

'Why'd you stop travelling? Did you get married or something? Have kids?'

'No, I've never been married and I don't have any children. I suppose I stayed home for longer stretches when Mum and Dad got older. Then Mum was on her own after Dad died and I stayed put permanently to look out for her. My twin brothers are a decade older than me and they had their own families and commitments and I guess Mum got to depend on me.'

'I'm *never* going to get married either,' Mia said. 'No. Way.'

I was washing the dishes I'd used to mix the muffins and she was drying. I nudged her with my elbow. 'Never say never. You might meet some gorgeous hunk you can't refuse.'

'Don't worry, Ruth, I'll be able to refuse,' she said flatly, sounding years older than a tender seventeen.

'What about school? You'll do Year 12, won't you? And then there's university,' I said. 'You'll need a job that pays well if you're going to do all that travel.'

'I will do Year 12 this year, but no university, not for me. Besides, Mum could never afford to support us both and Cody's the brains of the family. I want to do something hands-on, like hospitality. I wouldn't mind doing bar work or waitressing. I love working here, Ruth. It's such good experience for me.' She smiled and it lit up her whole face.

I regarded her for a moment with a new and burgeoning respect.

Here was a teenager who clearly knew her own mind. Such a lot going on behind the quiet reserve.

'It's almost nine,' I said. 'Everything's ready out there so why don't you open up and I'll finish off here? George starts at ten. You do the coffees until then.'

'Okay,' she said, shoulders squared.

It wasn't long before I heard Mia talking to the first customers. We sold out of the ham and cheese croissant special well before midday.

★ ★ ★

Early Tuesday afternoon, out for a jaunt on my day off, I bumped into Angie Daniels in a dress boutique in Kadina, the regional centre half an hour's drive north from Cutlers Bay. I'd been browsing through the racks with no real intention of buying anything, deliciously squandering my free afternoon.

I liked Angie. It didn't matter who you were, a homeless person or the mayor, she treated everyone with respect and kindness. She'd been over forty when she'd given birth to her daughter, Lily. The pregnancy was unplanned and Angie and Zach Cooper, Lily's father, had navigated some pretty bumpy terrain before they'd settled down and become a family.

'Ruth!' she said when she spotted me. She was on her own and appeared flustered. 'Just the person I need to see.'

My eyes must have widened at that because she laughed. Then she dropped her voice to a hoarse whisper. 'I need something special to wear but everything I look at is *so* expensive, even the so-called cheaper stuff. And you always look nice.'

'In a polo shirt and a pair of cotton capris? Plus or minus an apron?'

'And? You manage to look stylish, the way you turn up the collar and with your hair in that fancy twist. And always wearing bright-coloured lipstick.' She drew back and gave me a critical once-over. 'That dress you're wearing now is lovely.'

I glanced down at my coral-coloured linen shift. 'I've had it for years.'

'But I'll bet you didn't buy it from an op shop.'

I hadn't, rather an exclusive boutique in Sydney, although it most definitely would have been on sale. 'What's the occasion you're shopping for?'

She blushed and leaned in closer to whisper, 'Me and Zach are getting married.'

'Angie! Congratulations. That explains why Zach's been grinning like a loon of late.'

'Yeah, he has, hasn't he? He asked me and I said yes, mainly for Lily. Personally, I don't think it's important to be married, not if you're committed to the other person and the life you're making together. But in some circles it still seems to matter that a child's parents are actually married, even though a serious chunk of those marriages are unhappy and will end up in the divorce court.

'And although it's not a secret, we're not broadcasting it either. We're having a small civil ceremony and then lunch with family. It's a fortnight away and I still have nothing to wear,' she said, the last words rising with panic.

I looped my arm through hers and gently shepherded her towards the entrance. 'Let's go and sit somewhere, have a drink and talk about this. Who knows? I might be able to help.'

We found a cafe and ordered. I always enjoyed being this side of the counter for a change.

'Did you have anything particular in mind?' I said as we took a seat. 'A dress, trousers and a silky blouse, leggings and a colourful, floaty top, a skirt and jacket? Do you have shoes you want to match? What's Zach wearing? A suit? I take it you're not going with the traditional white—'

Angie reached across the table and gripped my forearm. 'Look at me, Ruth. Have you not noticed in the years you've known me that I have absolutely no fashion sense and my wardrobe reflects that? I own three pairs of jeans, an assortment of shorts and a bundle of T-shirts, but only one dress. I've owned that dress for over a decade and have worn it to several weddings, a funeral, out to dinner for my fortieth birthday and on my first real date with Zach. Unless I find something else soon, I'll be wearing it to my own wedding. And did I mention that I bought it at an op shop?'

'No, you didn't mention that. I'm sure we'll work out something. Trust me.'

The waitress came with our order. Angie eyed the ice cream–topped chocolate concoction put in front of her. 'Oooh,' she said with glee and rescued the dollop of whipped cream as it began its slow slide off the ice cream.

By the time we'd finished our drinks, we'd agreed that Angie would come by the flat sometime in the next few days and browse through what I had in my wardrobe.

'I'm almost one hundred per cent certain we'll find something suitable. You're only a fraction taller than me and roughly the same build. If what you chose needs to be altered, I have a sewing machine and I know how to use it.'

When I'd moved to Cutlers Bay it'd been in a rush and I'd thrown all my clothes and shoes into boxes and suitcases holus-bolus. There hadn't been time to sort through and discard what I'd never wear again, which would have been well over half of it. When it had all been unpacked, the clothes filled the wardrobes in my bedroom and the spare room to bursting. There were dresses, tailored skirts and trousers with matching jackets and all manner of party frocks and after-five wear, a lot of them bargain buys purchased during my travels. So many of the outfits I hadn't worn in an eon. And was never likely to wear again in the foreseeable future. The outings I'd worn those clothes to were another facet of the Ruth I'd almost forgotten had ever existed. The Ruth before Rosie's Cafe. That Ruth would never have entertained the idea of only wearing polo shirts and capris.

'Wow, was I ever lucky to bump into you,' Angie said. 'I'd about given up and resigned myself to wearing the grey number again. I can't bear the thought of spending my hard-earned cash on an outfit I might not like that much and would only ever wear once. Such a waste.'

'You're right. My clothes are just hanging there gathering dust. Not much call for after-five wear in Cutlers Bay.' At least, nothing that included me.

'Thank you, Ruth,' Angie said. 'I'd better go.' She gathered up her well-used daypack and stood. 'Zach has Lily and his afternoon shift starts in an hour or so.'

★ ★ ★

Back home, the first thing I did was go into the spare room, open the wardrobe and start pulling out any garments I thought might suit Angie. The wardrobe in my room yielded several more. I laid them all out on the spare bed, leaving them on their hangers. Some were still encased in the filmy plastic covers from when they'd last been dry-cleaned. I surveyed the selection with satisfaction; it'd give Angie a place to start. She was sure to find something here and knowing that made me feel good. Just because I might never wear the clothes again didn't mean others couldn't benefit from my excellent taste.

That thought made me laugh. I'd never considered myself a committed clothes horse, however, the array spread out before me suggested otherwise. And there was a large suitcase on the shelf above the hanging space packed to the brim with knitwear and accessories. Somewhere in there was a vintage Coco Chanel cardigan I'd purchased in Paris. Could be worth a bit now, along with a handful of other designer items. Money that could come in useful down the track, when the clothes wouldn't.

13

Ruth

The weather remained hot and everything wilted, including me. The herbs and tomato plants in tubs on the patio drooped in the heat no matter how much water I poured onto them. In the cafe, ice creams and cold drinks were all anyone wanted. We ran out of bottled water and I had to scurry to the supermarket to buy more. The start to summer had been mild and we'd yet to acclimatise, or that's what I'd been telling myself and anyone else who'd listen.

By Friday afternoon, Allie's usual bounce and optimism was at an all-time low. She was trying hard, I could see that. She hadn't mentioned her ex-husband again and I hadn't asked if he was still staying in her sleep-out. She came the closest to being her usual self when she commented on how cheerful Mia had been.

'She was like a different kid when she came home on Sunday. She actually spoke to me first. Then on Tuesday she went out, said she was putting her name down for night fill at the supermarket on top of the days she's working here. Okay in the holidays, I said, but definitely not when school starts again. She'll need to knuckle down if she wants to get through Year 12 with reasonable results. It doesn't come as easily to her as it does to Cody.'

'What does she want to do when she finishes school?' I said, with a twinge of guilt because I already knew and I was prying.

'She'll go to university,' Allie said as if there wasn't any other option. 'A tertiary education will give her the opportunities I missed out on.'

'Is uni what Mia wants?'

'No,' Allie said and winced. 'All she wants to do is see the world. God knows where she gets the travel bug from. Whenever I broach the subject of university, we argue and she storms out and won't talk to me for the rest of the day. Or the week, depending on how heated the argument was.'

'For what it's worth, Allie, I did go to university because it's what my parents wanted for me. It was okay, but it was the hospitality and bar course I did at TAFE that took me around the world, not the arts and communications degrees. And I didn't need a university education to establish and run a successful small business.'

'Yes, but you've had that education and no one can ever take it away from you. A university education will open doors for Mia that have always remained tightly closed for me. And I don't just mean employment opportunities.'

I took in Allie's mutinous expression. No question where Mia's stubborn streak came from. I wanted to smile but I didn't.

'Mia is a good worker. She has plenty of drive and determination. I'm sure she'll make a success of whatever she does. The point is that a university education is not the be-all and end-all some people make it out to be. I'll admit that, during my working life, some of the jobs I've had wouldn't have been possible without a university education. On the flip side, I wouldn't have made Rosie's work without the experience I'd had in the hospitality industry.'

Allie's expression was hard to read. Had I gone too far? Should I apologise for butting into something that was none of my business?

Then she said, 'Point taken, Ruth. A parent only ever wants to see their children flourish and hopefully not make the same mistakes as they did.'

'Of course,' I said. 'And you know, you're never too old to go to university.'

That brought forth a bark of laughter from her and a smile from me. An unexpected influx of customers sent us back to work and I think Allie was relieved.

After she'd left for the day, not noticeably happier than she had been, and Laurie had done the floors and taken out the rubbish, Angie turned up with her arms full of my clothes. She'd come by on Wednesday morning and I'd shown her to the spare room, pointed to the bed and told her to help herself. 'If nothing there takes your fancy—' I'd said as I slid open one side of the double wardrobe, '—you're sure to find something here.'

Her eyes had nearly popped out of her head. 'So many clothes,' she'd whispered and given me a wide-eyed look of wonder. 'Have you actually worn them all?'

'Why else would I have them? Mind you, I haven't worn many of them in the last five years. More's the pity.'

She'd blinked and her mouth had moved as if she'd wanted to say something but didn't quite know what. An hour later she'd left laden with a selection to try on in front of her own bedroom mirror.

'I think I've found the perfect dress,' she said now, her eyes sparkling. 'It's a tad tight but I had a quick squizzy and I think there might be room in the seams. Okay if I take these through and put them back in the wardrobe? And then see what you think about what I've chosen?'

'Just leave them on the bed. Do you have time to try it on now? I'll finish up here and come through.'

'I have about half an hour. Lily's with Zach. They're getting tea. She watches him, entranced, and they eat half the vegetables raw.'

'What a cutie,' I said. I held open the doors and she went through to the house and into the spare room.

Five minutes later, I joined her. She had her back to me when I walked into the bedroom. Gone were the shorts and T-shirt she'd been wearing. She turned around slowly.

'What do you think?' she said, head tilted to one side.

'Ooh, don't you look lovely! Zach won't be able to take his eyes off you.'

She'd chosen a silk cheongsam in swirling blues and greys. It'd been custom made on a visit to Hong Kong. I couldn't remember when I'd worn it last … at least fifteen years ago. It was perfect for her colouring, highlighting her blue-grey eyes, and the simple style suited her shapely figure. It looked better on her than it ever had on me. But she was right: it was a snug fit, especially around the middle. I could see the seams straining when she lifted her arms.

'Comes with having a baby,' she said, dropping her arms and patting her barely there tummy.

'Slip it off and let's see what can be done. And leave the other clothes, I'll put them away.'

Fifteen minutes later, Angie left with me promising to make whatever alterations I could over the next few days. The fit would remain firm but at least she'd be able to breathe and move about without the risk of a seam splitting. We'd talked shoes and accessories and what she was having done with her hair. She was grinning from ear to ear when she waved goodbye.

'Thanks, Ruth. Am I ever so glad I ran into you in Kadina. I want to look special for Zach and if it had been left up to me, I'd probably have been wearing the grey dress again.'

'You will look gorgeous for him,' I said and felt a bit of a lump in my throat.

In the wake of Angie's visit, I felt decidedly flat. She'd radiated a quiet calm and joy. If ever she'd had any qualms about giving up her single, transient lifestyle, which I believe she had, there was no evidence of it now. Although I was thrilled for her, I could acknowledge the sliver of envy that accompanied the benevolence. Not that I'd ever wanted to marry or have children; I simply hadn't. It wasn't her offspring I coveted; it was her joyfulness. The unambiguousness of it and the way she'd said she wanted to look special for Zach. That was what I envied: there was another person in her life that she cared about enough to want to look special for them.

It came to me while I was returning the clothes to the wardrobe. I'd last worn the cheongsam out to dinner with someone I'd wanted to look special for. Clearly my take on how special I'd looked was different from his because there hadn't been a repeat invitation. Then again, he'd turned out to be nothing special. That'd clicked when he said, 'Isn't that one of those dresses Asian women wear?' The way he'd said *Asian* had had the hairs on the back of my neck prickling.

As I slid the wardrobe closed, I caught my reflection in the mirrored door. My inclination was to avert my eyes and walk away, but I didn't: I met my eye in the mirror. And then before I could dissuade myself of the whimsy, I'd stripped off the work-worn polo shirt and capris and slipped into the cheongsam. The silk was cool and smooth, sliding across my skin with a gentle sigh. It fit like a glove; looser, if anything. I stared at my reflection, not consciously thinking, not until the first tear squeezed past my defences. What had happened to the Ruth who'd once worn this dress to look special for someone else?

'Gone, that's where,' I whispered to my reflection and scrubbed away the tear. 'She's long gone.'

Angie had said I always managed to look stylish, even in my work gear. I'd taken it as a compliment. Apart from Mum, and she'd been dead nearly six years, I could not recall a single time in the past decade when anyone had made a sincere, positive comment about my appearance, not before Angie said what she did. How sad was that? Did it mean that no-one really noticed me any more? That I was just *there*? Taking up space? Visible to others only if they'd decided I could be of service them? What a depressing thought.

I changed back into my work clothes, carefully arranging the dress on a covered coat hanger. There were a few chores left to do in the cafe and then I'd hunt out my sewing machine and oil it up, ready to alter the dress for Angie. I hadn't used the machine for months. Aprons to wear in the cafe were the last items I'd sewn. The sewing machine was just another thing that had been left to collect dust and become dry with disuse.

14

Hamish

In the first week of January a young professional couple made an offer on Hamish's apartment, twenty thousand more than the asking price. Unashamedly bemused, Hamish said to Brooke, the estate agent, 'I thought the idea was to offer less than the asking price and then we'd negotiate?'

'If you have your heart set on negotiating, we could ask for more,' she said. He must have looked skeptical or downright dubious because she continued, 'They've done their homework, Hamish. They like it and don't want to miss out. They're in a sound financial position and they're not going to the bank cap in hand—always positive for the vendor, which in this case is you.'

'And you know this because?'

'It's my job to know,' she said and he was hard pressed not to be irritated by the condescension in her tone. In his opinion, she was young and cocky. Over-confident. But her reputation preceded her and if the sale went through as smoothly as she was predicting, she'd have lived up to that reputation.

Hamish didn't sleep much that night. He tossed and turned and worried that he was doing the wrong thing, that he'd been impetuous because he'd felt unhappy and dissatisfied. If the sale went through he'd have six weeks to find a place to live. Where that might be, he had no idea. In the years before and after his marriage the places he'd called home had been determined by where the work was. Post-divorce, this apartment and the imagined lifestyle that went with it had been the ultimate goal. The light at the end of a lifetime of damned hard work in the most inhospitable places imaginable.

Around five he drifted off, only to awaken a couple of hours later feeling heavy-eyed and morose. Being the weekend and with nothing much on his agenda, he made himself stay in bed until eight; his golfing mates were holidaying with their respective families. Idly, he wondered what the Cutlers Bay Golf Club had to offer. He'd driven past the golf course several times and it appeared well tended and utilised.

After he'd risen and showered, he wandered down to Melbourne Street and claimed a table at his usual cafe.

'Macchiato, Hamish?' asked the server when he presented himself at the counter. She was a regular, always ready with a smile and, although he'd never say it out loud, he thought of her as a cleanskin: one of the few servers who didn't sport sleeves of tattoos.

'Thanks, Brittany. And two slices of toast with Vegemite while you're at it.'

'You've got it. Outside?'

'Yep.'

'I'll bring it over.'

He picked up a newspaper on the way to his table, but didn't read it while he waited, rather, he stared moodily at passers-by. People were out and about before the day heated up.

Brittany came with the toast and coffee. 'Cheers,' she said and laughed. 'Excuse me for saying this, Hamish, but you look as if you partied hard last night.'

'Nothing as exciting as that, Brit. I just didn't sleep well.'

'Yeah, totally hear you. My grandad says the same thing: that as he's got older, he doesn't sleep as well. Have a nap in the afternoon. That's what he always does.'

She winked and bounded off. Hamish gaped after her. Grandad? Father he could have accepted, but *grandad*? He swore under his breath. The woman at the table next to him, around his age, had obviously heard the exchange and openly smirked. Hamish took a deep breath and started in on his breakfast. Then he read the paper until a heavy hand clapped him on the shoulder right before a familiar voice said, 'Mate, when you weren't home, I thought I'd find you here.'

'Pete. What's up?'

'Nothin' much. Want another coffee? I'm gonna order one of those latte things.'

He was back in a matter of minutes and pulled up a chair opposite Hamish. He was wearing Stubbies and a T-shirt, with sneakers on his feet. No socks. The T-shirt had seen better days.

'You're not on the outer with Nat again, are you?'

Pete shook his head. 'Nah. She wanted some "me time" this morning because she's looking after her grandchildren this arvo. Robyn's brats.'

'Aren't they your grandchildren as well?'

'Not today,' Pete said and folded his arms. 'Any news on the sale of your joint?'

Hamish updated him, pausing when Brittany appeared with their coffees. Pete had ordered a pear and flaked almond friand to accompany his latte.

'What's with the girlie food?' Hamish said.

'I'm getting in touch with my feminine side.'

Hamish blinked. 'Seriously?'

'Yeah, well, Carmel suggested I try that and then I might understand more where her mum's coming from. As it is, mate, most of the time I don't have a freaking clue where she's coming from.'

'Carmel wasn't taking the piss?'

'Sort of, but I took her point. Bloke's gotta do his bit.'

Hamish glanced at the friand and then at Pete. 'Let me know how it goes,' he said.

'I wouldn't put money on it.' Pete grinned and bit into the friand. Three bites amid a shower of almond flakes and it was gone.

'Actually, that was quite nice,' Pete said and nodded sagely. He dumped two packets of sugar into the latte, stirred it vigorously and then downed it in one swallow. He frowned at the empty glass. 'That didn't even touch the sides. Might have to go again. You?'

'Okay, but let me,' Hamish said and took a twenty dollar note out of his wallet.

Pete came back after ordering and said, 'This fancy stuff is expensive, for what you get. Might have to stick with pies and iced coffee after all.' He put the meagre change onto the table in front of Hamish. 'Thanks, mate.'

Hamish folded the newspaper and pushed it to one side. 'How's work?' he said. Pete delivered rainwater tanks for a manufacturing company in the suburbs. He was often on the road for days at a time.

'Busy. Never lets up. I'm off to the Riverland on Monday, back Wednesday.'

'Do you ever get fed up with it? Ever wanted to do something different?'

'Nope,' Pete said, without hesitation. 'Great way to see the countryside. I've been everywhere, man.'

'Do you reckon it puts more stress on your marriage? Being away like you are?'

'Nah, not from where I'm sitting. If anything, it's the opposite. Gives us a break from each other.'

A waiter came with Pete's second latte and an apricot Danish. He deposited it on the table without speaking or smiling and shambled off.

'I said the same to Andrea once and did I ever get a mouthful. She said that might have been true if we'd ever spent long enough together in one hit to need a break from each other.'

Pete chuckled. 'You never were around much. Lucky you didn't have kids.' He picked up the pastry. 'You want half?'

Hamish shook his head. 'And there was no luck about it. I knew from the get-go that she didn't want children and I didn't care much one way or another. Would you still be with Nat if you hadn't had children?'

Pete stopped his vigorous sugar-stirring to stare at Hamish. 'Never thought about it. We both knew we wanted kids,' he said and the teaspoon clattered onto the saucer. 'But, mate, isn't it lonely on your own? Nat can be a pain in the arse, but we sometimes have a good laugh together.'

'So what was that all about, you know, when you took off to Cutlers Bay a couple of weeks ago? If you don't mind me asking.'

Pete's cheerfulness faltered. He took a sip of the coffee and carefully returned the glass to its saucer. 'Like I said, she can be a pain in the arse and she didn't like it that I had a few beers with Baz. Dunno if it was the beers or the fact I didn't go to lunch with you blokes that upset her the most.' Pete sighed. 'I'd had enough of her sniping that day. We were there to farewell your old man. And then Baz kept lining up the beers. Seemed like the right thing at the time, although I didn't think so the next morning. Haven't been that hungover since my twenty-first.'

'Are your parents still alive?' Hamish said, ashamed for not knowing or remembering. 'Nat's probably told me ...'

'Yep, they're both still going strong. They live in Mount Gambier and I do a run down that way with tanks every so often.' Pete stacked his crockery, pushed it into the centre of the small table and stood. 'I'll catch you later. Thanks for the coffee. I'm on my way to Bunnings to get a few things. I'm putting up more shelves in the shed. I hope everything goes smoothly with the sale. Keep me posted.' He pushed his chair into the table.

'Will do.'

He paused. 'Made any plans for another trip to Cutlers Bay? Clear out a bit more of your parents' junk?'

'No immediate plans. I'll need to be around for the next few days to sign whatever the agent needs me to sign. Plus I'd better get started packing up the apartment.'

'Yell out when you need a hand to move,' Pete said. 'I've got a six-by-four and we could hire one of those U-Haul trailers.'

'Thanks, Pete.' First he'd need a place to move everything to.

Hamish watched his brother-in-law amble off down the footpath. Nat wasn't the easiest person by a long shot and good on Pete for doing whatever he could to smooth things over in his marriage. He had to give the bloke credit for trying. Sadly, Hamish couldn't claim the same. Had he even wanted his own marriage to work? He accepted that he'd never given it a fair go. He hadn't made much of an effort, not when it'd really counted. He was beginning to believe that Pete was right: it was lonely on your own. The vision of how the future might pan out for him wasn't something he liked to dwell on, but if he stayed on the course he was on, the most the coming years would bring was greater isolation and loneliness.

What his father had done to staunch his loneliness and downward spiral to total dependence horrified Hamish. Nevertheless, the longer he ruminated on it and the more parallels he could draw with his own life, the closer he came to assimilating the reasons why his father might have chosen the path he did. Hamish could lay no blame, but that did nothing to absolve his own remorse. Could he have done more for his father over the years? *Should* he have done more? And what about Jonathon, his younger brother? How had Hamish failed him? *Had* he failed him? The cold, hard facts were that Hamish had little in his life to be proud of. Sure, he'd been a hard and conscientious worker, respected in his trade, but the only person who'd ever benefited from that had been himself.

Hamish stacked his empty cup with Pete's. He could linger a while longer, put off the inevitable return to the empty apartment. But sitting there cogitating wasn't good for his mental health. And he'd already had three coffees and it was Saturday morning and there were people waiting for tables.

15

Ruth

Wednesday morning rolled around again and I felt refreshed in the wake of two glorious days off. I'd barely flipped the sign on the front door to open when Audrey Franco was on the doorstep ready for a coffee and muffin. The festive season had been a brief hiatus and now life was returning to normal, the new year rapidly gathering momentum. Christmas with my brothers was a fond but distant memory. Some folk would holiday at the beach for a while longer, perhaps until school went back. But from the second week in January, the early-morning tradies' vehicles had returned, parked haphazardly out front of the hardware shop, the hospital admin girls were back at work, stopping in each morning for a coffee, and the op shop had reopened.

Audrey's mouth pinched up like a cat's bottom as she said, 'You wouldn't believe the junk people dump in the op-shop collection bins over the break. That's why I'm working again today, and Reg is loading the trailer to take to the transfer station as we speak. The most annoying part is that what they can't jam into the bins, they just leave in the alley.'

'That's a bit cheeky,' I said and went on making her coffee.

'Disgusting is what it is. The lazy so-and-sos. If the wind picks up it blows stuff everywhere. If we don't clean it up post-haste, some busybody will report us to the council and next thing we know we have them breathing down our necks.'

'Then why don't you do away with the bins all together? Tell people they can only bring their goods when you're open and then if you decide it's garbage it can bounce right back home with them. Let them take it to the transfer station themselves.'

Audrey's eyes nearly popped out of her head. 'Ruth!' she said. 'That's not like you at all.'

'What's not like me?' I said, genuinely curious.

She twitched a bit, uncomfortable with being put on the spot. 'It's not like you to be … outspoken. You're generally so amenable.'

So I was. But did everybody think that because I never voiced an opinion, I didn't have one? And that meant I agreed with whatever they said? How mistaken they were. 'I've heard you say all this before, Audrey, and I agree, why should you have to clean up other people's garbage?' I fixed the lid onto her to-go cup and slid it across the counter towards her. 'I can't understand why you've never done anything to try and change it.'

Audrey pinned me with a gimlet gaze. 'If we took away the bins they'd just dump it by the door or in the alley.'

'What about security cameras?'

'You think the church can afford the likes of security cameras?'

'If you can't afford the real thing, buy some of those fake ones. Put up signs saying the place is under surveillance. It might deter people.'

She nodded slowly. 'You know, you're right. Why should we put up with it? None of us is getting any younger and we're all volunteers. Well, everyone except Daphne. The church pays her ten hours a week to do goodness only knows what. The roster takes her all of ten minutes, the amount of thought she puts into it.'

'Then ask Daphne to make the suggestion to the powers that be. Go to them with a plan. They might even fund real security cameras.'

'I can't see that happening, but it's food for thought just the same.' Audrey pointed at the muffins under the net on the counter. 'What sort are they?'

'Orange with a lemon curd filling. The lemons came from Claire Cross's tree.' In the lull between Christmas and New Year, we'd cleaned out the freezers and I'd discovered several jars of lemon curd.

'They do look delicious. I'll have one … No, make it two. Reg can have one with his cuppa. He's been a real trouper, helping clear out the bins and doing the dump runs. It's given him something to think about other than his bowels, or the dog's bowels.' She shuddered.

I thought it prudent not to comment. Besides, what was there to say? I popped two citrus muffins into a brown paper bag. 'There you go,' I said and put the bag alongside her coffee. 'Enjoy.'

She paid me, gave a brusque nod and swept up her purchases. 'I'll see you again tomorrow, Ruth. Daphne wants all hands on deck until we've cleared up this mess.'

Audrey marched off and an image of her bursting into a lusty rendition of 'Onward Christian Soldiers' popped into my head. I almost laughed out loud. I rearranged the muffins to fill the empty spot. It wasn't long before there were more coffees to make and the morning's pace picked up.

Nine thirty came but Allie didn't and no message to say she'd be late. Fifteen minutes later, when I'd begun to worry, she rushed in. I was at the grill flipping toasted sandwiches.

'Sorry, Ruth,' she said, frazzled. She threw her handbag into the cupboard, pulled her hair into a ponytail and washed her hands. 'I went to put a load of washing on only to find the laundry floor flooded and no hot water. Have you ever tried getting a plumber in this godforsaken place? The local bloke's on holidays, would you believe? Now, where are we up to?'

'Tables two, three and seven have their coffees and the food's almost ready.'

'I'm on it,' she said.

I plated the sandwiches and she whisked around to the other side of the servery window. When she picked up the orders, I noticed her hands were trembling. Was there more going on here? More than a broken-down hot water service? Even if that were the case we had no time to chat about anything until the lunchtime crowd moved on. And there had been a crowd. Lasagne and salad was the special and it sold out; I'd expected it to last more than a day when I'd baked the two large dishes yesterday. Not that I was complaining. Or was I? Now I'd have to make more this afternoon. I usually stuck with the same special for two or three days.

'At this rate I'm going to have to do a supermarket run for more salad stuff to tide us over until the next delivery,' I said. 'And the butcher for more minced meat.'

'I'd offer to go but the plumber's coming and I need to get home to let him in.' It was already after three.

'You go then. I'll pop out after we close when Laurie gets here,' I said. But where were Allie's kids? Why couldn't one of them let the plumber in? And what about the ex-husband? Was he still camped in the sleep-out?

'Mia's at Mum and Dad's for a few days and Cody's staying with a mate,' Allie said, as if I'd voiced the questions out loud. 'I wanted to take them to Adelaide for a weekend before school goes back. Go to the movies, eat out, do a bit of shopping.' She closed her eyes and shook her head. 'Unlikely, especially not now that I could be up for a new hot water service on top of everything else.'

I stopped what I was doing and looked at her. 'Apart from the hot water service, is everything else all right?'

'Not really,' she said eventually.

'Don't think you have to tell me anything, Allie, but I'd have to be blind not to notice that you haven't been your usual self, not since Cody and Mia's dad showed up.'

She pushed the heels of her hands into her eyes and made a sound somewhere between anger and despair. 'I've got him out of the house but he's still in town. He insists he has no money, doesn't have anywhere else to go and says this town is as good as anywhere else.'

'Where's he staying?'

Her arms dropped to her sides and she gave a brittle laugh. 'At the pub. And would you believe he's got work there? Not in the bar, but all the restocking, yard work and the likes.'

'Yeah, Leon's not up for much since he had the heart attack and someone said he'd sacked the bloke who did all that. Caught him with his fingers in the till, apparently.'

'So Brett said. It's early days but he says he likes the work so far and Leon seems like a fair boss. My worry is that Brett'll insinuate himself further and further into the kids' lives and I'll be left with the fallout when he moves on—because trust me, he will.'

The front door squealed. Allie bobbed down and peered through the servery window. 'Going out not coming in,' she said. 'Which is exactly what I must do. The plumber is on his way from Kadina. I can't afford to miss him.'

I grabbed a cloth and a tray to clear the recently vacated tables. 'See you tomorrow,' I said. 'And if you need a hot shower tonight you're welcome to come around to my place and have one.'

Allie smiled. 'That's decent of you, Ruth. Thanks. I might take you up on your offer. If this hot water service is buggered and I need a replacement, it could take several days. Cold showers are okay in this weather, until you have to wash your hair.'

She left. I chatted to the few remaining customers while I cleared the tables. They were out-of-towners. Not grey nomads, because I hadn't noticed them slip any unused sugar sachets into pockets or purses. Turned out they had beach houses further down the coast.

They kept calling me Rosie and I couldn't drum up the energy to correct them. The three women prattled on about the quaintness of the cafe and how marvellous it was that they could get a decent cup of coffee this far from the city. Several inappropriate responses hovered, but I bit my tongue and smiled and made idle chatter about the weather and such instead until they left.

It was almost four when I flipped the sign behind them and pulled a face in their general direction. Audrey was *so* wrong. I remembered the other Ruth, the one who wasn't a cafe owner. She'd had opinions about many things and could be outspoken on occasion. But then she'd moved to Cutlers Bay and opened a cafe called Rosie's and that's how people here came to know her. To them she'd only ever been 'Ruth from Rosie's Cafe'. They didn't know the other Ruth, the person who'd had friends and had fun, who'd enjoyed having a few drinks and eating out before taking in a show or a movie. That Ruth used to laugh a lot.

Standing there staring out at the familiar streetscape I experienced a visceral yearning to be that Ruth again. I missed her. These days the only times she ever emerged was with family and old friends and that wasn't anywhere near often enough.

Later that evening, after Allie had been for a shower and I'd made more lasagne, I called Robert and then Elliot. If either was surprised to hear from me, they didn't voice it; they sounded genuinely pleased to hear from me. And Elliot laughed when I gave him a potted version of my day followed by a rant about everything I hated about small country towns.

'You need to get out more. Come for a stay, any time. We'll eat out, have a few wines, take in a show. You know you're very welcome,' he said. He was still chuckling when we disconnected.

Yes, I knew I was always welcome, especially at Elliot's, and I did need to get out more. Dip a toe back into the world of that other Ruth. Up to me to make it happen, wasn't it?

16

Hamish

'I thought you were all about clearing out the place to sell it and here you are bringing in boxes. What gives?'

From where he stood at the tailgate of his ute, Hamish glanced over his shoulder to see Zach Cooper walking through the gate towards him. He was in uniform and the police vehicle was parked on the opposite side of the street.

'Ah, Sergeant Cooper,' Hamish said. 'A slight change of plans, you could say. I've sold my apartment in North Adelaide and I need somewhere to store my possessions until I find another place to live. At this stage, I've got no idea where that might be and here's as good a place as any.'

'Plenty of storage units in Adelaide, I would have thought. That's a lot of books you've got there.'

'I like to read and do you know how much they charge for those storage units?' Hamish set down the box of books he'd been unloading. 'And from the few enquiries I've made locally, real estate doesn't move particularly fast in Cutlers Bay, so I think I'm pretty safe storing stuff here.'

Zach nodded, rasping a hand along his jaw. 'If the town was actually on the beach and not at the top of a windy cliff, things would be different, I dare say.'

Hamish folded his arms and regarded the policeman. 'So what can I do for you?' he said. 'You didn't stop by to chat about local real estate and the location of the town.'

Zach smiled and shoved his hands in his pockets. 'About a week ago, I was having a quiet beer at the pub and my ears pricked up when I heard a bloke mention your old man's name.'

Hamish frowned. 'And?'

'Turns out it was to do with his car, the Commodore.' Zach scanned the front yard and the garage. 'Everything where it should be? No sign of anyone poking around uninvited?'

Hamish's frown deepened. 'Not that I've noticed, but I haven't been here long and I can't say I've looked around the whole yard.'

'Did you check that the vehicle was in the shed?'

'No,' Hamish said, already on the move towards the garage. It was a galvanised iron structure with room for two cars and sliding doors at the front. The padlock had been firmly in place when he'd been here after Christmas. And it still was. For a moment, Hamish couldn't decide whether to feel relief or disappointment. If the car had been stolen there wouldn't be the need to offload it; it was a constant and grisly reminder of how his father had chosen to end his life. Hamish had had a brief conversation with the executors and their advice had been that if he came up with a local buyer to let them know.

'Padlock's all good,' Hamish called out to Zach.

The policeman had swiped off the dust from the louvred window at the side of the garage and was peering in. 'Car's still there,' he said. He straightened up and dusted off his hands.

'Maybe the bloke you heard talking wants to buy it. I could forward his details to the solicitors.'

Zach gave a mirthless laugh. 'No, mate. He doesn't have a driver's licence and he wouldn't have two bob to his name, that's why I was so intrigued when I heard him talking about the vehicle.'

'Pity,' Hamish said.

Zach nodded. 'You around for long?'

'Thought I might stay tonight and then see how I feel in the morning. Decide whether I stay for the weekend.'

'I'd say let's have a beer, but I'm getting married tomorrow,' Zach said and grinned.

'Congratulations.'

'Three years it's taken me to talk her into it. And if it wasn't for our daughter, Lily, I'm pretty sure we wouldn't be walking down the aisle now, nor ever.'

'Good for you,' Hamish said. He was a tad envious. Not because he wanted to get married again, but because Zach was getting married and he looked over the moon about it. Hamish couldn't bring to mind the last time he'd been over the moon about anything. It certainly hadn't been when he'd married Andrea. Come to think of it, he couldn't remember how he'd felt then—if he'd felt anything. Why *had* he married her?

'Yeah, it's gonna be a blast,' Zach said, still grinning. 'All my family's coming. Angie's mother can't make it but her brother flies in from Port Hedland today and she's gone to pick him up. I've never met the bloke but he sounds all right.' Zach laughed. 'Listen to me, will ya? Back to business: Like I said to you earlier, put a quiet word out at the pub and I reckon you'd find yourself a ridgy-didge buyer for the vehicle in no time at all.'

'I'll give it a go. I see there's a community notice board down the main street. Could put something up there … but I'll wait until I'm going to be around the place for a few days. Best of luck tomorrow. Hope the day goes well.'

'Thanks, it will, and we'll have that beer sometime.'

'For sure,' Hamish said.

After Zach had driven off, Hamish went back to unloading the last few boxes and stacking them in the second bedroom, the room he'd been sleeping in. There was only a single bed and he'd shoved the wardrobe and chest of drawers to one side to free up a wall to stack the boxes against. Even as he worked, he wondered at the wisdom of bringing his belongings here. He hadn't mentioned it to his sister. She was sure to have plenty to say because he hadn't consulted her first. Hamish couldn't put a finger on why he hadn't the same compulsion to be rid of their parents' home as Natalie did. But then her motivation was simple: she wanted her share of the money. His motive for holding back? He hadn't fully considered what that might be, but it could have something to do with his feeling of being untethered. More so since the apartment had sold, even though the longer he'd lived there, the more he'd felt his post-retirement existence was a sham. But at least living there he had the pretence of a life and he wouldn't even have that for much longer. In a way, his parents' house provided a prop of sorts; something to anchor himself to until he decided where he wanted to be. *Who* he wanted to be.

Hamish's initial intention had been to unload and stay for the night and sort through more of his parents' paraphernalia. Maybe drop a few bags off at the op shop and fill up the wheelie bin with rubbish ready for the next collection. But by the time he'd unloaded, all he wanted to do was turn around and go home, even if that home didn't quite belong to him anymore. This fickleness of purpose was so unlike him. So much of how he was feeling of late was out of character.

He didn't dwell, instead he locked up, turned off the power and replaced the key under the pot.

He drove to Rosie's Cafe. It wasn't quite four and he'd skipped lunch. A takeaway coffee and something to eat was necessary before he made the long journey back to Adelaide.

Ruth was at the counter and she looked up when he walked in.

'Hamish,' she said and her face lit up with a smile. 'What brings you back to town?'

Her smile was catching and it briefly lifted his mood. 'Quick turnaround is all. Wanted to pick up any mail and check everything was ship-shape at the house.'

'Coffee?'

'To go, if you don't mind. Make it a long black. And something to eat. I missed lunch.'

'A sandwich? The fryer and grill are off but the bread's fresh.'

'Whatever's going.'

She went to the kitchen. While he waited, he looked around the cafe. Several women sat at a table by the window, deep in conversation. An older gentleman drank tea and read the newspaper. Hamish suddenly understood why his father had become a regular here: there was a welcoming feel about the space, a homely atmosphere. Towards the end, his father's twice-weekly visits here would have been the full extent of his socialising. A lump grew in Hamish's throat and wouldn't be swallowed away.

No sooner had he wished that Ruth would hurry up so he could get out of there did she appear with a bulging brown paper bag.

'I hope you like roast beef,' she said and then she stilled. Their eyes met across the counter and he knew she read the grief and confusion in his face for what it was. 'I'll make your coffee. And what about a sweet treat for afters?'

'Thanks,' he said and the lump in his throat loosened.

She made the coffee and slipped a piece of pecan pie into another paper bag, along with a paper serviette. 'It's nicer warmed with ice cream,' she said and wrinkled her nose. 'But pretty good without, even if I say so myself.'

Hamish was on the road minutes later. The sandwich was delicious, the perfect amount of filling that didn't spew everywhere when he

held it in one hand. Ruth was right, the pecan pie was excellent. And
of course the coffee was up to her usual standard.

★ ★ ★

Hamish was tired in body and spirit when he let himself into the
apartment almost three hours later. The traffic had been horrendous,
even for a Friday evening. Everyone in a hurry, no-one giving an
inch. The day had been hot and the apartment was warm and stuffy.
He opened the balcony doors and turned on the overhead fans, went
to the fridge for a beer and sat down to watch the ABC News.

Nat rang just as the weather came on. He cursed but took the call.

'What's happening?' she said.

'Not much.'

'Is there something you want to tell me?'

'Like what?'

'Like your apartment being for sale?'

'Pete knows.'

'Yeah, but you could have told me.'

'Not a secret, Nat. I just didn't think you'd be interested.' No
response from her end so Hamish continued, 'We've never exactly
shared the goings-on in our lives, have we?'

'No,' she said, bluntly. 'And now we have no parents to keep each
other in the loop.'

Hamish had never considered it that way but their mother and to
a lesser extent their father had always filled him in on any significant
happenings in Nat's life. Did this mean he'd need to communicate
with her more often in the future? Or would they drift apart even
further until they'd lost touch altogether?

'So what are you going to do when the apartment sells? Where
will you live?'

'Er, I don't really know,' he said, disconcerted by where his thoughts had taken him. 'I have considered going back to work.' Why he didn't tell her that the apartment was under contract, he couldn't explain, nor that he hadn't a clue what he was going to do. He just didn't. Habits of a lifetime weren't that easily broken. *When the sale settles*, he told himself, *I'll tell her then.*

'Why go back to work? It's not as if you need the money.'

'Work's not only about the money, Nat.'

She laughed, a harsh, bitter sound that made him wince. 'That's a good one,' she said. 'When are you going to Dad's next?'

'I went today, as a matter of fact. Everything appeared to be in order.' He didn't mention the car or the conversation he'd had with the local copper.

'You could have told me you were going. The property's half mine.'

'Spur of the moment decision. Woke up this morning and felt like a drive out.' Not really a lie, but not the complete truth either. Definitely a pattern here … He'd have to think about that some more.

'We need to give those solicitors a hurry on to get the house on the market, Hamish. Houses deteriorate rapidly if they're not lived in.'

Hamish put his empty beer can on the coffee table. He toyed with the idea of having another and decided not to. Easier to stop at one. 'The place needs a significant amount of tidying up before it goes on the market. The garden, if you can call it that anymore, is a mess. The woodwork needs a coat of paint. And there's a heap of stuff left to clear out.'

Nat cleared her throat. 'I can't take any holidays just now.'

'No-one's asking you to. I don't mind doing it, but it'll be at my pace. I've done most of Dad's clothes but that's all. Did you want any of the furniture? Kitchen stuff? Sheets? Towels? Knick-knacks? Does Pete want Dad's fishing gear?'

'I don't know, not without asking him. Maybe Pete and I should drive over and have a look. Soon.'

'Maybe you should, after all, it's half yours. Let me know when you do decide to drive over and I'll make sure I'm there. Might be best if we go through the contents together, then there'll be no misunderstandings. Not that I need any of the household stuff, but there are books and lots of other things.'

'I suppose that's reasonable. I'll talk to Pete, let you know what we decide.'

'Fair enough. That it?'

Nat grunted with what he took to be a yes—and a goodbye, as it turned out, because she'd already hung up. Had he just had a reasonably civil conversation with his sister? Perhaps there was a chance that their relationship could take a turn for the better.

He sat and pondered many things until the sun had well and truly set and the only light in the living area was that cast by the flickering, muted television. Disappointingly, his musings did not bring forth the epiphany he was hoping for.

When he showered and went to bed he was no closer to knowing what his next move could or should be. Hamish had no memory of ever feeling as bereft as he did right then.

Blessedly, he slept.

17

Ruth

Allie was still without hot water by the weekend. Mia and Cody were home again and I'd offered the use of my bathroom, but Allie declined, saying they'd manage. 'A bit much to have the three of us traipsing around to your place and the plumber promised me he'd have the new unit installed on Monday,' she'd said when she left work on Friday afternoon.

Saturday morning, Mia showed up early for work. I was glad because I'd woken with a headache and was slow to get moving. I'd wanted nothing more than to put my head back on the pillow and let sleep take over again. Instead, I'd forced myself out of bed, had a shower and taken painkillers. They'd dulled the thumping to a manageable throb. A cup of tea and food helped a bit.

'How was the holiday with your grandparents?' I asked Mia as we took down chairs and topped up the sugar sachets on the tables.

'So-so,' she said. 'Nanna's a bit bossy, but Poppa's always fun. He played golf and I tagged along with him. That was okay. One day we went for a hike in Morialta Conservation Park. It was so hot. I wanted to go into Rundle Mall to the shops and to the movies, but—' She shrugged and rolled her eyes. 'They really have no idea. They took me to *McDonald's*.'

'That bad, huh,' I said.

'Yeah. I've never liked McDonald's, not even when I was a kid. It's junk food. Cody loves it. But then he is such a *boy*.'

'Can't say I've ever been a fan,' I said. 'But my brother Elliot, who's over seventy, still enjoys a Big Mac from time to time, with fries.'

Mia paused, cloth in hand. 'Wow, that's old to still be eating junk food.'

'He's not *that* old, Mia, and I don't think age has much to do with what we like to eat. He'd tell you he was still young at heart.'

She snorted. 'Not with all that fat and cholesterol in his system.'

'I'll tell him you said so,' I said, eyes wide.

'Is he your favourite brother? I remember you said you had twin brothers.'

'I suppose he is, not that I've ever really thought about having a favourite. Robert's okay but he can be a bit prissy and his second wife, I find her difficult to warm to.'

'What's prissy?'

'Prim, proper, basically a pain in the bum.'

Mia laughed. 'Which twin is the oldest?'

'Elliot, by seven minutes. They're not identical and although they're close, they are very different in looks and personality. Robert's a lot like our dad was and Mum used to say Elliot took after her father.'

We'd finished the tables and chairs and moved to the kitchen. The grill and the fryer were on. I had water heating ready for poached eggs. Saturdays were always busy and cooked breakfasts popular. George would be in at ten to help. Mia went out to top up the dogs' drinking bowl.

'Might as well open up,' I said to her when she came back through the kitchen door. She bounded off to unlock the front door and turn around the sign. I surveyed the cafe, ready and waiting for another onslaught. More of the same. The throbbing in my head worsened suddenly and I was struck by a wave of nausea that made me salivate. *Not now!* the voice in my head screamed. I stepped out the kitchen door and gulped in a few lungfuls of fresh air, vowing I'd make an appointment with my Adelaide GP on my next days off. I'd drive down and stay overnight with Elliot and maybe even look up an old friend, see if they were free for a coffee or lunch.

Feeling much better, I went inside just as Mia put in the first food order.

★ ★ ★

The headache hung around for most of the weekend. I'd kept the worst of it at bay with regular painkillers. First thing Monday morning, I rang for a doctor's appointment. If I wanted to see my usual GP for a long consult on a Monday or Tuesday, the earliest appointment wasn't until the middle of the following month—four weeks away. I was taken aback. I'd wait a couple of weeks before I let Elliot know I was coming to stay overnight, otherwise I'd be inundated with suggestions of what we could do while I was there. And it would all involve drinking wine.

Instead of doing housework and putting on a load of washing, I went for a drive. I could do all the chores tomorrow. A pity to waste such a beautiful summer's day, hot and sunny, with a steady breeze blowing in off the ocean. Uncanny how much better I felt the further away from Cutlers Bay I drove. When I stopped at a cafe in Wallaroo, down near the jetty, my headache had almost disappeared. After choosing a table outside, I ordered a pot of tea and scones with jam and cream and whiled away the next hour watching the activity happening around me. It was a pleasant way to pass the afternoon but if I was completely honest with myself, it was lonely on my own. How much nicer it would have been to have company, real company,

another person who wanted to be with me, not just the chatty waiter
filling up the empty space for a moment. Would this be the script for
what remained of my life? Tea and scones for one?

The tide was out so when the chatty waiter began throwing me
the kind of looks I threw people when closing time rolled around,
I went back to the car and drove until I found a spot where I could
walk on the beach—anything to put off returning to Cutlers Bay for
a while longer.

It was going on five when I trudged back to the car and shook
the sand off my feet before wriggling into sandals again. I headed
for home. Did I feel better after my afternoon out? Marginally, but
there was still the housework and washing to do. I told myself this
was all Graham Wurst's fault. If he hadn't decided to retire, I would
have kept on keeping on. Satisfied with who I'd become and what
I was doing.

Halfway home my phone pinged with a message; I didn't glance
at it until I was parked in my driveway. It was from Angie Daniels,
or was that Cooper now? It said, *THANK YOU!!!!!!!* and had a
photo attached: Angie and Zach on their wedding day, both of them
beaming. She looked so lovely in my silk cheongsam. I sent a reply
saying just that. A message bounced back: *Thanks … Is it okay if Zach's
sister borrows the dress? She loves it and has an important work do coming up
and nothing suitable to wear and no surplus funds… A bit like me.*

Without hesitation I wrote: *Of course she can!*

And Angie was back in the blink of an eye: *Thanks, Ruth, from both
of us. A xx*

The warm glow generated by having done a good deed lasted all
of five minutes. No sooner had I let myself inside than the phone
rang. It was Allie.

'I'm sorry, Ruth, but I won't be able to open up in the morning,
or work at all, actually.'

'Oh, bugger,' I said, the words out before I could censor them.

Her response was brisk and defensive and, when I thought about it later, a tad over the top.

'This is the first time I've ever needed a day off at short notice, Ruth, in all the years I've worked for you and I *am* only casual. I'll be back on Wednesday and Mia has offered to work in my place tomorrow. Unless of course you want to ask someone else.'

'No! Of course not.' What I wanted to ask was if she was all right, if there was anything I could do, but I didn't. Instinct warned me against it. And she was right in that she'd never taken an unplanned day off. So all I said was, 'Tell Mia to come in at ten, thanks. And you take care.'

'Thank you, Ruth. I'll see you Wednesday.' The line went dead.

I raised my eyebrows at the phone in my hand and said, 'I wonder what that's all about?'

By five past ten the following morning, I knew.

'Dad went and hurt his back,' Mia said without a trace of her usual reticence. 'Mum had to take him to Adelaide for a scan and then back to see the doctor in Kadina.'

'Did he do it at work?'

'No, unfortunately. Mum said if he had, he'd at least be on compo. She is *so* pissed off. He can't work or even stay at the hotel because he can't get up and down the stairs. Mum wanted to go in his car to save some wear and tear on hers, but it isn't registered. He's been driving Cody all over the place in an unregistered car. When he told Mum that, I thought she was going to do something really bad, like kill him.' Mia's eyes all but bugged out and then took on a glassy sheen.

'Oh, sweetie,' I said and opened my arms. She willingly stepped into them. I hugged her tight and she hiccoughed loudly, then drew back and blew her nose and gave me a soggy smile.

'I'd better get out there,' she said. 'I just heard a customer come in the front door.'

'Before you go, where's Cody now?'

'Oh, he went with them. Mum said she was less likely to kill Dad in front of either of her children. And Cody knows how to work the GPS in the car.'

Mia went out to the counter to serve, leaving me in a stunned silence. How easy my life was by comparison. I glanced at the food orders I'd been making a start on when she'd burst through the kitchen door and then I set to work.

It was a standard Tuesday, dead as a doornail after lunch. I was scanning the order from the wholesaler—it'd seemed a bit light-on—when Mia cleared her throat. I looked up from the sheet of paper in my hand.

'Ruth,' she said and blotches of colour stained her cheeks. She rolled her lips together and looked everywhere but at me.

'Promise I won't let on to your mum anything you've told me,' I said, taking a punt on the cause of her embarrassment. 'You're all having a tough time now, but it'll pass, believe me. And remember, calm seas don't make skilled sailors.'

She frowned and then her face slowly relaxed. 'Ah … I get it.'

'Here,' I said and went to the freezer to retrieve the half-dish of lasagne left over from last week's special. 'Take this home for your dinner. Throw a salad together, make some garlic bread—'

'I'm on it. And thank you, Ruth.' Sometimes she could sound like a woman twice her age, other times the vulnerable teenager she was.

After I'd closed up and Laurie had been and done the floor, I went home and did housework and two loads of washing without complaint.

18

Hamish

Hamish spent the weekend packing up his apartment. If he took all the books out of the equation, there wasn't a huge amount. Settlement was mid–February but he wasn't the type to leave the packing until the last minute. He'd been debating what to do with all the furniture when Brooke called late Tuesday afternoon.

'The buyers have asked if any of your furniture is for sale,' she said, straight to the point, as was her style. 'They love it.'

'Funny you should say that,' Hamish said, hardly believing his luck. He pivoted slowly and took in the expensive leather sofa and lounge chairs, the flat screen TV, the empty bookshelves, glass-topped coffee table, dining table and chairs … and couldn't imagine where else they might belong other than an apartment such as this.

'Hamish? Are you still there?'

'Yep, and it's all for sale,' he said.

'Excellent. Work out how much you want for each item and give me a few dates and times and I'll arrange for them to have another look.'

'The place is a bit of a mess right now. I'm in the process of packing up.'

'I'm sure they'll understand.'

There and then he decided to take another load to Cutlers Bay first thing the following morning. 'What about tomorrow or Thursday? I'll tidy up the place and make myself scarce for a couple of days.' There'd been nothing from Nat about when she and Pete might travel across to Cutlers Bay so he might as well carry on with his own plans.

'Done. If that doesn't suit the buyers, I'll get back to you soonest.'

Hamish breathed deeply and slowly. This was all becoming very real. With a pang of something that felt a lot like guilt, he scrolled to Nat's number. There were two of them in this tango; he'd at least tell her he was travelling to Cutlers Bay in the morning.

But she didn't answer and he didn't leave a message.

Hamish paced through each room of the apartment. It didn't take long and there wasn't an overabundance of furniture. He thought back to when he'd bought it all, not much more than a year ago. The wife of one of his golfing mates was an interior decorator and she'd helped him pick it all out. Truthfully, she'd picked it out and he'd agreed with whatever she'd chosen. Minimalist, she'd called the style. It was perfect for the apartment but, as it turned out, not for him.

The contents of the kitchen cupboards reflected that Hamish wasn't a cook. He could scramble eggs, open a tin of beans and throw a steak on the barbecue. As a result, there were only the most basic of utensils, crockery, coffee mugs, half-a-dozen wine glasses and a few other odds and ends. He'd had plans of entertaining when he'd moved in, had even considered cooking classes to improve his sadly lacking skills. He laughed at that now, the ridiculousness of it, the sound loud and grating. Takeaway pizza with the boys from golf had been about as good as it got. Maybe he'd throw the kitchen stuff in with the furniture, see if they wanted it all. They could have it for nothing.

Using a borrowed trolley, he took the last few boxes of books and the like down to the ute and stacked them in the back. The car parking was secure and he had no qualms about leaving them loaded overnight.

On his way back to the apartment, he bumped into a woman he'd seen several times over the months he'd lived there. They'd never moved past the nodding and saying hello stage of acquaintance. She was a decade or so younger than him and drove a late-model silver Audi. No wedding band; corporate attire.

Today she stopped and said, 'I see you've sold your apartment ... I couldn't help but notice you've been loading up your ute.'

He pulled up and propped a foot on the trolley. 'Went way quicker than I thought, for a lot more than I expected. But how did you know it was for sale? There wasn't a sign.'

She smiled and he noticed it was an attractive smile. 'I'm in the business,' she said. 'This is a very sought-after area. And I'm not surprised it sold as fast as it did.'

'If I'd known, I would have come to you,' he said with a shrug. 'But I don't even know your name ...'

She hesitated. For a split-second, he thought she was going to tell him. Then she shrugged and said, 'Never mind. Good luck with the move.'

'Thanks.'

She headed off in the direction of her car and he steered the trolley across to the lift and pressed the up button. While he waited, he watched her drive off. That banal exchange had been the longest conversation he'd ever had with anyone who lived in the apartment block. And it had come right when he was moving out.

★ ★ ★

Hamish got away the following morning before the sun had topped the ranges. A night of fitful sleep had left him feeling grumpy and gritty-eyed. He stood at the kitchen sink and drank coffee as the eastern sky lightened into a palette of pastel pinks and powder blues streaked with gold. Outside it was cool, the air fresher than most mornings, and the traffic light. It was barely after eight when he drove through the gate of his parents' place. He climbed out of the ute, stretched and sucked in a lungful of tangy sea air. He'd unpack the ute and then take himself to Rosie's for breakfast. His stomach rumbled in agreement.

The front door key was in its usual spot under the plant pot. When Hamish opened the screen door something dropped onto the verandah. He bent and picked it up: a realtor's business card and not the local bloke. Odd, but then he supposed word got around in small country towns. Or perhaps now that probate had been granted the solicitors were finally getting their act together. He flipped the card into the pot with the dead geranium and let himself into the house. Thirty minutes later, he'd locked up again and was on his way to the cafe and breakfast.

When he pushed through the front door, Ruth was busy at the coffee machine, chatting to two women waiting at the counter. They wore office garb and sneakers. He reckoned he'd seen them in here before. Several tables were occupied and customers sipped on their morning brews. The aroma of coffee and freshly baked muffins made him salivate. He perused the menu board. The two women, clutching insulated cups, nodded with vague recognition on their way out.

'Good morning,' Ruth said. 'Back again and so soon.'

'Couldn't keep away,' he said. 'Coffee, please, and the smashed avocado on sourdough with poached eggs. And one of those muffins.' He jerked a thumb at this morning's offering: apple and cinnamon.

'Done,' she said. 'Coffee first?'

'Please. Long black, thanks.' He paid and wound his way to the table where he'd sat on every other occasion, except the day the family had come here to eat after the cemetery. Two more people came in after him and Hamish wondered where Ruth's sidekick was.

When she brought his coffee, she put it down and said, 'This is the table where your dad always sat.'

'I didn't know that. Did he just sit here on his own and stare out the window? Like I'm doing now?'

'He'd read the paper, eat his raisin toast and yes, he'd stare out the window for a bit.'

'No helpers today?'

'Allie. She'll be here shortly. The regulars know I'm on my own until nine thirty and they're usually patient. That said, I'd better get moving.'

Hamish watched her wend her way back to the counter. She scooped up empty coffee cups on the way. He liked the way she moved. The job kept her in shape. He couldn't imagine she'd have time for much else. The more he considered it, the more he realised he wanted to know more about her, like what she did in her free time. Why she'd ended up in Cutlers Bay in the first place.

Disappointingly, it was Allie who delivered his food, not Ruth. 'Sorry about the wait,' she said.

The meal was delicious, the poached eggs firm on the outside but runny in the middle and well worth the wait. Ruth hadn't emerged from the kitchen when he left.

Back at his parents' place there was an unfamiliar sporty-looking cherry-red hatchback in the driveway. Hamish frowned and parked alongside the kerb. He peered up the pathway and saw the front door was open. His frown deepened. When he went inside, the passage light was on. The musty staleness he'd become accustomed to when the house had been closed up for days had dissipated. Whoever it was had been here for a while.

'Hello?' he called.

Footsteps and then a slight woman with big hair emerged from the main bedroom.

'Who are you? And what are doing in here?' he said.

She was holding a tablet, reading glasses perched on the end of her nose. 'I could ask the same of you,' she said.

'This is my parents' house. I have every right to be here.'

'Oh,' she said, drawing out the syllable. 'You must be Hamish.' She extended her hand and stepped towards him. 'Terri Longbottom, Longbottom Realtors, Kadina and Wallaroo.'

The card he'd thrown into the geranium pot. He shook her hand. 'You still haven't told me what you're doing here. Today isn't your first visit.'

'Natalie requested an appraisal on the property. She wants the place sold as soon as possible. I'm taking photos today. Didn't she mention that to you?'

'No, funnily enough, she didn't and it's not *hers* to sell. It's part of our parents' estate and it's in the hands of the solicitors appointed to act as executors.'

'Oh.' Her eyes widened. She licked her lips. 'My apologies, I must have misunderstood your sister.' She tucked the tablet under her arm. 'I'll make myself scarce.'

'It's okay, Terri. Probably not all your fault.' He moved to one side so Terri could pass. 'The key?' he said.

'On the kitchen table.' She paused when she reached the front door, swivelled around to face him. 'It is a solid old home. Good bones. Plenty of potential. No salt damp. Needs a bit of TLC before it goes on the market, if you want the best price. If the opportunity arises, I'd be more than happy to work with the executors.'

Hamish stood on the verandah until she'd driven away. He pulled out his phone and hit his sister's number. Sure enough, it was busy. What's the bet Terri pulled over as soon as she was out of sight and rang her client? Former client, maybe? He wandered around the outside of the house looking for what the realtor had seen but he'd never taken the time to notice. She was correct, it was sound and free of salt damp. He surveyed the generous backyard. Plenty of room to extend the house. A new kitchen, living area, wet areas … He was envisaging such a renovation when his phone rang.

'Nat,' he said. 'Is there something you wanted to tell me?'

'All I wanted was a rough idea of what the house was worth.'

'So you gave a complete stranger permission to fossick around when no-one was here. Take photos.'

'Not exactly. And you're there now.'

'You didn't know that I would be here. And you must have told her where the key was.'

Nat sighed. 'We need the money, Hamish. We still have a mortgage on the house and it needs a new roof and we want to install solar panels and batteries at the same time. The cost of electricity is crippling us—'

'Yeah, but what would you have done if Dad hadn't died? He could have gone on for a few more years yet.'

'But he didn't,' she said, 'and I want what I'm entitled to.'

'And you'll get it, in due course. We're only talking weeks, maybe a month to two, not years, until it's all sorted.'

'So what are you doing there again?' she said.

Now was his chance to come clean. 'I've started packing up my books for when the apartment sells. I'm storing them here until I have somewhere else to put them.'

Nat surprised him by not having a go because he hadn't run it by her first. He just never knew with her.

'So do you think your apartment will sell quickly?'

'I'm optimistic. There's been interest.' Why couldn't he just tell her it was under contract?

'Maybe when it sells and you're flush you can give us a loan,' she said in a jokey sort of way, but they both knew she wasn't really joking. And then it struck him: *There* was the reason he hadn't told her his apartment was as good as sold and for more than the asking price.

19

Ruth

The next few days in the cafe were tension filled. Allie arrived for her shift right on the dot each day and did her work with her usual efficiency, but her heart wasn't in it and smiles were rare. A couple of times, I came very close to snapping at her and asking her to lighten up and leave the problems at home. The only highlight was that Hamish was in town again and seemed in no hurry to leave. He'd worked out that generally the cafe was quiet after three and I was on my own and would have time for a chat.

Allie was filling in her timesheet before she left for the day on Friday afternoon and I was flipping through recipe books. A customer had generously given me a bucket full of yellow-flesh peaches off his tree and I was desperate for something to do with them. They wouldn't keep for much longer. Allie cleared her throat and I looked up. Her bag was slung over her shoulder and she had her phone in one hand.

'Ruth, I'm sorry I've been such a grump this week. Things at home are quite challenging at the present and although I try hard not to bring it to work, it's not always that easy.' Her attention shifted to the phone and she fidgeted with it. 'You've always been a terrific boss, which makes me feel even worse about the way I've been.'

'Well then, let's hope the situation rights itself pretty soon,' I said. I wondered if she wanted me to say more but I wasn't about to say it was all right, because it hadn't been. She'd been like a sullen black cloud and the customers had noticed.

'Yes,' she said and slipped the phone into her pocket without making eye contact. 'See you next week. Oh, and thanks for the lasagne you sent home with Mia. It was generous of you. It would have been spaghetti on toast otherwise.'

'You're welcome.'

She threw me a rueful smile and left. I stared at the kitchen door after it clunked shut behind her. My gut told me there was much more going on with Allie than what Mia had confided about was happening at home. My head started to ache; distant drums again. With eyes closed, I massaged my temples. What if Allie quit? But why would she? She needed the job. Unless a better-paying job with more hours came along. The drums came closer.

Then the rarely used bell on the counter dinged. I pushed myself upright, pasted on a smile and went out to attend.

Hamish strolled into the cafe at three thirty just as I finished making iced chocolates for two kids itching to spend their pocket money. I squirted on an extra dollop of cream and they both grinned. 'Which table are you sitting at? I'll bring them over.'

'By the front window,' they chorused, already halfway there.

I carried the drinks to table one and turned to greet Hamish. 'Coffee?' I said and he nodded. 'What have you been up to?'

'Would you believe Zach Cooper's found a buyer for the car? I've been cleaning it out.' He shuddered.

'That would have been awful! I don't know of anyone in town who details cars. I wish I could offer you something stronger than coffee. You look as if you could use it.'

'You don't have a piece of that pecan pie left, by any chance?'

'No, sorry. It's one of the most popular things on the menu. There are brownies with macadamia nuts.'

'Sold.'

'Warm, with ice cream?'

'Yes and yes. I would never describe myself as a sweet tooth but you are a persuasive woman, Ruth.'

Hamish sat at table three to eat and drink and read the paper. The kids noisily slurped their iced chocolates and when they were finished, they left just as noisily. Four o'clock came and I flipped over the sign, locked the front door and went on with my usual routine. Hamish brought his plate and cup through to the kitchen.

'Is Laurie not coming? Shall I start putting up the chairs?'

I glanced at the clock. It was well after four thirty. I frowned. Unease fluttered in my stomach. 'Laurie's never late.' There were no messages or missed calls on my phone. I scrolled through to his home number. It rang out. Hamish watched me do all this. He quickly picked up on my anxiety.

'Does he live on his own? What's his address? I could slip around there, see if he's okay.' He said it casually, as if it were no bother. I knew he'd be thinking about his own father.

'Are you sure?' I said.

He nodded firmly, aware of the subtext.

I tried Laurie's number again with the same outcome. 'Number seventeen Third Avenue,' I said, along with brief directions.

'What's your mobile number?' Hamish was poised, ready to enter it into his phone. I rattled it off.

He left and I paced, peering every so often through the front door, never sure what I was looking for. The ambulance? Zach's police ute? Try as I might, I couldn't recall Laurie's son's name or where the farm was. I looked up the White Pages and found seven Randalls in and around the area. *Not good enough*, I told myself. Laurie wasn't exactly an employee but I should have known these details.

Fifteen minutes passed and I began stacking chairs onto tables to distract myself.

I had six chairs to go when my phone pinged with a message: *Laurie ok.*

'Thank god,' I murmured, lightheaded with relief. I sent back a thumbs up, pocketed my phone and finished the chairs. Hamish came in just as I was filling the mop bucket with hot water, detergent and a splash of vinegar.

'He'd had a bad night so after lunch he laid down for a nap. I rang the front doorbell and when he didn't answer I went around and knocked on the back door. Took a bit to rouse him. He couldn't believe what time it was.'

'Next time I see him I'll get his son's phone number. Thanks for going around there.' I rested the mop against the cupboard and focussed on Hamish. His expression was bleak. 'Are you okay?' I said.

He lifted his shoulders and gave the tiniest shake of his head. 'Just thinking how it must have been for Zach Cooper when he went around to check on Dad, not knowing what he'd find. I suppose for him it wouldn't have been the first time he'd stumbled across a worst-case scenario.'

'Goes with the job, I guess. Not something I could do.'

'Me either. Hats off to the people who do.'

We reached for the mop at the same time.

'Let me do it,' Hamish said when I refused to relinquish my grip on the wooden handle.

'It's okay. I did it for years before Laurie came along.'

'And I'm offering to do it now in lieu of Laurie. He still wanted to come and do it but I promised him I would and I'm a man of my word. He believes you work too hard.'

I laughed and reluctantly let go of the mop. 'He is a dear man. Another lonely soul left to fend for himself after his wife died. They seem to gravitate to this place. Or the front bar of the hotel.'

'I get why they come here, Ruth. I've sat at Dad's table often enough now to have worked it out.' He raised his eyebrows before he trundled off with the mop and bucket and I set about unloading the dishwasher and putting out supplies for the following morning. I tip-toed across the wet floor when I went to the storeroom. I loved the vinegary freshness left in the wake of the mop.

'Come for breakfast in the morning,' I said after he'd emptied the bucket down the grate outside the kitchen door. 'On the house.'

'I will come, but I'll pay,' he said. He washed his hands at the hand basin. Large, capable hands, neatly trimmed fingernails. Used to hard, physical work, if the calluses were anything to go by.

'No, you won't. Laurie does the floors and I feed him. That's the deal.'

Hamish smiled and I decided I definitely liked his smile. 'Fair enough,' he said, drying his hands on the paper towel. 'I'll see you tomorrow morning. And don't work too hard. Can't have Laurie worrying about you.'

I gave an exaggerated eye roll as I locked the kitchen door after him.

I peeled and sliced peaches to make peach and honey jam and then put together the dry ingredients for tomorrow morning's peach and coconut muffins. While I worked, I pondered how it might be for Hamish going back to his parents' place, unaccompanied except for his memories. More from what he hadn't said rather than what he had, I'd gathered all had not been well between Hamish and his father. On that front I'd been lucky: nothing but happy memories of my dad. I'd been doted on. Robert and Elliot being a decade older meant that I'd virtually been an only child, which probably had a lot to do with it. Basically, I'd lived something of a charmed life. There'd been the usual challenges: not getting jobs I'd wanted; relationships that hadn't worked out; being broke in New York and not knowing

how I'd get home. Trivial stuff, most of it. Losing Dad and then Mum
a decade later had been king hits, but my brothers, particularly Elliot,
were always there in the background, if and when I needed them. So
nothing out of the ordinary, really, not like what Hamish and his sister
would be trying to come to grips with. And Natalie's children and
grandchildren, losing their grandfather in such a way. How would it
be explained to them? And then to have to clean out the car where
his father had taken his own life? That was the part that left me with
a lump in my throat.

It was late by the time I'd made the jam, poured it into sterilised
jars and cleaned up. Peach and honey jam would go nicely with
scones and whipped cream. I put aside a jar for Allie, thinking a sweet
treat might cheer her up for a bit.

20

Hamish

'The car's been sold,' Hamish informed Nat. They were talking on the phone late Saturday afternoon. 'The bloke picked it up after lunch.'

'How much did you get for it?' Nat demanded and Hamish could have hurled the phone across his parents' kitchen.

'Is that all you can think about? The money? It was me who picked it up from the police station in Kadina and drove it back here and then I cleaned out the damned thing, Nat. Take a moment to consider what that might have been like.'

'He didn't die in the car, he died at the hospital,' she said.

'Splitting hairs, Natalie.' He told her how much the car had sold for and that the buyer had paid the money directly into an account nominated by the solicitors. He didn't mention the sixty bucks he'd spent on a slab of Pale Ale for Zach. He'd willingly bear that cost just to be rid of the Commodore.

'When are you coming back to Adelaide?'

'Don't know. I might stay and clean out the garage now that the car's gone. If there's anything I think you or Pete might want, I'll put it to one side. Any idea when you'll drive across?'

Natalie took a moment to process all of what he'd said. 'Maybe next weekend. If Pete's not away.'

'Will you overnight it?'

'Let me talk to Pete first, see what he wants to do.'

'Your call.'

'Will you be there? Have you sold your apartment yet?'

Hamish cleared his throat. 'A few things in the pipeline. I should know more soon.' Fibbing for sure, but with only the faintest tinge of remorse this time. He'd tell her when he was good and ready.

'Terri gave me a ballpark figure of what the place should fetch, depending on how much work we do first to tidy it up.'

We? With a flare of annoyance, Hamish said, 'So when are you planning to do some of that tidying up? If you're going to benefit, isn't it only fair you do your share?'

He could almost hear Nat's hackles rise, but what she said next surprised him.

'I hate being there, Hamish. It's too sad now that Mum and Dad have both gone. I wouldn't care if I never saw the house or Cutlers Bay ever again. You probably don't understand because you weren't as close—'

'Quit while you're ahead, Nat,' Hamish said through gritted teeth. 'You know nothing about how I might feel.' And as bizarre as it might sound, when he was here, he felt closer to his parents than he had when they were alive.

Nat sniffed but held her tongue.

'I'll keep working here while I wait to see what happens with the apartment. Who knows what might lie just over the horizon?'

'Nothing more than what's on this side of it,' Nat said. 'You ought to know that by now, you've been looking for most of your life. I'll talk to Pete and he might come up on his own. He'll know what things of Mum's I'd want to keep. Dump the rest.'

After the call ended, Hamish sat at the kitchen table and stared at nothing. Was Nat right? Had he always been so busy chasing what was just over the horizon that he'd missed what was right in front of him? Sobering thought, if it had even a grain of truth in it. He stretched and yawned, contemplated a beer but put the kettle on instead. His stomach rumbled. Ruth's big breakfast was all he'd eaten today and that was hours ago. Coffee in hand, he went outside and sat on the back step. It'd been a nice day, the heat tempered by a gentle sea breeze that seemed to pick up around mid-afternoon on days like this. The neighbour over the back was mowing grass and a dog barked off in the distance. Hamish drew in a long breath and then let it out slowly, willing himself to relax along with it. The backyard was a peaceful spot with its requisite gnarly old lemon tree and leaking galvanised-iron rainwater tank. Remnants of what had once been a vegetable patch took up a large corner of the yard, a carefully chosen spot protected from the scorching late-afternoon summer sun. Next to it a small garden shed housed a lawnmower, wheelbarrow and other gardening equipment. None of it would have seen the light of day in a long while. By the tap, a coiled, faded hose with a sprinkler on the end was tangled up with weeds. Testament to these observations was the back lawn: long ago browned off and now dead from lack of water. Hamish sighed and leaned back against a verandah post. While he sipped the coffee he went back over the conversation with Nat.

He didn't know what to make of her admission that she'd prefer not to visit Cutlers Bay ever again. Hamish's snarky self reckoned it was nothing more than Nat being Nat, a veteran at avoiding unpleasant situations and things she didn't want to do. It'd been like that when they'd been growing up. Being the youngest, their parents had shown Nat far greater leniency than either he or Jonathon had experienced. Then, after Jonathon's death, in the eyes of their father everything had been Hamish's fault. Hamish had always found Natalie difficult and hard to like. He'd searched for understanding but found he had none. If you took away their parents they really had nothing in common. In the cold light of day, when the house sold and the estate was settled there would be little reason for him to pursue an ongoing relationship with his sister. The thought left him feeling vaguely regretful, but steadfast.

★ ★ ★

Hamish heard raised voices in the pristine stillness of early morning. He paused to listen. It was Sunday and he'd been up since dawn, methodically piling half a skip load of junk in the driveway in front of the garage. He heard the muffled thud of a slammed door and then nothing more. He shrugged and kept on with what he was doing. Several minutes later, he noticed a dark-haired teenager hurrying along the opposite footpath, her arms tightly crossed, shoulders hunched. He recognised her as the L-plate driver. Had the raised voices come from where she lived? What had it been about? Hamish chided himself for being nosy. Not enough going on in his own life if he had the time and inclination to be curious about what was happing in the lives of the neighbours.

Having worked up an appetite, he was looking forward to another one of Ruth's big breakfasts, but the cafe didn't open for the best part of an hour. He took a video of the growing pile in the driveway and sent it to Nat with a message: *See anything here you want?*

Moments later a reply whooshed back.

Is that a table tennis table leaning against the shed?

Yep.

Mum and Dad playing table tennis???

Hard to imagine. There's a crate with bats and balls, nets, etc. Do you want it?

NO! I'm just surprised. I had no idea.

And with you being so close— Hamish paused and then deleted the words and wrote: *If you want anything in the pile let me know asap.* Nat responded with a thumbs-up emoji. He carried on adding to the pile.

Rosie's Cafe was humming when he let himself through the front door some time after nine. Ruth was at the coffee machine and he was surprised to see the young woman he'd seen earlier scurrying along the footpath ferrying coffees and teas to waiting customers. Hamish didn't dwell on how pleased he was to see Ruth or how disappointed he was to see table three taken.

'Good morning,' he said. 'Looks busy.'

'Just your average summer Sunday morning. What can I get you?'

'Same as yesterday, thanks. And who's the girl waiting tables?'

'Mia, Allie's daughter. Why?' Ruth regarded him with a steady gaze.

'No reason, except that she walked past Dad's place earlier this morning. She was probably on her way to work.'

Ruth nodded and returned her attention to the drink she was preparing and the girl called Mia flashed past and scooped up the two waiting cappuccinos. A young man with slicked-back hair and a blindingly white T-shirt came in through the kitchen door.

'George! Not a minute too soon,' Ruth said. 'Take over here, please, and I'll get back to the kitchen.'

'Sure thing,' George said, tying on a waist apron.

'And how are you?' Ruth added and pointed out the order she was up to.

George nodded. 'I'm good, thanks.' They switched places.

'Now, Hamish. The big breakfast? Long black or macchiato?' Ruth scanned the dining area. 'Table one okay?'

'Yep, and make it a macchiato.' He paid and made his way to the table. It felt strange not to be sitting at table three but the couple there appeared firmly ensconced with their bacon sandwiches, coffees and newspapers. Mia was on her way back to the kitchen with her hands full of empty cups and crockery. Hamish scrolled through the morning's news headlines on his phone and it wasn't long before Mia was there with his coffee and breakfast cutlery.

'Hi,' she said. 'I'm Mia Thomas. Ruth told me where you're staying and that we're practically neighbours. Who knew?'

'Hello, Mia. I'm Hamish and yes, we are. My parents lived at number thirty-four before they died.'

'I heard about your dad. I'm sorry,' she said.

'Did you know them?'

Her mouth turned down. 'Not really. The old lady—I suppose she was your mum—anyway, when I was younger I'd see her in the garden and she'd always say hello. And then later, sometimes she'd be up the street or in the park in her dressing gown and slippers and she couldn't remember where she was. Me and my brother Cody would take her home and the old man—your dad, I guess—well, he could be a bit cranky with her.'

'Mum had dementia and Dad looked after her. It wouldn't have been easy on either of them.'

'That's exactly what my mum said. She said your dad used to come into the cafe but not on the days I work.' Mia flashed him a smile. 'Nice to meet you, Hamish. I'd better get on or I'll have the boss on my back.'

'Yeah, right. Nice to meet you too, Mia, and thanks for telling me about my mum. She loved her garden.'

'It used to look really pretty,' she said, gathering up empties as she went.

Hamish's appetite deserted him. He stared down at the cooling coffee and fought the urge to get up and walk out. Get as far away from this place as he could, back to wherever he'd been when the neighbour's children had been walking his forgetful mother home to an uncertain reception. Nat might be right in never wanting to come back to Cutlers Bay. Then there'd be fewer reminders of how often and how deeply he'd failed his parents, especially his mother.

21

Ruth

'Something wrong with your coffee, Hamish?' I put the laden plate on the table in front him. He was sitting with his arms folded and he hadn't touched the drink Mia had delivered at least ten minutes earlier. There was a pallor beneath his tan that I hadn't noticed earlier. His eyes were glazed. He squinted and blinked a couple of times.

'No, definitely not,' he said, as if he'd been someplace else.

'You look as if you've seen a ghost.'

He made eye contact and then glanced away again. 'I suppose I have, in a roundabout sort of a way.'

'Is there anything I can do? I'm a good listener and sometimes it helps to just talk.' After a quick scan of the bustling cafe, I felt compelled to add, 'Not now, of course, but we close at two.'

When he didn't answer, I wondered if he'd heard me, or was pretending he hadn't to avoid embarrassment.

'Do you know where my parents lived?' he said.

I nodded.

'Come around for a drink after you close. I'm cleaning out the garage and when I've finished there I'll start on the yard. Any excuse to down tools will be welcome.'

'What about I bring leftovers for a late lunch or an early tea? The cafe's closed tomorrow and some things won't keep.'

He smiled, not his most vivid smile, but he'd lost the haunted look of minutes earlier. 'Sounds perfect.'

'Let me make you another coffee. This one will be cold.' I reached for the cup.

He stayed my hand with his own. 'It'll be fine, Ruth, thanks.'

'See you later then,' I said, mainly to confirm to myself that I was actually seeing him later. At a place other than the cafe, where there was always the counter between us.

'Looking forward to it,' he said and reached for the pepper grinder.

'Enjoy.' I hustled back to the kitchen and the waiting orders, but not without a quick peek over my shoulder to reassure myself he was eating the food I'd put in front of him. He was.

By two o'clock, the cafe was empty, George had gone and although I'd told Mia she could go too, she appeared to be in no hurry to leave, leisurely stacking chairs onto tables. I locked the front door and turned the sign. She mightn't be impatient to go, but I was. For the first time in forever, I had a place to be other than here, never mind I'd all but invited myself. After I'd mopped the floor, I'd put together the food: leftover frittata, salad and an assortment of sweet treats. Then I'd have a shower and change clothes before I went. Didn't want to go out smelling like fried food.

'Do you want me to mop the floor?' Mia said. 'I don't mind.'

'What's up? You're usually the first out the door on Sunday afternoons.'

She gave a dramatic sigh and said, 'Nothing to go home to. Cody's at a mate's place and Mum and Dad do nothing but argue. And when they're not yelling at each other, the silence is nearly as bad.'

'Is your dad's back getting better?'

'That's what they argue about! He won't do what the doctor and the physio say he should do and Mum's just desperate for him to get better so he can leave.'

'What do you think?

She rolled her shoulders into a sort of a shrug. 'I dunno,' she said. 'Cody likes having Dad around. They do things together, you know, Xbox and stuff like that. I can take it or leave it.' She screwed up her face. 'But if him leaving means Mum's mood improves, I'm all for that. When she's not picking on Dad, it's me or Cody in the firing line.'

'Oh dear, things sound tough. Is there anyone you could talk to? A close girlfriend? Maybe your grandma?'

She shook her head vehemently. 'No!' she said. 'It's not their problem, Ruth,' she continued, sounding just like her mother. 'Mum would *die* if she knew I'd mentioned anything to you. She hates people, especially her mother, knowing our business. But her and Dad yelling at each other this morning? Everyone in Cutlers Bay would have heard *that*. It's why I came to work early.'

'In the unlikely event that Allie says anything to me, you have my word that I won't repeat what you've told me. Not a word of it. Okay?'

'Okay,' Mia said in a small voice, looking at her feet rather than at me. My guess was she was already regretting sharing so much with me.

'And Mia—'

She looked up.

'You did a great job today. If you're still good to mop the floor, please do, and put an extra thirty minutes on your timesheet. I'll finish off in the kitchen.'

'Cool,' she said and went off to fetch the mop and bucket.

★ ★ ★

It was closer to four o'clock than three when I set off on the short walk to East Terrace. The afternoon was hot and I'd changed into tangerine-coloured linen shorts, a cream-coloured tank top and my favourite sandals. My hair was in a French braid and I wore lipstick the colour of the shorts. The picnic of leftovers was stowed in an insulated bag. I didn't drive because I suspected wine might be involved. Besides, it wasn't far.

There was no sign of Hamish in the garage or the front garden when I arrived. But he'd been there, because a pile of junk took up the full width of the driveway. I knocked on the front door. The flyscreen sported a hole bigger than my fist.

'Come in … door's unlocked,' he called. 'Make yourself at home. I'll be out in a sec.'

I let myself in and followed the passage through to a dimly lit kitchen. I heaved the bag of food onto a faded green and white formica table. The reason for the dimness soon became obvious: a creeper of some kind crowded the outside of the kitchen window, restricting the natural light. I peered out the window to where I could see the end of the garage and an elderly rainwater tank.

'The ivy will have to go.' Hamish stood in the kitchen doorway. He flicked on the overhead light, towel-drying his hair with one hand. 'Not that it'll make much difference. A skylight is what's needed.' He wore khaki-coloured shorts and a black T-shirt; thongs on his feet. He paused and my face quickly warmed beneath his steady gaze. 'You look nice,' he said.

'Thank you. So do you.' We each sized up the other. Then he said, 'Is that the food?' and the spell was broken. Or maybe I'd imagined it in the first place.

Keep things in perspective, Ruth. Here is an attractive, interesting man who will have no reason to be in Cutlers Bay after the disposal of his parents' estate. And a woman who used to be interesting and attractive but is tied to Cutlers Bay for the foreseeable future.

'It'll stay cold in there for a while.'

He slung the towel over the back of a chair and opened the fridge.

'Beer? Or would you prefer a glass of wine? There's white or red.'

'White, thanks.'

He produced a stubby of beer and a bottle of Pikes Clare Valley Riesling.

'Perfect,' I said 'Glasses?'

'To the left, cupboard above your head.'

I took down the finest of white wine glasses and carefully placed it on the table.

Hamish raised his eyebrows. 'A surprising find in Mum and Dad's kitchen, to be sure. Would have been Mum not Dad. She didn't mind a glass of wine. Dad was a beer man, the rare times he drank.' He unscrewed the lid from the wine, poured me a generous amount and returned the bottle to the fridge. 'Shall we take our drinks outside? It's not too bad on the back verandah this late in the afternoon.'

'There's cheese and crackers.' I unzipped the bag. The cheese board had survived the walk intact.

'Pretty flash leftovers,' he said.

'Allie warned me the blue cheese dressing wouldn't be popular and she was right, hence the leftover blue. The cheddar is a staple in my fridge, as are the Tasmanian brie and the olives.'

'My lucky day,' he said and picked up the cling-wrapped board along with his beer. 'Grab your wine and follow me.'

We settled in two ancient armchairs with an upturned milk crate between us to serve as a table. 'From the heap of stuff in the driveway, I gather you've made serious inroads into the clearing out and cleaning up. Are you on holidays?'

'Retired,' he said. He cut a piece of blue and loaded it onto a cracker. 'It seemed like a good idea at the time.'

'Retired from what?'

'Diesel mechanic,' he said and I automatically glanced at his hands. He chuckled. 'Retired long enough to get the grease out from under my fingernails.'

'The day you first came into the cafe I wondered if you worked outdoors ... because of your tan,' I added when he raised his eyebrows. I hoped he didn't notice the flush of colour creeping up my neck. You were never too old to be embarrassed.

'That'd be the golf course,' he said, 'but before I retired, I worked primarily in remote areas ... seismic crews, oil and gas fields, stations. Money was good. If you know what you're doing, a bloke could be gainfully employed twenty-four-seven, if he wanted to be.'

'And are you having second thoughts now, about retiring?'

'Kind of,' he said. 'It took me about a year to discover that everything I'd strived for wasn't what I wanted after all. I was like a square peg in a round hole. So much of who we are is tied up in the work we do. You take the job out of the equation and what's left?'

'A good question. To the people in this town, I'm "Ruth from Rosie's Cafe". They've never known me as anyone else and they don't give a thought to who Ruth might be without Rosie's Cafe. I'm beginning to wonder myself. Fuzzy memories tell me she was okay ... obviously not without her flaws. You know the bit that scares me the most?'

He shook his head.

'When the time comes to hang up the apron, I won't know who to be.' I gulped a mouthful of wine. And then another. 'So I do understand what you're getting at.'

'Maybe what we need to do when we retire,' Hamish said after a thoughtful pause, 'is reinvent ourselves. Whether we realise it's what needs doing and actively do it, or just let it happen over time. Try something and discover it's not for you, so try something different until you find what fits.' He leaned forward and rested his elbows on his thighs. He looked as if he had the weight of the world on his shoulders. 'And all the while you're getting older, less able and coming to realise you've let some of the most important things just slip through your fingers.'

'You sound as if you've been giving this a bit of thought,' I said. With a mild shock, I realised my glass was empty.

He shrugged and cast me a sideways glance. 'Probably not before time.' He sat back in the chair and closed his eyes. 'Mia said something this morning that touched a raw nerve. She said we were neighbours and I asked her if she'd known my parents. She replied that yes, she had.' He swallowed hard. 'She and her brother used to bring my mum home when they found her out wandering, not a clue where she was. When they brought her back, Dad would be cranky with her. And I thought, Hamish, where the hell were you when all this was happening? And why weren't you there to help out sometimes so that the neighbour's kids weren't the ones bringing her home?'

'And where were you?'

'Working, with no-one other than myself in mind. Any wonder my marriage went down the tube the way it did. My sister *kindly* pointed out to me recently that's there only room in a relationship for one selfish person and of course I thought she was referring to Andrea, my ex. But now I'm pretty sure she meant me.'

So he had been married. I stood. 'I'm going to get a glass of water and more wine. Do you want another beer?'

'Thanks.'

In the kitchen, I paused and took a deep breath, then I found a glass and filled it with tap water and drank it. What Hamish had recounted explained why he'd looked as if he'd seen a ghost this morning at the cafe. How should I respond? Real, meaningful conversation with someone I hardly knew but wanted to know better was something I'd forgotten how to do. What he'd shared with me deserved more than a trite or clichéd response. I grabbed another stubby and the wine bottle from the fridge, told myself to slow down on the wine and went outside, hoping that whatever I said would be the right thing for the circumstances.

22

Ruth

I woke at seven on Monday morning with a doozy of a headache and a roiling stomach. This time it was definitely not a migraine, but a hangover. After drinking the best part of a bottle of wine the previous evening, what else could I expect? I drank two glasses of water, swallowed paracetamol and went back to bed. After three more hours of sleep, I felt much better. If only the cafe were open, I'd ask Allie to make me a greasy bacon and egg sandwich and a double-shot expresso. But I made do with cheese on toast and two coffee pods.

While I was sitting at the kitchen table, still in my dressing gown, wool-gathering while I drank a second coffee, the phone pinged with a message. Hamish.

Have you forgotten your offer to help me pull down the ivy today? It's nearly lunchtime.

Hardly. But I had forgotten my offer and I was in two minds about how clever I'd be spending too much time in his company. I'd enjoyed yesterday evening immensely and, unless he was an accomplished actor, so had he. He'd told me about selling his apartment and how he was considering all his options, including going back to work out bush. Wouldn't be wise to get attached only to have him evaporate into the Never-Never. From where I sat I could see how easily that attachment could happen. Pikes Clare Valley Riesling wasn't the only thing that had given me an attack of the giddies. But then, what the hell? At my age, opportunity didn't present often, if at all. And there was always the chance I'd misread the signs and all he was after was a brief distraction. Did I want to find out?

I quickly tapped in a reply: *Give me an hour. Not at my finest this morning.*

Ha! No rush. See you when I see you.

I finished the coffee and dragged on a well-worn pair of cut-off jeans and a tatty T-shirt. Sneakers on my feet. Straw hat, sunglasses, sunblock and gardening gloves and I was good to go. But not without a swipe of lipstick. On my way past, I watered the pots of herbs on the patio. They weren't what you'd call flourishing and that was totally my fault. To flourish, they needed regular food and water, just like every other living thing.

Hamish was hard at it when I arrived and I had to dodge trails of falling ivy. A tangle of green cuttings wilted in a heap near the rainwater tank. 'This is a mongrel of a job,' he said from his perch up the ladder. I squinted into the sun and watched him climb down. 'There's another pair of secateurs there, if you wouldn't mind cutting up what I've pulled down and shoving it in the green-waste bin.'

Hands on hips, I looked at the heap and then at the bin.

'I know it won't all fit in there but it's a start. I'm organising a rubbish skip to be delivered.' He mopped at the sweat on his face with the bottom of his T-shirt. The man had a sixpack. Well, I'll be. Then he smiled and there was that giddy feeling again. 'Thanks for coming over,' he said. 'I half-expected you to renege on your wine-fuelled offer.'

'Tempted to, but a gardening workout will do me the world of good.'

'You do look a tad seedy. Or is that something I shouldn't mention?' His smile widened. 'There's plenty of cold water in the fridge. And we have the leftover leftovers from last night.'

I grabbed the secateurs and set about the task at hand, thankful I'd brought the gardening gloves. It was the most work they'd ever done.

It wasn't long before the band on my straw hat was sticky with sweat and I could feel moisture trickling between my breasts and soaking into my bra. The bin was full to overflowing, so I started piling whatever he cut down and sawed off in a heap. The main trunk of the ivy was thicker than my arm.

'A chainsaw would be bloody handy about now,' he said. He'd discarded his T-shirt and rivulets of sweat ran down his chest as he used a handsaw to chew through the main trunk. Then he dropped the saw to the ground. 'Let's go in and have a cool drink,' he said. 'I'm about buggered. Are you hungry?'

'Thirsty more than anything.' I mopped my face with the bottom of my T-shirt and followed him into the house. I couldn't decide whether to be disappointed or relieved when he pulled his T-shirt back on. I got a whiff of the pungent sourness of his sweat as it mingled with my own. 'Tell me again why you're getting rid of the ivy? You could have trimmed it back around the kitchen window. I think it looked quite nice. Added to the ambience of the place.'

'True, but it'd completely choked up the gutters on that side of the house. There's water damage from when it rains and the gutters overflow. A bit of rot in the woodwork.'

'Oh, I see. But aren't you just going to sell the place anyway? You could have left it to whoever buys it to decide.'

He filled two large glasses with cold water and slid one across the table towards me. 'We'll get more for it if it's structurally sound and neat and tidy. I think I'll paint the outside woodwork.' His gaze swept around the kitchen. 'Been a while since the place has seen a lick of paint anywhere. From what I can see, I don't reckon Theo was big on home maintenance. He never was that handy and Mum was the gardener.'

'What did he do for a living before he retired?'

'Pen-pusher in some government department. Took a payout when computers got too much for him. He was quite bitter about it, by all accounts.'

I took a long drink of water and then pressed the cool glass against my face. 'So do you enjoy all this handyman stuff? Painting and the likes?'

He leaned against the kitchen sink, crossed his ankles. 'I dunno. I've never thought about it, just do what's gotta be done. But I do enjoy working with my hands and none of what needs doing can be too hard, if a bloke uses his common sense and YouTube.'

That made me smile. 'Where do you think I learned to change a tap washer?' I said. 'And unblock drains and replace stovetop elements. Plumbers and electricians are notoriously expensive and in my kind of business, you do whatever you can to bolster the bottom line.'

'I can imagine,' he said. 'From what I can gather, the past few years haven't been kind to small business. You must be doing something right to have survived. How much longer do you reckon you'll stick at being Ruth from Rosie's Cafe? Before you hang up your apron, as you so aptly put it.'

Biding my time, I reached for the water jug and refilled my glass. How could I admit that I had no exit strategy? That my life's savings were tied up in the business and I was too young for the aged pension. Hamish held out his empty glass and I topped it up for him. I sipped more water. His scrutiny became uncomfortable.

'Simply put,' I said, 'I don't have a retirement plan. Remiss of me, I'm beginning to realise.'

'Not necessarily. Look at me, I had a meticulously planned retirement strategy, only to discover twelve months down the track it was completely the wrong one. And now? I'm no closer to an answer about what I'll do or where I'll live when I have to move out of my apartment. I can see myself going back to work.'

'But wouldn't that be a backwards step? Unless of course you needed the money.'

'Nah, I don't need the money,' he said. 'If I went back to work it wouldn't be for the money.'

'Lucky you,' I said. If I was as well set up, hanging up my apron once and for all would be a cinch.

He put his empty glass on the sink, refilled the water jug and returned it to the fridge. The mood in the room had shifted, subtly but definitely, cooling by a degree or two. He stepped across to the kitchen window.

'Hasn't made much difference, has it?' he said and I knew I hadn't imagined his withdrawal. He didn't want any more talk about the future. Or was it talk about money that made him uncomfortable? Was he expecting me to hit him up for a loan because he had plenty? Or ask if he wanted to go steady? I almost snorted at that idea.

'I don't follow you,' I said, except for the obvious and blunt change of subject.

'The light. In here. The bulk of the ivy's gone but it hasn't made much difference.'

'Oh, I see what you mean and you're right, it hasn't. Maybe a skylight would be the way to go.' I went to the sink, rinsed my glass and upended it on the draining board. 'I might get going,' I said.

'What about the leftover food? I thought you'd stay for lunch.'

'You eat it. Besides, I'm not that hungry and I have jobs to do.'

He looked put out. Too bad. I felt a sudden and inexplicably urgent need to get out of there.

★ ★ ★

Elliot rang after tea that night. I'd settled in for an evening of mindless television-watching in my dressing gown, a bowl of freshly made popcorn on my lap.

'What's happening out there in the sticks, old chook?' he said, true to his usual form.

And true to my usual form, I resisted a tart comeback that would have gone something like: *If you visited me more often you'd know.* 'Not a real lot,' I said instead. 'Business has been steady, keeping me on my toes. Are you okay?'

'I'm very well for a man of my advanced age. You sound tired.'

'Advanced age?' I scoffed. 'Perhaps I had one too many wines last night and that's why I sound tired. Or it's because I am tired. After five years running my own cafe I am *very* tired. I'm up before six most mornings and the days I bake it's six in the evening, or after, before I shut up shop.'

'Why don't you sell up? Retire. Enjoy life for a bit. Before you know it, you'll be old and decrepit like me.'

'I'm too young to retire. I've recently rejigged things a bit so that I can have two days off every week.'

'Who says you're too young? If you retired now you could have seven days off a week instead of two. I retired when I was sixty and you're what? Going on sixty-three?'

'Yeah, well we're not all uber-successful like you,' I said, aiming for banter but not quite making it.

'True,' he replied, sounding pompous.

I laughed because that's what he'd expect me to do, but I didn't find it a bit funny. Not that I begrudged him or Robert their apparent financial successes; they'd both worked extremely hard. But then so had I and right now I was feeling a bit touchy about the whole retirement and money subjects. I'd said too much already. I had my pride.

'Let's talk about something else,' I said and stuffed a handful of popcorn into my mouth. It was barely lukewarm.

'So, when are you coming to stay, now that you have all this time off?'

'On the fourteenth of February. I've booked in for a check-up with my GP.'

'Ruth, what's going on? Are you unwell?'

'No, except for the occasional headaches. I'm sure it's nothing, but I haven't had a serious check-up since I moved to Cutlers Bay. I'm long overdue and while I'm not unhealthy, I could probably be healthier.'

He grunted. 'Talk to Robert. He's always lecturing me on what I should and shouldn't do, what I should eat, or more to the point, what I shouldn't eat or drink. And that I should exercise more. He can list all the maladies that run in our family, from high blood pressure to haemorrhoids. Downright morbid, if you ask me.'

Intrigued, I pushed myself upright and shifted the bowl of popcorn to the coffee table. 'Tell me, do you have high blood pressure or is it haemorrhoids that are bothering you? Or maybe both?'

'Not something I'm prepared to discuss with you, or anyone else for that matter, except perhaps my physician.'

'Sounds like you should talk your doctor. You need to get to the bottom of whatever it is that's bothering you,' I said and sniggered.

'How very droll,' he said. 'Now, provide me with dates and times to allow me to prepare for your imminent arrival.'

'It's three weeks away, Elliot, and please don't go to any trouble. No dinners and shows and the likes. I would much prefer to spend a couple of quiet evenings with you.'

'You really have gone to seed out there in Hicksville, haven't you? However, your wish is my command. Evenings in it will be. Pizza and red wine. And not my best red either. Not with pizza.'

We talked for a while longer and he filled me in on the latest family goings-on. Robert was training to run another marathon and my niece Stacey's husband Chris was having gastric bypass surgery.

'Last resort,' Elliot said mournfully. 'The poor bugger has tried every diet under the sun and then some. Stacey is at her wits' end with him. You know his mother always has been a big woman.'

The only time I'd met Chris's mother was when he married Stacey. I didn't remember her at all, never mind what size she was. Shortly after that we said goodbye.

For no real reason, Elliot's call left me feeling down in the dumps. We were all ageing, every one of us, and the older we got, the more tenuous our grip on life became. What would Elliot do when he couldn't manage on his own anymore? I couldn't imagine him settling into a retirement village or the likes. And an aged-care facility? Unimaginable. Is that where I'd end up? A horrifying thought. When Mum couldn't manage Dad at home after he'd fallen over and broken his hip, he'd spent several weeks in a nursing home. Visiting him in that place had been awful enough. The idea I might end my days in an aged-care facility was beyond the pale. I needed to get my act together, make the most of the years I had left before it was too late.

23

Hamish

Hamish was on his way back to Cutlers Bay. He glanced in the rearview mirror at the load in the back of the ute and asked himself for the umpteenth time *why* he'd bought a skylight to install in the kitchen of the old house—along with watching back-to-back video clips on YouTube describing how to install it. He felt confident that he could do the job, no sweat. What he wasn't feeling confident about was why he'd bought the damn thing in the first place when all he'd planned was to tidy up the property so it could be sold. And what about the hundreds of dollars' worth of paint and accoutrements packed in the back alongside the skylight? External *and* internal paint. Plus the new poly rainwater tank he'd ordered. He sure had let himself be carried away at Bunnings.

After Ruth's precipitate departure the previous Monday afternoon and then the news the rubbish skip wouldn't be delivered until the end of the week, he'd packed up and driven back to Adelaide that same day. The skip delivery was out of his control and try as he might, he could not fathom why Ruth had up and left like she had. He'd been enjoying her company and even though they hadn't talked much, it had been nice to have someone working alongside him. Had he said or done something to upset her? He'd replayed the scene in the kitchen over and over and hadn't come up with a feasible explanation. That had been one of Andrea's favourite gripes about him: how clueless he was when it came to understanding women. What man did?

It had been late when he'd let himself into the apartment and he'd wished he'd stayed in Cutlers Bay, as contrary as that sounded. First thing the following morning he'd powered up his laptop and discovered that Brooke had emailed, saying the purchasers had been back to look and would take all the furniture except for his bed, the fridge and the kitchenware. He decided it could all go to his parents' place. He'd boxed up the kitchenware that afternoon.

With the road stretching out in front of him, Hamish's mood began to lighten the closer he travelled towards Cutlers Bay. When he turned into East Terrace, he felt remarkably upbeat, the streetscape invitingly familiar. Finding the rubbish skip completely blocking the driveway and having nowhere to park except on the street did nothing to dampen his mood. The skip would be there for a fortnight and Pete had agreed to drive up on Sunday, chose whatever he wanted to take back with him and help Hamish fill the skip with the remainder. There was a high chance he'd need to get the skip back a second time.

He spent the remainder of the afternoon removing what was left of the ivy, digging out the stump and throwing it all into the skip. At around six he packed away his tools, showered and shaved and took himself off, on foot, to the hotel for a meal and some company. Rosie's Cafe was closed but when he walked past he did peer in through the front window for any signs of life. The interior was dim and the only light came from the drinks fridge. He told himself he wasn't disappointed but knew that he was. He hadn't heard a peep from Ruth since she'd walked out the front door Monday afternoon.

Had he expected to? He hadn't made contact with her, hadn't told her he was off to Adelaide again or when he might be back. Should he have? The Sunday evening they'd spent together had been fun. They'd talked about anything and everything. She'd surprised him by how extensively she'd travelled in her younger years. He'd totally enjoyed himself. Did he want to repeat the experience? Yes, he did.

So there was his answer: he should have messaged her to tell her he'd gone back to Adelaide.

He crossed the street to the pub, but then caught sight of Cutlers Bay Fish & Chips & Takeaway. A burger and chips versus a schnitzel and chips? He vacillated briefly. Did he really feel like making beery small talk with the front bar regulars? Was that the sort of company he was after? An emphatic no.

Mind made up, he changed course and recrossed the road. If he had a hankering for a beer there was plenty in the fridge back at the house.

Stepping into the fish and chip shop was like stepping into a sauna. An extraction fan thundered away above the deep fryers, and a young man hunched over one: chips in, chips out. Several customers waited with their backs to the wall opposite the counter, heads bent, thumbs busy. Hamish felt in his pocket for his phone and when he didn't find it, panicked before remembering he'd left it on the bathroom cabinet.

The middle-aged woman at the grill caught his eye and said, 'What'll it be, love?'

'Hamburger with the lot and a minimum chips, thanks,' Hamish said.

'Drinks?'

He shook his head and stepped back to join the ranks of the others waiting for food. There were no tables, only two plastic chairs that had once been white. In front of the cash register, the vinyl floor tiles were worn right through. The shop was clean and the drinks fridge stacked but, like the woman flipping meat patties, it had a tired and time-worn feel about it.

Two customers left with bulging, sweaty plastic bags. Another customer came in and Hamish saw it was Mia Thomas.

She grinned when she recognised him. 'Hi, Hamish.'

At the sound of her voice, the young man at the fryers glanced over his shoulder.

'Hi, Rory,' Mia said with a little wave. 'See you back at school next week?'

Rory nodded, blushed scarlet and went back to the chips.

The woman at the grill raised her eyebrows and went to the bain-marie, where several paper-wrapped parcels waited. She loaded them into a carry bag. 'There you go, love,' she said and handed the bag across the counter to Mia. 'Tell your mum I'll put aside a roast chook for her tomorrow.'

'Thanks, Peg.' Mia paid and turned to Hamish. 'Are you on foot?'

'How did you know?'

'Your ute's parked out the front of your dad's place. Do you want a ride home?'

'Your order's only a couple of minutes away,' Peg said, helpfully.

'Okay,' Hamish replied, because how could he not?

Mia grinned. Peg winked at him. He had the distinct feeling he was missing something. Peg wrapped his burger and then scooped golden, salt-encrusted chips into a grease-proof bag.

Clutching his plastic bag, he followed Mia out to the maroon SUV parked in front of the shop. 'Is this your car? I've seen you drive past in it.'

'Nah, it's Mum's.'

'But don't you only have your Ls?'

'That's right, but Mum had to go next door and now you're with me, so I'm okay.'

She laughed when Hamish said, 'I feel used!'

The trip took all of three minutes and then Mia was carefully easing the SUV into the kerb behind his ute. 'I'm working at the cafe tomorrow. Saturday and Sundays are my days. Will you be coming in for breakfast?'

'There's a high chance of that, if not for breakfast then for coffee. And thanks for the ride.' He reached for the door handle. 'But don't make a habit of it, not until you have your Ps. You wouldn't want Sergeant Cooper to catch you.'

'No! Are you staying here for a few days, or going straight back to Adelaide?'

He paused, one hand on the door handle and the other clutching his dinner. 'My ute,' he said, nodding slowly. 'You noticed it had been gone for a few days?'

'Yep. Can't help but notice, not when I'm up and down this street every day.'

'So there'd be no getting away with anything in this town, not with you out and about,' Hamish said and arched an eyebrow.

Mia shrugged but didn't smile.

'I can't help it if I notice things,' she said. 'I'm not a stickybeak, I just notice.'

'Nothing wrong with that. You drive carefully, Mia, and I might see you in the morning.'

'Bye, Hamish. Enjoy your burger. Peg's are the best.'

She puttered off, the L-plate nowhere to be seen. He watched until she'd indicated and made the turn into her mother's driveway. The two lads on pushbikes he'd seen before wheeled through the gate moments after her. Laughter and voices drifted across the road before the front door slammed behind them.

Teenagers learning to drive, taking unnecessary risks behind the wheel of their parents' car. A circumstance he wasn't sorry he'd missed out on. The closest he'd ever been to being behind the wheel of any car his parents had owned was to clean it out. A year into his apprenticeship, he'd bought his first car and taught himself how to drive. There had been risks taken, although they hadn't seemed unnecessary at the time.

He walked around to the back door, which he'd left unlocked, and wondered what had happened to Mia's father. The man didn't ever get a mention by anyone.

★ ★ ★

Pete arrived Sunday morning when Hamish was in the front garden watering the few surviving rosebushes he'd discovered in the tangle of weeds and dead shrubs. He turned off the hose and walked out to meet his brother-in-law.

'You must have been up at sparrow's fart,' he said and eyed the four-by-two trailer hitched behind Pete's ute.

'Something like that,' Pete said and folded his arms. 'Nat wants her mum's display cabinet, the one that's in the lounge room, and the pine dresser in the kitchen,' he said and kicked the closest trailer tyre.

'Fair enough. They should both fit on the ute and you can put anything else you want in the trailer. Did you bring ropes and stuff?'

Pete jerked a thumb at the bulging hessian bag in the back of the ute. 'All in there.'

Hamish headed past the rubbish skip towards the garage and Pete followed him. 'See that pile?' he said. 'The one closest to the garage? I've stacked anything I thought you might want there and I've put all Dad's fishing gear together over there. You're welcome to poke through everything and what you don't take will go into the skip.'

'Don't you want anything?' Pete ambled over to the pile with the fishing gear.

'Not really, except for a few tools, garden implements, the lawn mower and anything else that I think will come in useful here.'

Hamish went inside and left Pete to sort through his father-in-law's belongings and the memories that went with them.

When Pete came in a while later, he meandered in and out of the rooms and surveyed the boxes of Hamish's belongings stacked up along the passageway. 'You look as if you're moving in, mate,' he said.

'Settlement's in a fortnight and I have to be out of my apartment. Here's as good a place as any to store things.' The bed, bedding and the towels in the bathroom, along with a few clothes, were all that was left to collect from the apartment. He'd sold the fridge to a friend of a friend and they'd picked it up the same day.

In the kitchen, Hamish flicked on the electric kettle. 'Coffee? Have you eaten?'

'I thought we could grab breakfast at that cafe down the street. Bloody good tucker those times we ate there after Christmas.'

'Rosie's doesn't open until nine on weekends.'

'Suits me. I'll finish poking around outside. Then I'll need to empty out the dresser and the cabinet in the lounge. What shall I do with all the crap that's in it? Nat said she didn't want any of it.'

Hamish slowly stirred his coffee and tried not to grit his teeth. It was his first coffee for the day. He hadn't slept that well and he felt irritable. 'That's a bit harsh, mate, they're the things Mum kept because they were precious to her.'

'Yeah, well ...' Pete said and shuffled his feet. 'You know what they say: What's precious to one bloke is junk to another.'

'Sure,' Hamish said and shrugged. 'What about your girls? Would they like a keepsake or two from their grandma? Did Nat ask them?'

Pete rolled his tongue around the inside of his mouth as if he was searching for an answer to Hamish's question.

When he came up with nothing, Hamish said, 'What say we take photos of what's in the cabinet and the dresser and send them to the girls? Let them decide?'

Pete's face screwed up as if he was in pain. 'What if they all want the same things? And Sally's got no place to store stuff. Neither has Carmel. It'd all end up at ours and Nat would go ballistic.'

'They're grown-ups, Pete. Let them sort it out among themselves.'

Pete's face relaxed and his head bobbed up and down like a bobble head dog. 'They might not want anything.'

'Won't hurt to ask. Let them decide. Too late after it's all been offloaded to an op shop or a secondhand dealer.'

Pete grinned slowly and slapped his thigh. 'Job's done. On that note, let's go eat breakfast. It's past nine.'

They walked to the cafe and Hamish spent the time considering what he'd say to Ruth when he saw her. Yesterday he'd bought a few groceries from the supermarket and made his own toast for breakfast. He hadn't wanted company and had enough insight to know he was better off on his own when he felt like that. Hamish recognised his potential to become a grumpy old man. Sometimes he suspected he was already halfway there. Maybe that's what had scared Ruth off. That and him assuming she'd wanted to help him tear down the ivy in the heat on her day off and her offer hadn't been just the wine talking.

There was a queue at the cash register, not long, but a queue nevertheless. Mia was taking orders and an older woman he didn't recognise was delivering food to the couple sitting at his table.

'Why don't I grab us a table? I'll have what I had last time,' Pete said and, with remarkable agility, wound his way to the only unoccupied table in the back corner.

Hamish scanned the menu board and when it came to his turn, Mia took his order with a faltering smile. 'There might be a bit of a wait,' she said. 'Sorry.'

'Short-staffed?'

She nodded vigorously and held out the EFTPOS machine for him to tap his credit card. 'George'll be here soon and Lorna's good but she's not Ruth.'

'Where's Ruth?'

Mia bit her bottom lip and her gaze flicked around to see who might be in earshot. She leaned over the counter. 'One of her twin brothers … he's in intensive care at the Royal Adelaide, but Mum said they don't expect him to live.'

'Shit,' Hamish said, his gut tying itself into a knot. 'When did this happen?'

'Friday afternoon. Mum was about to leave at the end of her shift when Ruth got the call.' Her eyes widened. 'Mum said she thought Ruth was going to faint when they told her.' She passed Hamish his receipt. 'What table are you sitting at?'

'The one in the corner.'

'Table four. I'll get to your coffees soon.'

'Thanks, Mia. No rush.'

When he sat down, Pete said, 'What's up?'

'Ruth's in Adelaide. One of her brothers is in intensive care, not expected to live.'

'Bugger me. That's cruel. She seemed like a nice woman.'

'She is a nice woman,' Hamish said. He took out his phone and tapped out a message. *Ruth, I just heard about your brother. I'm sorry.*

Her response was immediate: *Thanks. Things not looking good. Waiting for his children to arrive.*

'Who're you messaging?' Pete said.

'Ruth,' Hamish answered. *Look after yourself,* he wrote in reply. It felt inadequate but what did you say to a friend in the circumstances? He wasn't even sure if the short time they'd spent together meant they *were* friends. All he knew was that if she needed anything from him, he would willingly oblige. He hit send and then wished he'd said what he'd just thought.

Pete tapped his fingers on the tabletop and Hamish looked up to find his brother-in-law watching him speculatively.

Mia came with their coffees. 'Is she okay?' she asked Hamish as she put the mugs on the table.

'I think so. But how did you—'

She touched his shoulder. 'Like I said, I notice things.'

She left and Pete coughed and cleared his throat. 'Mate, you must come in here pretty often.'

'Coffee's good and the food's always excellent.'

24

Hamish

Ruth's brother died in the early hours of Monday morning. Hamish knew this because when he woke at six am, the first thing he did was reach for his phone. There was a message from Ruth. He sat on the edge of the bed and rang her because he needed to say more than could be said in a text message. But when the call went to message bank part of him sighed with relief. What did you say to someone whose brother had just died? Then he realised how early it was and with Ruth being up half the night, she was probably trying to snatch some sleep. He sent a brief message that fell way short of what he wanted to say if only he could have found the words.

He hadn't heard from her by lunchtime and told himself that of course she was with her family and had more important things to do than talk to him.

By mid-afternoon, he was resigned to not hearing from her at all. Resigned and disappointed.

The day was overcast and marginally cooler than it had been, so he took the opportunity to climb onto the roof. He'd been meaning to do it for a while; from the ground, the roof appeared to be in reasonable condition, no rust or loose sheets of iron, but he wanted to take a closer look and scope out where the skylight would go. It was from this vantage point that he watched an unfamiliar and nondescript car slow down and park behind his ute. When the driver climbed out and he recognised who it was, he nearly lost his balance.

'Ruth,' he yelled. 'I'm up here. I'll be right down.'

She looked up, shading her eyes with her hand. 'What on earth are you doing up there?'

He scrambled across the galvanised iron roof and down the ladder.

She was waiting at the bottom. Her eyes were red and puffy and she looked as if she hadn't slept for days. She probably hadn't.

He dusted his hands on his shorts. 'I thought you'd still be in Adelaide.'

'It's been awful … a nightmare …' Her bottom lip quivered and she blinked back tears. 'But I needed to come home and sort out a few things and collect more clothes. The funeral's on Friday morning.' She dragged in a lungful of air, closed her eyes and held her breath.

'Ruth?' he said and gripped her shoulder. The breath shuddered out of her and he dropped his hand when she opened her eyes.

'I'm all right,' she said. 'What I was going to say is that I'll work tomorrow, Wednesday and Thursday and if I can't find enough staff to cover Friday and Saturday, I'll close the cafe. I'll leave for Adelaide again Thursday afternoon, as soon as Laurie's been to do the floors.'

'Have you got time to come inside and have a drink? Hot? Cold?'

'A cup of tea would be wonderful, if you have it. I've drunk too much coffee over the last couple of days and nights. I feel as if I'm floating in it.'

'There's tea, nothing fancy, your standard Liptons. I've been waiting for the weather to cool down before I went climbing up on the roof. I need to see what condition it's in.' Hamish held open the back door and she preceded him inside. 'Excuse the mess,' he said when they entered the kitchen. Chaos reigned. The table and cupboard tops were covered with crockery, vases, empty jam jars, everything taken out of the pine dresser before he'd helped Pete load it onto the back of his ute.

'Where did that gorgeous dresser go?' Ruth said, aghast.

'You noticed the dresser?'

'Of course. I was going to ask if you wanted to sell it, but then I thought I might have sounded a bit crass ... You know, so soon after your dad died.'

Hamish just stared at her. 'Pete took it for Nat. Yesterday. That and Mum's display cabinet. The only two pieces of furniture that were actually worth anything, come to think of it.'

'I suppose she was entitled to have them, if you didn't want them.'

'I didn't, but if I'd known you wanted the dresser—'

'It doesn't matter, Hamish. I'd pictured it in the cafe, that's all, and I would have got rid of that cupboard where we keep the spare cutlery and other stuff. I bought that at the op shop for twenty dollars, slapped on a coat of paint.'

Hamish cleared a spot at one end of the table. Ruth sat down. He made tea for her and coffee for himself and took a chair opposite her. 'He was one of twins, wasn't he?'

'Robert was the youngest by seven minutes and Elliot is devastated. We all are. He was seventy-two, seventy-three in July. Too young.'

'How many kids?'

'Two and a wife and an ex-wife. Three grandchildren.' Ruth fiddled with the handle of the bone-china mug. 'If it'd been Elliot, none of us would have been overly surprised because he does not look after himself, never has. Eats too much, drinks too much. But Robert? He ran marathons and didn't eat red meat. Made smoothies that had kale and other green stuff in them. Alcohol only ever on special occasions.'

'Often the way of it. What happened?'

'He collapsed while he was training for the "big marathon". Luckily he runs with a bloke who's a paramedic, otherwise he would have died on the side of the road. Ruptured cerebral aneurysm is what the specialist in intensive care told us. He didn't ever regain consciousness and they only kept him on life support to give Charlotte and Oliver, his children, time to get there. They both live interstate.'

'Bloody hell,' Hamish said and then winced, wishing he'd come up with something better. Something comforting. But suitable words eluded him. He really was out of his depth here. No experience saying comforting things to anyone, that was the trouble.

Ruth sipped her tea. 'Did your brother-in-law only come for the day? I see the skip's almost full.'

'He was here by eight and gone by three. We loaded his trailer with bits and pieces and then worked on filling the skip. Had breakfast at the cafe, that's how I knew you were in Adelaide. Mia told me.'

'Were they busy?'

'Flat strap. She said they had been on Saturday morning as well. Mia certainly knows what she's on about. A good worker.'

'She's her mother's daughter, no doubt about that.' Ruth finished her tea and stood. 'I'd better go. Apologies for not getting back to you this morning. I took Elliot home from the hospital and grabbed a few hours of sleep. He's a bit of a mess. I feel as if I should have stayed but in the end, he was as anxious for me to leave as I was to go.'

'Is anyone there with him?'

'The woman in the townhouse next door has become a friend. She's a single mother and she works from home and promised to keep an ear out for him. If I need to go back, she'll let me know. She has my mobile number.'

'Who's looking out for you, Ruth? He was your brother too.'

She finished rinsing her cup at the sink before turning to face him. 'It is kind of confronting, Hamish. It's sad when your parents die but you expect them to go long before you do. When one of your siblings dies, it gives you a real jolt.' Her eyes glistened with tears. 'It makes you think of all the things you should have said to them and done with them but didn't because you thought you had plenty of time. And then, just like that, you have no time at all.' She smiled a watery smile. 'But I'm not telling you anything you don't already know, am I? Your dad hasn't been gone long at all.'

'No,' he said quietly. 'But regret takes you nowhere good, unless of course you use it as motivation not to make the same mistakes in the future.'

'Ideally. Thanks for the tea,' she said. 'I'll see you later. Are you around for a while?'

'I think so.' Hamish walked out with her. 'A lot of jobs to do here and there's nothing much left in Adelaide. Another load and that'll be it. I have this ridiculously large bed that I don't know what to do with except bring it here and store it in the garage. It won't fit into the bedroom.'

'Why didn't you sell it?'

'It's extremely comfortable and I like it.'

'Reasons enough to keep it.'

'Possibly. And Ruth, seriously now, if you need help with anything, please call me. I can turn my hand to most things.'

'So I've noticed,' she said. 'Bye—and thanks.'

She climbed into her car, executed a perfect three-point turn and waved as she drove off. The sun had come out and the afternoon was warm. It would be hot on the roof so Hamish went inside instead. He'd found a stack of newspapers in the garage and used them to wrap and pack his mother's precious things into cardboard boxes. He put aside a few things to keep: a vase he remembered as his mum's favourite; a gold-embossed decanter and set of matching port glasses that had been his grandmother's; and the bone-china mugs. Ruth had admired the one he'd served her tea in.

Since Pete's visit Hamish had come up with a better idea than sending photos of the items to Nat and the girls: the next time he went to Adelaide, these boxes would be going with him and he'd deposit them on his sister's front verandah. He'd leave it up to her to decide how to dispose of the contents. It was the least she could do.

25

Ruth

I'd been running on adrenaline and caffeine and not much else since the phone call on Friday afternoon. Back in Cutlers Bay and with home in my sights, I'd begun to flag at Hamish's place. When I let myself into the flat, it was warm and stuffy and something was on the nose: rotting banana peel and an empty yogurt container. I hadn't emptied the bin in the kitchen before I'd rushed out. Was that only three days ago? It felt like a lifetime. Life as I'd known it would never be the same again because one of my brothers was dead. The realisation stunned me anew and I dropped onto the sofa, closed my eyes and took stock of how I was: tired from the inside out, my head thick with fatigue, and sad beyond any sadness I'd ever felt before, even after Mum died. She'd been ninety-two. At her ninetieth birthday celebrations, she'd said she considered herself to be living on borrowed time.

Elliot and I had been the last to leave the hospital this morning. We hadn't wanted to desert Robert, even though he was no longer in the land of the living. Lana, Robert's second wife, had left not long before us. My belief was that she'd hung on until then because she'd been determined to outstay Corrine, Robert's first wife, and the mother of his children. Elliot had been of the same opinion. We liked Corrine. In a way, she'd been Robert's Hazel while Lana was his Blanche d'Alpuget. Nevertheless, although I wasn't overly fond of Lana, it would have been difficult for her because, to some extent, Charlotte, Oliver and Corrine had pushed her to the fringes at every opportunity. Unintentionally, I hoped, but I suspected it'd been the opposite. Elliot had just shaken his head, stunned into speechlessness by the sheer enormity of what was happening.

When the stuffiness of the living area and the smell of days-old banana peel could be tolerated no longer, I dried my eyes, flung open doors and windows and set about the chores I'd come home to attend to. As I ticked off each task, it was hard to ignore the sharp tug of guilt whenever I thought of Elliot, which was most of the time. Distance had brought clarity and I knew now I should have stayed with him.

I sat down and rang him. His voice was slurred when he said hello. Had I woken him or had he been drinking?

'How are you?' I said.

'How do you think I am?' he barked and I kicked myself for asking such a redundant question. I knew how heartsick I felt.

'I've done most of what I needed to do here, only the wholesaler's order to ring through and then find staff to cover. Do you want me to come back tonight?'

He made a choking sound, half-laugh, half-sob. 'What and have you kill yourself on the road because you fell asleep at the wheel on your way back?'

'I'll be careful.'

'Ruth, do not even think about getting in your car again tonight. I'm fine. Corrine sent Oliver over to keep me company and luckily he enjoys a red as much I do. Tomorrow we're going through all the photos to choose the ones for the service.'

I barely knew the adult versions of Robert and Corrine's children, my niece and nephew. I'd never been close to them. A few hours over the occasional Christmas lunch or family get-together were the only times we were ever in the same place at the same time. Elliot's daughter Stacey and I had had a short spell of closeness when I'd first moved to Cutlers Bay, before she and her partner had taken off for Queensland. But when you lose a close family member the ones remaining become more precious.

'That was thoughtful of Corrine, to send over Oliver. Have you heard from Stacey? Will she be down for the funeral? How did Chris's gastric bypass go?'

'Yes, no and smoothly,' Elliot said. 'She won't leave him, not so soon after his surgery. And of course there're the kids.'

'Surely they're old enough to look after themselves? Are you disappointed she's not coming down?'

'Of course I am, but I fully understand. I'll fly up and see them when the dust settles. What about, you old chook, how are you?'

'Tired … sad … still can't believe he's dead. I'd only spoken to him once since we were together on Christmas Day. He didn't mention training for another marathon, it was you who told me he was.'

I yawned widely and Elliot said, 'Ruth, do what you have to do and go to bed. Please. I'll cope. If you can't get back here until Thursday, I'm in good hands.'

'I'll call you tomorrow. Goodnight, Elliot.' I'd wanted to tell him that I loved him but the words had stuck to my tongue. Not because I didn't love him, but because we'd never said that to each other before. Not ever. Why not?

After our conversation, I found it hard to get going again. My body was reluctant to do what I asked of it. The wholesaler's order was the only task that wouldn't wait until the morning. The order was late as it was and I'd rung them, promising to have it in within the hour. I attended to that, had a hot shower and tumbled into bed.

I think I was asleep before my head hit the pillow.

★ ★ ★

I woke the next morning and luxuriated in that sublime feeling of being totally refreshed after a solid sleep, that handful of precious seconds before reality kicks in. And so it did, viciously reminding me that one of my brothers was dead. This time a week ago he'd been very much alive; he'd been a husband, a father, an older brother, friend and colleague, and training for a marathon. If I hadn't witnessed his heart's dying pulse, that last blip of life as he lay prone in the ICU hospital bed, I would not have believed he was gone. He'd been so alive, so vital, always reaching for the next challenge.

If I could have, I would have pulled the sheet up over my head and gone back to sleep, anything to avoid facing the inevitability of another day. From experience, grief was something that must be endured; left to take its course because it would not be denied. But face the day I must and six forty-five was too early to call Elliot, or anyone. And yet, on the bedside cupboard, my phone vibrated with an incoming call.

'Hamish, good morning.'

'I expected you'd be up. How are you?'

My brother's raw response when I'd asked him the same question the evening before sprang to mind. 'Much better after a good night's sleep,' I said, because I was. 'You?'

'Yeah, I'm good. You looked wrecked yesterday. I'm glad you had a good sleep. If I can be of help in any way at all, please yell out.'

'I will and thanks. What are you up to today?'

'Scraping woodwork and emptying the old rainwater tank. I'm going to take it to the dump. Do you know anyone with a trailer I could borrow or hire?'

'Laurie Randall has one and so does Zach Cooper. I'm sure either one of them would loan it to you.'

'Perfect. I'll ask Laurie. He might even give me a hand to load the tank onto the trailer.'

'Have a good day, Hamish, and thanks for the call.'

'You too. Go easy on yourself, Ruth.'

Yawning, I dragged on my dressing gown, went to the bathroom and then made coffee. Officially, this was my day off and Allie would be opening up this morning. Lorna had been rostered to start at ten, however I'd talked to her yesterday evening and she'd agreed to work later in the week instead. 'What about on the weekend?' I'd asked.

'I'm working at the supermarket on the weekend, because they're short-staffed,' she'd said.

I needed to talk to Allie before I offered shifts to any of the other staff. She'd get a surprise when I showed up at ten instead of Lorna. I had planned to call Allie last night but decided it would be better to talk to her in person. She'd been so prickly of late and I was reluctant to ask more of her, regardless of her earlier comment about wanting to work extra hours.

I needn't have worried, because when I went through to the cafe, Allie was expecting me. 'Lorna rang,' she said in response to my questioning look. She was at the grill, bacon and eggs sizzling. Silly me for forgetting the efficiency of an employee grapevine. 'I'm sorry about your brother, Ruth. How are you?'

There was that question again. 'Up and down,' I said. 'Work will be a useful distraction. Shall I take over at the grill or would you prefer me to be out front?'

'You can take over here if you like.'

'Thanks,' I said. She enjoyed cooking but it'd be easier for me to hide away in the kitchen, especially today. I tied on a clean apron and scanned the next orders. Allie plated the eggs and bacon alongside toasted sourdough and then whipped out to deliver them. Moments later, I heard the whirr of the coffee grinder followed by the hiss of steam.

As usual, it wasn't until after the lunchtime rush that we found time to have a genuine conversation.

'Robert's funeral is on Friday,' I said. 'My original plan was to drive back to Adelaide on Thursday after the cafe closed, but I talked to my nephew briefly this morning and Elliot isn't doing too well, so I would like to go back earlier if I could.' I paused, hoping she'd pick up and offer whatever extra hours she could fit in.

To my consternation she didn't speak, she simply stood there wringing her hands.

'Allie?' I said and frowned.

She cleared her throat. 'I need Thursday off, Ruth. Sorry. I've already asked Lorna if she'd work for me. I can do all day tomorrow and Friday.'

Lorna hadn't mentioned anything about already working Thursday for Allie. 'What about Saturday? Lorna's at the supermarket.'

She shook her head and my head started to pound properly. 'It's my birthday on Saturday and Mum and Dad are coming for the day. Mia has asked Suzie to work for her. It was sort of a last-minute thing for Mum and Dad to come up … and we didn't want to bother you with the changes to the roster. It's my fortieth.'

'Oh, nice. Happy birthday for Saturday,' I said, not sounding as if I meant it, but I did.

How *was* I going to work this? There were other casuals on the books but me and Allie—and Lorna, at a push—were the only cooks. I didn't want to have to come home late Friday so I could open the cafe on Saturday morning. My plan had been to spend the weekend and my two days off with Elliot. It would have been good for both of us. I know I'd told Hamish I'd close the cafe if necessary but I'd honestly thought I'd find staff willing to help out. That is, Allie would be willing to step into the breach, because she was the only other person who knew all that needed to be done. I'd even shown her how to deal with the day's takings.

'I'm sorry, Ruth,' she said.

Why did I get the feeling she was apologising for more than not being able to work Thursday?

'Never mind. I'll sort something out, even if I have to close the cafe. Just come in at the usual time tomorrow and then if you can do the full day on Friday, I'd appreciate it.'

Allie nodded. She scooted off to clear recently vacated tables and I took a minute to lean heavily on the edge of the sink in the hope my fulminating headache would ease. I was busy scraping down the grill when Allie returned with a tray full of dirty dishes.

'Ruth,' she said.

I paused and glanced over my shoulder at her.

'I have an idea. What if I started early on Saturday to do the muffins, Suzie came at nine and I worked until George started at ten and then I came back at two to sort out the till and whatever else needed doing? I could do the same on Sunday but with Mia.'

'Do you think George and Suzie would be all right here on their own for four hours? Two juniors? On a Saturday morning? It's one of our busiest times and neither of them cook. Thanks for the offer, Allie, but I've thought about it and the best thing will be to close the cafe on Thursday and then I'll come home in time to open on the weekend. I'll ask Lorna to work with you on Friday. And of course Gayle will be in over lunch.'

I couldn't read Allie's expression, but she nodded and got on with loading the dishwasher.

At three o'clock, I went home. There were a few customers lingering over coffees but we'd done most of the cleaning up. I felt frustrated and frazzled on top of the nausea and aching head. Not having had any lunch might have had something to do with it, but that wasn't all.

My place was with my family at a time like this. It's where I wanted to be and instead my responsibilities kept me in Cutlers Bay. If I didn't do something soon to ameliorate my situation, I'd begin to resent being here and that'd be unhealthy for me and my staff.

26

Ruth

Hamish appeared well after three on Wednesday afternoon. Allie had long gone and the cafe was almost empty. He took one look at me and said, 'Please don't tell me you're driving to Adelaide this evening.'

'I hardly slept so, no, I won't go tonight.' I felt on the verge of tears. It'd been like that all day. I'd be okay one minute and have tears welling the next. I ducked down and finished restocking the milk fridge to give myself a steadying minute. Getting through the day had taken every ounce of energy and determination I possessed. Deciding not to open the cafe tomorrow was a sound decision—I needed to be with Elliot. I'd already posted a notice in the window. 'Do you want me to make you a coffee?'

'No, thanks. I'm here because Laurie's at the dentist.'

'I thought his appointment was next week.'

'A cancellation. They called him when he was helping me with the tank and I told him to take it, that I'd do the chairs and the floor.'

'Right. I can manage if you have other things to do.'

'Ruth, just say "Thank you, Hamish". And later I'm going to make you an early dinner because I'll bet that you haven't eaten a decent meal for days. And although I don't cook per se, I'm a dab hand with a steak, potatoes and a barbecue plate.'

'There's a barbecue at your dad's? I didn't notice it.'

'It's nothing flash. I found it in the shed and bought a gas bottle at the hardware.'

'Shall I bring a salad? And what time?'

'Whenever you're ready and a salad would be … healthy.'

'Wine?'

'You decide. I'll lock the door, turn the sign around and start on the chairs. Have you wiped down the tables?'

'No, let me do that first. And Hamish—'

Already halfway to the front door, he stopped and turned around, raised his eyebrows.

'Thank you,' I said.

After I'd finished up in the cafe and before I left for Hamish's place with the salad and a bottle of red, I packed a bag ready for the morning. It'd be the last thing I'd feel like doing after a glass or two of red wine and I wanted to be away early. Robert had been a traditionalist, so I chose a black summer-weight wool jersey dress and heels for the service. A colourful scarf to add a touch of brightness to the sombre outfit. I hung the dress in the bathroom to air overnight. I'd worn it last when Mum's only surviving sibling had passed away. Aunty Del had been eighty-nine. My funeral dress.

Hamish had instructed me earlier to message when I left home and he'd start the food. Hence the mouthwatering smell of barbecuing meat drifted down the driveway when I turned in the gate. The rainwater tank was gone and a pile of rubble was all that remained of the stand. I paused to ponder the stone wall where the ivy had climbed. It was a lighter colour to the remaining walls.

Hamish appeared while I pondered. 'It'll weather up and be the same as the rest of the place in no time,' he said. He reached for the insulated bag I was carrying. 'Bloody hell, Ruth, what have you got in here?'

'It's the glass salad bowl, one of Mum's, and it's heavy … along with the bottle of wine.'

He wouldn't have me do anything and was such undemanding company I felt myself relax for the first time since that dreadful phone call last Friday. Our conversation was sporadic and limited to comments about the food and the weather, which seemed to suit us both. The meal was delicious, the steak perfect. By eight o'clock I was nicely mellow and yawning widely.

He said, 'Go home and go to bed, Ruth.' He offered to drive me but it was still daylight so I walked, the insulated bag much lighter on the return journey. 'All the best for Friday,' he'd said when he'd waved me off at the front gate. I just wanted it to be over.

★ ★ ★

The service was well scripted, very Robert and Lana, and after the requisite tea and bikkies, immediate family traipsed out to Robert and Lana's place in the foothills. Although not to my taste, it was a beautiful home and Lana was a gracious host. My understanding was that Lana had brought a fair share of wealth to her union with Robert. How Corrine felt being in her ex-husband's home was anyone's guess. She still lived in the three-bedroom brick-veneer in the western suburbs she and Robert had bought in the first year of their marriage. The children had grown up there.

Much to my dismay, Elliot partook readily of Robert's extensive liqueur cabinet and drank himself into a stupor well before the sun was even close to going down.

'I'm sorry, Ruth, but I can't stay with him tonight,' Oliver said after we'd manhandled my drunken brother into the passenger seat of my car. 'My flight's early tomorrow morning and I want to spend tonight at Mum's with Charlotte.'

'Totally understandable. I'm grateful for what you've done, Oliver. Don't give it another thought,' I said. I gave him a hug. 'It's been terrific to see you, I'm just so damn sorry about the circumstances.'

'Me too,' Oliver said. 'I don't think it's hit me yet that my dad's dead. I'll probably fall in a heap when I get home.'

Elliot was belted in and snoring, oblivious to everyone and everything. That being his primary objective, I assumed. I slammed the passenger-side door much harder than necessary.

'How will you manage him at the other end?' Corrine said from behind me.

I swung around in surprise. 'Fair question. His neighbour's son is a strapping young lad. If he's home, I'll ask him to help. Otherwise, Elliot can sleep it off in the car. At least until I need the car to drive myself home so I can open the cafe in the morning.'

'Take him to my place,' Corrine said and I didn't miss Oliver's surprised gasp. 'He can sleep it off there.'

'Thanks, but I wouldn't do that. You enjoy your evening with Oliver and Charlotte.'

Lana came down the steps holding out a large empty ice-cream container, along with its lid. 'Take this,' she said. 'You might need it.' I had the feeling she'd done this many times before, only it would have been Robert taking Elliot home.

'I'll kill him if he spews in my car,' I said baldly. Lana winced. I opened the car door and thrust the container onto Elliot's lap. 'Hold that,' I said. He pushed away the container and mumbled something. I closed the door again. 'Do you know what? I've just had a brilliant idea. I'll take him home with me. I have a spare room and he has stayed with me once before.'

Corrine laughed. 'Go, you! You've always been the one with the most spunk, Ruth. Robert could be a pedant and Elliot is a lush, a nice bloke but a lush nevertheless. Totally get why Gloria left him and Stacey moved to far north Queensland.'

'Mum,' Oliver said through gritted teeth. 'I think we should leave. Now.'

Lana stood by silently, her arms folded as if she was hugging herself tightly. I wondered if she was thinking about the unfairness of it all; that the wrong brother had died. She was taken aback when I reached out and hugged her.

'Take care,' I said.

'You too, Ruth,' she answered quietly. 'Robert helped Elliot temper his excesses. The poor man's on his own now.'

'So are you.'

'Not in the same way, Ruth. I have friends, family and lots of outside interests. Elliot had Robert.'

Lana stepped back and Corrine hugged me. 'Bye, love. Keep in touch.' She opened the car door for me. 'Good luck,' she said. 'When will you bring him back?'

'After the weekend. The cafe's closed on Monday and I have Tuesday off.'

She nodded. I started the car and reversed out of the driveway.

Elliot rallied momentarily. 'Where the hell are we?' he said.

'On the way home,' I said. Not a *big* lie.

He grunted and went back to sleep.

The sun set as we hit the motorway, a fiery ball swallowed by the sea. Elliot snored and snuffled in the seat beside me, drool dribbling down his chin. We'd stopped by his townhouse and he'd slept in the car, oblivious, while I'd thrown a few clothes into a suitcase for him and grabbed my own overnight bag. I didn't bother to change clothes or wake him to see if he needed the bathroom. But I had checked that the gas was turned off and the rubbish bin in the kitchen was empty.

The kilometres flashed past and I kept glancing sideways at my sleeping brother. When had he become such a drunk? Since he'd retired? He'd always liked a drink but I'd assumed he knew when to stop. Apparently not. And my read of the earlier situation was that no-one was putting up their hand to take Robert's place in keeping his twin on the straight and narrow. That left me.

I couldn't think about it just now. System overload.

We were soon at Port Wakefield and I followed the signs to a public toilet. Elliot fought against being prodded awake. Somehow I managed to get him out of the car, but the nearest bush was as good as it got. He dribbled urine all down the front of his underpants and trousers. I wanted to cry and then shake him until his teeth rattled. He fell into the car seat, mumbling. I buckled him in. 'Do you want a coffee?' I said, but he didn't answer me. I left him in the car and dashed in to get myself one at the first service station I came to.

Never had I been more glad to see the twinkling lights of Cutlers Bay. Leaving him in the car, I unlocked the flat and turned on every light. I shook him awake, not as gently as I could have, and he appeared more with it than he had been at Port Wakefield. I wondered what had happened to his suit jacket and tie. Probably still at Lana's place.

'Elliot, we're home. At my place.'

'What the—' he said and looked around blinking blearily.

'You were too drunk to leave on your own and I had to come home. I'll take you back on Sunday or Monday. Plenty of time to sober up and give your liver a break. Now, can you please get out of the car and we'll go inside. You can have a shower and go to bed.' My patience was gossamer thin.

After several false starts, he managed to lever himself out of the car seat. I carried our bags inside and took his through to the spare room. It all went swimmingly until the shower. He didn't want one but there was no way he was getting into the clean sheets on my spare bed reeking of urine. With my help, he managed to undress and get into the shower. He was a head taller than me and probably weighed at least thirty kilos more than I did, so it wasn't easy. Who'd be a nurse or a carer? I set the water going and then hovered outside the open bathroom door talking to him every minute or so. He'd grumble something in return, until he didn't and then I heard a splashy, slapping sound followed by a grunt. When I ripped open the shower curtain he was slumped on the floor in the shower recess, snoring. That's right, snoring, with tepid water drumming down onto him. Tempted to leave him there until the water went cold, I turned off the shower but couldn't rouse him enough to get him up. When I shook him he told me to go away, but not as politely as that. By now I *was* in tears. I threw two towels at him, hunted out my phone and rang Hamish.

'Ruth,' he said after the second ring. It was late and I was so relieved he wasn't asleep.

'I need your help,' I said and choked back a sob.

'Where are you?'

'Home. Come down the lane behind the cafe.'

'I'll be there in five,' he said and he was.

I met him at the door.

'What's up?'

'Follow me.' I led him through the living area to the bathroom. 'Hamish, meet Elliot, my brother. I can't get him up.'

'Is he sick?'

'Drunk.'

'Did he fall?

'No, I don't think so, he just kind of slid down the tiles.'

Hamish didn't ask questions, simply said in an authoritative voice, 'Elliot, mate, you need to get up before you freeze your balls off.'

Remarkably, my brother opened his eyes and focussed on Hamish, but not without difficulty. 'Who the hell are you?'

'Hamish Adams, a friend of Ruth's. I'm here to help you up and get you to bed.'

Elliot swore and tried ineffectually to sit up. 'Where's my sister?'

I peered around Hamish. 'I'm here, Elliot. Now will you please let

Hamish help you? It's late and I need to be up early.'

'All right, all right,' he said and slithered around the shower recess. I'd never unsee that image.

'What's say we dry you off first,' Hamish said and proceeded to do just that.

'His pyjamas are on the hand basin. I'll go and see to the spare bed,' I said and sped off without waiting for a response from either man. I grabbed an extra pillow from the linen press and was folding back the top sheet and doona when Hamish guided Elliot through the bedroom door.

Together we settled him into bed. I'd put Lana's ice-cream container on the floor beside the bed and I pointed it out to Elliot.

'Do you want a cup of tea? Glass of water?'

'Water, thanks,' he said, abashed. He looked dreadful. My heart squeezed with love and despair.

He was asleep when I went back with a bottle of water—I didn't trust him with a glass. I put it on the bedside cupboard and turned off the light.

Hamish had tidied the bathroom and hung the towels outside on the clothesline.

'Thanks,' I said, heartfelt, when he came back inside. 'Do you want a cup of tea? Beer? Cold water?'

'Tea would be good, if you're up for it. What happened?'

I filled the kettle and switched it on. 'One or six too many at the wake. He lives by himself and I had to come home and there was no-one to stay with him so I brought him with me. I'll take him back after the weekend.'

Hamish propped himself against the kitchen cupboard and watched as I made the tea.

'Milk?'

'Just a dash. No sugar. Is he always a big drinker?'

'Worse than I thought. Robert's wife is concerned about him.

Her words went something like, "Robert tempered Elliot's excesses". And Robert's not here anymore.'

'I see.'

We stood in the kitchen and drank our tea. 'Thank you so much, Hamish,' I said. I was embarrassed for my brother and for myself.

'Think nothing of it. Not the first time I've helped put a drunk to bed.'

'Oh. And has anyone ever had to help put you to bed?'

'Nope. I like a beer as much as the next bloke but I haven't been legless since I was a teenager. Don't see any point to it.'

'I enjoy a wine or three on occasion, as you might have guessed. But I don't enjoy feeling seedy the next day. I don't have time for it.'

Hamish left after he'd finished his tea. 'I'll come in for breakfast tomorrow,' he said. 'See you then.'

'Okay. Goodnight and thank you again.'

'You're very welcome, Ruth. I'm glad you called me and didn't try to get him up on your own.'

I locked the door and turned off the outside lights. It was almost eleven and all I wanted to do was crash. I'd be up again at five. Before I went to bed, I checked on Elliot. He was dead to the world and his sleep appeared more peaceful.

I left the lamp on in the living area and closed my door. Exhausted, physically and emotionally, I immediately fell asleep.

27

Ruth

Audrey Franco was the first customer over the threshold on Saturday morning, which was unusual. Suzie had messaged to say she'd be half an hour late. Although I'd slept, I felt hungover even though all I'd had to drink at the wake was mineral water.

'Ruth,' Audrey said. She stepped around the counter to where I stood by the till and took one of my hands in hers, giving it a firm squeeze. Her hand was cool and clammy. I did my best not to shudder. 'My sincere condolences, you poor, poor girl. Brings you up short when one of your siblings passes, doesn't it?'

'Yes, it does,' I said and gingerly extracted my fingers from her moist grip. The community grapevine was obviously doing its job. 'And thank you, Audrey, for your kind words. What can I get you this morning?'

She blinked and her attention shifted to the morning's muffins under the mesh cover. Chocolate chip, warm and fragrant. 'Hmm. Seeing as how I'm here, I might as well have a muffin and a cappuccino.'

'Why not? Sit yourself down, Audrey, I'll bring it over.'

She paid and sat down by the window at table one, her back

ramrod straight. She wore powder blue capris and a matching floral blouse, her blue-rinsed hair freshly permed. I wondered if she ever relaxed.

The front door opened just as I delivered Audrey's order. It was Hamish and my heart gave a crazy little skip, which I did my best to ignore.

'Good morning, Ruth,' he said and smiled.

'Hello,' I said to Hamish and 'Enjoy,' to Audrey, who was now more interested in this unknown man with the killer smile than her muffin and cappuccino.

He followed me to the counter. 'How's Elliot this morning?'

'Embarrassed, remorseful, annoyed that he's here and at my mercy, not that he's said anything.'

'Hungover?'

'Not as much as he should be. Coffee?'

'Please, and a bacon and egg sandwich.'

'Have here or take away?'

He glanced at Audrey and then around at the otherwise empty cafe. 'I'll have it here. Thanks. Table three.' He took out his wallet.

I shook my head vehemently. 'No way, Hamish. Not after what you did to help last night.'

He reluctantly put his wallet away.

Suzie arrived at nine thirty full of apologies, but no explanation. Then the usual Saturday morning crowd began steadily trickling in and it wasn't long before I was inundated with food orders. George came in like a breath of fresh air and took over at the coffee machine while Suzie zipped around delivering food and drinks. Too busy in the kitchen, I managed to gulp down a coffee and a toasted cheese sandwich, made with the crusts of course, and I didn't notice when Hamish left. What Elliot was up to, I had no idea.

Some Saturdays I didn't mop the floor at the end of the day. Today was one of those days. We'd almost had to chase out the hangers-on when two o'clock came and went. George left and Suzie minutes after him. She'd been subdued all shift. I wondered what dramas she had going on in her young life. There was always something.

I was dead on my feet when I eventually turned off the kitchen light in the cafe and went through to the flat. Elliot hadn't popped into the cafe for a coffee and breakfast, which I'd offered for him to do, and I was trying not to think the worst, that is, that he'd popped across the road to the hotel instead.

Except for the hum of the refrigerator, the flat was silent. No sign of Elliot inside or out. No note. My concern upped a notch. I rang his mobile number and immediately heard its shrill ring. It was on the bedside cupboard in the spare room, charging. The bed was made. His suit trousers were flung over the back of a chair and the dress shoes he'd been wearing yesterday were beside the bed. I'd thrown in a pair of sneakers when I'd packed his bag, along with shorts, track pants and a couple of T-shirts and pyjamas. There was no sign of his wallet.

The hotel, that's where he'd be, propped up at the front bar with the other regulars. I groaned, the sound loud in the silent room. So what if he was at the hotel? He was an adult and I wasn't his keeper and neither did I want to be. It wasn't my job to find him and bring him home.

Anger, red hot and searing and aimed mainly at Robert for dying, flashed through me. Remorse followed immediately. If Elliot wasn't home in half an hour I'd go searching for him. In the meantime, the list of jobs I had to do was endless. Best I get started.

★ ★ ★

Almost an hour passed before Elliot crossed my mind again. Lucky for him, I wasn't his keeper, because it turns out I wasn't very good at it. My phone rang just as I was contemplating where I'd begin the search. It was Hamish.

'Ruth, Elliot's here with me, in case you were wondering. He went for a walk and happened upon me out in the front yard. Serendipitous really ... he's been helping me install the skylight. You didn't tell me he was an engineer.'

'I don't remember you asking,' I said, waspishly and without self-reproach. It's how I reacted when I felt I was being ganged up upon by men. Just ask my brothers—make that *brother*. Tears prickled and I blinked them away.

'Ruth, are you all right?'

'Tired and bereaved but otherwise okay. Please ask Elliot if he'll be home for tea.'

Hamish cleared his throat and I did feel a moment's remorse for being a bitch. It was Elliot who should be on the receiving end of my ire, not Hamish. He'd been nothing but kind and he was grieving too.

'I'm sorry,' I said.

'Don't be. Do you want to go to the hotel for a counter meal tonight? You've been cooking all day.'

'Thanks, but no, Hamish. All I want is a quiet evening at home followed by an early night.'

'Fair enough ... hang on a sec—' he said and I could hear Elliot's voice in the background. 'Right, the plan is this: we'll finish up here and then grab a counter meal. Okay?'

'Tell him I'll leave the door unlocked.'

'He said he won't be late, Ruth.'

'Sure ... Thanks and I'll see you later.'

The day had been clear and hot; mid thirties. Not much of an afternoon sea breeze. The tea towels on the clothesline were dry an hour after I'd pegged them out and I stood and folded them into the basket. The cement was warm under my bare feet.

After folding the tea towels, I soaked the sad-looking pot plants with water and picked a handful of ripe cherry tomatoes and a sprig of basil, crushing a leaf with my fingertips and inhaling the spicy smell. The tomatoes accompanied by a wedge of cheddar, olives and a few crackers was all I wanted to eat.

The seven o'clock news was on and I was ironing my 'uniforms' when Elliot came in looking sheepish.

'How was the pub meal?'

'Fair,' he said. He peeled off his sneakers and put them outside the door. 'I might have a shower. I've been up a ladder in Hamish's ceiling space and it was hot as Hades.' He padded through to the spare room. His complexion was pasty grey, his thinning hair in sweaty spikes.

He was almost to the door when he stopped and turned to face me.

'I need to apologise for yesterday, Ruth. I must have been awful and you were so gracious. I would have left me to sober up in a ditch, but you took care of me. And this afternoon, I was only going for a walk around the block to stretch my legs, but then I went further than expected and ran into your bloke ... realised I didn't have my phone.'

'He's not my bloke, Elliot. He's just someone who comes into the cafe from time to time. And he's been kind to me.'

'If you say so. Towel?'

'Yours is the striped one behind the bathroom door.'

His lips quirked into an almost smile. 'You're more like Mum the older you get. You even sounded like her just then.'

'Not a day goes by that I don't think of her and miss her. The cakes I bake for the cafe are all her recipes. I flick through her recipe book at least two or three times a week. It's almost as if she's there with me. There's only you and me left now, Elliot. Doesn't that feel weird to you? Mum and Dad and now Robert.'

'Bloody horrible is how it is. I feel as if half of me has been ripped away, the good half. Robert always was the better person.'

'But you're easier to get along with.'

'Then it's lucky for you I'm the one you're stuck with, as unfair as that feels to me right now. But you probably would have been better off having Robert around. And Lana didn't deserve to be widowed.'

He looked lost, forlorn, a seven-year-old boy not a seventy-something man. I went to him and hugged him.

At first he stood rigidly in my embrace. I didn't let go and slowly his muscles loosened, his arms slid around me and he hugged me in return.

28

Hamish

Sunday morning, Elliot returned as promised to help Hamish finish off the skylight. He looked so much better than he had on their first encounter in the shower recess at Ruth's on Friday night. Despite Elliot's enthusiasm, Hamish kept in mind that Ruth's brother was a decade older than he was and not the fittest of specimens. But now they had successfully installed the skylight, the difference to the kitchen was remarkable. Except that, with all the extra light, he could see how desperately the room needed a coat of paint and just how shabby the cupboards were.

'Ideally, the room needs gutting,' he said to Elliot. They were sitting at the kitchen table having a cold drink and a sandwich for a late lunch.

'But why would you bother? Let whoever buys it do what they want.' Elliot finished his sandwich and wiped his mouth with a folded handkerchief he pulled from the pocket of his shorts. 'If it were me, I'd knock out part of that wall, demolish the tacked-on laundry and build out. New kitchen, large living area. Glass along the back … Given it's north-facing, it could all be glass. New wet areas that included a laundry and a second bathroom.'

Hamish nodded. He filled the kettle and switched it on. 'Tea? Coffee?'

'Tea. White and one. Why don't you buy out your sister, renovate the place and then sell it? You'd have a place to live while you did it and you could make yourself a tidy sum when you sold. It'd be a project that'd keep a bloke occupied and out of the pub.' Elliot paced around the kitchen, pausing to peer out the window. 'Decent-sized block. Your main concern would be not to overcapitalise. Cutlers Bay isn't exactly Kensington Gardens or Norwood.'

'I had noticed,' Hamish said.

Elliot chuckled. 'Beggars belief why Ruth sank all her money into a business in a place like this.'

Hamish dropped the tea bag he'd been dunking into the bin. He put the mug of tea onto the table along with the milk and sugar. 'Cutlers Bay isn't *that* bad,' he said. 'Mum and Dad lived here happily enough for a lot of years. Golf course looks half-decent and you can even get a proper cup of coffee in town.'

'You play golf, do you?'

'Don't mind a hit every now and then. You?'

'Ah,' Elliot said and sank down onto his chair. He doctored his tea and took a sip. 'Rob and I used to hit a ball around at least once a week. He did it because he enjoyed the game and he was damned good at it. I did it because I needed the exercise and it helped pass the time. God knows what I'll do now to fill in my days.'

Hamish didn't say anything, too busy teasing out Elliot's comments about the house. To use Elliot's own words, it would give him something to do, a project. Not that keeping himself out of the pub was an issue for Hamish; his issue was more about being *bored* to death. There were only so many games of golf a bloke could play. He didn't enjoy it *that* much. He liked to read, but there was a limit to how long he could sit with a book before restlessness set in. And buying out Nat's share of their parents' house would get her off his back. She'd be happy—ecstatic, more than likely.

When they'd talked on the phone the day before, she'd hinted at him paying rent, given he was virtually living in the house and it was half hers. His response had been something along the lines of: Not as long as my arse points to the ground, given the work I'm doing to clean up the place. She'd quickly backed down and he'd reiterated to himself that once their parents' estate was settled there would be little need for him to communicate with her at all. Something about that notion both appealed and appalled, and left him feeling empty inside. She was all that was left of his immediate family. It was a pity she made herself so hard to like.

But to buy out her share of the house? Hamish had made some inquiries and had a rough idea what the asking price for the property would be. Settlement for his apartment was ten days away and he'd be fully cashed up with no need to delve into his superannuation. Really, there was nothing to hold him back. He liked the town well enough, although he shouldn't discount how much a certain cafe owner factored into that.

Elliot coughed and jerked him out of his musing. 'I'll be on my way, if you don't need me for anything else. Ruth said she'll drive me back to Adelaide this afternoon, after the cafe closes. Thanks for lunch.' He stacked their dirty plates into the sink.

'Don't worry about the dishes and thanks for your help. I'd still be fiddling about with the skylight if you hadn't come along when you did.'

'Happy to help. I'll see myself out.'

They shook hands. Elliot frowned but didn't say anything more. He had already apologised profusely for the unusual and embarrassing way they'd met.

Hamish cleared his throat. 'Next time you're up visiting Ruth, chuck in your sticks and we could have a hit.'

Elliot's expression brightened. 'I could do that,' he said. 'Next time I'm across this way.'

After Elliot had gone, Hamish wandered about the house and yard, thinking, imagining, calculating. He'd never renovated anything before. No old cars, motorbikes, stationary engines, not like a lot of mechanics he'd known over the years. To overcapitalise and never realise the money spent on the renovation would be an easy and costly mistake. He was handy and a quick learner but he didn't have the skills required to do some of the work, tradesmen would need to be contracted for that. None of it would be cheap and the more he did himself, the better. From what he'd picked up over the years, anything involving building or renovation notoriously blew out the most carefully constructed budget. He would certainly need to do his research first.

But even before that, was it what he wanted to do? Could he afford another wrong turn? Did he have time for it? With any luck, he still had a lot of good years left. Regardless, it was imperative he set himself up over those years for the final decade of his life, because by all accounts, that was when everything came unstuck.

★ ★ ★

He was on his way into the Cutlers Bay real estate agent's office on Tuesday afternoon when who should be coming out? None other than Ruth. He didn't know who was the more surprised. Probably him.

'You're home,' he said. 'How was the city?'

'Hot. Relentless. The traffic is worse every time I visit and there was smoke everywhere from a bushfire in the hills.'

'So you enjoyed yourself, then?'

She laughed, which pleased him. Of late, her eyes had lost their sparkle.

'How was Elliot?'

'We talked. I told him he was welcome here any time. This morning I had a coffee with Lana, Robert's widow. She puts on a stoic face, but underneath that? Her grief is very raw. She's going to have Elliot over for a meal later this week.'

'What about you?'

'Oh, I'll be fine. Robert and I never featured hugely in one another's lives and although I'll miss him, it won't be the same for me as it will be for Elliot and Lana. I didn't appreciate how much time Robert and Elliot spent together. Lana indicated that they saw each other most days and Elliot was there for a meal two or three times a week. Would have been hard on a new marriage, not that she sounded at all bitter.'

Hamish glanced at his watch. Ruth noticed. 'Am I holding you up?' she said.

'No, you're not. But I need to catch Bryan before he leaves for the day and that's in about ten minutes.'

'Okay, I'll see you later then.'

He wanted to ask her to come around for a drink this evening but Bryan opened the door.

'Hamish Adams?'

'Yep, that'd be me,' he said and the moment was lost. By the time Bryan ushered him inside, Ruth was already halfway across the street and walking towards the supermarket.

'Remarkable woman,' Bryan was saying when Hamish finally tuned in. Bryan wasn't a big man—wiry was the word that described him—but he had an aura of unleashed energy about him. 'Now, what can I do for you?'

Hamish sat in the proffered chair. 'It's about my parents' place, 34 East Terrace,' he said and went on to describe briefly the current situation with the property. 'And to cut a long story short, I've decided that I will offer to buy out my sister's share, if she's willing, which I'm certain she will be. I've had a conversation with the solicitors acting for the estate and you're to expect a request from them for a property valuation, including your costs.'

Bryan nodded. 'They didn't want an independent bank valuation?'

'Nope. But if my sister wants to get her own independent valuation, she's free to do so.'

'Fair enough. When you do agree on a price, transfer of ownership shouldn't take more than a couple of weeks. You have a conveyancer?'

'I do.'

Instead of going home after the appointment, Hamish made for the supermarket. If he was going to be in Cutlers Bay indefinitely he needed to feed himself better than he had been. Sandwiches or toast most meals wasn't a balanced diet, not by anyone's standards. And while he liked Ruth's food far better than what he prepared for himself, he couldn't show up at the cafe every day.

Disappointingly, there was no sign of Ruth in the supermarket aisles. She must have whipped in and out while he was talking to Bryan. Making the most of her day off. He grabbed a few vegetables and salad items, bread, milk, meat and whatever else took his fancy and cursed to himself when he had to pay for more bags to carry the groceries home. There was already a pile of them back at the house. He needed to get better at this.

His phone rang while he was loading the groceries onto the back seat of the dual cab. He wished for it be Ruth, but no, it was Nat. He didn't answer. He guessed why she'd be calling: the solicitors would have contacted her regarding his offer to buy out her share of the house. She'd be bitching because he hadn't mentioned it to her first. But he would do this by the book, leave no room for her to come back at him any time into the future. He'd return her call later.

29

Ruth

The first day of my working week was off to a stellar start: the gas ran out, both bottles empty, which meant there was no grill or hot water. The worst part of it was I couldn't recall when I'd turned over the bottles. There were two gas bottles and the routine was that when one bottle emptied another was ordered. That way we avoid the situation I found myself in at eight-oh-five on a Wednesday morning when the first customer of the day ordered a bacon and egg roll. After talking him into a toasted ham and cheese sandwich instead, I took out the sandwich press and, while it was heating, I rang the local depot. Of course replacement bottles couldn't be delivered until I'd been online and ordered the gas first. Then I discovered the milk fridge hadn't been restocked and salad sandwich fillings were low.

When Allie came in to start her shift, the gas bottles had been delivered. Her face paled as I recounted what had happened. 'Oh, Ruth,' she said. 'That was me. I turned the gas over ages ago and forgot to write it on the white board. Sorry.'

'It could as easily have been me who forgot. Don't worry about it. Bryan came in for coffee and watched the shop while I went to the office to order it. Were you busy yesterday?'

'Steady,' she said. 'But Lorna had to go at one thirty. Her mum had a fall. The lady next door heard her calling out and she phoned for the ambulance. I was on my own after that.'

'I hope she didn't break any bones. That'd be awful for her and for Lorna.' And me, if it made Lorna less available to work.

The bell at the counter tinkled and Allie and I looked at each other. 'I didn't hear the door,' I said.

'Me either. I'll go.'

Lorna leaving early the day before explained why the milk fridge hadn't been restocked and the sandwich fillings were low. While I shredded lettuce and sliced tomatoes, I sifted through the casual staff I had on the books, wondering if one of them might be prepared to learn the cooking side of things. If Lorna quit, I'd need a backup. It might be a good contingency plan regardless.

After the bumpy start, the week progressed along similar lines to every other week. Allie was more her old self but didn't let on at all how things were at home, except to say that her fortieth birthday celebrations had been a success. Luckily, Lorna's mum hadn't broken anything. She spent one night in hospital under observation and Lorna stayed at her unit with her for the next couple of nights. I knew this because, as I'd discovered, Allie and Lorna talked often. It didn't matter how well I got on with the staff and how easygoing I tried to be, I'd always be the boss and rarely privy to everything that went on.

Elliot and I talked a couple of times during the week. Brief conversations, mainly to ascertain the other's wellbeing. My GP appointment was on Tuesday and I'd be staying with him overnight. I'd see then how he was genuinely faring. It'd brought me up short to admit how little I knew about his life and how he filled in his days.

The only significant change Robert's death had brought about for me was that my concern for Elliot's welfare had escalated. Honestly, before Robert died, I hadn't given my brothers' welfare much thought at all. The day I'd driven Elliot back home to Adelaide, his good humour had been over the top. He hadn't fooled me and I'm sure he realised that, because when he'd waved me off, he'd said, 'You mustn't worry about me, old chook, I can look after myself.' Of course that meant I'd worried.

Friday afternoon, Hamish came into the cafe minutes after Allie had left. I wondered if he'd been watching and waiting for her to leave. A ridiculous thought. There were a few customers dawdling over afternoon tea, so I made Hamish a coffee and we went through to the kitchen so I could continue the perpetual cleaning up and preparing for the next day.

'How's your week been?'

'So-so,' he said. 'Quick trip to Adelaide to sign papers, drop off a few boxes of Mum's stuff to Nat and pick up the last few belongings from my apartment. And the bed. Had a helluva job moving it. Had to borrow Pete's trailer in the end. He came down and helped me. I organised for the electricity meter to be read. Settlement's next Wednesday.'

'How does that feel?'

'A relief more than anything.' He grabbed a tea towel and started drying the dishes I'd washed. 'I was going to overnight it, you know, the last night I'd spend there and all that, but in the end I couldn't be bothered.'

I left Hamish to the drying up and ducked out to see if the customers were happy. Peg wanted another cappuccino. She'd sometimes come in for coffee and cake and sit for a while before the fish and chip shop busied up in the late afternoon and evening.

'I see the bins have gone from the op shop,' she said when I delivered the second cappuccino. 'Bit of unrest over it. And I hear it was your idea.'

'My idea? Who told you that?' I said and laughed. 'Audrey Franco has been carrying on about those damned bins and the rubbish people dump in the alley for as long as I've lived in this town. If something isn't working, any sensible person would change it. Find a solution that did work.'

'You and I know that but unfortunately not everyone has our common sense. And let me warn you: those women at the op shop will need someone to blame if the change doesn't work out.'

'But how could they possibly lay the blame at my feet? All I did was make a suggestion. I'm not involved in any way with the op shop. I've never even taken stuff there.'

Peg tutted and waggled a finger at me. 'Ruth, you would have discovered by now how small towns work. Let me tell you how I learned my lesson. Years ago, I was offered locally caught fish. I refused to buy it and I won't go into the reasons why but they were all valid and I was in the right. "Someone" dumped a drum of rotting fish guts into our front yard. I swear that, to this day, I can still smell it when it's stinking hot.'

'You're joking?'

'Not in a heartbeat,' Peg said. 'In my experience, people whinge, but the bottom line is, they do not like change, they just like to bitch. You have my word that when I hear anything about the op-shop bins, I'll be sure to set them straight about your role in it.'

'Thanks, I think. Should I say something to Audrey? It must have been her because I haven't said a word to anyone else. Why would I?'

'Up to you, but as you've probably worked out, she's not the sharpest knife in the drawer, that one. By the way, you make excellent coffee, Ruth, and the muffin was pretty good too.'

I went back to the kitchen shaking my head. Had Peg just warned me to stick to what I knew best: making coffee and baking muffins? Surely not.

'What was that all about?' Hamish said. He'd been watching from the kitchen doorway.

'This town,' I replied and rolled my eyes. 'One of the few times I've ever said what I thought! Is it closing time yet?'

The door opened and a cluster of teenagers surged inside, laughing and stirring each other. School was out so no, it wasn't closing time yet. Unfortunately.

'I'll leave you to it,' Hamish said. 'If you feel like a drink and a debrief later, come around. I'm not going anywhere. I can rustle us up something to eat.'

'I'll message you,' I said and fronted up to the counter to take orders. The kitchen door clunked shut behind him.

It wasn't until two-and-a-half hours later when I went home to the flat that I remembered Hamish's invitation. The school kids had been cashed-up and hungry and I hadn't ended up closing until well after four. Then Laurie was uncharacteristically chatty when all I'd wanted to do was complete my prep for Saturday morning. Now, as per usual, I had at least a dozen things I needed to do before bedtime. A drink with Hamish really was out of the question.

See you shortly, I messaged anyway, because I needed an hour away from my responsibilities. And I wanted to know what he'd been doing at Bryan Chalmers's office on Tuesday afternoon.

Because I'd been on my feet all day, I drove the short distance to East Terrace. The rubbish skip was gone and the front yard was immaculate. The man was a machine.

He came to the door just as I lifted my hand to knock. 'No sign yet?' I said and glanced back over my shoulder.

He pushed open the screen door. The hole had been patched. 'I'm not with you?'

'The For Sale sign? Wasn't that why you were seeing Bryan?'

'Ah,' he said, an amused gleam entering his eyes. 'Not exactly. Come in and I'll pour you a glass and tell you all about it.'

Intrigued, I followed him down the passage and into the kitchen. 'My goodness,' I said. 'Light and airy.' I took in the skylight.

'Certainly has made a huge difference. You have been busy.' The kitchen cupboards were devoid of clutter and the stainless steel sink almost sparkled.

'Elliot helped with the skylight. Would have taken me twice as long on my own. He's pretty clever.' Hamish fetched a bottle of white wine out of the fridge along with a stubby of beer. I took down a glass and he poured me a generous serve. We were both still in our work clothes.

'Outside?' he said and I nodded.

'When do you sleep?' I said as we sat on the verandah. I was amazed to see that the backyard had been tidied up and the pad for a new rainwater tank halfway prepared.

'Plenty of daylight hours this time of the year and Laurie gave me a hand another day. He worked damned hard all day and I offered to pay him but he wouldn't hear of it.'

He produced a bag of salted mixed nuts, ripped it open and put it on the upturned crate between us. It was a mild evening, not a breath of breeze, and on the drive around I'd noticed billowy clouds building on the western horizon.

'We might be in for a storm,' I said.

He cast his eyes upwards. 'Fingers crossed that the roof doesn't leak around the skylight when it rains.'

'So,' I said, angling myself towards him. 'Is the house on the market or not?'

'Or not,' he said. He stretched out his legs and crossed his ankles. 'I'm in the process of buying Nat out of her share. My plan is to renovate the place and then sell it. That gives me somewhere to live and plenty of time to decide what to do with the rest of my life.'

'Oh, I didn't see that coming. I thought you were anxious to offload the place. Leave Cutlers Bay behind you.'

He took a long pull on his beer. I took a sip of wine. It was cold, crisp and dry. Perfect. I was hungry and if I wasn't careful, I'd be tipsy after one glass, on top of the headache that had lurked in the background all day. I put down the wineglass and poured myself a handful of nuts. Hamish held out his hand and I filled it.

'I thought I was too, but I like the old house.'

'Is it because you're not quite ready to let go of the final link to your parents?'

'Hadn't thought of it in those terms, but maybe. And the more I do around the place, the more potential I see in it. The trick will be to know when to stop spending money I might never recoup when it sells.'

'Renovating anything always costs more than you think it will. Trust me on that.'

'Yeah, but I'll be able to do a lot of the grunt work myself. I've been asking around about tradesmen and the likes. A mate I play golf with in Adelaide is a builder, has his own business. He's offered to drive across and have a look at the house. I have lots of ideas and he'll know if they're structurally doable.'

His tone was positive and his animated expression suggested he was excited about the project. Or perhaps about *having* a project. I remembered vividly what that excitement had felt like when I'd bought the building I'd turned into the cafe. It had been thrilling and fulfilling when it all came together. *But not anymore,* said the voice in my head. Something bit me on the ankle and I swiped at it.

'Mozzies? I'll get a coil.' Hamish disappeared into the house. He came back a few minutes later with a box of mozzie coils and matches. 'I thought with the old tank and the ivy gone, the mozzies would bugger off as well.' He lit a coil and put it on the cement between us.

'What does your sister think about your offer? Was she surprised?'

'This way she'll get her share sooner rather than later and that's a win-win for her. Wants the place valued by two independent agents. Thinks I'm going to rip her off, or some such rot. It's all in the hands of the executors, which she just does not get.'

'You're not close?'

'Nah. Top-up?' He pointed to the almost empty glass dangling from my fingers.

'A glass of water, if you don't mind. I've had a headache hanging around all day, probably because I haven't drunk nearly enough water.'

He came back with a jug of cold water and two glasses. 'Now, before I fire up the barbecue,' he said, filling a glass and handing it to me, 'I've told you why I was talking to Bryan Chalmers. Why were you?'

I laughed. I couldn't help it.

Hamish frowned. 'What's so funny?' he said.

'A letter addressed to Bryan was in with my mail so I took it over to him. It'd been sitting on the bench for a couple of days and I kept forgetting to do it.'

'That was all?'

His scepticism was not misplaced, because along with the letter, I'd taken the opportunity to ask Bryan a few business-related questions, in confidence, of course. Bryan had been affronted that I'd assumed he wouldn't automatically keep any business discussion we had totally private.

I tilted back in the seat so I could look up at Hamish. It was an hour or more until sunset but the back verandah faced east and it was swathed in shadows, making his expression difficult to read. He stood still, silent and watchful. I opened my mouth to speak and then straight away closed it again. The pressure inside me built. I wanted— needed—to confide all the things I was grappling with, but that went so completely against the grain and old habits were hard to break. I'd basically been doing it solo for most of my adult life. If ever I'd opened up to Mum, she'd listened but never interfered. And there'd been occasions along the way when I'd desperately wished someone had been involved enough to want to interfere. A trustworthy person I could have shared with, used as a sounding board. Especially with the more gnarly decisions, like whether to buy a rundown building in a small country town and turn it into a cafe, using up all my savings and having no plan for how I would support myself into retirement.

I took a slow sip of water, mainly to moisten my dry mouth. Hamish didn't budge. I think we both knew we'd reached a significant juncture in our developing friendship. If I lied, denied or obfuscated, it would set the tone going forward.

'I've decided to sell the cafe,' I said, testing how the words sounded out loud. 'I asked Bryan a few questions about the process.'

He nodded slowly. 'Any specific reason why you've decided to sell now?'

'Oh, I could give you one hundred reasons, but what they all boil down to is I just don't want to do it anymore. I'm over being Ruth from Rosie's Cafe. I just want to be plain old Ruth again, whoever she might be.' I closed my eyes and sank deeper into the armchair. 'If I have to keep working at the pace I am for much longer, I'll get to resent it and then hate it and that wouldn't be good for anyone.'

'What did Bryan say?' His chair creaked as he sat down again.

'What options I have, but he didn't sound overly optimistic about any of them, but then that's Bryan and he's been in the business a long time. To realise anything near what I've invested, I'd need to sell the shop and the flat and the business as a going concern.'

'You would have kept the proper records—everything you'll need to sell it—to demonstrate it's a viable business?'

'Of course I have,' I said. 'I built the cafe from nothing and it is a reliable small business, if you're prepared to work hard and not pay out too much in other people's wages. Bryan knows this, but he also understands how challenging it is to sell such businesses in country towns like Cutlers Bay.'

'Might be prudent to sell the business and keep the real estate. Live in the flat and lease the shop to the new owner. What about the woman who works for you? Allie? She seems capable.'

'She is extremely capable, but she's bringing up two teenage children on her own and has her fair share of problems, financial and otherwise. I've made a living out of the cafe, but there's only ever been me to support and I haven't had a holiday in the whole five years I've owned the damned place.'

'What's a holiday?' Hamish said. 'More nuts?' I held out my hand. 'A long weekend on Kangaroo Island is the most holiday I've ever had and I was on my honeymoon.'

'I bet the new wife wasn't impressed.'

He snorted. 'She was the one who couldn't take the time off. The more I think about it, the more I wonder why we ever got married in the first place.'

'The clarity of hindsight,' I said. When I swiped at another mosquito Hamish said, 'Do you want to move inside?'

'I'm okay if you are. It's pleasant sitting out here.' We lapsed into silence. Then I cleared my throat and said, 'In the interests of full disclosure, the thing that keeps me awake at nights is what happens if I can't sell any of it. Because there's only that business and the real estate between me and the poorhouse. Minimal savings, no superannuation to speak of, no rich relatives and not eligible for the aged pension for years. Like you and your marriage, if I'd known half a decade ago what I know now about running a cafe in a small town, we wouldn't be having this conversation.'

'You wouldn't have done it?'

'Not necessarily, but I would have planned an exit strategy and I would've held back some of my savings, not spent every cent when the cost of the renovations blew out.'

'If you seriously want out, I suppose if the real estate doesn't sell and no-one wants to buy the business, you could shut it down, sell off whatever you could and get a job. At least you'd have a place to live.'

'Yeah, right,' I said. 'I'll bet there are unlimited employment opportunities waiting for someone like me. The wrong side of sixty and used to being her own boss.' I was beginning to sound like a whiny old woman but I didn't for one moment regret sharing with him. 'And what if one of the reasons I want to sell up is because I don't want to live in Cutlers Bay any longer? What if I want to be closer to what's left of my family?'

'Make a list of your options, Ruth, the most favourable outcome through to the least favourable. The pros and cons of each. I'll bet the person you bought the building from never imagined they'd sell it. How long had it been on the market?'

'Six-and-a-half years, that's why it was such a bargain. In the end, the renovation, buying the stock and covering the start-up costs was way more money than what the building alone cost. Making the flat liveable didn't take much. I did the painting.'

'How long since anyone had lived in the flat?'

'Only about two years. The owner rented it to an elderly relative. My understanding is she eventually went into care and it was empty after that.'

He pushed himself to his feet. 'I'll fire up the barbie. You look as if you need to be fed. Fish tonight. Caught at Rocky Point.'

'Your brother-in-law?'

'Yep. That meal I promised you ages ago.'

'What can I do?'

'Make the salad. That would be overextending my culinary skills. There's green stuff in the fridge.'

I threw together a salad and microwaved potatoes, adding dollops of butter. The fish had bones but the meal was tasty.

'Next time, come and have dinner at my place,' I said to him as I left. 'I'll make you something other than Vegemite toast or a big breakfast.'

'It's a date,' he said.

On the drive home, I tossed those words over a few times. Is that what we were doing? Dating? I wasn't sure, nor was I certain if that's what I'd hoped we were doing. The idea of a trustworthy friend appealed to me more than anything. He was an attractive man but I wouldn't know what to do with a romance.

30

Hamish

It was done. The keys to the apartment had been handed over and the money transferred to Hamish's bank account, giving him a balance that had his heart pumping fast for several seconds. He celebrated by himself what he was beginning to think of as the next chapter of his life: Retirement, Take Two. Buying out Nat's share of the house would take time to be finalised, but the ball was rolling. Bryan Chalmers had appraised and valued the property and Terri Longbottom was coming in the morning to do the same. Of the two agents, Hamish believed that Bryan's valuation would be the lower of the two and the most realistic, but knowing his sister the way he did, he accepted without qualms that she'd push for his buyout to be based on the highest valuation. In the end, the solicitors would decide.

He settled into one of the tatty old vinyl-covered armchairs on the back verandah with a beer and a bag of peanuts and decided the only thing that would make the moment more right was if Ruth was sitting in the adjacent chair, sharing the special time with him. He'd always been a loner, so that realisation in itself was novel for him. As he gazed out onto the backyard, he thought about his parents.

Had they often sat out here and enjoyed a warm summer's evening? Chatted about their day? Given the armchairs had already been firmly ensconced when he'd arrived, perhaps they had. The depth of the dust and cobwebs he'd cleaned off the chairs led him to believe his father hadn't sat out here on his own. There wasn't a lot left to look at in the backyard, not since Hamish had dispatched the rainwater tank to the dump and taken out every dead plant and shrub and the remains of the long-neglected vegetable garden.

He was into his third beer and feeling mellow when the lengthening shadows disappeared altogether. The sea breeze had dropped, the evening stilled, and tomorrow was forecast to be another hot day. As he sat there, Hamish pondered the unexpected direction his life had taken and what the future might hold. Jeff, his mate the builder, was driving across on the weekend. He was looking forward to that. It would be good to catch up with Jeff, but even better to discover which parts of his renovation imaginings could be realistically accomplished.

On the crate beside him, his phone rang. He glanced at the illuminated screen hoping it'd be Ruth, but no, it was Nat. It continued to ring and vibrate itself towards the edge of the crate. He snatched it up the second it would have toppled over the edge and onto the cement. It stopped ringing before he answered and he heaved a sigh of relief, short-lived, because it started up again.

'Nat,' he said.

'You're going to have to advance me money in lieu of my share of the house,' she said and sounded out of breath. 'Twenty thousand at least. Maybe thirty. Immediately.'

'And why am I going to have to do that? And who says I have money I can advance you, immediately or otherwise?'

'I know you've sold your apartment and I know how much you got for it so don't bullshit me, Hamish.'

'How do you know that?'

'You can find just about anything you want online, if you know where to look.'

Hamish shifted in the seat. His mouth turned sour. 'I'm not giving you a cent, Nat, not until we have an agreement on what your share of the house is and it's all been made legal.'

She made a sound somewhere between a sob and snort. 'Robyn pranged my car. I need a car to get to work, pick up the grandkids from school and all the other things I do to keep this family afloat.'

'Is Robyn all right? Was anyone else in the car? Why was she even driving your car?'

'She's fine, but the car's a total write-off. And it's none of your business who drives my car.'

'Insurance?'

'You're kidding me? Who can afford insurance? It was probably as much as the car was worth.'

'And you need thirty thousand? That's a pretty nice replacement you have in mind. What about Pete's ute?'

'He uses that,' she said, getting shriller by the syllable.

'Only to and from work. Lots of people manage with one car.'

'It's a ute. Where would I put the grandkids? In the back? Stop being an arsehole, Hamish, and just transfer me the money. You can afford it and it's only part of what's mine anyway. If I was a total bitch I'd contest the will because you don't deserve half, the little you did for Mum and Dad. I'll text my bank details.'

Hamish's jaw tensed. 'Not gonna happen, Nat. You only have two weeks at the most to wait before you'll have your *fair* share and you can spend it on whatever you please. In the meantime, borrow Robyn's car.'

'Why are you being such a bastard, Hamish?'

'I don't think I am and if I was, it might have something to do with the fact that the only time I ever hear from you is when you want something, usually money.'

'It's not as if you don't have enough—'

'Natalie,' he said, 'we are not having *that* conversation again. So unless you want to talk about something different, like how the kids are, how I am, what Pete's up to or what's happening in Cutlers Bay—'

She hung up, just like he knew she would. He stood, stepped over to the edge of the verandah and emptied the stubby onto the bare garden bed. His mellow mood had evaporated. Contest the will? He'd given up trying to understand why, when it came to him, his sister had always been a grasping and unlikeable person. She'd been an irritation as far back as he could remember, although she'd become less likeable with age.

He went inside and opened the fridge to scan the contents, settling for cold lamb chops left over from last night's barbecue. Two tomatoes and bread completed the meal. While he ate, he debated whether or not to call Ruth. He decided against it. She'd be worn out after a long day on her feet. They'd had a brief phone conversation the previous Tuesday evening, not long after she'd arrived home from Adelaide and she'd sounded distracted and worried about Elliot. 'I wanted him to come home with me again, but he refused,' she'd said. 'I had coffee with Lana this morning and she said he'd come to dinner and got rolling drunk. She'd managed to pour him into a taxi. And one day she'd popped in and he was still in bed, at two in the afternoon!'

A lesser person might buckle under the strain. The last thing she'd need right now was to hear him banging on about what an ungrateful bitch his sister was and always had been. So Hamish did what he always did when he didn't know what else to do: he went back to work. This time that meant removing the mantelpiece and surround from the fireplace in the lounge room. He hadn't decided yet whether he'd brick in the fireplace completely or strip the layers of paint off the mantelpiece and decorative framework and restore it all to its former glory.

★ ★ ★

Jeff arrived bright and early Saturday morning astride a Harley Davidson motorcycle, the one that Hamish had only ever heard about.

'Mate,' he said, circling the chrome-encrusted classic. 'Business must be booming.'

Jeff grinned, resting his helmet and gloves on the seat while he peeled off his leather jacket. 'Boys and their toys is what the wife says.'

'Come in and I'll show you around. Coffee?'

'Let's do the house first.'

Two hours later, Jeff had inspected the house from top to bottom, photographed everything and taken a ream of measurements. He raised his eyebrows when Hamish handed him several drawings outlining his ideas the best he could.

'I'm a diesel mechanic,' Hamish said and shrugged, 'not a draftsman.'

Jeff pored over the drawings for several minutes.

'Well, what do you think?' Hamish said when he couldn't contain himself any longer.

'Ambitious,' Jeff said. 'You might want to rethink the size of the extension when you get the quote. If you're doing it purely as an investment, you don't want to overspend. But if you intend living here for the duration, it would make it into a very liveable home.'

'At this stage, an investment is what I have in mind. And to mitigate costs, I intend to do as much of the work as I can.'

Jeff nodded. 'We can turn these into real plans, if that's what you want, then you'll have something solid to work with and I can give you an idea of what it might cost.'

'Yep, it's what I want. Now, there's a decent cafe in town. Why don't I buy you a coffee and something to eat and you can fill me in on what I'll owe you for drawing up the plans.'

Jeff took out his phone and glanced at the time. 'I've got about another hour before I need to be back on the road. The lad plays cricket this afternoon and I promised I'd be there to watch him.'

They walked to the cafe, Jeff happy to stretch his legs.

Mia was at the counter taking orders and she gave the men a bright smile. 'Hamish, what can I get you?'

They ordered coffee and toasted sandwiches and, as luck would have it, table three was the only table free. Hamish made a beeline for it.

'You obviously come here often,' Jeff said and sat down. 'Even have your own favourite table.'

'Coffee's good, food's good, what's there not to like?'

Jeff glanced around the cosy cafe. 'Never thought I'd see you living out in the sticks. Not after that flash joint you had in North Adelaide. But I'm beginning to see how the place could grow on a bloke.'

'It's not a bad spot,' Hamish said and then described the golf course. 'Haven't had a hit yet, but plan to soon.'

Mia came with their coffees and a few minutes later Ruth arrived with the toasted sandwiches. Hamish introduced her to Jeff.

'And does a motorcycle go with the leather trousers, or do you just like leather?' she said and Jeff laughed.

When she was on her way back to the kitchen, he gave Hamish a sly glance and said, 'Yeah, I can see how the place could grow on a bloke.'

Hamish didn't comment, concentrating on his toasted sandwich instead.

Back at East Terrace, Jeff donned his leather jacket and helmet. 'Should have something to you in a couple of weeks,' he said, patting the pocket where he'd slipped the list of measurements along with Hamish's drawings. The Harley started with its trademark rumble and, anonymous now behind the tinted visor of a helmet, Jeff lifted his arm in farewell.

That's when Hamish spotted the two boys astride pushbikes on the opposite side of the street. He'd seen them around before, heedlessly riding their bikes up and down the street. They were barely teenagers. He'd wanted to shout to them to take more care; that it only took an instant of inattention for lives to be changed irrevocably. Hamish waved and they scooted across the street, without looking both ways first.

'Was that a Harley?' the sandy-haired taller of the two said. He vibrated with excitement.

'Sure was,' Hamish said. 'Twenty-eighteen Low Rider.'

'Awesome. Is he your mate?'

'Yep.'

'Is he coming back?'.

'Not today,' Hamish said.

'Bummer,' he said, unimpressed. 'Do you know when he is coming back? Maybe he'd take us for a spin around the block, eh, Cody?'

The other boy nodded, his straight dark hair flopping over his forehead. Hamish guessed that Cody was Mia's brother. There was definitely a resemblance.

'Sorry, fellas, but I couldn't say when Jeff'll be back this way with his bike.'

Resigned, they skidded off the footpath and onto the road, spitting up gravel as they went.

'Watch out for traffic,' Hamish yelled, sounding a bit demented even to his own ears. The sandy-haired lad glanced back over his shoulder, scorn written all over his face.

31

Ruth

After I'd closed up and finished the usual mundane chores on Sunday, I sat at the kitchen table with a leftover muffin, a pot of tea and a notepad and pencil to make the lists Hamish had suggested. It was my first chance since I'd discussed selling the cafe with him.

No doubt the best outcome would be to sell the building, the flat and the business all in one hit and have the new owner take over quickly so the business didn't lose momentum. Then there was the question of what I'd do in those circumstances, where I'd live. Was I serious about wanting to leave Cutlers Bay? About going back to Adelaide? I'd always assumed that's what I'd do. But now, with my thinking cap on and pencil poised, what was there for me now other than Elliot? The housing I'd be able to afford would determine where I'd live. Not the most ideal of circumstances.

Bryan had voiced that the option he thought most likely to succeed was the one where I sell the business, with or without the name, and lease the building to the new business owner. Much like Hamish had said. And that option gave me somewhere to live and an income stream. And if I decided not to stay here, I could lease out the flat as well.

I drew up columns and filled them with the various alternatives, along with their pros and cons. I left until last the option where nothing sold and I had to carry on until I dropped dead of exhaustion. Or, as Hamish had intimated, I closed the cafe and sold off whatever I could in what would effectively be a fire sale. Sadly, I could clearly envisage this scenario playing out when all else had failed.

How depressing to think I could end up living out my days here, in a poky two-bedroomed flat at the rear of what would be a gutted shopfront. People would walk past and say, 'Remember when there used to be a lovely little cafe here, great food, great coffee, but the owner ran out of steam and then couldn't sell it so she had to close it down and now she lives out the back with her cats …'

I shuddered at the sequence of events all too easily imagined. Except for the bit about the cats. I'd never owned a cat and couldn't see myself ever going down that pathway. A dog? Maybe, when I had more time to walk it.

The subject of selling the business was constantly on my mind. Apart from Bryan, Hamish was the only other person I'd discussed it with and only that once. I had thought I'd bring it up with Elliot when I'd stayed over before the doctor's appointment, but he'd been too caught up in his own concerns to give any thought to mine.

My GP had been thorough. She'd gently rebuked me for leaving it so long between health checks. 'You're over sixty now, Ruth, you need to take better care of yourself. Exercise. Eat well. Don't neglect your emotional health and wellbeing, especially important in view of your recent bereavement.'

'Of course, but who gets time for exercise? I'm on my feet all day as it is.'

Going by her expression, she'd been disappointed by my response.

My blood pressure was up a fraction but she wouldn't commit to what she thought might be causing the headaches. 'Let's get more information first,' she'd said and ordered a raft of blood tests. Some of them fasting, so I'd had to find out where I could have the blood taken in Cutlers Bay. 'And make another appointment to see me in a fortnight.' That had been an order. 'We'll discuss the results and where to from there.' Then she'd scribbled something on a slip of paper and handed it to me. I hadn't looked at the note until I was back sitting in the car. It said: *Prescription for exercise: At least 2 x 30 minute brisk walks per week OUTSIDE in the fresh air, preferably with company.*

I hadn't known whether to laugh or crumple up the 'prescription' and dump it. In the end, I'd fixed it to the fridge at home with a magnet. I'd had the blood taken but I'd made no attempt to 'fill' the exercise prescription. I could see myself out with a torch walking *briskly* the night before my next doctor's appointment, which was only a week away now. Then I could at least report that I had been for a walk, even if it was in the dark and on my own. How sad was I?

★ ★ ★

I hadn't seen or heard from Hamish since he'd come into the cafe with his leather-clad mate on Saturday morning. If he'd been on his own, I would have asked him around for a meal on my days off. But here it was Tuesday afternoon, days off almost over, and I hadn't even made the effort to ring him. I could remedy that right now. The phone was on the table beside me so I grabbed it and scrolled through to his number.

'Ruth,' he said when I'd been about to hang up. I could hear he was breathing heavily.

'Have I caught you at a bad time?'

'No! I was up a ladder, that's all.'

'Do you want to do something this afternoon? Something that's not work?'

'What did you have in mind?' He sounded wary.

'A drive out to Rocky Point … a walk on the beach. I could pack a picnic and we could watch the sunset …' My certainty that this was an inspired idea withered the further along I went without any sounds of encouragement from his end. 'Only if you're not too busy,' I said.

'What time does the sun set?' he said, when I'd begun to suspect I'd lost him completely.

'Around eight.'

'I'll pick you up at six. You supply the food and I'll bring the drinks.'

When we arrived at Rocky Point, the sea breeze had picked up and my imagined pleasant but brisk walk along the beach turned into a trudge with us pushing hard into a headwind with sand blasting our shins. Even the seagulls were having trouble staying airborne.

Because it was so windy, we picnicked in the cosy comfort of Hamish's dual cab. The sunset was spectacular.

It was dark when he dropped me off at home, just shy of nine. 'Thank you, Ruth. I had a good time.'

'You sound surprised,' I said.

He chuckled. 'I suppose I am, a bit. I've never considered myself to be a walk on the beach and watch the sunset kind of a bloke.'

'You've never done it before?'

'Maybe once.'

'Let me guess, the honeymoon weekend on KI? Under duress?'

He groaned, closed his eyes and bumped the back of his head against the headrest several times. 'Am I so predictable?'

'Don't worry, I've lived in Cutlers Bay for years and I haven't walked on the beach that often. The first time was when I visited my niece and the cafe was barely an idea. But lately I've been thinking how there used to be more to my life than just work.'

'Beware, because I've tried it the other way around, you know, without the work, and the boredom nearly drove me batshit crazy.'

'I'm not ready to stop work altogether. I can't see myself doing nothing. I just need to find a better balance.'

'Let me know when you do.'

'I'm working on it, pardon the pun. We've one more weekend to go with Sunday trading for this summer and then I'm considering having three days off. That's if Allie's prepared to carry on working all day Tuesday.'

'I thought you were going to sell up?'

'I am, but I'm under no illusions that it'll happen overnight. It could take months. Years, even. Bryan made sure I understood that in the discussion we had.' Had a fortnight passed since I'd talked to him? My goodness. 'I'd better go,' I said, conscious the car engine was idling and, like every other day, I had jobs to do before bed. I opened the door and the interior light came on. 'Sorry about the sand.'

'Part and parcel of a trip to the beach, or so I imagine.'

'Lasagne's the lunch special this week.'

'You've twisted my arm. I'll come for lunch one day. Not sure which day it'll be. I need to shoot down to Adelaide to Bunnings and I haven't decided when. Let me know if there's anything you need.'

'At Bunnings?'

'Not just at Bunnings, Ruth—anything at all.'

★ ★ ★

Allie was early the following morning. I was busy at the coffee machine when she arrived. There were already several food orders waiting. I'd slept well and felt more my sanguine self than I had for weeks. Could today's improved mood be attributed to the picnic and the walk on the beach with Hamish? Possibly. That and the cooler weather that had blown in overnight. There'd even been a sprinkle of rain.

'What are all the garbage bags doing outside the kitchen door?' she said as she came in and my buoyant mood faltered.

'What do you mean?'

'There's about half-a-dozen chock-a-block black garbage bags, the ones with the yellow ties, and a cardboard box of old toys.'

'You are kidding me.' I tapped the jug of frothed milk on the counter, much harder than I needed to. 'Take over here will you, please,' I said in a tone of voice Allie would never have heard before.

'Okay,' she said, eyes wide. She picked up the jug of hot milk.

I dashed out the kitchen door into the service lane and her description had been spot on, except that there were five bags, not six. Hands on hips, I stood there struggling to get my thoughts in order, my stomach roiling. How ridiculous and petty was this?

Allie poked her head out the door. 'There are two more food orders, Ruth.'

'I'm coming.' I went inside, washed my hands and got to work, all the while fuming. Allie asked me what it was about and I gave her the condensed version, hardly believing the tale even as I recounted it.

'I'd dump them right back on the op shop's doorstep. Let Audrey Franco deal with it, the cow,' she said.

'What would that solve?'

'Do it in the dark and they wouldn't know where the bags came from.'

Tempting, but not my style. And what if they *had* installed security cameras? 'I'm going to ring Zach Cooper when I get a minute. Explain the situation to him and ask him what I should do.' I thought of Peg and the fish guts and how easily this could get out of hand. 'I just can't believe that someone has done it!'

'There are some strange people in this town,' Allie said. 'Any town, I guess.'

As it happened, Zach came into the cafe for a coffee an hour later. He was in uniform and Allie directed him out to the kitchen while she made his coffee.

'What's up, Ruth?' he said. He was tall and big and the kitchen suddenly felt overcrowded.

I explained. He stepped out into the service lane. When he returned a few minutes later, he was scratching his head. I kept on making the salad that we'd serve with the lasagne, chopping the vegetables with unwarranted ferocity.

'I had a look in the bags and they're full of old clothes, towels and stuff like that. I think your conclusion about why they're there is more than likely correct. I'll chuck it all into the back of the police ute and take it around to the op shop, have a chat with them.'

'I just don't get why anyone would do such a thing, Zach.' I frowned. My head had started to pound and I was on the verge of tears. 'Audrey and I had the conversation while I made her coffee and all I did was offer a solution to a problem that she's been banging on about forever. And now all of a sudden I'm the bogey man because someone—and I can't be one hundred per cent certain it was Audrey—said the bins had gone and I was behind it.'

'Here's your coffee, Zach,' Allie said and passed him a large takeaway. 'And I made one for you, Ruth.' She put the steaming mug on the bench beside me.

'Thanks,' I said. I couldn't drink it at the moment because it would more than likely make me sick.

After she'd scuttled off, Zach took a sip of his drink and sighed. 'My first one of the day,' he said. 'And, Ruth, all I can say is that sometimes there is no rational reason why people do the things they do. In my experience, most people resist any upset to the status quo, even if the status quo is not fair or just.'

'Yeah, Peg told me the story about the fish guts,' I said. 'Did you have to deal with that one?'

'I've heard her story. Luckily, it was before my time.'

'So what should I do? I've never had anything like this happen all the while I've been here. And I can hardly bear to serve Audrey when she comes in as it is, not since Peg told me what she'd heard.'

Allie passed through a food order. I glanced at it and started to gather the fillings for the sandwiches.

'And since then this is the only instance you've had junk dumped here?'

'Yes.'

'Does anyone else use the service lane?'

I shook my head. 'It belongs with this building. It's my property.'

'You might want to think about a gate. Something high and secure that you can lock.'

'I'll look into that.'

'ASAP would be my recommendation. And Ruth, we'll probably never discover who the culprit is.'

'Aren't there security cameras somewhere?'

'You jest.'

'Thanks, Zach.'

He stood back and finished his coffee, watching me make the sandwiches. 'They look good. And your lasagne is one of my all-time favourites.'

'Do you want something to eat? I can whip up a sandwich or put a serve of lasagne in a container for you to have later.' Way back, when Zach was single and had no inclination to cook for himself, I used to do for him what I now did for Laurie. Of course, Zach paid me in cash.

'Thanks, but no,' he said and patted his flattish stomach. 'Easy to put on and almost impossible to get off, especially at my age, as my dear wife keeps reminding me.'

Try as I might I couldn't quite recapture the upbeat mood of earlier. Every time I served a customer I couldn't help but wonder if they were responsible for dumping the bags in my service lane. Three o'clock came and frustratingly Allie left before I could ask her if she was interested in keeping the full-shift Tuesdays when summer Sunday trading ceased. I'd work the shorter shift, or no shift if that worked financially.

Laurie arrived promptly at four thirty to do the floors. I asked him what he thought about a gate at the service lane entrance.

'A damned sound idea. Why there's not something there already, what with the gas bottles, rubbish bins and all, beats me. Kids these days seem to have too much spare time to get up to mischief.'

My stomach plummeted. I hadn't thought of the gas bottles being vandalised; they were chained and padlocked into place.

'Is that something you could do, Laurie? I'd pay for everything, and your time of course.'

'I'm sorry, Ruth, but I don't have the tools for a job like that, or the confidence, if the truth be known, not anymore. What about Hamish? Bloke's pretty handy and he has the tools and the confidence, in bucketloads. I'd willingly help him with it.'

★ ★ ★

Thursday began like any other, except that Hamish was there at seven measuring up for the gate. We'd spoken the previous evening and he'd quickly agreed to help out. He looked pretty good in washed-out denim jeans and a navy blue cotton-drill work shirt, a thick pencil shoved behind his ear. He gratefully accepted the coffee I took out to him.

'I didn't know you wore glasses,' I said.

'Reading and when I don't want to get any measurements wrong. I reckon the best way would be to build in the end completely and have a solid wooden door with a keypad lock. You could do the same with Colorbond but it wouldn't look as neat, in my opinion.'

'A keypad lock's an excellent idea. No mucking about with keys. You must put everything on my account at the hardware,' I said and took out my phone. 'I'll ring Bob right now and tell him you're on your way.'

Hamish headed to the hardware shop across the road—I'd convinced him of the wisdom of shopping local rather than at Bunnings—and I let myself back in the kitchen door just as the timer on the oven beeped. The muffins were ready.

I was in the middle of lifting them onto cooling racks when there was a tap on the kitchen door. 'It's open,' I called, thinking it'd be Hamish, but it was Allie. 'You're early,' I said brightly in an attempt to disguise my instant apprehension.

'I needed to talk to you, Ruth, and we never get the chance during the day.'

'No, we don't,' I said, lifting the last muffin onto the rack. 'And I wanted to ask you about shifts, now that February's almost over and Sunday trading with it. I was thinking—'

She held up a hand, a serious expression on her face. 'Perhaps I'd better say what I need to say first,' she said. 'Because when I do you might not want to say what you thought you did.'

I wiped greasy fingers on my apron. 'Out with it then,' I said, more calmly than I felt.

She held out an envelope I hadn't noticed she'd been holding. 'It's my resignation,' she said.

Myriad emotions swept through me but all I could do was blink and fiddle with the hem on my apron. She placed the envelope on the bench. 'I need more work, Ruth, a lot more work, permanent work that comes with sick leave and annual leave and a greater ability to accumulate superannuation.'

'You have another job?' I said with difficulty because my mouth was so dry.

She nodded.

'And you didn't ask me to be a referee?'

She rolled her lips together. 'I wanted to but Lo— that is, a friend advised against it in case I didn't get the other job. She thought it might make the situation here a bit tense and that's the last thing I wanted. I've loved working here. I couldn't have asked for a better boss, but I'm forty now and I need to get my house in order and part of that involves preparation for the future.'

What she said sounded well rehearsed. That was okay. I wished I'd had such an epiphany when I'd been her age. 'Can I ask what the job is?'

'Catering and hospitality support services at the hospital,' she said with a hint of defiance.

'Congratulations,' I said and she drew back in surprise. 'You'll be an asset to any organisation, Allie.'

Her eyes narrowed as if she didn't quite believe me, and she'd prepared herself for a much different response. But I meant what I'd said and I'd deal with the panicked chaos in my head later. 'I think we made a good team and I'll miss you.'

She swallowed, pressing her fingertips briefly to her lips. 'It's not that I don't like working here, I do—I love it. But it's not enough anymore, not now the kids are getting older. I can't rely on Brett for anything. I thought about a second job …' She sighed and her shoulders slumped. 'Well, I've been looking, Ruth, and there's not much on offer. Cleaning, bar work, that sort of thing, if you can get it, and it's all after hours when I need to be at home with the kids. Then this job at the hospital came up.'

'Timely,' I said.

Her mouth flattened into a rueful smile. 'I know I've been lucky.'

I reached for the envelope. 'How much notice have you given me?'

She flinched. 'Next Wednesday will be the last day I'm available. I start the new job the following Monday.'

There went any plans I'd had for extra time off. 'Are you okay to do the full shift next Tuesday? Lorna's on the roster to do your usual shift.'

'I'll be here. And I'm sorry, Ruth, to leave you in the lurch when I know how tired you are.'

'Don't be sorry. You need to take care of yourself and your family. I'll see you back here at the start of your shift.' There was more both of us could say but we'd only be going around in circles. I needed time to process and decide what I was going to do.

'Shall I go through the front and unlock?'

'Is it that time already? Okay, thanks.' With an ear out for the squeal of the front door, I rushed through the last-minute preparations, purposefully pushing aside the staffing problem Allie had just dropped on me. I was annoyed, but not really with her. I'd seen this coming, even thought about upskilling one of the casuals to cook. Had I done anything about it? No. Robert's death and Elliot's floundering had derailed me in so many ways.

I heard the front door. Showtime. The muffins could cool on the rack for a few minutes longer.

My quickly pasted-on smile slipped when I saw who the first customer of the day was: Audrey Franco.

She fidgeted with the lid of her to-go mug and wouldn't meet my eye. 'No muffins today?' she said.

I imagined myself saying, *No muffins today, Audrey, and the coffee machine is broken,* and sending her on her way. But instead I said, 'They're cooling in the kitchen. Apple and cinnamon.'

'Ooh, I do like those. I thought I could smell cinnamon.'

'The usual?'

She passed me her to-go mug but then didn't let it go. 'I'm so sorry, Ruth. I should have kept my big mouth shut. I had no idea what people would make of the things I said.' The words spilled out in a plaintive gush. She raised her gaze to mine and then released the mug. Undeterred by my obvious bewilderment, she ploughed on. 'Sergeant Cooper came into the shop yesterday, told Daphne and me what had happened. Daphne was so shocked she had to sit down and take one of her heart pills. Sergeant Cooper didn't mention any names but I know he knew it was me who'd been, er, gossiping.' She folded her arms, hugging herself. She looked dreadful, as if she hadn't slept. 'I was awake all night worrying and Reg insisted that I come in first thing this morning and apologise to you.'

I started on her coffee, mainly to give myself a moment and take strength from the familiar routine and the delicious smell of coffee beans being ground. I would accept her apology, but she could sweat for a bit.

When I handed her filled cup across the counter, I said, 'Thank you for your apology, Audrey. And good on Reg for insisting. Now, would you like me to fetch you a muffin?'

'Yes, please,' she said with a tentative smile.

To my immense relief, there was no time for any more stilted conversation because, right on cue, the admin girls burst in the door.

32

Hamish

The malicious pettiness of whoever had dumped their cast-offs at Ruth's door had astounded Hamish and that didn't happen often; as a rule, he approached his ponderings of the human condition with detachment. What nagged at him the most about what had happened was that Ruth had not deserved it, whichever way you chose to look at it. And the incident had certainly rattled her.

That's why, without reservation, he'd put his work on hold to build the frame and hang the door to make the service lane safer for her and the staff. With Laurie's help he'd almost completed the job by the time the cafe closed on Saturday afternoon. The trickiest part had been installing the lock and keypad, but they'd worked it out between the two of them.

Ruth had come out to take stock of their achievement.

'All that's left to do is to paint it,' Hamish said, proudly.

'I can do that.'

'I'm sure you can, but I won't consider the job complete until it's painted. First thing tomorrow morning the primer goes on and then

the paint on Monday. Same colour as the woodwork at the front of
the shop.'

'It looks terrific. Much more secure. Thank you both. I don't know
why I didn't do it years ago. Let me shout you and Laurie dinner at
the pub tonight?'

'I'm up for it,' Hamish said and Laurie readily agreed. They packed
up the tools and arranged to meet at the hotel at six.

As pubs went, the Cutlers Arms was functional, if old and shabby.
Because it was the only operating hotel in town, it was well patronised.
Hamish elbowed his way through to the bar and ordered a beer. He'd
barely taken the first mouthful when Laurie pushed in beside him,
looking spruce in slacks and a dress shirt, with what was left of his
hair slicked back over his bald patch.

'My buy,' Hamish said, raising his voice over the rabble.

'My lucky day,' Laurie replied and clapped Hamish on the back.

Ruth was a few minutes late. Hamish had been watching out for
her and he had several seconds to take her in when she stepped
into the hotel foyer before she clapped eyes on him and waved. She
looked good.

Laurie nudged him with his elbow. 'Scrubs up all right, eh?' he
said, a twinkle in his eyes. 'If I was fifteen years younger myself—'

'She *is* a remarkable woman,' Hamish said, half to himself, recalling
that's how Bryan Chalmers had described her.

Ruth gestured that she'd see them in the dining room and then she
pushed through the frosted-glass doors and disappeared from view.

'Is there anywhere else you can eat out in this town?' Hamish
asked Laurie as they strolled through to the dining room, furnishings
circa 1970s. 'Apart from the cafe and the fish and chip shop, that is.'

'The motel has a pretty flash restaurant. They tell me the tucker's
not bad but pricey. The golf club used to do meals on a weekend, but
not anymore. Covid put the kibosh on a lot of things in the country.'

The dining room was empty except for a family of four. Ruth was studying the faded historical photographs hanging around the walls: the Cutlers Arms and Cutlers Bay in their heyday.

'That's our table there,' she said and made her way over to it. Her name was scrawled on a laminated reserved sign. 'When I rang earlier to book, Leon informed me it was the lucky last table.'

Hamish's sceptical gaze slid around the near-empty dining room.

A slim—no, make that skinny—woman in a black skirt and grey polo shirt zoomed into the dining room. 'You blokes ready to order?' she said to the family of four. She whipped out a notepad and waited, pencil poised.

Hamish noticed that the small dining room bar was unattended. 'Do you want something to drink, Ruth? Another beer, Laurie?'

'I can take your drinks order in a sec, Ruth,' the woman said with a quick glance their way. 'After I've sorted out these blokes.'

'Okay, thanks, Gabby,' Ruth replied.

Hamish sat down and passed around the laminated menus. He expected them to be sticky with fingermarks and food but they weren't. Ruth sniffed and when he glanced her way, she was smiling. She leaned towards him and he got a whiff of the perfume or shampoo she favoured. He liked it.

'The pub might be old and rundown but you can't fault its cleanliness,' she said in a low voice. 'Gabby wouldn't have it any other way.'

'Does the publican own the hotel?'

'Leasehold,' Laurie said, peering over his reading glasses. 'East-coast city folk own it and they couldn't care less about the upkeep of the place. As long as it meets licensing requirements and makes 'em money.'

Gabby took their drink order: beer for Hamish and Laurie and a dry white wine for Ruth. 'Put them on the bill, please,' Ruth said and Gabby nodded.

'I'll take your food orders when I come back with the drinks,' she said and zipped off.

Hamish wondered what the rush was all about, but then the diners began to steadily trickle in. Not long after they'd ordered their meals, the dining room was full and another waitress had appeared.

'It's like the cafe,' Ruth said. 'Fills up at mealtimes, is hectic for a couple of hours and then they all disappear.'

'I take it the slow-food movement has yet to reach Cutlers Bay.'

'It's your typical pub fare, Hamish. Most of it deep fried and not meant to be lingered over,' Ruth said.

When the time came, Hamish had eaten better schnitzels, but he'd also eaten a lot worse. At least the chips were hot and crispy and the salad fresh.

'They've got a new cook,' Laurie said. 'Business certainly has picked up.' After he'd demolished his chicken parmigiana, he thanked Ruth for the meal, wiped his mouth with the paper napkin and stood. 'But if you don't mind, a couple of my mates are in the bar and I'd like to have a beer and a catch up with them. And before you ask, I walked down.'

'No dessert, Laurie? Not like you at all.'

'Couldn't fit it in, but don't let me stop you.' He ambled off towards the front bar.

'Another drink?' Hamish was in no hurry to leave. 'Or dessert?'

No sooner were the words out than Gabby materialised at their table.

'Nothing wrong with your hearing,' he said and she smirked. 'I'll have another beer, light this time.'

'And another glass of wine for me, dry white. I take it there's a second sitting for dinner?'

'Yep,' Gabby said.

Hamish blinked and she was gone. 'Amazing,' he said. 'Do you eat here often?'

'No, but if you want a meal that won't break the budget that's not takeaway, the hotel is your only choice.'

'Not that it's necessarily what I think, but a person couldn't be blamed for thinking the town hasn't got a real lot going for it. Hope I've done the right thing, buying Mum and Dad's house. What if I spend a bucketload of money on it and then can't sell it when the time comes?'

'My employer at the time said something similar when I told him I'd bought an old shop in the country and was going to turn it into a cafe. He said I was crazy, that I was putting all my eggs into one basket and I'd be trapped here if I couldn't sell it when I decided I'd had enough.'

'Was he right? Do you feel as if you are trapped?'

'I hadn't, not until Graham Wurst from Cutlers Bay Financial Services retired and I started thinking about my retirement plan— that is, that I didn't have one. Is it too late for you to change your mind? Not buy out your sister?'

Gabby came with their drinks. 'Yell out when you're ready for your bill, Ruth. No rush.' Gabby flitted to the next table, tucking the tray under her arm and pulling out pencil and pad to take orders.

Hamish gazed at his glass of beer, pondering what Ruth had asked. 'It probably isn't too late to pull out.' He grinned slowly. 'And almost worth considering, just to see the look on Nat's face when I tell her.'

Ruth rested her chin on her hand and studied him. 'Why do you dislike your sister so much, if you don't mind me asking?'

'You've met her. Did you like her?'

'She was a bit … abrasive, but your dad had just died. And I don't *know* her.'

'Trust me, she gets more abrasive the better you get to know her.'

Ruth sat back and sipped up her wine. 'Robert used to irritate me, drove me batty, if you really want to know. He was so pedantic about everything, but I miss him, more for his wife and Elliot than for myself.'

'You're a much kinder and more generous person than I am and probably ever will be.'

She tilted her to head to one side. 'Oh, I don't know, I reckon you could surprise yourself if you let yourself go. You've been kind and generous to me,' she said. Then her gaze shifted and she smiled moments before a heavy hand dropped onto Hamish's shoulder.

'Fancy seeing you two here. Cosy,' Zach Cooper said and wiggled his eyebrows. 'Mind if I pull up a pew for a sec?'

'Be my guest,' Hamish said and Ruth nodded.

Zach pulled out the chair Laurie had vacated and sat down. He wasn't in uniform, but his presence was intimidating nevertheless. 'Ruth, it's you I wanted to talk to. Laurie said you were in here. It's about what we discussed the other day.' Zach's attention shifted briefly to Hamish.

'It's okay, Zach, you can say whatever you need to say in front of Hamish. He knows the whole story. And by the way, Audrey Franco apologised to me yesterday.'

'I don't think her intention ever was to be malicious, Ruth. Anyway, I tracked down who did it and you can rest assured they won't do it again.'

'How did you manage that?'

'I wish I could say unparalleled police work, but Daphne Russell thought she recognised a corduroy jacket in one of the bags.' He laughed with genuine mirth. 'And, believe it or not, in another bag there was an addressed envelope in the back pocket of an old pair of jeans. I took it from there. I wish all policing was that simple.' Zach pushed away from the table and stood.

'Thank you, Zach. It's a relief to know you've tracked down the culprit. I can stop being suspicious of everyone I serve at the cafe!'

'Cheers. I'll leave you to it. I told Angie I'd only stay for one beer.'

The noise level in the dining room had steadily increased as the tables began to fill again while they'd talked to Zach. Ruth pushed away her half-finished wine. 'That's not the same drop I had the first time around. Way too sweet for me.'

'Shall I get you another wine? Or something else?'

'No, I think I'll head home, thanks. Are you going back to the bar?'

He shook his head. 'I'll walk you home.'

'I'm only across the road, Hamish.'

'Don't argue.'

'All right, you can walk me home, the long way. Then I can report to my doctor that I've been for *two* walks in the fresh air and with company. Finish your beer while I go and pay the bill.'

Hamish waited for her in the foyer. He didn't miss the curious interest displayed by the locals as he and Ruth left together. Ruth didn't appear to notice—or to take any notice if she did—and Hamish found the inquisitiveness didn't bother him one iota. Let them speculate to their hearts' content.

33

Ruth

When I showed up at Elliot's place on Monday afternoon he'd forgotten I was coming. Forgotten I had a follow-up doctor's appointment the next day. 'But I rang you on Friday night and reminded you.'

'Did you?' He was flustered and blustery because he hadn't remembered.

'You'd had a few red wines, I reckon.'

'These days there's not much else for a bloke to do.'

The townhouse was disgusting. Dirty dishes in the sink and the bin overflowing, and I counted seven empty wine bottles lined up by the back door. The place reeked of decaying food and unwashed old man. 'You could try cleaning up,' I said, flinging open the sliding door onto the patio to let in the fresh air. 'You look as if you've lost weight. I don't suppose you've been eating properly.'

'Haven't felt hungry.' Elliot dragged a shaky hand across his stubbled jaw. His eyes were red and rheumy. He looked awful; a decade older than he had before Robert died. My heart lurched. 'But now that you're here I'll shower and shave and we can go out somewhere nice to eat. That Italian place on The Parade. I'll make a booking. Now where the hell did I leave my phone?'

I grabbed his arm before he stumbled off in search of his phone. 'Should I be worried about you, Elliot? You're all the immediate family I have left.'

His bottom lip quivered. 'I'm sorry, Ruth. Losing Robert so suddenly … I feel as if I've been cut adrift. I'd counted on being the first one of us to pop off our perches.'

I closed my eyes, took a steadying breath and tried to put myself in his shoes. 'You go and have a shower and a shave. I'll start cleaning up the kitchen and what's the bet I find your phone?' I scanned the shambles in front of me. 'Didn't you have a cleaning lady once? What happened to her?'

'Knee replacement. She'll be back on deck in another few weeks. You are an angel, Ruth.'

Angel or not, I gritted my teeth, rolled up my sleeves and set to work, stacking the dishwasher first. Was this my destiny, to be forever cleaning up kitchens? I found the phone on charge beneath a newspaper and a half-loaf of sliced bread, dried out because the bag had been left open. At least the phone was fully charged.

We ate early and ended up having a pleasant evening. The food was excellent. Elliot limited himself to two glasses of red wine and I stayed with sparkling water. Alcohol would have put me to sleep and I was driving. Over the meal, I prattled on about the cafe, how my most reliable staff member had resigned and I'd spent the morning ringing around anyone who'd ever worked for me, enquiring if they were looking for a job. Erin Saunders, a cheerful young thing who'd briefly been on the payroll in the very early days of the cafe, had been the only one interested. I'd emailed her an application form and we'd arranged for her to come in for a chat on Wednesday, after the cafe closed. Elliot grunted every now and then to prove he was listening.

On the drive home, more his loquacious self after food and wine, he turned to me and said, 'I don't know why you're bothering to waste time and energy looking for more staff, Ruth. Put the place on the market and come back to Adelaide. Move on.'

'It's not quite that simple, Elliot. The local estate agent advised me that the more robust the business is when it goes on the market, the more likely I'll be to sell it. Now tell me, how's Lana?' I changed the subject because I really did need a break from all things Cutlers Bay. Wednesday would be the last day I'd work with Allie and I felt sad about that.

'Lana? She was fine the last time I spoke to her. And how's that bloke of yours? Hamish? Is he the reason you're not that keen to sell up and come back to the city?'

'He's not *my bloke*. We're friends, that's all. And I am going to sell up.'

'He seems like a good sort, pretty handy and not afraid of hard work. You could do a lot worse.'

'Can't we talk about something else?'

'You know, Robert and I could never understand why you didn't partner up permanently and have children when you could. I know you're probably rolling your eyes the way you always do when I raise the subject.'

'All right, I won't roll my eyes, but have you ever considered that I didn't partner up permanently because I didn't want to?'

'What about children? Didn't you ever want a family?'

'Not really and then my eggs ran out. You and Gloria only had Stacey. Didn't you want more kids?'

'Perhaps, but it didn't happen,' he said, a trifle sadly. 'Gloria wasn't well after Stacey was born, postnatal depression is what they called it. When she recovered, we half-heartedly talked about trying for another child, but I was forever working and Gloria didn't push it. She admitted years later, around the time we split, that she'd been terrified of going through again what she'd been through after Stacey was born. Can't say that I blamed her for that.'

We were home. I stopped the car and we sat in the semi-darkness, neither of us moving, as if we didn't want to destroy the fragile cocoon of closeness we'd created through the sharing of confidences.

'I didn't know she'd had postnatal depression. Are you ever in contact with her these days?' I said, my voice loud in the quietness.

'She lives in Melbourne now, she moved after Stacey left home. Corrine keeps in touch but I don't. No need, not after Stacey left the nest.'

'Gloria knows about Robert?'

'Corrine told her. I thought she might have come to the funeral. She always had time for Robert, more than she had for me, as it turned out in the end.'

'I haven't seen her for decades.'

'You were always off travelling, having a splendid time in exotic places that we could only ever dream of.'

'I made my choices, Elliot, and you made yours. And you eventually visited some exotic places.'

Elliot laughed, a mellow sound that warmed me. 'Ah, Barbara, what a year that was. Barbie was an exotic place, in and of herself.'

'Enough,' I said and held up my hand. 'There are things about your life I do not need to know.'

'Every man needs a Barbara in his life, somewhere along the line.'

'And every woman needs a summer in Paris and an Alexandre,' I said, goodness knows why.

He nudged me with his elbow. 'Tell me more!'

'Most definitely not,' I declared, pulling the key out of the ignition and climbing out of the car. He followed suit and I said, 'That is all I will ever say on that subject, Elliot. But just because I didn't partner up permanently, as you so eloquently put it, doesn't mean I haven't had my moments.'

I slammed the car door and the sensor light on the porch blinked on in time for me to see my brother gawping at me over the expanse of the car roof.

★ ★ ★

The two-plus hour drive home on my own after my appointment and early dinner with Elliot provided the perfect opportunity to overthink what the doctor had said and pick over my concerns about my brother. I desperately did not want to do either of those things, so I slid a CD into the player and listened to Carole King belting out old favourites. Music got me as far as Port Wakefield, where I stopped to use the public amenities and of course that brought back the memorable trip home with Elliot following Robert's funeral. After that, not ruminating on current problems was out of the question.

Ten minutes from Cutlers Bay, I summarised my mulling: While I felt a certain obligation towards my older brother, the more time I spent with him, the more convinced I was that I could never pick up where Robert had left off. Nor did I want to. Not that Elliot had in any way hinted that was what he expected. Being a much younger sister was a huge leap away from being a twin brother and it would get messy only if I let a sense of obligation skew expectations—mine and Elliot's.

It was after ten when I drove into my carport and I'd barely made it in through the sliding door when my mobile rang. Hamish. And there were two earlier missed calls from him.

'Are you home yet?' he said and yawned.

'Only just.' I dumped my bags onto the sofa. My head still thrummed with the noise of the road.

'What did the doctor say?'

'That I'm reasonably healthy and the headaches are most likely stress related. She said I need to seriously reconsider my work–life balance.' I laughed but without any real humour and flicked on the kettle. 'At least I could tell her I'd been for two walks. How are you?'

'Good. The rainwater tank arrived today and I've hooked it up, just in case it rains. Had to get PVC pipe and a few fittings from the hardware. Bloody expensive.'

'Is rain forecast?' I took down a mug and dropped in a chamomile and spearmint teabag.

'Nah, I'm just forever hopeful.' He yawned again.

'Go to bed, Hamish. Thanks for the call.' I meant that. Check-in phone calls had ended when Mum died and I hadn't realised I'd missed them.

'Goodnight. Glad you're home safely. Oh, before you go, how was Elliot?'

'A bit of a mess when I arrived, much better when I left. The test will be if he can sustain it. I really don't know if grief's the reason he's not coping, or if he's genuinely losing the plot. Hard to determine when I'm so far away. I feel like I should go back next weekend.' My shoulders sagged. I already had so much to do.

'Suggest to Elliot that he drives across to Cutlers Bay for the weekend. I'll happily put him to work.'

'That's an idea. He might be up for it.' After a second round of goodnights, I put the phone down on the table and rubbed my eyes. I felt as if I'd been run over by a truck. Tea, hot shower and bed, in that order. Unpacking of the overnight bag could wait until tomorrow.

34

Ruth

Allie's last day was unremarkable, except for the fact that it was her last day. I'd bought her a gift in Adelaide: a copy of a cookbook on my shelf that she'd admired several times. *All the best*, I'd written in the card. She'd been glassy-eyed as she'd unwrapped the gift. When the kitchen door snapped shut behind her at three pm, I felt bereft; a glimpse of what it must feel like to be abandoned. But the customers did not allow me to wallow for long.

An hour later, after I'd closed the cafe, Erin came for her interview. I invited her through to the office. As we went she explained that her children were at school now and she was eager to re-enter the workforce. That's when it came back to me why she'd only worked for me briefly when the cafe had first opened: she'd had a toddler and had been pregnant with her second child and found it all a bit too much.

'The thing is,' Erin said when I got down to the nitty-gritty of days and hours she could work, 'Liam, my husband, isn't as pumped as I am about me getting a job. I was wondering if I could start with two days a week and if that doesn't cause any disruption at home, I'd be willing to increase to three days. What do you think?'

My eyes narrowed. Not exactly what I'd had in mind, but then Erin was different than I remembered her. Not as bright and bubbly, nor as trim. 'And if it does cause too much disruption at home, what then?' I said.

On the opposite side of the desk, Erin shifted in her seat, crossed and then uncrossed her legs, the hiss of fabric against fabric. 'I'd have to quit,' she said, unable to meet my eye.

At least she was upfront. 'What about school holidays? Would they be a problem?'

She fidgeted some more, twisting a thin gold band I assumed was a wedding ring around her finger. 'I couldn't do school holidays. Sorry. Liam's mum will help out every now and then but she definitely won't do school holidays. She says it's not her job to bring up her grandchildren.' This said in an almost-whisper, eyes flicking to the office door as if she expected her mother-in-law to burst through at any second. 'And I couldn't start until the week after next.'

I felt like stamping my foot and wailing. I had hoped for more, much more. Solving the staff shortage was proving more problematic than I'd foreseen. Lorna was willing to do extra, but only in the short term and her hours were always dependent on how her mother was coping. George was back at uni; Mia and Suzie were at school and only available on Saturdays. Gayle and Liz, my two other reliable casuals, weren't interested in any more hours than they already did, that is the short shifts over lunchtimes on Thursdays and Fridays. If I said no to Erin, I'd have to advertise and manage on my own for longer stretches than I did now. Simple as that.

'Erin, what if we try Tuesdays and Wednesdays to begin with? Ten am until three pm?'

I held my breath when she screwed up her face. 'I'd need to finish by two thirty at the *very* latest to give me time to get to the school to pick up the children.'

'Okay,' I said slowly. The school was ten minutes away, max. 'Erin, are you sure you're ready to go back to work?'

'Oh, yes,' she said, nodding vigorously. 'I really liked working here before. I feel as if I have a lot to offer.'

I shelved any misgivings—and there were a few—and we agreed on a starting date the following week when she could come in for a couple of hours of orientation. She'd let me know which day worked best for her.

After she'd gone, I dropped my head into my hands and groaned. What happened to the good old days when the employers had dictated their employees' terms?

Although I tried hard not to feel despondent, I did. The cafe just wouldn't be the same without Allie.

With a burst of energy that came of a visceral need to do something—anything—proactive, I scrolled through to Bryan Chalmers's number.

The call went to messages.

'Bryan, I would like to talk further about what we discussed the other day. When would be a good time? Thanks.'

It was amazing how much better I felt after I'd done that.

★ ★ ★

That night I sat down on the sofa with a cup of tea and a notebook and a pen. I would begin to make lists of everything I needed to do to prepare the cafe and flat for sale. Then I'd do at least one of the jobs on the list every day. I opened the notebook and stared at the blank page for a futile few minutes. Where to start?

I put the notebook down on the sofa and reached for the tea. That's when I spotted the parcel that had been delivered with this morning's mail and I'd dropped onto the arm of the sofa when I'd come in from the cafe. It was a plastic postbag and whatever was inside was soft. I ripped it open. Wrapped up in layers of silver tissue paper was the silk cheongsam I'd loaned to Angie and that her sister-in-law had asked to borrow. The return address on the postbag read: *Steph Cooper, Wallaby Way, Broome, Western Australia*. I'd assumed her sister-in-law was local, not that it mattered. There was a thank-you note sticky-taped to the tissue paper. It was brief and sincere and the garment had obviously been dry cleaned. I messaged Angie to say the cheongsam had arrived from Broome. She rang me and launched straight in.

'Steph said she'd posted it. Did I not mention she lived in Broome? Oops. She was *so* grateful to have something beautiful to wear. She's a single mum. Speaking of which, Joanne, who I know from Lily's playgroup, has something important coming up and nothing suitable to wear. She tried the op shop but they send all the decent stuff to their metro outlets, or so the story goes.'

'Send her around and I'll see what I can do.'

'Thank you! She's around my size. Skinnier, if anything. And, Ruth, please don't think I'm trying to turn your wardrobe into a community wardrobe. But I know what it's like when you need to look good and don't have much money and the last thing you need is to spend on an outfit you might never wear again.'

'I honestly don't mind so long as the clothes are clean and in good shape when they're returned to me.'

'I'll pass that on to Joanne and she can decide whether to come and see you. You might even recognise her. She's been into the cafe a few times.'

Lying in bed that night, my head buzzing with all the things I needed to do but hadn't been able to think of when I'd had the notebook open in front of me, I thought about Angie's comment. A community wardrobe? I'd never heard of such a thing. But Angie was right about how often clothes were purchased on a whim or for a special occasions or the likes and then never worn again. Sometimes they were never worn at all. I'd been guilty of that, sending clothes to Salvos with the tags still attached.

35

Hamish

Melancholy was a frame of mind not foreign to Hamish. He didn't experience it often, but when he did, he knew to keep busy, distract himself and not dwell on the likely causes of his low mood. That particular Friday, he'd struggled to focus and keep busy and not mope. When Laurie Randall rang at four that afternoon and asked him to do the floor at the cafe for Ruth, he'd jumped at it.

At four thirty, he knocked on the kitchen's screen door. When there was no answer, he peered through the mesh and tried the handle, only to find the door locked. He knocked again, harder this time, making the whole door rattle on its hinges.

'Laurie?' Ruth came from the cafe into the kitchen.

'No, it's Hamish. The door's locked.'

'Oh, sorry,' Ruth said. She was frowning. She unlocked the door and he came inside. 'Where's Laurie?'

'Said his knee blew up last night, like a balloon. He's been to the doc and needs to keep it up for a bit. I'm filling in for him.'

'Oh, dear. He was limping yesterday and the day before. I told him I'd do the floors, but he insisted. Who does he think did them before he came along? And I don't expect you to do it in his place.' She sounded brusque, at the end of her tether.

'What's up?'

She threw up her hands. 'Everything … nothing … Working with Lorna now Allie is gone is driving me crazy. She never stops talking! Now Suzie, the junior who works with me and Mia on Saturdays, is sick. I've been trying to find someone to replace her, but it looks like it'll be Mia and me on our own.' She closed her eyes and groaned. 'Saturdays are short but often the busiest day.'

'I'll do the floor now,' Hamish said, at a loss as to what else he could offer. 'Any problems with the door to the service lane?'

'No, it's great. I only locked the screen door because I was in the office. And you haven't given me your bill, Hamish. I need to pay you so that you can pay Laurie.'

Hamish didn't want Ruth's money, for no particular reason other than he'd wanted to do something for her. She worked hard and was always doing stuff for others. He pushed his hand through his hair and, avoiding her eyes, said, 'Laurie has a few maintenance jobs around his place that he can't manage anymore and I've offered to do them for him, you know, like a trade for his help with the door. And you keep feeding him, so I reckon we're all square.'

'Well, I don't! You spent several days on that job and we agreed that I'd pay you for your time.'

'I don't remember agreeing to that. You've paid for all the timber, the door, the lock and the paint. Consider my time a gift. Besides, Elliot helped me with the skylight and he's your brother.' He raised his eyebrows, daring her to argue. It was the most alive he'd felt all day.

Ruth's expression made him want to laugh. 'What's Elliot being my brother got to do with any of this?'

'Is he coming up for the weekend?'

'No. His daughter is flying down from Queensland for a visit. She arrives on Sunday and she'll be there for the week. He'll be on his best behaviour.'

'Are you going to see her?'

'Next Saturday. I'll leave as soon as I close the cafe. We're having a family dinner on Saturday night and I'll come home Sunday after I've taken her to the airport. She's flying to Melbourne to spend a week with her mum and then home.'

'Good on her,' Hamish said. 'Now, the mop and bucket?'

'Outside, next to the gas bottles. Detergent and vinegar under the sink. But you don't have to do it, Hamish.'

'I know I don't, Ruth.'

She looked as if she was going to argue but then she huffed out an exhausted thank you. 'I'll be in the office. And don't think for a second I didn't notice how skilfully you changed the subject. Please tell me how much I owe you for your time, Hamish.'

Hamish chuckled to himself after she'd gone. He had no intention of taking her money.

He'd filled the bucket with hot soapy water and made a start on the floor when she emerged from the office. 'Any luck?'

She shook her head. 'I tried George, but he won't be back at the farm until semester break. He said he'd be happy to work then, if I still needed him. At least I don't have to worry about Sundays for the time being. If I had to go back to one day off a week it wouldn't be long before they'd be carting me off in the padded van.'

Hamish smiled. 'Thanks, Ruth.'

'For what?'

'Cheering me up.'

'Sharing all my problems has cheered you up? Are you okay?'

'I think so,' he said and the mop stilled. 'Just feeling a bit down today. Happens every now and then. Same goes for most people, I'd guess.'

'Sure, but during the last four or five months you've had a huge amount of change and upheaval in your life.' She propped herself on the edge of a table, careful not to knock a chair onto the floor, and folded her arms. 'Losing a parent the way you did … Beats me how you'd ever come to grips with something like that. Then you sold up and moved, took a risk buying your parents' house, alongside the task of clearing out their belongings. What an emotional soup that must have been. Plus dealing with the troubled relationship you have with your sister. Enough to wear the toughest person down. And all on top of you retiring and that not turning out as well as you'd hoped it would. Do you talk to anyone about this stuff?'

'You,' he said. 'And Jeff, the mate with the Harley. He's a bit younger than me but both his parents are dead. We've had a couple of chats about parents dying, that sort of thing.'

'Is it enough? There are professional people you can talk to.'

'I know there are but, so far, what I do has been enough. I'm going to take my clubs out tomorrow and have a round of golf. Haven't had a hit since before Christmas. Do you play?'

Ruth sputtered with laughter. 'Not lately,' she said. 'I'm not what you'd call a sporty type, in case you hadn't already noticed. Swimming, the odd game of tennis, that's about my limit, and I haven't done any of either in the past five years. Out of the three of us, Robert was the fit one, the sportsman, and he died first. How fair was that?'

'Not fair at all,' Hamish said. He dunked the mop into the bucket of water. 'I'd better get on with this before the water goes cold.'

'And I'd better get on with the hundred and one things I have to do. Buy you a drink later? I've got beer in the fridge, and wine. And there's always food, plenty of pizza slice left over. Unless you'd rather go to the pub?'

'Not unless you do.'

'I'd have to shower and change and I really haven't got the energy.'

'We could always go for a walk afterwards. If you felt like it.'

'Are you serious? I can hardly drag my feet around now.'

'Out in the fresh air, taking in the sights. We had a decent walk that day on the beach. I enjoyed it.'

'You are serious? Okay, we'll walk, but only after I've sat down for a while. And we'll head in a different direction this time. There's a clifftop walk, I've been out there several times. And at the end of Clifftop Drive there's this amazing old Queenslander. It looks as if it's just been plonked there, out in the middle of nowhere. Fabulous garden.'

'Done,' he said.

★ ★ ★

Hamish woke in the early hours of Saturday morning, mouth dry and pulse racing and with a vague memory of a dream he hadn't had for a long time. It involved his brother Jonathon and it had never made any sense, not now nor any of the other times he'd woken with his heart pounding. While he lay there waiting for it to settle, what Ruth had said the afternoon before came to mind. The bit about professional people being available if he needed to talk. His brother's death was a subject he'd never really discussed with anyone except his mother, and that had been before he left home as a teenager. Nat's niggling at him from time to time about it was just that, her trying to rankle and get a rise out of him. They'd never actually *talked* about what had happened to Jonathon. How did she manage the memories? Did she miss him? After all, Nat was closer in age to Jonathon than Hamish had been. He'd know these things if they'd ever talked about it. If not for the few dog-eared photos of his brother he'd found in an old and dusty album on the bookshelf in his parents' lounge room, it would have been as if Jonathon had never existed.

In the early days of his marriage to Andrea, they'd visited his parents and afterwards he'd attempted to explain to her why his relationship with his father was the way it was. The more he'd laboured over the explanation, the more disinterested she'd become, so he'd stopped and never mentioned it again—and she'd never asked. It was a tragic event in his childhood. As an individual, the experience had played a part shaping him into the man he'd become. As a family, they'd all been affected and changed by Jonathon's death, they'd just never talked about any of it. And if they didn't discuss it, they could pretend it hadn't happened. That pretence had been no panacea at all. Furthermore, if it had never happened, why had Theo never stopped blaming him? The older and wiser Hamish had become, the more convinced he was that his father had given up blaming him for the actual accident, because how could he not? It had been an accident. What he'd continued to blame Hamish for was being alive when Jonathon wasn't.

Wide awake now, Hamish threw back the bedclothes and padded barefoot to the kitchen for a glass of water. Moonlight streamed in through the window and the skylight, making electric light redundant. He stood at the window, gazing out into the night past the rainwater tank and towards the neighbour's fence. Hamish knew his mother had never stopped grieving for the son snatched away so cruelly. When he'd visited his parents, on what turned out to be the last time he saw his mother alive, Theo had left the two of them and gone for a walk. By then her dementia had progressed to such a stage that all his mother ever did while she sat in her special chair was stare, not at him but through him, her lips moving and her arthritis-ridden fingers fidgeting with the towelling bib around her neck. Hamish remembered feeling compelled to talk about Jonathon, so he had. His mother's fingers had stilled, her lips had stopped moving. For the whole half-hour his father was gone he'd talked about his brother, as many memories as he could cram in before he heard his father let himself in the front door.

At the sound of Theo's voice, his mother had started fidgeting again and picking up the silent conversation she was having with whoever.

Hamish had wondered then—as he wondered now—if suppressing all that grief and the memories of Jonathon was what had pushed her towards dementia in the first place. Who would ever know?

He went back to bed but it was a while before he dropped off to sleep again.

36

Ruth

I managed to get through the next week relatively unscathed, partly because Mia worked on Wednesday (a pupil-free day at the high school), which meant I only had one whole shift with Lorna. I was well and truly ready to see the back of her. A genuine Cutlers Bay local, Lorna wasn't exactly lazy, but she loved a chat and I had to constantly remind her of her duties. I was sure those social butterfly tendencies were why she wasn't keen on cooking—there was no-one to talk to in the kitchen. I decided I'd see if I could manage with just the short-shift casual on Thursday and Friday. Lorna had appeared as relieved as me when I'd told her I wouldn't need her for the remainder of the week.

When Erin had come in on Thursday morning for her orientation, she'd proved to be a quick learner, which lifted my spirits. Fingers crossed there'd be no 'disruption' at home when she began her shifts proper. If I could only convince Liz and Gayle, who did the short shifts week-about, to increase their shift by half an hour, I'd cope with Thursdays and Fridays on my own; not ideal, though, and more work for me. Then on Saturday—when Hamish had surprised me by turning up at our busiest time to clear tables—Mia offered to work for an hour each day after school to help clean up and prep for the next day. It was a tempting offer.

'Does your mum know you were going to suggest this to me? And what about your job stacking shelves at the supermarket?'

'They've cut back my hours and it is dead boring. Not to mention the pimply-faced youth I work with *lets* me do everything. I'd rather work here.'

'Pimply-faced *youth*? And you're what, seventeen?'

'He's only fifteen and he has acne, like really gross acne. And he picks—'

'Stop right there,' I said.

She laughed. 'Mum said I could ask you but if I slacked off on my homework, that was it.'

'All right, we'll give it a try. Four until five?'

'Thanks, Ruth. And school holidays? I can work whenever.'

'We'll see. You need some time to rest and relax. How was your mum's first week at the new job?'

Mia frowned and pulled at her bottom lip. 'I don't think she likes it much. She starts at seven so me and Cody get ourselves off to school, which is fine, because, like she says, we are more than capable. But she's tired and grumpy in the evenings, and in bed by nine.'

'She'll probably get used to it. It's a lot more hours than she was working here. On her feet the whole time.'

Mia shrugged. 'I heard her tell Dad that a couple of the women she works with are real bitches.'

'That's a shame. But you be careful who you go repeating that to, Mia. You know what small towns are like, everybody knows everybody else.'

'Or they're related.'

'That too. Now, I need to get a move on. I'm off to Adelaide for a family get-together. And I'll see you on Tuesday at four. I've told you the code for the service lane door?'

'Yep. You have a good time tonight.' She grabbed her polar fleece out of the cupboard. The mornings were getting chilly.

'Mia, before you go,' I said, 'is your dad around permanently now?'

Her face took on a mutinous expression. 'One would assume so,' she said. 'But of course me and Cody will be the last ones to know, officially.'

'Is he still living with you?' I was prying but felt justified, because I did care about Allie and Mia. My best employee had resigned and if you joined the dots, the downward spiral had begun at the return of the erstwhile husband.

'In a caravan, out the back. Someone Mrs Giles knows loaned the caravan. It's a piece of junk, but now that he's out of the house, Mum's a lot calmer. See ya.'

The plan was to be on the road by four, in time to meet everyone at the chosen venue sometime between six and seven. I'd booked myself into a motel overnight because Stacey was staying with Elliot and I didn't fancy sleeping on Elliot's over-sprung couch. It had been three or more years since I'd seen my niece and I was excited about the catch-up.

An hour later, congratulating myself for being right on schedule, I almost didn't believe it when I put the key in the car's ignition, turned it and nothing happened. I tried again, but all the engine did was make a clunking, grinding, not very healthy sound. I would have a screamed if I'd had the energy. My phone rang from the depths of the handbag on the passenger seat.

'All ready to go?' Hamish said when I answered.

'Except that now my car won't start,' I said, enunciating each word carefully. 'I'm looking for my roadside assistance card ... I know it's in here somewhere.'

'I can be there in ten minutes.'

'It's okay, Hamish, this is why I pay for roadside assistance. Besides, aren't you playing golf?'

'I am, but I'm nearly done and it's not as if I'm competing in the Australian Open, and I wanted to catch you before you left.'

Distracted, I upturned my wallet and shook out all the cards onto the passenger seat. Half of them I didn't even recognise. Another job to add to the list. 'Finish your game, Hamish. You don't need to rescue me every time. I'll ring the RAA.' I spied the card and pounced on it.

'Fair enough,' he said and the phone went dead.

I paused and stared down at it. No mistaking the cool tone nor the abruptness with which he'd ended the call. 'Oh, shit,' I said after I'd replayed my side of the conversation. He'd probably thought I didn't appreciate everything he'd done for me. I rang him back. He didn't answer and I didn't have time to leave a message. I rang roadside assistance and waited forty minutes for Gordon, the local mechanic, to come and tell me I had a flat battery and that maddeningly, I hadn't closed one of the back doors properly and that would have been enough to do the damage.

Of course he didn't have a replacement battery with him but he jump-started the car and I was on my way, albeit an hour late. 'You should be right,' he said. 'The battery doesn't look that old but if it is on the blink, you'll need to bring the car in and I'll replace it.'

As much as I was tempted otherwise, I kept to the speed limit because I couldn't afford the fine if I was caught. But I broke the law regardless when I picked up my phone to glance at it at regular intervals. But there was nothing from Hamish.

By the time I'd reached Gepps Cross I'd convinced myself that perhaps it was better this way. Let things cool off a bit between us. It was kind of him to offer to cut his golf game short but I was used to managing on my own and I didn't need him to gallop to my rescue every time. At least, I didn't think it was what I needed, or wanted, as gratifying as it was when he had. Both of our futures were uncertain and having him there, ready and willing to bail me out, could become addictive.

When we'd walked to Clifftop Drive the week before, the tide had been out and we'd clambered down the crumbling cliff and onto the beach. I'd stumbled and he'd taken my hand to steady me and hadn't let go as we'd walked on the beach. I hadn't minded at all; his fingers had been warm and strong, the skin tough and callused and it'd felt right to have them intertwined with mine. But where to from there? Did I need a man in my life? Did I even *want* a man in my life? Pertinent questions which I did not have answers for, except to say that I hadn't found Hamish's company at all onerous—quite the opposite. I liked him as a friend but I couldn't pretend, not even to myself, that I hadn't noticed him as a man, and that's when I floundered.

When it came to relationships, I had very little experience to fall back on and I suspected that Hamish didn't either. And what was so special about a relationship that would make it worth all the bother? I did a mental flick through the people I knew in long-term relationships, married or otherwise, from Audrey and Reg Franco to Allie and her estranged husband; my brothers and their attempts at marriage and togetherness; the handful of friends I'd kept in vague touch with over the years. None jumped out as matches made in heaven, although Robert and Lana had appeared content, in a reserved, unambiguous sort of a way. One Christmas, unobserved, I'd watched Robert. He couldn't take his eyes off his wife. They'd not long been married and, in that moment, I'd witnessed just how deeply he cared for her. I'd felt like an intruder.

But in the end, how much did any of it matter? Robert was dead and Lana was on her own again. I'd lived my adult life on my own and been content enough. The car behind me tooted and with a start I saw the lights had turned green and I was holding up the traffic.

By the time I arrived at the inner-city hotel, Elliot and Stacey were well into their main courses. Parking had been a nightmare and I'd ended up having to walk several blocks.

Stacey beamed when she spotted me. In her early forties now, she reminded me so much of her mother, or how I remembered her. We hugged.

'So good to see you, Ruth. You look tired. Dad said you had car trouble. You're not still driving that beat-up old station wagon?'

'It's been a long day and who can afford a new car?'

'I've ordered you the garlic prawns,' Elliot said. 'I thought they'd be the quickest option. Just let them know you're here.' He was animated and rosy-cheeked and recklessly waving about a half-full glass of red wine.

'Just the three of us? What happened to Lana? And Corrine? I thought they were coming?'

'Aunty Corrine rang earlier saying she'd woken up with the sniffles. But it's okay, because I spent Tuesday afternoon with her and caught up on what Oliver and Charlotte have been up to. And I had lunch with Lana on Thursday,' Stacey said. 'She was good, considering it's barely six weeks since Uncle Robert died.'

Elliot didn't comment, swirling the wine in the glass, his face an expressionless mask. Had he chosen not to accompany his daughter on these visits or had he not been invited?

Stacey didn't want another drink and Elliot still had a third of the bottle to go, so I went and sorted out my food and detoured to the bar for a drink. While I waited to be served, I debated whether or not to have a glass of wine. I did feel tired and disgruntled. The tiredness was a given, but who knew where the other came from?

Don't kid yourself, Ruth, of course you know.

I checked my phone again. No missed calls or messages from Hamish. There was the source of my disgruntlement and the reason why I didn't do relationships. Life already threw up more than enough day-to-day challenges and uncertainties—why go and pile on another layer?

★ ★ ★

On the drive to the airport on Sunday morning, Stacey swivelled in her seat and said, 'How's Dad really doing, Ruth? He says he's fine, all hale and hearty, but I dunno …'

Gritty-eyed and sleep deprived after your typical motel stay, it took me a moment to compose a response. 'Like you said last night, it's barely six weeks since Robert died and Elliot misses him.'

'They were close, weren't they? Mum said she sometimes felt like a third wheel when the three of them were together. Dad used to share more with his brother than he did with her. I guess it made her feel a bit redundant as a wife.'

'She told you that?' I said, with a quick sideways glance her way. Not that I was surprised.

'Don't get me wrong, Mum really liked Uncle Robert and he was always terrific to her and me, even after Mum and Dad split up.'

I yawned and Stacey grinned.

'You looked wrecked, like you drank most of the bottle of red, not Dad. Thanks for coming, Ruth. It was excellent to hear about life in Cutlers Bay. Unchanged by the sounds of things. Fingers crossed the business and the building sell quickly and you can get on with your life.'

'Yeah, although what that life might look like is yet to be determined.'

'I can't wait to retire!' Stacey said.

She insisted I drop her off at the terminal. 'Are you sure you don't want me to come in and have a coffee with you?'

'Thanks, but I'm going to phone home again. Chris sounded a bit down earlier. While he made it through the surgery without any problems and he is losing weight, he's not finding any of it easy. And two teenagers can be trying at the best of times.'

In the pick-up and drop-off zone, I humped Stacey's suitcase out of the back of the wagon and onto the footpath. We hugged each other. I was caught unawares by the strength of the connection I felt between us and how much I didn't want her to go.

'When you sell the cafe, come up for a holiday,' she said. 'There's heaps of things to do and some fabulous resort-style accommodation. If you come in the off season you can get packages quite cheap.'

'Now there's an idea … a week or even a fortnight of pampering in a five-star resort. Who knows what lies down the track? Give my love to Chris and the kids.'

'Will do, and, Ruth, please ring me any time, especially if you're worried about Dad. I'm a long way away, but sometimes it helps to talk and he is my dad and I love him.'

'Did he say anything about flying up to you for a holiday?'

She shook her head. That's when I noticed the officious-looking security guard begin to move in our direction, pointing at the nearby sign and then at the timepiece on his wrist. The traffic was banking up and he'd had his eye on us for a few minutes.

'I'll go,' I said. 'We'll talk soon.'

Stacey was halfway across the concourse, dragging her suitcase behind her, before there was a big enough gap for me to merge into the traffic.

Instead of turning north towards home, I headed east and back to Elliot's place. I'd have lunch with him before the drive home and we could talk. There was a conversation we needed to have: What *were* his expectations of me? In the longer term, having his younger sister butting into his life uninvited might be the last thing he wanted or needed. A similar conversation with Hamish might be advisable if I wanted to avoid any future misunderstandings. And if he was still talking to me at all.

Elliot's garage door was up and the garage was empty. I didn't drive in. He hadn't said anything about going anywhere when I'd picked up Stacey earlier, not that he had to tell me everything. I chastised myself for not calling ahead. I put the car in park and pulled on the handbrake to search for the phone. This morning at the motel the car hadn't started and the young man with a Ned Kelly beard and a pierced eyebrow from the room next door kindly jump-started it for me. Hence I wasn't game to turn off the ignition until I was safely home. I'd accepted I was up for the cost of a new battery.

My call to Elliot went unanswered. I shrugged, left a message and did a U-turn to point the car in the direction of home. I'd have just enough petrol to get me there.

37

Hamish

When it came to women, Hamish's track record was far from exemplary and he was in a quandary about how quickly and easily the situation with Ruth had spiralled out of control. He admired her and enjoyed her company and had found himself wanting to *support* her in whatever ways he could. Not *rescue* her, as she'd so flippantly implied on Saturday. The response suggested her interpretation of the situation between them was at odds with his own. She was definitely not a woman who needed rescuing; her independence and straightforwardness had been what had attracted him from the get-go.

He sat at the kitchen table late Sunday afternoon, empty coffee mug in front of him, mobile phone next to it. He picked it up and the screen burst into life. He stared at it for several seconds and then carefully placed it down beside the coffee mug. He'd lost track of the number of times he'd followed the same sequence since he'd as good as hung up on Ruth. He wanted to contact her, but the age-old fear that she might reject him again held him back. *Let her be the one to make the next move*, he'd told himself more than once. But she had made the next move—she'd rung back seconds after he'd hung up and he'd ignored the call. Why hadn't he answered? Out on the seventeenth hole, he'd held the phone in his hand and let it vibrate, all the while knowing it was Ruth. She hadn't left a message.

When he couldn't dance around the truth any longer, he'd finally admitted to himself that he'd been hurt and angry. He'd felt as if he'd given of himself, only to have it thrown back in his face. But then stealthily, over the ensuing hours, reason had prevailed: she would have been worn out after a busy Saturday in the cafe; she had a long drive ahead of her and was anxious to be on her way; she would have been stressed and frustrated because her car wouldn't start. In hindsight, what a mature adult would have done was quit the game of golf and driven to her place to help, regardless of her protestations. But he hadn't been a mature adult; he'd had a little tantrum. And now he was uncertain what his next move should be.

Nothing in his life felt anything like inspiring. He'd heard not a peep from his sister, not since the money to buy her share of the house had been deposited into her credit union account. Done and dusted and proof that he'd been right all along: he only ever heard from Nat when she wanted something, usually money. What disappointed him more was that he'd heard zip from his brother-in-law. He'd thought that their relationship had strengthened in the aftermath of Theo's death, but not so. Was he going soft, letting himself be distracted and disappointed by such things?

Work on the house had come to a standstill. Jeff was yet to send the promised plans and without them, Hamish's hands were tied. Not one to stand still for long, he was itching to get the project moving. But there was no point knocking out doors and windows and tearing down walls before he had plans he was satisfied with. Not to mention the required building approvals. Sure, there were umpteen jobs he could do in the back and the front gardens, but when the renovation was in full swing, the place would morph into a building site and anything he did to the gardens now would inevitably need redoing.

More to the point, he'd made the decision not to spend another dollar on the property until he had the plans and a clear idea of what the renovation would cost.

Who could blame him for feeling bored and dissatisfied and becoming fidgety with it?

Hamish grabbed his wallet and car keys. He'd cheer himself up with one of Peg's hamburgers and a side serve of chips. He'd treat himself to a beer with it.

On the drive to the takeaway, he passed the workshop of the only mechanic in town. A decades-old white Holden station wagon was parked to one side. He shot around the block again, slowed to a crawl when he came to the workshop and confirmed that, yes, it was Ruth's car. How long had it been parked there? Had she even made it to Adelaide to see her niece? The thought gave him pause and a little twinge of something else. Guilt perhaps?

It was dusk when he returned with his meal, the cab of the ute smelling like the inside of Peg's shop. He turned into his street and his headlights flashed on something bright and shiny and there was Cody and his mate, only metres away in the middle of the road, fooling around on their bikes—no lights, no helmets. Hamish's heart did a loop inside his chest. He slammed on the brakes and the vehicle shuddered to a halt. His mouth went dry. He jammed the ute into park and pulled on the handbrake, unclipped his seatbelt and threw open the door.

'Have you blokes got a bloody death wish?' he yelled, advancing on them.

They sniggered. Cody's mate gave Hamish the finger and then they fishtailed their bikes and took off into the gloom, their insolent laughter trailing behind them. Seized by an impotent anger, Hamish shook his fist at them.

The porch light of the house adjacent flicked on and he heard a door open. 'Is everything okay?' a male voice called.

'Yeah, just some idiot kids on their pushbikes.' In that moment he felt old and ridiculous.

A grunt and the door closed again with a thud. Hamish climbed into the ute and slowly drove the short distance home. Tomorrow he would visit Cody's mother and talk to her about her son's reckless behaviour.

★ ★ ★

Monday afternoon he'd loitered in the front garden, on the lookout for the maroon SUV Cody's mother drove. Via Leslie Giles, his back-fence neighbour who was always up for a chat when she spotted him in the backyard, he knew Allie's shift at the new job finished at three pm. When he clocked her car go past, he was across the road in a flash to bail her up before she'd reached the front door.

'Allie, can I have a quick word?' he called and she swung around, surprised.

'Hello, Hamish. What's up?'

'I've come about Cody and the lad he hangs out with,' he said, out of breath by the time he reached her.

She stiffened. 'That'd be Noah Collins. What have they been up to?'

He thought she looked weary and not at all happy. He tried to lighten his demeanour. 'I almost ran into them last night, messing about on their bikes in the middle of the road, no lights or helmets.'

'Cody does have a helmet,' she said, 'but because it's not the latest, you-beaut style, he refuses to wear it.' She shifted the bag she was carrying from one hand to the other. 'Did you say anything to them?'

'Yes, and it wasn't very well received, believe it or not.'

A corner of her mouth tipped up in half a smile. 'I'd believe it. All I can do is talk to him. As far as Noah goes—' The smile faded. 'He's a hard nut, that one.'

A stocky man in denim jeans and a faded blue singlet barrelled around the corner of the house. 'What's going on, Alison?' he said and then directed his belligerence towards Hamish. 'And who the hell are you?'

Hamish introduced himself. 'I live on the other side of the street, a few doors down.' He held out his hand. The man ignored it.

Allie blushed. 'This is Brett, Mia and Cody's dad,' she said.

'Howdy,' Hamish replied, with effort. 'I'm here about your son. He'll get himself killed if he doesn't take more care on his pushbike, him and that mate of his.' Allie winced. Hamish ploughed on regardless. 'No helmets, no lights—they're an accident waiting to happen.'

'What's it to you?' Brett said, his mouth contorted with defiance.

'I'll tell you what it is to me,' Hamish said, clenching his hands into fists. He took a step closer to the other man and jabbed a finger at him. 'I don't want to be the poor mutt whose life is turned upside-down because he comes around the corner one night and knocks one of those idiots off their bike, all because they don't have lights, helmets, hi-vis vests or anything!' He was practically shouting when he felt a firm hand grip his forearm.

'Hamish,' Allie said, 'I—we will talk to him, won't we, Brett?'

Brett moved back a pace and folded his arms across his hairy chest. 'You need to get that anger under control, mate,' he said, self-righteously. Allie rolled her eyes.

A powerful urge to be away from there hit Hamish like a freight train. 'Thanks for your time,' he said brusquely. He took off, gravel crunching underfoot, desperate to put as much distance between himself and these people as fast as he could. What was the matter with him? First, the dream had come back and now he'd had a gross overreaction because he'd let some bogan push one of his buttons.

'What the effing hell was that all about?' he heard Brett say as he rounded their gate post and struck out onto the footpath. He hadn't heard Allie's hissed reply but his fertile imagination didn't take long to conjure up several likely responses, none of them favourable to him. Didn't people understand how whole lives could be changed in as many seconds as it took a hapless—or drunk—driver to careen around a corner and into unsuspecting boys on bikes?

He went inside and slammed the front door, then went from room to room and drew the blinds at the front windows. While he was doing it, he craved a return to multistorey living for the first time ever. One of the few positives of a fifth-floor apartment was that being high in the sky made him oblivious to the happenings down on street level.

He went into the bathroom and splashed cold water onto his face and hoped he wasn't beginning to unravel completely.

38

Ruth

Mia showed up at the cafe after school on Tuesday as we'd arranged. She dived into the tasks I allotted her with an enthusiasm I envied. The hour passed far quicker than it would have if I'd been on my own. Laurie's knee was giving him ongoing strife and I'd demanded he take the week off from doing the floors. I wasn't expecting Hamish to show up in his place and when he didn't, I had a job convincing myself I didn't feel a sliver of disappointment. On Monday, after I'd picked up my car with its new battery, I'd stopped by Hamish's house. I'd had time to consider all things Hamish on the return drive to Cutlers Bay. We had a lot in common: both single and around the same age; no children or other hangers-on; and, from several childhood memories he'd shared, his suburban upbringing had not been hugely dissimilar to my own. I'd also considered just how well Hamish actually *was* doing since his father's death and had become reconciled to the fact that if I wanted the friendship back on track, it would be up to me to make it happen. Of course I didn't say all that in the note I left when he didn't answer the door, I simply apologised for any misunderstandings and invited him around for a meal on Friday night.

On Thursday, the weather changed. Mild, gloriously sunny days had heralded in autumn but in the space of twenty-four hours, wintry weather hit. The cafe smelled of damp clothing laced with mothballs. I turned the air conditioner to heat mode. I'd had no reply from Hamish and I'd begun to worry. Was this his way of telling me it was over, whatever *it* had been? I couldn't believe he'd be that callous. It just didn't mesh with what I knew of the man. Had he even found my note? A gust of wind could easily have blown it away.

When Mia arrived after school it was still blustery and raining. She whipped through the floors and restocked the fridges.

'You haven't seen Hamish in your travels, have you?' I asked when she came into the kitchen. I was preparing ingredients for tomorrow's special: vegetable soup and chicken-filled toasties.

She shook her head. 'Can't say I've even noticed his ute in the driveway, but then I'm out at school all day and then here. Maybe he's gone to Adelaide or something.'

'Maybe,' I said, not convinced.

She started wrapping cutlery in paper serviettes and we worked side by side in companionable silence, the rain thrumming on the roof. Every now and then there was a gust of wind that rattled through the building and the swishy, splashy sound of a vehicle passing by on the wet road.

'I've messaged Mum to come pick me up,' Mia said when her hour was almost up.

Not long after, there was a loud knock on the kitchen door before a dripping umbrella preceded Allie inside.

'What a day!' she said, propping the soggy brolly in the handbasin. I hadn't clapped eyes on her since the last day she'd worked for me and I couldn't believe how pleased I was to see her.

'How are you?' I said and wiped my hands on a tea towel.

Myriad expressions crossed her familiar face before she settled on a resigned smile. 'Fair to middling. It's good to see you, Ruth.' She glanced around the cosy kitchen. 'I miss this place more than I ever imagined I would.'

'How is the new job?'

She made a so-so motion with her hand. 'The politics of the place! Just unbelievable.' She cast a furtive glance her daughter's way. Mia was hanging on her every word. 'I'll get used to it,' Allie said and forced a bright smile. 'You ready to go, sweetie?'

'Yep. Mum, have you seen Hamish lately? I haven't. Ruth was asking.'

For a split second Allie looked like a deer in the headlights. She cleared her throat. 'Not since Monday afternoon,' she said. She pulled a fifty-dollar note and a slip of paper out of her pocket. 'Mia, be an angel and pop to the supermarket for me?' She held out the money and the note.

Mia screwed up her face. 'But it's raining,' she said, sounding just like a whiny teenager.

'Take the umbrella. I'll pick you up out front in fifteen minutes,' Allie said in what I recognised as her 'don't mess with me' tone.

I looked from mother to daughter. I could tell Mia was on the verge of arguing, but then she didn't. She snatched the money and note from her mother's outstretched hand, grabbed the umbrella and slammed the door on her way out. Allie gave her head a tiny shake.

'What's going on?' I said.

She ran her tongue around her teeth and then proceeded to tell me about an altercation Hamish had had with Brett on Monday afternoon, apparently over Cody and his mate's reckless behaviour on their bikes. 'Without a doubt, Brett acted like a moron, but Hamish's reaction was over the top, or so I thought,' she said. 'Cody's a good kid, but that Noah Collins ...'

Now was not the time to disclose what I'd witnessed when I'd ducked out to the supermarket the afternoon before: Cody and his mates had been huddled together in the area beside the public amenities and I'd swear on a stack of bibles they were vaping. When Cody saw me, he'd quickly hidden something behind his back. Cody probably was a good kid, but he was also a teenager in a peer group of kids who might not be as well behaved because they hadn't had a mother like Allie.

'Perhaps Hamish has gone away. It's just that I left him a note on Monday afternoon and I haven't heard from him.'

'Like I said, I haven't seen him since Monday afternoon when I got home from work. But now that I think about it, his place has been all shut up, the blinds drawn. Why don't you ring him?'

'I might pop around later, see if his ute's in the garage. Anything can happen when you live on your own. Maybe he's sick.'

Allie frowned. 'I never thought of that. He always looks so fit, but there is a pretty bad stomach bug going around. Does he have anyone who checks in on him every now and then?'

'I honestly don't know. He has several mates, a sister, nieces, but I get the impression none of them are close.' And me. I hadn't been a very good friend to him, had I? He'd check in to see if I was okay and I knew he kept an eye out for Laurie. How had I not thought to repay his kindness by checking in on him?

I grabbed my phone off the bench and scrolled through to his number. He didn't pick up. I ripped off my apron and threw it on the bench. 'Something's not right. I'm going around there right now.'

Allie didn't appear surprised. She left through the kitchen door and I locked up after her. After I'd turned everything off, I hurried through to the flat to collect my car keys. And would you believe it, the *damned* car would not start. Dead as a doornail. Didn't even make the grinding, clunking sound it had before. If Gordon had been there I would have strangled him.

Luckily, the rain had eased, but a fine drizzle had set in. I donned a raincoat and rummaged through the laundry cupboard for the umbrella I hadn't eyeballed since last winter. It took ten minutes for me to power around to East Terrace. I dodged puddles along the way. Motorists had their headlights on in the dreary, drizzly streets.

Hamish's house looked particularly dismal and when I peered in through the garage louvres and found an empty space, my legs almost crumpled with relief. Not that I'd thought for a second— or perhaps I had, subconsciously. After what Allie had told me and Hamish's own admission days before that he'd been feeling down … No. Never. But then I didn't know him all that well, did I?

The front and back doors were locked, even the screen doors, and the note was where I'd left it. Autumn leaves had swirled in onto the verandah.

'No-one home?'

I spun around at the sound of Allie's voice. I hadn't heard her walk up the driveway. She had on a bright yellow raincoat and a black beanie.

'The garage is empty,' I said. 'The bin hasn't been put out and there's not much rubbish in it.'

'Aren't you the detective?' She nudged me with her elbow. 'I'd say he's gone to see friends or family for a few days.'

It was beginning to appear that way. We walked along the driveway to the gate. 'I'm glad I came around,' I said, mainly for my own benefit.

'I would have offered to stop by and investigate except that I had Mia with me and she's too curious by a mile. Where's your car?'

'Bloody thing won't start. I just bought a new battery for it. Gordon will be hearing from me.'

'Come with me and I'll run you home,' she said.

'Thanks, but I'll walk. The exercise will do me good, or so my GP says. Thanks for coming over. I guess he'll be back, eventually.'

Allie's eyebrows disappeared under the edge of her beanie but she didn't comment and I was grateful for that. She'd know all about men who came and went whenever they chose and the confusion left in their wake.

39

Ruth

Bryan Chalmers popped in for a second coffee on Friday afternoon, not long before closing time. Business had been slow, the day overcast, cool and miserable, and the cafe was empty. Mia had messaged saying she couldn't come after school and I was debating whether to mop the floor today or leave it until tomorrow. Or never.

'Wishing you'd kept the nine-to-five paying job?' Bryan said— smugly, I thought.

I handed him his coffee: two shots, white and one. 'Am I that easy to read?'

'Not at all, Ruth. But you have the look of someone who's had enough. You didn't return my call. Have you changed your mind about selling?'

'Sorry. I meant to ring you again but I'm afraid so many other things have been demanding my attention.'

'I heard Allie Thomas quit and Erin Saunders is working here a couple days a week. How's she going?'

'Early days. How do you know all of this?'

'The wife. She's born and bred Cutlers Bay and knows everyone and everything. So, what have you decided?'

'Have you got a minute now?'

'Yep.'

I went to the front door and locked it, flipping the sign around to closed. The cleaning up could wait. 'Come through to the office, that way we can avoid any prying eyes.'

'Good thinking,' Bryan said. We both knew that if we were seen in here together having a cosy little tete-a-tete when the cafe was closed it'd be around the town in a flash.

I took the seat behind the desk and Bryan the visitor's chair. He sipped his coffee but I didn't miss his covert scan of the cluttered room.

'I want to sell everything,' I said. 'The sooner the better.'

'You sound as if you've made up your mind.'

'I have, and not without considering your suggestion of only selling the business and leasing the building to whoever bought it. The thing is, Bryan, I'll need the money from the sale of the business *and* the building to set myself up somewhere else.'

'You won't stay in Cutlers Bay?'

'Honest answer? I don't really know. My older brother is the only immediate family I have left and he lives in Adelaide. He's on his own now.'

'You do realise that if we manage to sell it all, which I wouldn't count on, what you'll end up with will seriously limit where you buy in the city?'

'Yes, unfortunately, I'd worked that out for myself.'

'You could always stay here. There are worse places to retire. In fact, folk move here to retire.'

The beginnings of a headache punched at the backs of my eyes. 'You know what? Let's get it on the market and let me worry about where I'll live if and when it sells.'

Bryan crossed his legs and rested the coffee mug on his knee. 'All right, I'll draw up an agency agreement for you to sign. What you'll need to do is get on to your accountant and have them prepare a Form 2. When I have that, I can value the business. We sign off when you're happy and that's when the real fun starts.'

'Will you advertise?'

'I'll ask around locally first, off-market and confidentially. There are several folk in the district who've indicated an interest in small business, if ever anything came up. If that goes nowhere, then we advertise.'

'I won't have to have a for-sale sign in the window, will I?'

'Not if you don't want to. But folk will talk, no matter how we go about it, and that's not always a bad thing. But you need to be prepared because there are some who'll ask you questions that are none of their business.'

'Like what?'

'How much you make, what you're asking for it, why you're selling, that kind of thing. Up to you how you answer but my advice is the less said the better. If you think they are genuinely interested, refer them to me.'

'And the building and flat are advertised separately, on different internet sites?'

'That's correct. Who's your accountant?'

I named a firm in Kadina. 'And Selina Martin does my books.'

Bryan nodded. 'Expect them to take at least two to four weeks to prepare the Form 2. Ring them Monday and ask what documentation they'll need from Selina.'

We talked for a few minutes more about timeframes and when and what I'd tell the staff. I felt nauseated when I let him out the kitchen door and my head was pounding. I swallowed painkillers with a glass of water. My GP was right: the headaches were stress related. By six I'd cleaned up and done the prep needed for Saturday. Twice I'd picked up my phone ready to ring Bryan and tell him I'd changed my mind. To forget all about it. I'd keep plodding on here until I couldn't plod any longer. But how ridiculous was that? I wanted out and this was the only way it was going to happen. If not now, it'd be in a year or two when I was older and even more over it than I was now.

Too late, I realised that, with everything else going on, I'd forgotten to ring Gordon about my dead car. Tomorrow was Saturday and his workshop closed at midday. I swore and felt better after venting.

I went through to the flat and hopped straight into the shower, washed my hair and put on a pair of comfortable track pants and a T-shirt. When I thought about food and what I might eat for my evening meal, it struck me that tonight was the night I'd invited Hamish to dinner. Tomorrow it'd be a week since I'd spoken to him and he'd sort of hung up on me because I'd been preoccupied and thoughtless along with it. Although we hadn't discussed it, I knew Allie would let me know if he came home. She probably wondered what was going on between us, but like me with her and Brett, no matter how interested she was, she'd never ask. If anyone did ever ask, what answer would I give them? As far as I could see, there wasn't anything going on between Hamish and I. Not anymore.

★ ★ ★

Lana rang right in the middle of my pre-bed preparation when I had a mouthful of toothpaste.

'Hang on,' I said. I put the phone down, spat out the toothpaste and wiped my mouth.

'Is this a bad time?' she said when I picked up again.

'As good a time as any.' Lana didn't ring me, ever. Unease raised the hairs on the back of my neck. 'What's up?'

I heard her breathing and then she gave a ladylike little cough, into the back of her hand, I'm sure. 'I don't know exactly how to say this,' she said, 'and I wish with all my heart that I didn't have to—'

'Just tell me, Lana.' *Do like I've just done with the toothpaste and spit it out.*

'I didn't want to worry you, Ruth.'

'A bit late for that, given it's ten pm and you've never called me before. Is this about Elliot?'

'I thought I was doing the right thing, meeting him for coffee and then having him around for a meal, but now he won't leave me alone. Every day he rings or texts, wants me to go out for lunch … dinner … a drink. I've asked him not to ring me anymore but he keeps doing it. If I don't answer, he drives to my house, allegedly to see if I'm all right.'

'He's lonely. Doesn't know what to do with himself since Robert died.'

'I understand that, Ruth. You think I'm not lonely too? But when he showed up earlier this evening, he'd been drinking and I was afraid of him. I don't want to go to the police, but I will if he doesn't stop bothering me.'

'I'll talk to him. Tomorrow. I promise. I'm so sorry, Lana.'

'It's not for you to apologise, Ruth. He's a grown man, responsible for his own actions. But who else was there for me to call? I'm sorry it had to be you.'

'I was there on the weekend, but I didn't spend much time with him. He seemed okay. I mainly went to catch up with Stacey and I know she's worried what'll happen to him long term.'

'Please don't mention this to her. She is a lovely girl and doesn't need this problem dumped in her lap.'

And I did? 'Leave it with me then, and feel free to ring if he bothers you again. My only caveats are I'm two-and-a-half hours away and he doesn't listen to much of what I say anyway. Calling the police might be the most expedient option, if it ever happens again.'

40

Ruth

The alarm woke me from a deep and dreamless sleep. It took moments for me to orientate to where I was and when it was and then all I wanted to do was pretend I was someplace else at least a thousand miles away and go straight back to sleep. Recklessly, I closed my eyes and imagined what the morning might look like if I didn't have to get up and open the cafe. Of course I dozed off and woke with a start, shocked to see the time: under an hour until the cafe opened. I flew out of bed and into my clothes after the briefest of washes. Hair into a twist, tinted moisturiser, lipstick and I was good to go. The muffins needed to be into the oven … no, today was Saturday and it was croissants. In my haste to get the oven on I left my phone on the kitchen bench where it'd been charging overnight.

Six hours later I was back in the flat after a hectic shift in the cafe. I picked up the phone and there were four missed calls from Elliot and nothing from Hamish. Why hadn't it been the other way around? The phone clattered back onto the bench. I needed a cup of tea and a sandwich to fortify me before I returned Elliot's calls.

Alas, he beat me to it by half a sandwich.

'Have you been talking to Lana?' he barked, in lieu of a greeting.

'I didn't ring her, she rang *me*. And I'm not the one who's been pestering her. You need to stop it, Elliot. She'll call the police next time, which she has every right to do.'

'Is that what she said? That I was *pestering* her?'

'I think the word she used was bothering.'

'I thought she was lonely, enjoyed the company. Wanted to talk about Robert, the good times we'd had.'

'And that would be fine from time to time, but not every day. You need to back off, let her grieve in her own way, in her own time, *on her own*.'

'All right for you to say. You have plenty to occupy your time, people around you every day. All I do is sit and brood.'

I drew in a long breath and willed myself to remain calm. 'Elliot, would you like to come and stay with me for a few days? A change of scenery might give you a boost and I could use some help, now that I've made the decision to put the business on the market.'

'What sort of help?'

'Tidying up the garden, sorting out stuff, the odd maintenance job, some painting.'

He grunted. 'I'll think about it.'

'Shall I drive down next weekend? We could eat out, see a movie?' If I could get Gordon to fix my car first.

'Why would you do that if I'm coming up there?'

'Okay. When do you think you'll come?'

'It won't be this week. Dentist and eye appointments. I think I need new glasses. I might bring my clubs and have a hit of golf with Hamish.'

Good luck with that. 'The spare bed will be made up and ready. And please promise me you won't bother Lana, not at all.'

Nothing but empty silence from the other end of the phone.

'Elliot? Promise me. I don't want to be bailing you out of jail.'

'All right. You have my word, old chook,' he said.

My chest tightened. He might have agreed but the defeat in his voice heightened my unease. Mindlessly, I chewed through the remains of the chicken sandwich, washing it down with lukewarm tea. For a few minutes, I seriously contemplated ringing Stacey, ignoring what Lana had asked. Stacey was family, Lana wasn't, not really. But then, what could Stacey do except worry? It'd spoil the last days of her stay in Melbourne with her mum. Then she'd be home and three thousand kilometres away again. I frowned. What would Gloria make of all this? Could I talk to her? She'd been married to Elliot for a couple of decades. If anyone knew him, it was her.

I dropped my head into my hands. What was I thinking? Gloria divorced him *because* she knew him so well. Dumping on her wouldn't be fair at all. I cursed again, under my breath. Then my phone pinged.

A message from Allie flashed onto the screen: *He's back, A.*

I picked up the phone, fumbled the password. Allie answered on the second ring.

'When?' I said, my heartbeat a rapid tattoo in my chest.

'Just now. I went outside to bring in the bin that no other bugger thought to bring in yesterday and I saw him pull into his driveway. Funny thing is, a few minutes later he left again.'

'Oh,' I said, and for some uncanny reason I glanced over my shoulder and there was Hamish at the door, hand raised and about to knock on the glass. 'He's here.'

'Ah, so that's where he was going in such a hurry. Bye.'

I stood, took the three steps required to reach the door and slid it open. 'Hamish,' I said, through the screen.

'Ruth.'

We stood there, either side of the flimsy flywire. I didn't know what to say. It was as if all the spiels I'd rehearsed for a situation such as this had vaporised.

His hand rasped across his mouth. 'I got your note,' he said. 'I need to explain.'

I flicked open the flyscreen and gestured for him to come inside and he stepped past me. He smelled of sweat, his jeans were grubby, his shirt was crumpled and his hair was a matted mess. Red-rimmed and bloodshot eyes suggested he hadn't slept in a while. Had he lost weight?

'Coffee?' I took down two mugs.

'Love one.' He stood awkwardly by while the coffee machine powered up.

'Do you want something to eat?' My default mode: offer food when you don't know what else to do.

'Nah, thanks.'

When I put the mug of coffee on the table he sat in the chair I'd vacated, his back to the door. I propped myself against the sink and took a sip. It was hot and chocolatey, my favourite dark roast blend. Late in the day for coffee, but I didn't care.

'It's hard to know where to start,' he said.

'At the beginning?'

His laugh was hollow; humourless. 'That'd be my childhood, I guess.'

I glanced pointedly at the kitchen clock. 'The abridged version, perhaps?'

This time the corners of his eyes crinkled when he laughed. 'The abridged version it is.' The clock ticked as he visibly collected himself. Should have I braced myself? Was I in for a shock?

He cleared his throat. 'When I was fifteen, my younger brother Jonathon was knocked off his bike by a drunk driver and killed. He was eleven. Natalie was nine. I was with him when it happened, but I didn't actually see it happen. Nevertheless, Dad blamed me for *letting* it happen. I was the oldest, I should have been looking out for him, blah, blah, blah.

'Mum never held me responsible, not for one second. Even in the depths of her grief, she saw it for what it was: a tragic accident. As you can imagine, my family was never the same after that.' He fiddled with the handle of the coffee mug then picked it up and drank what was left in one gulp.

I was speechless. What family would be the same after experiencing something like that? But to blame a teenage boy for such a tragedy?

He carefully placed the mug back onto the coaster. 'Over the years, and in my defence, Mum chipped away at Dad, finally getting him to see that it had been an accident, not my fault at all. But Dad still blamed me, I think just for being alive when Jonathon was dead.' He leaned back in the chair and folded his arms. 'So, Allie's lad Cody and his mate are often out on the street fooling about on their bikes. Sunday evening I went out for a hamburger and when I came back, I could have easily cleaned up one—or both—of them. It was nearly dark, they were in the middle of the street, no lights on their bikes, no helmets, no hi-vis … Scared the shit out of me. Monday, I went across and caught Allie when she came home from work. We had a civilised discussion about it and she said she'd talk to them, but then—'

'Brett came along,' I said and sat down across the table from him.

He nodded. 'How did you know?'

'Allie told me.'

He wasn't surprised. 'Pushed my buttons, big time. I came this close to punching the dickhead. Ruth, I've never so much as raised a hand to anyone, ever. I went home feeling quite rattled. I threw my swag and a few other bits and pieces into the ute and went bush. I needed to get away from here—from everything—for a few days. Life's been full on since Dad died. Talk about things never being the same again.'

'Did you tell Allie about your brother?'

'Nope. Apart from an aborted attempt to explain to Andrea in the early days of our marriage why I had such a dysfunctional relationship with my father, you're the first person I've ever told.' He sat forward and rested his forearms on the table.

'What about your sister? You've never talked about it with her?'

'Not in a constructive way. And as a family, we never discussed it. Mum and I did, very occasionally. I dunno if not talking about it was the only way Dad could deal with it. I'm convinced Mum's dementia was partly caused by the stress of suppressing all that grief. If it weren't for a handful of photos I found in an old album, it would be as if Jonathon had never existed.'

'I wonder what your sister remembers?'

'I've always wondered if she actually saw the accident happen. She didn't have a pushbike so she wasn't with us, but we were out on the street not far from home. And she was a sly kid, always popping up where you'd least expect her to be, knowing stuff she shouldn't.'

'Do you think you should discuss it with her? It might help you both.'

'Yeah, I've thought about doing that but decided it'd be pointless, now that Mum and Dad are both gone. Plus I'd never be one hundred per cent certain that she'd told me the truth.'

'Truth based on the memories of a nine-year-old would be a pretty wobbly thing, if you ask me. I can't even remember being nine.'

He frowned. 'No, but then your brother wasn't killed when you were nine. You don't forget something like that.'

'Not unless you wanted to forget because you were somewhere or doing something you weren't meant to be and the memory is too traumatic.'

'Truthfully, Ruth? If she does have baggage or demons or whatever, she can deal with them however she sees fit, just leave me out of it. No happy endings in the dealings I've ever had with her.' He rubbed his eyes and yawned.

'Another coffee?'

'No, thanks. A shower and a solid night's sleep is what I need. But

I found your note when I got home and I wanted to apologise for being such a jerk last Saturday. You were already under pressure and I put you under more.'

'Not all your fault, Hamish. When you rang, I was preoccupied, trying to get my head around my car not starting because, after all the planning and rushing around, I was going to be late anyway. And I'm so used to solving my own problems. I don't expect you or anyone else to bail me out whenever I get into strife. You have your own life. I have mine.'

'But we're friends, aren't we?'

'I'd thought so.'

'And friends should be able to expect certain things of each other, within reason? Isn't that a part of what good friendship is about?' He stood and pushed the chair into the table.

He was waiting for me to reply but I didn't know what to say. Had I forgotten what it was to be a good friend? Or was I just out of practice?

He gave a wry smile. 'It's okay, Ruth. Five nights out under the stars with no internet gave me ample time to navel gaze. Thanks for the coffee. I'm in dire need of a shower and a change of clothes because I stink. I'll see you later.'

I didn't dispute what he'd said or offer a raincheck for the missed meal invitation in the note. Sure, he'd apologised and so had I, in a roundabout sort of a way. Mostly we'd justified our actions and behaviour. No mention of when we might see each other again.

His visit left me feeling oddly unsettled and not at all happy.

41

Hamish

True to his word, Jeff emailed preliminary plans for the proposed renovation by the end of the week. Jeff had offered two options, including one that would be way cheaper than the other. Hamish was torn. The more expensive proposal appealed; in it, Jeff had captured everything Hamish had imagined. But he needed to be realistic. The time away in the bush had given him the clarity he'd been lacking. He had no idea what the future might hold, no clear vision of what he wanted it to hold. He'd thought he had but it'd turned out to be nothing more than a mirage.

He spent Sunday morning poring over the plans, walking through the house, contemplating each room; tromping around the yard, thinking, imagining, dreaming, common sense always bringing him back down to earth with a thud. When he thought about Ruth, which he often did, he wished he could ask for her take on Jeff's ideas. But he felt as if she'd drawn a line in the sand when he'd visited her on Saturday afternoon, a line that indicated she was committed to her independence and saw reliance on others as unacceptable. It wasn't dissimilar to how he'd lived his own life, relentlessly self-sufficient. He drafted an email to Jeff outlining his decision, but didn't send it. He'd sleep on it, see if he felt the same way in the morning.

He was up well before the sun on Monday morning. After a coffee watching the sun rise from the back verandah, he booted up his laptop, reread the email and sent it. There would be no renovation, at least not now.

Builders were early risers so he wasn't surprised when a return email dropped into his inbox within minutes: *No worries, mate. And you don't owe me anything except a couple of beers. I enjoyed the ride across. I believe you've made the sensible decision. If you've no plans to live there long term, why spend money you're unlikely to recoup? Tidy it up, paint it and sell it. Keep in touch. Cheers, J.*

By eight he was at Laurie's place, mowing the older man's lawns as promised. It was a beautiful day, clear, warm with a gentle breeze. Hamish cleared the house gutters and trimmed back a bush that was encroaching on the driveway. Around ten, Laurie hobbled out with a cuppa for them.

'How's the knee?' Hamish said, pulling up an empty milk crate to perch on. There was a plate with slices of fruitcake. It only took one bite for Hamish to know Ruth had made it.

Laurie sat himself down in an old cane chair and propped his foot on another milk crate. 'Physio's satisfied with the progress. Slow but sure, she says. I have to take her word for it.'

'You're not still doing the floors at the cafe, are you?'

'I couldn't, as much as I want to, but Ruth insisted on bringing food around yesterday even though I hadn't earned it. Thank goodness that young Mia is helping her after school.'

Hamish hadn't known that. What else was happening at the cafe that he didn't know about? And why did not knowing bother him so much?

'Ruth should sell that cafe, get out before she runs herself completely into the ground. It's a younger person's game, working a business like that,' Laurie said and eyed Hamish expectantly.

Oh no. Not going there. He was beginning to get the gist of how things worked in country towns like Cutlers Bay. The lowdown on Ruth's future plans for the cafe would not come from him.

When Laurie accepted there'd be no inside info from Hamish, he reached for a second piece of cake. 'She's done the town proud setting up the cafe and carrying on for as long as she has. It's a credit to her.'

'You'll get no argument from me. Is there anything else you need me to do while I'm here?' Hamish said.

The older man cleared his throat and shifted in the seat. 'Not for me as such, but Esme next door, she could do with a few jobs being done. Jobs I'd normally do for her and will again when I'm fit and able.'

'Her lawn and what else?' Hamish had noticed the overgrown patch of grass next door.

'Trim back the salvias along the fence and pull a few weeds. With that drop of rain we had last week and now the sunshine, you can almost watch the damn things grow. Use my mower and edge trimmer and anything else you might need. She's not short of a bob and she pays me by the hour. I'm sure she'll be more than willing to do the same for you.'

'What about that bloke I've seen around the town, the one with the beat-up old Falcon ute and trailer? Mower and all the gear on the back?'

'That'd be Chris Lehman. Not much older than you would be my guess, but the poor bugger needs two knee replacements. Old footy injuries. He still does a few jobs but only for his long-term clients.'

'I see. I guess I could help your neighbour out, this once.'

'Good on ya! I'll ring her now,' Laurie said and Hamish did a double take when the man pulled a sleek new iPhone out of his shirt pocket. He stood and wandered to the end of the verandah to give Laurie privacy.

'What about tomorrow morning? Nine?' the older man called out moments later.

Hamish gave him a thumbs up.

Another short exchange and Laurie pocketed the phone, a satisfied grin on his ruddy face. 'You'll get real coffee over at Esme's, a cut above my Blend 43.'

After lunch and before he began clearing out the front sitting room ready to paint, Hamish forced himself do something he'd been putting off for a long time. The thought of doing it now knotted up his insides and made his palms sweat. But it was time.

He took out his wallet and flicked through until he found the tattered business card he knew was in there; had been for about five years. *Lenard Schiller, Psychologist*, followed by a mobile phone number and an email address. No website or social media. Hamish knew this because he'd checked every now and then over the years.

Way back, when he'd done work servicing diesel generators and the likes for an outback earthmoving company, he'd often overnight in one of the construction fly camps. One evening he'd been chatting with the company medic, who was also the safety officer. He couldn't remember what their conversation had been about except that she'd sought him out in the mess the following morning at breakfast and handed him this card. She'd winked and said, 'His books are closed but mention my name and I reckon he'll open them for you.'

Five years was a long time. That Lenard Schiller was out there some place practising as a psychologist was a long shot. That his contact details had remained the same after five years was an even longer shot. Hamish picked up his phone and dialled the number on the card.

★ ★ ★

Hamish was shifting furniture into the middle of the sitting room when Ruth knocked on the front door. With the curtains gone and the Holland blind pulled up as far as it would go, he'd watched her walk up the driveway carrying an insulated shopping bag.

'I've been baking for the cafe,' she said when he opened the screen door. 'Pecan pie. I thought you might like a piece for afternoon tea.' She sounded hesitant.

'A man would be a fool to say no to a piece of your pecan pie. Come in. I'll put the kettle on.'

She paused at the sitting room door and scanned the chaos within. 'You're prepping ready to paint? Somewhere I have a stack of old sheets I've used to cover furniture when I've painted. You can borrow them if you like.'

They went through to the kitchen. 'Ah, so you've bought yourself a coffee machine,' Ruth said, eyeing the compact appliance on the cupboard and the rack of coffee pods beside it. 'I guess we won't be seeing you in the cafe anymore.'

Hamish shrugged and took the kettle to the sink to fill. 'An impulse buy,' he said. 'I was in Port Pirie Saturday morning on my way home and they were on special.'

Ruth smiled but Hamish noticed that it didn't quite reach her blue eyes. 'You don't have to explain to me,' she said. 'After all, Rosie's is only open five days a week and coffee is a seven-day-a-week addiction.'

'So, what'll it be? Tea or coffee?'

'Tea, please.' She put the bag on the table and lifted out the pecan pie. 'A piece each for now and two for you for later.' She held up a jar of whipped cream.

'You spoil me,' he said.

'It's my way of attempting to put things right.'

He opened his mouth to protest but her serious expression stopped him.

'Let me finish. I defended the way I'd behaved but I didn't apologise for my part in the misunderstanding. I'm sorry, Hamish. My life has been devoid of close friends for so long I've forgotten how to be such a friend.'

The kettle boiled and switched itself off. Hamish ignored it. 'I don't think that's entirely correct. I'm a bit out of practice in the friendship department myself. And I have baggage, lots of it.'

'We're in our seventh decade, Hamish. No-one gets this far in life without accumulating baggage, but time is running out and we shouldn't waste another moment of it. Now, are you going to make that tea? And do you want whipped cream with your pie?'

He watched her collect two plates from the cupboard and add a generous dollop of cream to each slice of pie. He made the drinks. They sat outside and had afternoon tea. Ruth brought him up to date with her progress towards getting the cafe on the market.

'The hardest part will be telling the staff. They'll all be worried about their jobs, naturally,' she said. 'I've got no idea how the community will react. I don't know if I should care about that or not.'

'Not something you can control, Ruth, so I wouldn't worry about it at all. I know one person at least who'll fully support you. People notice how hard you work.'

'And who would that one person be?'

'Laurie—and me, so really that's two.'

'He said you were mowing his lawn and seeing to a few jobs. That was decent of you.'

'Not especially. He's helped me out a lot and that's probably added to doing his knee in.'

'Not to mention mopping my floors. But he says helping us lifts his spirits. Swings and roundabouts.'

On her way out, Ruth said, 'Come by and pick up the old sheets whenever you like. I'd offer to drop them off but my car's kaput again. Gordon took it away earlier.'

'But didn't you buy a new battery?'

'Turns out it wasn't the battery after all. Earth leakage or some such thing, or so Gordon thinks. Let's hope he'll be able find what's wrong and fix it. Expeditiously and economically.'

'Fast and cheap?' Hamish folded his arms and frowned. 'If it is earth leakage it could take a bit for your mechanic to locate and isolate the problem. Depends how good he is. You might end up needing an auto electrician.'

'That all sounds like wonderful news, not to mention expensive,' Ruth said, with a familiar hint of sarcasm.

'If he's competent at what he does, he'll sort it, no problems.'

'One can only hope,' she said.

It was on the tip of Hamish's tongue to offer her the use of his ute if the need arose, but he kept silent. The last thing he wanted was for her to think he was out to rescue her again.

42

Ruth

I procrastinated. There was no other word for it. Bryan had given me the agency agreement but I hadn't signed it yet. I'd thought he'd been joking when he'd offered to post it, but no. 'People will speculate enough as it is,' he'd said, 'without them seeing me hand you a large envelope when I come in for my morning coffee. No need for them to get a head start before you've signed on the dotted line.'

We'd compromised and he'd slid the plain white envelope under the cafe door on Monday afternoon. The document was languishing on the bedside cupboard. I'd read and re-read it while I'd been lying in bed at night and then wondered why I hadn't slept well.

I desperately wanted to not procrastinate any longer, nevertheless signing was a huge step for me to take. Rosie's Cafe had been my focus for over five years. Every ounce of energy had been channelled into making it a profitable business, one I'd built from the ground up. How would I fill my days without the cafe? Who would I be when I stopped being Ruth from Rosie's Cafe? No longer a successful business owner and employer? Extracting myself was shaping up to be as big an upheaval to my life as making the original seachange had been.

Only now I was five years older and weary along with it. Considering all this made my dithering explainable and understandable, if only to myself.

Life went on. Customers still wanted warm muffins with their morning coffee. Audrey Franco found something else to moan about and the hospital admin girls both went down with Covid. Elliot did need new prescription glasses but his teeth were in good shape. My headaches had eased somewhat. Managing the stressors in my life by getting more exercise and eating a healthier diet was bound to be helping. There'd been no news from Gordon about the car and the carport remained empty. He'd had the station wagon for almost a week and because days could pass without me using it I kept forgetting to check on its progress. I'd see the empty carport when I went outside to peg a load of washing on the line or squirt some water on the long-suffering plants and it'd prompt me ring. Unfortunately, my forays into the backyard were always after five thirty when he'd already closed for the day.

Thursday, after Liz had left for the day, I was clearing tables when a young woman came into the cafe with a toddler in tow. She hovered by the door, eyes darting around the room, finally settling on the menu. She looked familiar, but then when you owned a cafe in a small country town, most people who came through the door looked familiar. Giving her time to decide, I carried on through to the kitchen with a tray full of dirty dishes. When I returned to the counter, wiping my hands on a towel, she hadn't moved. The toddler was crawling around under table eight, weaving between the chair legs, giggling.

'Something I can get you?' I said. 'I've turned off the grill but I can zap a slice of quiche or toast a sandwich, if you're after hot food.'

'Are you Ruth?' she said.

'I am.' I was beginning to suspect she wasn't here about food or drink. I came around the counter, conscious that the two old biddies sipping Lady Grey at table four were all ears. 'How can I help you?'

She licked her lips, crossed her arms and said, 'I'm a friend of Angie Daniels and she said—'

'Oh, are you Joanne?'

'Yes! It's taken me this long to drum up the courage to come in, I thought you would have forgotten.'

If the old biddies leaned much further forward in their seats trying to eavesdrop they'd topple over onto the floor, face first. I grabbed a paper serviette and jotted down my mobile number.

'Here,' I said and handed it to her. 'I can't leave the cafe now but I close at four. Ring me and we'll work out something.'

She clutched the flimsy serviette and nodded vigorously. 'Thank you so much,' she said. The toddler crawled out from under the table, as if he'd sensed his mother was on the move again. I beamed at the old biddies and went back to work.

I was mopping the floors when the phone rang. It was after four and Mia was refilling the dog bowl we kept outside. When I answered the call, Joanne told me she could come around on Saturday afternoon.

'What's the occasion?' I said. No answer. 'I'm not prying, Joanne. It'll give me a bit of an idea what clothes might be suitable.'

'Oh, okay. It's an … er … family thing. I need to look really, really good.'

'Day? Night? Formal? Smart casual?'

'Er … I dunno … just something that makes me look good?'

'Right. We can start there. I'll see you Saturday.' Bemused, I went back to the mopping. Going on the skin-tight leggings and baggy T-shirt she'd been wearing when she'd come into the cafe earlier, Joanne's fashion sense and style was likely similar to Angie's: practical and economical. Nothing wrong with that, for most occasions.

Mia finished at five. She'd topped up the sandwich-filling containers, restocked fridges and the sugars, sweeteners and condiments on the tables. I'd recently changed serviette brands and the new ones weren't as robust, but they were cheaper. Of late, every time I phoned through an order the total was more than the previous one, for basically the same items. If wholesale prices kept increasing I'd have to consider putting my prices up. Not a happy thought. Over five years I'd only made one across-the-board price increase. Coffee was different. The prices went up at least annually and there'd always be a backlash from a handful of customers.

It was nearly six when I turned off lights and went through to the flat. The days were rapidly shortening. The weekend after next would see the end of daylight saving. It wouldn't be long before soup was back on the menu every day. When I checked my phone there were two new voice messages: one from Bryan and the other from Gordon. Bryan wanted to know when I was going to sign the agency agreement and Gordon apologised for not getting back to me sooner about the car. He mentioned the words *auto electrician*, and I shuddered.

A cold, crisp glass of white wine was the ideal accompaniment to the Thai-style fish cakes with sweet chilli sauce I sampled for dinner. They were next week's lunch special and had arrived frozen from the wholesaler. The second glass of wine went down too easily. By eight thirty I was yawning and struggling to keep my eyes open in front of the television. I should have gone to bed.

The phone rang. It was on charge in the kitchen. I leaped off the couch to answer it and almost tripped over my feet.

'You sound as if you've been running,' Hamish said after we'd said hello. He was in Adelaide.

'Just getting up off the couch. I think my doctor might be right, I do need to get more exercise. What's happening?'

'Nothing of any real consequence. Had coffee this afternoon with Cate, my favourite niece. I have another appointment tomorrow afternoon and then I'll drive back.'

He didn't offer any more about what the appointments were and I told myself to be satisfied with that. I chattered on about Laurie's visit to inform me the physio had given him the all clear to start doing the floors again, Gordon's glacial progress with my car and whatever else popped into my head.

He cut across my prattle with, 'Have you signed the agency agreement yet?'

I blew out a breath and flopped back onto the couch. 'No, not yet.'

'Ruth, Rosie's is never going to sell unless you put it on the market.'

'I know, I know …'

'Have you changed your mind?'

'Bryan asked me the same thing. And like I said to him, no, I haven't changed my mind. There is no other choice than to sell, whether it's now or next year or the year after. The only difference is I'll be *totally* exhausted by then.'

'It's only the agency agreement, Ruth, you can still change your mind. What's really holding you back?'

Ridiculously, tears welled in my eyes. I scraped at them with the back of my hand.

'Ruth?' he said. 'What's wrong?'

'It's hard to let go, Hamish. I started Rosie's from nothing more than an idea and a dusty old building. And what am I letting go of it all for? It's not like I'm selling up because I want to go off travelling or because I want to buy a unit in a retirement village—not that I can ever see myself wanting that. Besides, I can't afford to retire yet and I haven't got a clue what I'll do to fill in my days when I don't have the cafe.'

I heard a door slam at his end, then voices followed by the tinkle of a woman's laughter.

'I've gotta go, Ruth,' Hamish said. 'Sorry. Can we talk more when I get back?'

'Sure,' I said, nonplussed, pushing myself upright on the couch. A woman's laughter. One of Hamish's appointments? I was intrigued. And a tiny bit agitated.

I opened my mouth to ask if everything was all right, but he'd already gone.

★ ★ ★

The golf ladies filed in, all ten of them, after eleven the following morning. They were in high spirits, with windblown hair and rosy cheeks. They dragged tables six and seven together and promptly ordered up a storm. I was on my own and found myself dithering about what to do first. Not like me at all. I stopped, took several slow breaths and began with the coffees, teas and cold drinks.

What would be a better arrangement, I decided as I ground coffee beans, frothed milk and mixed chai lattes, was if Erin worked at the end of the week and the short-shift girls did Tuesday and Wednesday, the slower days. Most people didn't mind waiting a bit, but only until they deemed they'd waited long enough. My aim for the cafe had always been to have something on the table in front of the customer within five minutes of them ordering, even if it was only cutlery or a glass of water. Today's influx made that impossible.

And then Liz was late. Only by five minutes, but when you have a full house with customers waiting, every minute counted.

When two o'clock came, Liz and I were in the kitchen. She'd barely cracked a smile all shift and was making moves to leave. 'Would you mind staying on for another half an hour?' I said, taking in the stacks of dirty dishes, the overflowing bin and the depleted supplies.

She wrinkled her nose. 'Ordinarily I would, but I'm off to the hairdresser. Sorry, Ruth.'

Rarely had I heard a more insincere apology. 'All right, but before you leave, would you be prepared to work Tuesdays and Wednesdays instead of this end of the week, if the others were willing? I have Erin for more hours and Thursdays and Fridays are the busier days.'

'Can't she work more days? Allie used to. And what about Lorna?'

'Lorna's mum isn't that well and Erin can only work two days at this stage.' My stomach clenched. Why was I explaining to her? She worked five hours a fortnight. She could either agree to what I'd asked or not. Or at least agree to think about it. 'It was just a thought, Liz. I haven't mentioned it to any of the others.'

Her mouth pinched up like a prune. 'There used to be three of us over lunch, Ruth. Today was ridiculous. Maybe you just need to bite the bullet and employ another casual.'

Her words were like a slap. 'Maybe I do,' I said, stretching my lips into the parody of a smile. 'But that is my decision.'

Her eyebrows lifted, only a fraction and I would have missed it if I hadn't been watching closely.

'I'll think about your suggestion, that's all I can promise,' she said. 'And I'll mention it to Gayle, if you like.'

'I'd rather you didn't. Let me talk to Erin first.' I knew full well she'd be scrolling through to Gayle's number before she was out the door. Out of all my employees, I liked Liz the least. She was a reasonable worker and relatively reliable—if everything went her way. Gayle was much more amenable. A more astute employer would have talked to her first. I could have kicked myself. I'd spectacularly sabotaged the idea before it had gained any traction. This is what happened when you opened your mouth before you'd thought things through.

There was a noisy throat-clearing out at the counter. Why people didn't ring the bell …

'I'd better get that,' I said. 'See you tomorrow. Don't keep the hairdresser waiting.' I sidestepped Liz and scuttled out to serve.

I had to practically shoo the last customer out the door at four o'clock and it was almost dark when I finished up and went through to the flat, back aching and feet burning. How many *more* times would I have to do all of this?

Before I was sidetracked, I fetched the agency agreement from the bedside cupboard and put it on the kitchen table with a pen alongside it.

When I fell into bed just before ten, I remembered that I hadn't made my daily call to Elliot.

★ ★ ★

Hamish came into the cafe for breakfast first thing Saturday morning.

'You look mighty pleased with yourself,' I said when I delivered his coffee. 'Good trip to Adelaide?'

'Productive,' he said. 'You look buggered.'

I glanced around. The closest ears were at table one. I leaned in and said in a hushed voice, 'Would you mind coming around later this afternoon? I need someone to witness my signature on a document.'

'What time?'

'Five?'

'Done,' he said. 'So you've decided to go ahead?'

'There was never any question about that. I just needed time to get my head around it. Even now—' The front door opened and a group of four regulars came in. It'd be full breakfasts all round. 'See you at five and thanks,' I said and whizzed off.

Mia was already at the coffee machine and Suzie would start at ten. Two staff—luxury. As much as I hated to admit it, Liz was right: I needed more help. Forget trying to save money on wages. Erin had been working for a fortnight and she was coming along nicely. She was certainly no dynamo but she'd quickly cottoned on to the routine and what needed to be done. The customers liked her. The same couldn't always be said of Liz.

Joanne came to the flat at three thirty like we'd arranged, only it'd completely slipped my mind until she tapped on the sliding door. And I hadn't sorted through my wardrobe for garments that might be suitable for her special occasion, as I'd promised I would.

'I can come back another day,' she said when I apologised. The way she shuffled her thong-clad feet and worried at the hem of her T-shirt, I knew she'd bolt if I said yes and I wouldn't see her again. That would be such a shame.

I invited her inside. 'Let's look together,' I said. 'When you get home you'll need to air whatever it is you choose. The clothes have been shut in the wardrobe and they get a stale smell about them, even though they're clean.'

'Like an op shop,' she said.

'Sort of.'

An hour later we'd settled on a pair of tailored black linen-mix trousers and an emerald-green silk shirt. She spun slowly in front of the full-length mirror, admiring her svelte silhouette.

'They fit as if they were made for you,' I said. 'Classic. An outfit like that is always in fashion. You can borrow the shoes as well, if you like.' I'd rooted out a pair of patent black court shoes for her to try on with the trousers.

'I'm okay for shoes, thanks. These are tight and they pinch a bit.'

Before she left with the outfit stowed in a plastic garment bag, we talked about how she might wear her hair on the day. 'And makeup?' I said. 'Do you wear much?'

'Nope, only lip gloss sometimes. Sunblock. Decent makeup is expensive. Do you think I should I wear more?' Her eyebrows knitted together with concern.

'No! You have lovely clear skin. Stick with whatever you're comfortable with.' She hadn't given me any more details about the occasion except that it was a week away, it was important and she was very nervous about it. 'Scared shitless' were her words.

I'd barely seen her out, insisting she didn't need to get the clothes dry-cleaned afterwards, that I'd see to them, when Hamish arrived. He drove his ute into my empty carport.

'Who was that?' he said.

I spread my arms and said, 'Welcome to Ruth's Community Wardrobe.'

'Say what?'

'Her name is Joanne, she doesn't have much and I've loaned her an outfit to wear for a special occasion she has coming up.'

'Very generous and community spirited of you.'

'I've got way too many clothes that I don't wear anymore but they're too good for the op shop. No way am I having the likes of Audrey Franco and Daphne Russell pawing through my precious cast-offs. I'll have you know, I have clothes I bought when I lived in Paris!'

I laughed at the look on his face.

'You sound pretty chirpy,' he said as he followed me into the flat.

'I have two days off starting now. Today we had a great shift all round. Mia is terrific to work with and Suzie can be fun, when she's not whingeing about whatever drama is currently taking over her life. And after yesterday—'

'What happened yesterday?'

'Just an awful, busy, never-ending day.' I sat at the kitchen table and picked up the pen. 'Thanks for doing this,' I said and signed on the dotted line, right where the iridescent arrow pointed. Then I pushed the document towards him and he sat down and followed suit. When he'd signed, I returned the pages to the envelope. 'Have you got time to stay for a drink? Hot? Cold?'

'Wouldn't say no to a beer,' he said.

I fetched him a beer, poured myself a glass of wine and put out a board with cheese and crackers.

'Now, where were you up to when we were talking on the phone Thursday night? When I had to go?' he said.

'I don't really remember what I was raving on about. Doesn't matter now because I've signed the agreement. I'll personally deliver it to Bryan first thing Monday morning. I don't care who sees me.'

He opened the beer and fiddled with the cap. 'I do get it, Ruth. It's one thing to think about doing something and quite another to actually do it. That takes courage, no matter how much you've convinced yourself it's the correct thing to do.'

Something about the way he said it made me wonder if he was referring to my situation alone. But I needed a break from thinking and talking about selling the cafe so I didn't press the issue. I changed the subject instead. 'How's the renovation coming along? Has your bikie mate come up with any plans yet?'

'Ah, the renovation …' He folded his arms and rested the beer bottle in the crook of his elbow. 'Think I might've got a bit carried away there. I've decided to shelve the idea—for the time being, anyway. Even the cheaper option Jeff gave was way more than I'd ever imagined.'

'Are you disappointed? You seemed intent on making the renovation your project.'

'I was, but then common sense reasserted itself. Seeing as how I've already bought the paint, I'll go ahead and paint the place, see what I can do to smarten up the kitchen and the bathroom, finish tidying up the front and back yards and then put the place on the market.'

'Well, you always were going to sell it. Sensible not to make the same mistake I did and sink all of your savings into it.'

'There's a difference, Ruth. You were passionate about what you wanted back then and you made it happen. It's served you well, until recently. It didn't take much for me to talk myself out of renovating the house, which makes me question whether it was the right decision in the first place.

'So, I'll mark time for a bit. Take it a day at a time. I've got nothing to lose, nowhere else to be at the moment. And there's more than enough to keep me occupied here. I'm even considering a holiday.'

'A holiday? Now there's an idea. The minute this place is off my hands I'm going to Far North Queensland to lie by a swimming pool, read, eat, drink and be waited upon. Trouble is, I might never come back.'

He smiled and held up his empty beer bottle. 'Go again?'

'Why not? Now that I've signed on the dotted line I feel in the mood to celebrate.'

43

Ruth

Bryan was delighted to receive the signed documents first thing Monday morning. When I rang the accountants, they offered to communicate directly with Selina after I'd briefed her.

After lunch I messaged Selina and then walked around to her house so we could talk face to face. She met me at the front door of their newish homestead-style home and we went through to the petitioned-off space in the family room she used as an office. Unlike the house, there was nothing out of place in her tiny corner.

'I'm having a coffee. Can I get you something?' she said on our way through.

'No, thanks.'

She gestured for me to sit down on the same old chrome and red vinyl kitchen chair she'd dragged in every time I'd visited. She made herself comfortable at the desk, picked up her drink and waited expectantly.

When I didn't speak immediately, her brow wrinkled and she said, 'Are you all right, Ruth? You look a bit pale. You're not coming down with something, are you?'

'No, I'm fine,' I said, caught unawares by how nervous I felt. I'd rehearsed what to say on the way over but instead of delivering the carefully prepared speech, I just blurted out, 'I'm going to sell the cafe. I've already signed an agency agreement.'

She nodded slowly, her mouth forming an upside-down U. 'Good for you, Ruth. Let's hope it sells quickly,' she said. 'And I guess you'll need me to prepare the financial statements for the accountant as soon as possible?'

'Yes, please. The person I spoke to advised that you communicate with this person.' I took out the slip of paper on which I'd scrawled the name and mobile number.

'Ah, yes,' she said. 'He's easy to work with. Gets the job done faster than others.' She pinned the slip of paper onto a cork board. 'When will you tell the girls?'

'This week. They'll be concerned about their jobs, which is understandable. All I can say to them is they'll have a job as long as I'm calling the shots.'

'Any new owner would be crazy not to re-employ them, at least when they first take over.'

'Especially if it's a novice like I was. I'd worked in cafes but never owned and operated one.'

'Is the building and flat up for sale along with the business? Do you want out of Cutlers Bay as well as out of the cafe?'

'Ideally, it all goes together: the business, the shop and the flat. That said, I don't know where I'll live if it does. The one thing I am certain about is that I don't want to be Ruth from Rosie's Cafe for any longer than necessary.'

'You'll have to reinvent yourself. How exciting.'

'Reinvent myself? I'll be happy just to rediscover the person I was before Rosie's took over my life. She used to have fun, she didn't have to censor every word she said and she lived a life that wasn't always about work.'

'Totally get what you're saying. I love how my life is now but that doesn't mean I don't look forward to the day when priorities shift and I'm Selina first, before I'm somebody's wife or mother or bookkeeper or general dogsbody.'

Her vehemence made me chuckle. 'Don't ever lose sight of that, Selina. But realistically, there won't be much for me to stay for once Rosie's is gone.'

'Don't underestimate the connections you've made, Ruth. You might be surprised by how many people regard you as a friend.'

'But what would I do if I stayed here? After I've had a holiday, which is non-negotiable. And I'll need a job.'

'You could always work for whoever buys the cafe.'

'Oh no, I *cannot* imagine that. No way! And the last thing a new owner would want is me peering over their shoulder.'

'What about volunteering? The Country Fire Service is always looking for volunteers and so is the ambulance. I know they don't pay anything but you get to know other people and that can lead to a paying job down the track. What else can you do besides run a cafe? Lots of transferrable skills there.'

'Right now my primary goal is to get through each day at a time.' What she said was true, but my brain was in overload. I'd noticed that about getting older: I couldn't keep as many balls in the air at one time, not anymore, no matter how many lists I made and how hard I tried.

When I left Selina's, the afternoon sea breeze was brisk. A line of fluffy white clouds clung to the western horizon. I set off for Gordon's garage. Supposedly, he'd fixed my car. I didn't use it all that much but I didn't like to be without it. The last time I'd spoken to Elliot, he'd given no indication he was planning to drive to Cutlers Bay any time soon and that meant I'd be visiting him on my next days off. Who knew how many more trips I'd make up and down that road? Lana hadn't called again and I took that as a positive; either

Elliot had stopped bothering her or she'd called the police when he had.

Gordon apologised profusely that it'd taken him a week to fix what he described as 'a relatively minor problem'. Suffice to say, the invoice he delivered along with the car was far from 'relatively minor'. Back at the flat I hosed the dust off the station wagon before I went inside and rechecked the wholesaler's order and phoned it through. Then I baked several slabs of pasty slice for the coming week. The meat and vegetable filling was seasoned with Mum's secret mix of herbs and spices and the fragrant aroma soon filled the cafe kitchen. Pasty slice was an autumn and winter favourite, along with homemade tomato sauce. By seven pm, I was ready to sit down with a cup of tea and put my feet up. In the interests of quality control I sampled a generous chunk of pasty slice and gave myself ten out of ten.

★ ★ ★

Erin baulked at my suggestion she change her shifts to Thursday and Friday. 'Liam is only just getting used to me not being there to get his lunch on Tuesdays and Wednesdays!'

Poor Liam … I remembered a time when employees were always on the lookout for more hours and you'd bend over backwards to do whatever your employer asked.

'You don't even want to think about it?' I said. 'Ask Liam if he minds? He could always come to the cafe for lunch.'

She screwed up her face. 'Nah, I don't think so. I get why you want me to change, but I'd rather leave things the way they are, if you don't mind. After all, this is only my third week.'

'Fair enough,' I said. It was the end of her shift. She slung her bulky handbag, a designer rip-off, over her shoulder. It was now or never. I took a deep breath. 'Oh, and by the way, Erin, Rosie's Cafe will be going up for sale in the next few weeks.'

Her cupid's-bow mouth formed a perfect O. 'You know, the clothes boutique took two years to sell and then the new owner went bust in less than a year,' she said in a breathy tone, a portend of doom.

I almost rolled my eyes, except that she might turn out to be right. 'Oh, well, none of us know what the future holds. Probably just as well.'

'But what will happen to my job?'

'Not for me to say, except that you'll all keep your hours while Rosie's still belongs to me.'

An hour or so later, Mia paused the mopping for a moment while I told her. 'Wait until I tell Mum. I wish she could afford to buy the cafe,' she said and went back to the task with renewed vigour.

Allie was knocking on the kitchen door at seventeen minutes past five. 'Ruth!' she said and burst through the door. 'Why didn't you tell me you were thinking of selling up? Not that you had to and I couldn't afford to buy it even in my wildest dreams.'

Mia had done well. The community grapevine was off and running. 'Come in, Allie.'

Allie sized me up. 'Now, you're sure about this, Ruth? It's all very sudden,' she said, sounding a lot like my mother.

'Not as sudden as you might think. Believe it or not, I was about to warn you I was seriously considering it when you handed in your resignation. After that there was no reason to tell you.'

She propped herself against the handbasin and folded her arms. 'It was Graham Wurst retiring, wasn't it? That's when I noticed a change in you. And then Theo died and Hamish came along.'

'What's Hamish got to do with any of it?'

She lifted a shoulder and let it drop. 'The chance of a life after Rosie's Cafe?'

'Hamish and I have become friends, that's all. He'll move on when he's fixed up his parents' place and it sells, which I think it will. It's a nice old place, lots of character, big block, plenty of potential. And who knows where I'll end up?'

Allie didn't comment, although she smiled as if she knew something I didn't.

I kept at my closing-up duties otherwise I'd never get home. 'I'd offer you a coffee only the machine's already done.'

'Thanks, but I was on my way to the supermarket when I got Mia's message.' She yawned and I noticed how tired she looked.

'Has the job improved?'

'A fraction. I'm beginning to feel less of an outsider. But five early morning starts in a row, week in, week out … I'm knackered by eight and in bed by nine. On weekends all I do is cook, clean, wash and iron and get everything ready for the next week.'

'You're not the first working woman to say that and you won't be the last. How's Brett's back coming along?'

'Slowly. Unfortunately, Leon had to give the job to someone else, not that I blame him. But there's not a lot of work to be found in a small town at the best of times and even less for a bloke with a bad back. At least Brett's helping out around the house a bit now. I think Cody prefers his cooking to mine.'

'How is Cody?'

'Good, for a teenage boy,' she said, her mouth a flat line. 'Brett can be tough on him. Our parenting styles are very different.' She closed her eyes as she gave a tiny shake of her head. 'He might be Cody's father but he hasn't been around much and it was only ever for the good times. Cody resents it if Brett tells him off and tells him how he should behave. I might just resent it a bit myself.'

'And I guess there's always a tension because Brett might up and leave any day.'

'That too,' Allie said. 'Cody's even thrown that in his father's face a couple of times when Brett's been laying down the law.'

'Tricky.'

'Part of me wishes he would just go. Life would be so much easier.

But then I feel guilty, because he is their father and once upon a time I loved him enough to marry him and have children with him.'

That would be the trickiest part of it all to my way of thinking. We surprised ourselves and hugged before Allie left. Was this one of the connections Selina had been talking about?

'If I thought it'd make any difference, I'd pray that the business sells in the first week it goes on the market,' Allie said.

When the door in the service lane closed after her, I stopped in my tracks: she hadn't asked me if I would stay in Cutlers Bay after the cafe sold.

44

Hamish

Esme McCann, Laurie's next-door neighbour, was effusive in her praise of the yard work Hamish did for her. So much so that, without his permission, she referred him to a friend, another older woman in need of an able-bodied person to mow lawns and clip hedges. Apparently, the friend had been a client of Chris Lehman's but not long enough to be deemed long term. Hamish tried to explain to Esme that he was retired, not looking for work and that he'd done her yard as a favour to Laurie. 'I don't have my own equipment or insurance or a way of billing people,' he said.

'Pfft,' Esme said, with a dismissive flick of her wrist. 'Take the cash. Everybody else does. I'll have you back again in a flash. Laurie shouldn't be tackling lawns anymore, not with that knee, and Marg Lehman said Chris goes into hospital next week for his first knee replacement. He'll be out of commission for weeks and that's if it goes well.'

In the end, more to get away than anything, Hamish agreed to mow her friend's lawns and trim her hedges. 'But, please, do not pass my name and mobile number onto anyone else.'

'But why not?' Esme said. 'You're very capable and you could have all the work you wanted. I could give you three names right now.'

'That's the thing. As I've said, I don't necessarily want the work.'

He left her thankful but crestfallen. When he returned Laurie's whipper snipper, he repeated the exchange.

Laurie snuffed out a laugh. 'I'd be willing to bet that Chris Lehman would sell you his outfit.'

Hamish threw his hands into the air. 'Why would I want to buy Chris Lehman's outfit? Apart from the fact that the ute's ancient and needs a new set of rings, and the trailer's riddled with rust—and that's probably just for starters.'

Laurie's eyes narrowed. 'Who said?'

'Mate, no-one needs to *say*, it's obvious when he drives past in a cloud of blue smoke. And the ride-on mower he carts around in the trailer has seen better days.'

'Haven't we all,' Laurie grumbled. 'But a bloke looking for work could do a lot worse.'

'Why all of a sudden does everyone think I'm looking for work?'

'Wishful thinking, I reckon. And you're good at it. There're a lot of elderly folk in this town who barely cope with their yards and home maintenance and they'll cope a lot less as the months and years pass. But they should be able stay in their own homes until the end, if that's what they want, and not have the place fall down around their ears. Me being one of them.'

Is that how it'd been for Theo? Had his dad managed less and less until he could see the time fast approaching when he wouldn't manage at all? Had he been too proud to ask for help? Money too tight to afford it? The rundown state of the house and yard and the meagre savings in Theo's bank account attested to just that.

Hamish felt a familiar squeeze of remorse. The situation could have—*should have*—been different.

'Aren't there some kind of assistance packages old folk can get from the government?'

Laurie snorted. 'You mean aged-care packages? Doesn't matter how many of them the government gives out, if there're no able-bodied people to do the work, they're a complete waste of time.' They traversed the short distance to the back verandah. 'Time for a cuppa before you head off?'

'Yeah, a quick one. The cans of paint beckon.'

On the way home, Hamish stopped off at Rosie's to buy lunch and say hello to Ruth. He parked outside the hardware shop and crossed the road. The cafe's door squealed, heralding his entry, and he was embraced by the warm and fragrant atmosphere of the cafe. A plump, fresh-faced young woman he hadn't met before delivered food to table five. As usual, Ruth was busy behind the coffee machine.

Her face lit up when she saw him. 'Hamish! Table three is free.'

'I'm after some lunch—takeaway if you don't mind—and I just had a brew with Laurie.'

She skilfully placed brimming cups onto their waiting saucers. 'How is he? The knee? He's having a go at the floor this arvo, but only if he's okay.'

'He's not limping anymore.' Hamish moved aside to let the young woman collect the prepared drinks.

'Erin, the two caps are table four, that one there is a weak one for the lady with the spotted top and the tea is for table two,' Ruth said.

Erin nodded and carefully picked up the cappuccinos, the pink tip of her tongue firmly gripping her top lip.

'I'm hoping speed will come with confidence. It's only day six,' I whispered when Erin had moved off to inch her way towards table four. 'Pasty slice is on today, with homemade tomato sauce.'

'If that's what smells so good, I'll have it.'

'Do you want it hot, or will you heat it at home?'

Hamish scanned the cafe. 'Bugger it,' he said. 'I'll have it here.' He glanced into the cake cabinet. 'And a piece of apple pie … and coffee.'

'Cream, ice cream or both with the apple pie?'

'Guess.'

'Hmm …' Her head tilted to one side. 'Ice cream.'

'Bingo!' he said and her eyes sparkled with amusement.

He made his way to table three. The woman in the spotted top with the weak cappuccino at table four stared at him every step of the way. He smiled and nodded. She turned away, her face the colour of a tomato.

While he waited he took in the cafe, every detail from its welcoming atmosphere to the simplicity of the decor. Hard to imagine anyone other than Ruth standing at the coffee machine. Would he patronise the place when it belonged to someone else? If they proved as formidable a barista as Ruth then of course he would. But only for takeaway.

On his way out, his stomach full, he stopped at the counter. 'I haven't paid yet,' he said to Erin.

'Yes, he has,' Ruth called from the servery window.

Erin's head swivelled from Hamish to Ruth and back again.

Hamish held up his hand. 'Don't worry, Erin, let me sort this one out.' He stepped around the counter and through to the kitchen.

Ruth was at the fryer shaking off hot chips. 'You haven't billed me yet for the alley,' she said without turning from her task.

'It was a gift, Ruth, my time was a gift. I wanted to do it for you.'

'Your time and your expertise. Not just anyone could have constructed that.'

'I enjoy working with my hands and it was a challenge.'

'Okay,' she said and glanced over her shoulder at him. 'Thank you. Now I'm going to show my appreciation by feeding you, free of charge, and it's something I'm good at.' She scooped chips into a bowl and sprinkled them with salt. She spun around, slid the bowl onto the servery window and tapped the bell for Erin to collect it then glanced at the next order. The oven timer binged. She grabbed a tea towel and went to open the oven.

He threw up his hands. 'All right, you win. I won't pay. By the way, the pasty slice was the best I've ever tasted. But you didn't bake the apple pie, did you?'

'No.' She paused long enough to look at him. 'Was it okay?'

'Yep. The average punter mightn't notice the difference, but I did.'

'Get away with you,' she said, grinning, and flicked him with the corner of the tea towel.

He laughed and let himself out the kitchen door.

45

Hamish

Hamish came home after a satisfactory eighteen holes of golf to find an unknown bright-blue SUV parked in his driveway. Even on a grey day such as it was, the car glowed with the patina of a new vehicle. Irritated, he parked on the street and went to investigate. The interior was as pristine as the exterior and gave no clues as to who the owner was. The acrid smell of a cooling engine told him it hadn't been parked there for long. He circled the house and thought it odd when he found no sign of anyone. He let himself in through the back door and was immediately assailed by the aroma of freshly brewed coffee.

'Natalie,' he said under his breath, much as he would a curse. And there she was sitting at *his* kitchen table, drinking *his* coffee and flicking through *his* Saturday *Advertiser* even before he'd had a chance to read it. Irritation morphed into indignation. 'What the hell do you think you're doing in here?'

'Hamish,' she said. 'And hello to you too.' She stood, went to the coffee machine, selected two more pods and refilled her coffee mug. 'Can I get you one?'

'How did you get inside?'

'I had a key. Mum and Dad had it cut for me way back.'

'But this isn't Mum and Dad's house anymore. It belongs to me. You've had your share and I presume the vehicle blocking up *my* driveway was purchased with some of that share.'

'You presumed right. She's a beauty, isn't she? I've never had a new car before. Pete's spewing because I haven't let him drive it yet. Where have you been?'

'Golf.' Hamish dropped his car keys onto the kitchen table and then poured himself a glass of water, drinking it down in one gulp.

Nat sipped her coffee and watched him. 'When did you start playing *golf,* the game of the rich?'

'What do you want, Nat?' he said, wiping his mouth with the back of his hand.

'Who said I wanted anything? I'm allowed to take my new car for a spin, visit my brother, see what he's done to our parents' home. And you have been busy, but I would have chosen a different colour paint for the interior. Cate said you were in town recently and you met her for coffee.'

Hamish blinked at the abrupt change of subject. 'I did and your name didn't come up, not once.'

Nat's mouth hardened. 'Why did I even bother driving out here to see you?'

'I give up. Why did you bother? You gave me the impression Cutlers Bay was the last place you'd ever visit voluntarily.'

'I was curious. And I thought you might have been glad to see a familiar face, stuck out here in the sticks.'

'I choose to be here, Nat. There's a difference.' He picked a banana out of the fruit bowl, peeled it and ate it in five bites, bracing himself for a comeback along the lines of, *A pity you didn't choose to be here more often when Mum and Dad were alive.*

But she left him gaping when she said, in a more conciliatory tone, 'The skylight looks great, makes a huge difference to the room. And thanks for delivering those boxes of Mum's odds and ends. I wouldn't have bothered with it otherwise.'

She moved away from where she'd been standing to gaze out the kitchen window, freeing up the coffee machine. The mug he'd used earlier for his first coffee of the day was upturned on the sink. He grabbed it and made himself coffee.

With her back to him, she said, 'The backyard is huge. Have you ever considered extending? You could add a family room and update the wet areas. With a bit of money, the place could be turned into a more modern home, big enough for a family.' Then she ruined it when she glanced over her shoulder and added, 'And you've got the money,' in the same snarky tone she used whenever she mentioned him and money in the same sentence. He'd been about to say that yes, he had considered it but after that salvo he ignored her.

Hamish sat down and swivelled the open newspaper so he could read it. Maybe she'd finish her coffee and go if he didn't talk to her. But no, she sat down again.

'How do you think life would have panned out for us if Jonathon hadn't been killed that day?' she said and he was grateful he was already seated. 'Do you think we should talk about it, Hamish?'

The vulnerability in her voice and expression caught him totally off guard. 'Do you *want* to talk about it?' he said, not certain that he did.

She leaned back in the chair and folded her arms. 'No, but that's not the question. The question is, *should we*? And why haven't we talked about it ever before? It's as if we never had a brother.'

'You'll get no contradiction from me,' he said and mirrored her posture. 'When I was sorting through stuff, I found a few photos of Jonathon in an old album on the bookshelf.'

'Yeah, Mum used to take them out to look at them when Dad wasn't around. She'd always end up crying and I wouldn't know what to do except cry myself. Now that I'm a mother and a grandmother I understand that what I should have done was hug her and not aggravate her by telling Dad.'

'You told Dad?' he said in a hushed voice because he didn't want to believe what she'd said.

Her silence was confirmation enough.

'What did he do?'

'He'd get angry, tell her that looking at the photos would only make her sad, wouldn't bring him back. He said we had to move on, move past it. I'm sure if he could have found the photos in the early days he would have destroyed them, but she always hid them. And I know I was a bitch for telling him she looked at them but I would *never* have let on where they were.'

'But they were just there, in the photo album with all the other photos of us as kids.'

'She used to hide them, back then.'

'Come to think of it, there aren't many photos that were taken after Jonathon died and they're only of you.'

'You left,' she said, an accusation not an observation.

'Not for a year and what was there to stay for?'

'Me. The place was like a morgue, but without the body because we weren't allowed to mention him. I don't remember hearing Mum ever laugh again, not until she began to lose her mind. And then she laughed at anything, funny or not.'

'You always were Daddy's girl, you didn't need me around. My presence did nothing but remind him of the son he'd lost. Or so he told me, in a dozen different ways.'

'He mellowed with age, Hamish. I won't say he was ever easy, because he wasn't. And after Mum's dementia was diagnosed, it was a bit like a return to the bad old days. He was always angry.'

'I know … I wasn't around often, but often enough. I don't think he knew how to deal with any of it, more so with Mum, because she was still alive and the loss was gradual, so he clung on to his anger.' Hamish had thought often about what Mia had said his father's reaction had been whenever she and Cody had brought his mum home from her wanderings. 'Have you ever wondered if all the accumulated stress from losing Jonathon and then not being able to grieve the way she should have been allowed to contributed to her getting dementia?'

Nat didn't answer.

Hamish glanced her way. She was frowning and picking at her fingernails. 'No, is the honest answer,' she said eventually. 'But now that you've put it out there, I wonder if that's what Dad thought? And if he did, imagine his guilt? No wonder he was always angry.'

'So what he did, taking his own life, might not have been only about being diagnosed with an incurable disease. Is that what we're saying here?'

Nat laughed, a hollow sound. 'How could we ever know? Perhaps? He's not here to ask. All I do know is that none of it is black and white, is it? And we should have talked about Jonathon a long time ago, Hamish. We should have insisted that as a family we talked openly about him and what happened. If we had, it might have saved what was left of the family and saved me a fortune in therapy sessions.' She stood, took her mug to the sink and washed it. 'I'll go.'

'Have lunch before you do,' he said, much to his own surprise. 'I can make a sandwich.'

'Thanks, but no thanks. I'd probably choke on it. Plus I don't know for how much longer I'll be able to keep my bitchy self at bay.'

When he went to stand she put a firm hand on his shoulder and said, 'Don't get up. I'll see myself out, via the loo. My house key is on the cupboard.'

He did as she said and stayed put. He waited for the sound of the toilet flushing. Then he listened for the slam of the front door, followed by the crunch of car tyres on the gravel driveway. He felt stunned and more than a little bit sad.

46

Ruth

I arrived at East Terrace right on five on Saturday afternoon, as per our arrangement. Hamish's bemused expression when he answered my knock hinted that me coming for a meal had slipped his mind.

'Am I early?' I said, when he pushed open the screen door for me to enter.

He glanced down at his paint-splattered hands and T-shirt. 'No, time got away from me. Sorry.' He sounded distracted, almost in a daze. 'Give me ten minutes to shower and change. The salad stuff's in the fridge if you want to make a start. Spuds are in the cupboard under the sink.'

I had a moment's déjà vu when he came into the kitchen a while later, smelling of soap and towel-drying his hair. I was at the sink peeling potatoes. I put down the knife and wiped my hands on the tea towel tied around my waist in lieu of an apron. 'Better now?'

'Much better, thanks,' he said. 'Busy day?'

'Not especially. Are you all right? You seem a bit preoccupied. Or is it the paint fumes?'

He shrugged and flung the towel over the back of a chair. 'Natalie came, just showed up out of the blue,' he said, curling his top lip. 'Wanted to brag about her new car and talk about Jonathon.'

'Your brother?'

'It was a Nat I've never encountered before. She was actually quite civil, after a bumpy start.' He went to the fridge and grabbed a beer, holding up a bottle of wine. I nodded and took down a glass. He filled it with riesling. 'Until today, the subject of Jonathon has always been taboo.'

'Did you ask her?'

'Ask her what?'

'If she saw the accident happen.'

'No, I didn't. But she did admit that she's been having therapy. She accused me of deserting her back then.'

'How so?'

'I suppose I did. Virtually the day I turned sixteen, I left home to start an apprenticeship and I'll confess I didn't give my younger sister more than a passing thought. I couldn't wait to get out of there. Nat described it perfectly when she said "the place was like a morgue, but without the body because we weren't allowed to mention him". And she knew about the photos of Jonathon, the ones I found in the old album. She said Mum used to look at them whenever Dad wasn't around and then she'd cry and hide them again afterwards. There's nothing right about any of that.

'I tell myself it was a lifetime ago, I wasn't much more than a child myself, and most of it was out of my control. None of it can be undone. That might have been true for teenage Hamish, but I grew up, became a man and I made so many choices that I see clearly now for what they were: self-serving and avoidant, just like my father.'

'Oh, Hamish,' I whispered. There were no words. I went to him and slid my arms around his waist, resting my head in the curve where neck meets shoulder. I felt him sigh and with it went any hesitancy he'd been hanging onto. He clung to me like a man drowning.

When it came time for us to step apart, I immediately felt bereft and then awkward, acutely aware of what a novice I was with intimacy such as this. And here I was in my seventh decade. What had I done with my life?

Hamish's half-smile suggested he had an inkling of how I might feel. Was it because he felt the same?

He reached for my hands and gently tugged me towards him. 'Thank you,' he said and dropped a light kiss onto my forehead. Then, without a moment's notice, he kissed me fully on the lips; a proper kiss, deep and with feeling and impossible to resist. I was sixteen again, finally kissing the boy I'd been crushing on for months.

This time when we parted there was an entirely different vibe between us. No less awkward but infused with another type of tension.

'And don't you dare imagine that came of gratitude,' he said. 'It's been coming for a while, don't you think?'

'I have wondered, even hoped on occasion, but had never been entirely certain, not about any of it.' I propped my backside on the corner of the table. 'But that could have been self-delusion, Hamish, because it's been decades since I've had a relationship that went any further than a couple a dates. And while I'm baring my soul here, there doesn't seem to be the same urgency as there was when I was younger. A desire to savour rather than gulp.'

'That's the funny thing about getting older: the less time I have, the more likely I am to bide it. But tell me, do you have at least a flicker of urgency?'

I laughed and reached up to wipe lipstick from his mouth with my fingertips. 'That colour doesn't suit you and, yes, I'd say there's definitely a flicker of urgency there.'

'Pleased to hear it,' he said. 'And speaking of appetites, I'll get the barbecue fired up.'

'Shall I do enough so you have leftovers for tomorrow? There looked to be plenty of steak.'

'Ruth,' he said, 'you certainly do know the way to a man's heart.'

★ ★ ★

The glow from my evening with Hamish carried me through the long and intermittently boring trip to Adelaide the following morning. Especially the part where he came out to see me off. I hadn't had a send-off like that for decades. Even now the memory sent a tingle right through me. His parting words had been, 'Imagine how good we'll get at this, Ruth, the more we practise.' I was looking forward to that, but not without a whisper of trepidation. Bodies change as they age. A targeted discussion with my GP might be a timely idea.

So far, the car had started perfectly every time and my confidence was slowly trickling back. At Port Wakefield, I stopped to stretch my legs and message Elliot, to remind him I was on my way. The servo coffee was disgusting, but I drank it. What I'd find when I reached my brother's place was anyone's guess; better to be caffeinated than not.

Elliot surprised me, yet again. The townhouse was spotless and if his cheerfulness proved real and not forced, I'd say he was doing way better than he had been.

'My cleaning lady has returned with a new knee and minus five kilos. Remarkably spritely and just as well, because I was about to disappear under the pile of dirty dishes and old newspapers,' he said.

And empty wine bottles, I thought but didn't say.

'You have a dishwasher, Elliot, and a recycle bin. How hard can it be?'

'I've decided I loathe housework, anything domestic, actually. That was one of the few positives about being married—Gloria did it all.'

'So you reckon it's women's work, do you? My bet is you being such a sexist was one of the main reasons Gloria left.'

'That's a bit harsh, old chook,' he said, taking a step back.

'Sorry,' I said, instantly remorseful. Although what I'd said held way more than a grain of truth. Gloria had never confided in me, but Stacey had. 'I didn't come to pick an argument, Elliot, you just pushed one of my buttons.'

'I've never imagined you having buttons,' he said, a study of uncertainty. 'You're always such an agreeable person.'

'Oh, I have buttons and opinions and everything! Plenty of them. I've even been called feisty, believe it or not. Five years behind a cafe counter agreeing with whatever customers say and not upsetting the staff has dulled my edge.' I went through to the kitchen and reached for the kettle.

He was right behind me. 'I thought we could go out for coffee … lunch perhaps? Have others wait on you for a change?'

'Yes, let's,' I said, rapidly warming to the idea. A slow lunch on a Sunday was something I'd relished in a previous life. 'Where did you have in mind?'

★ ★ ★

That night, sleep would not come. I'd slept in Elliot's spare room often enough for it not to be that. I felt tense, out of sorts, as if something untoward was about to happen. I couldn't think what. My life was moving along nicely. The business was only weeks away from being on the market and Bryan was cautiously optimistic; Elliot appeared to be managing well enough; my friendship with Hamish was heading in a direction I'd only ever considered fanciful.

And then, like a light bulb bursting, there it was, the root of my unrest: I was on the threshold of a total upheaval of life as I'd known it for so long.

47

Ruth

Elliot was up before me Monday morning. He complained of a headache. 'I had such an awful sleep,' he said. 'At my age, that's often explanation enough.' He yawned and made tea, shuffling around the kitchen like an old man, which I suppose in a way he was. After my road to Damascus moment in the early hours, I'd gone out like a light and slept for six hours.

Perched at the breakfast bar, I pulled out my phone and tried for a doctor's appointment, on the off-chance they could fit me in. The earliest non-urgent appointment was Thursday and not with my own GP. To see her, I'd have to wait three weeks. I made an appointment for then. Elliot raised his eyebrows. 'Women's business,' I said and he visibly flinched. Definitely not an enlightened male.

The day was cool and there'd been a shower of rain in the night. We took our mugs of tea through to the sitting room instead of the patio. Elliot was uncharacteristically taciturn. When I asked if his headache had eased, he said, 'I'm all right, just feel a bit fuzzy headed and tired.'

Later, I made us coffee and toast and he brightened up, reminiscing about Robert and all the things they'd done and those they'd planned together but now wouldn't get to do.

'When are you coming to stay with me?' I said when I'd packed up and was preparing to leave. It was almost one and we were standing in the kitchen. 'Hamish said you'd mentioned having a game of golf with him.'

'Has he had a hit there yet?'

'Several times. He likes it. The green fees are cheap, so he says.'

'Will he join the golf club?'

'No idea, but I'd doubt it. When he's finished with the house and he sells it, he'll be off.' Said lightly but with a sinking feeling.

'What about you, old chook, what'll you do when you don't have the cafe anymore?'

'Yet to be determined,' I said. 'Would you like it if I was closer to you, to look out for you?' Blunt, certainly, but it'd get any expectations out in the open.

He was aghast. 'Of course I won't need you to look out for me! Whatever made you think I would? That I'd even expect it? You have your own life—don't sacrifice what's left of it on me. I doubt I'd do the same for you.'

'Yes, you would. And who else have either of us got? It takes Stacey a day to get here, if the flights are available and she can get away.'

He swallowed, bright splotches of colour on each cheek. 'God knows why they had to move so far away. Just ridiculous when her mother and me are this end of the country.'

'Chris's family? They all live up there. Perhaps they wanted their kids to know both sides of the family?'

He huffed and puffed and blustered a bit more and then said, 'I do have friends, believe it or not. And if you must know, I have made preliminary enquiries about alternative accommodation. It'll be the stairs that eventually make this place unliveable, but that's a way off yet. Since Robert's death, I have updated my will, along with all the other required documentation. Copies are in the cupboard under the bookshelf. Satisfied?'

'I suppose so. Have you told all this to Stacey?'

'Not yet.' He fidgeted, obviously uncomfortable with the subject. 'And if you insist we talk about such morbid a topic, what about you? Have you made a will? The odds are on me going well before you, but then look what happened with Robert.'

'I have a will. Mum nagged at me until I made one. I'll update it when the cafe sells.' Another thing to add to the ever-increasing list of things to do. 'No-one likes discussing this stuff, Elliot, but that doesn't mean we shouldn't talk about it, so thanks for having the conversation with me.'

He grunted with what could only be described as ambivalence. He carted my overnight bag to the car and dumped it onto the back seat. 'Take care, old chook. Thanks for coming and we'll talk soon,' he said and pecked me on the cheek.

It hadn't escaped me that there'd been no mention of when he might visit me. No point pushing; he'd come when he was ready. Or not.

I climbed in, buckled up, but when I turned the key in the ignition, nothing happened. Not a thing. Nada. I swore and tried again.

Elliot frowned and yanked open the door. 'What's happening?'

'Nothing,' I said, mentally crossed my fingers and tried again, with the same outcome.

Elliot frowned. 'Didn't you say you had it fixed?'

'I thought I had. Five hundred and seventy-three dollars' worth of fixing.' The car had sat here in the driveway since I'd arrived yesterday. We'd cabbed it to lunch and in the evening I'd walked to the nearby strip of shops for bread and milk.

'I'd say take my car, but as you can see—'

Yes, I could see clearly what the problem was: his car was parked in the single garage and I was parked in the driveway behind it. 'I'll ring roadside assistance.'

'I'll put the kettle on and think of something for lunch.' He wandered inside.

I rummaged in my handbag for the phone. After the dead-battery experience with the car I'd added roadside assistance to contacts. I literally had my finger on the number when the phone rang. Hamish. Unbelievable.

'Hello,' he said and sounded as if was in a rush. 'Are you on the road yet?'

'No. Why? And hello to you.'

'I need a few things from Bunnings. Would you mind? I can phone through the order and pay for it, you'd only have to pick it up on your way through.'

'Ordinarily I'd say yes, be glad to, but guess what? My car won't start. I was about to call roadside assistance. Sound familiar?'

'Forget Bunnings. I'm down on Wednesday, I can pick the gear up then. Has Elliot got a car? Would he loan it to you?'

'Yes and yes, only it's parked in his shed and I'm parked behind him.'

'Oh, I see. Did you swear?'

'Several times and with gusto.'

His laugh was mellow, his smile easily imagined, and I felt instantly better. I wasn't in this on my own, not if I didn't want to be. And not only for the broken-down car, but for life in general. All a bit daunting, really.

'Keep me posted.'

★ ★ ★

The mechanic was diligent but he could not coax the car to life. 'Could be the electrics ... the computer maybe ...' He shrugged, scratching his head with greasy fingers. I was astonished that a car as old as mine had a computer. 'I can organise for the vehicle to be towed, just need an address.'

'My usual mechanic is over two hundred kilometres away,' I said.

He glanced down at the tablet in his hand. 'Oh, yeah, you're from the country.' Said as if it were a disease. He squinted at the screen. 'Know any mechanics in metro?'

'Let me ask my brother. Give me a sec.' I raced inside and yelled, 'Elliot! Where do you get your car serviced?'

He came through from the sitting room, rubbing his eyes. 'At the Audi dealership where I bought it,' he said. 'Where do you think?'

'Argh! Why is nothing simple?' Then I had a thought: Hamish used to live in Adelaide. He'd been a diesel mechanic. I whipped out my phone.

'Where does Elliot live?' Hamish said after I'd explained the situation.

'Kensington Gardens.'

'A mate of mine owns a garage at Parkside ... I'll give him a call, text you the address.'

'Just give me the number and I'll ring him,' I said. Elliot's eyes bulged at my impatient tone.

'Ruth,' Hamish said, patiently, 'this isn't me trying to *rescue* you, I know how incredibly well you manage on your own. This is me offering to *help* in what must be a frustrating situation for you. Now, do I ring Tony or not?'

I squeezed my eyes shut against an unexpected burn of tears. Why had I called him if not for his help? 'Yes, thank you, and sorry. I might never completely break the habit of needing to solve my own problems.'

He laughed that delicious laugh and my tension all but ebbed away.

'What's happening?' called the mechanic from the front door. 'I'm on the clock here. And if you want that tow today ...'

I held up my hand. 'Almost there!'

'Let me ring Tony and send through the address,' Hamish said and disconnected.

Moments later my phone pinged with a message: *Tony Gazzola, Auto Repairs,* followed by an address. I took the details out to the mechanic.

'Oh, yeah,' he said, 'I know Gazz. Good bloke.' He tapped away on the tablet and a few minutes later said, 'Tow's organised. They'll ring when they're on their way. Mightn't be for a couple of hours.' He walked to his van and was gone.

I collected my overnight bag from the car and went inside. I didn't know if I should laugh or cry. Elliot was in the sitting room, flat out in his recliner, feet up, eyes closed, with a half-eaten sandwich on the table beside him. He looked haggard. Did he often nap in the afternoons? He wasn't *that* old.

'How am I supposed to get home?' I mumbled, more to myself than anyone as the implications of being stranded in Adelaide sank in. A cafe to open tomorrow … the wholesaler's order to phone through before nine tonight and the need to be there in the morning when they delivered it.

'After they've taken your car you can borrow mine,' Elliot offered, but not as blithely as when his year-old Audi had been safely parked in by my twenty-five-year-old wagon.

'Then you won't have a car.' I dropped onto the couch and started googling car hire companies and then bus timetables. 'Hire cars cost a fortune,' I said.

Elliot murmured in agreement.

'The bus leaves the depot at five, but will only get me as far as Ardrossan.'

'Then you'll need to make a move soon. It's heading towards three.'

'I'll Uber it. You don't mind dealing when they come for the car?'

'Of course not.'

Would Hamish pick me up from Ardrossan? Or Allie? Mia had her L-plates and was always happy to drive. It would be dark though, around eight o'clock. I *hated* asking anyone but I was running out of options, not that I'd had many to begin with.

'Hamish,' I said when he picked up after the first ring. 'I'll get the bus home. Can you pick me up from Ardrossan? It's not far. Bus gets in about eight.'

'Weren't you going to borrow Elliot's car?'

'I'd rather not … he needs it.'

'Sure, I can pick you up from Ardrossan, or I can pick you up at Elliot's.'

'It's a long way for you to come and Bunnings will be closed.'

'Offer's there. You decide.'

So tempting. No tedious bus trip and I'd be home in plenty of time to phone through the wholesaler's order waiting on the kitchen table. And get a good night's sleep before an early start.

'Yes, please, that would be brilliant but only on the proviso that I pay for the fuel.'

'Ruth, let's discuss details later. See you in a couple of hours.'

'He's coming to get me,' I said to Elliot.

He tipped his head towards me, opened one eye and said, 'I thought he would. All you needed to do was accept his offer.'

48

Hamish

Word that Rosie's Cafe was for sale spread even faster than Ruth had envisaged. One morning Hamish was sitting at table three enjoying an early cooked breakfast when Audrey Franco burst in. She relayed the news to Ruth as if it wasn't her cafe that was for sale. It wasn't until Audrey started speculating about how much the asking price would be that the penny finally dropped. Without batting an eyelid, Ruth had patiently explained that if Audrey was interested in the business, she'd best discuss it with Bryan Chalmers. Audrey had blinked rapidly, opened and closed her mouth several times and then shifted her attention to the morning's muffins on the counter.

Paradoxically, the news had been good for business: according to Ruth, Rosie's had never been busier. And her car was back on the road. Hamish had taken her to Adelaide to pick it up, the colour draining from her face when Tony gave her the bill. She'd stayed to have lunch with Elliot and Hamish had moved on to an appointment of his own: another session with the psychologist.

He'd vowed that he wouldn't jump to any conclusions about the success or failure of unburdening himself to a professional until he'd had at least six sessions. Lenard had said at the beginning if it wasn't working for Hamish before then, he'd know, and he would willingly refer him to someone else. Now, after three fifty-minute sessions, Hamish could admit, cautiously, that he was making progress. There was a way to go yet and he still hadn't told Ruth what he was doing. Initially, that was because he couldn't see how it was any of her business, but as their relationship deepened, so did the feeling that he was holding something important back from her. That she'd be hurt he hadn't confided in her. After all, it was her openness and honesty after he'd shared his account of Jonathon's death that had prompted him to seek professional help, help he knew he needed but had only ever contemplated.

The days rolled into weeks. Easter came and went. Hamish spent as much time with Ruth as her busy life allowed. Operating a cafe was no mean feat and readying it for sale added to an already packed schedule.

Hamish concentrated on painting the East Terrace house's external woodwork. He needed to finish it before the first hint of winter's inclement weather. On top of that he did a few maintenance jobs at the cafe for Ruth. He helped her paint the inside walls one weekend after the cafe closed. Ruth fed them well and kept them caffeinated.

Laurie's knee had improved markedly, enough that he could continue mopping the cafe floor each afternoon, but Hamish insisted on mowing his lawn and whatever else he could do around Laurie's yard. It was on one such morning, after Hamish had finished mowing and they were sitting out back with a cuppa, that Laurie said, 'I hear Chris Lehman's not doing so well after his knee replacement. Got an infection, so I'm told. Ended up back in the hospital for a spell, on one of them drip things, with antibiotics. I saw him hobbling into the pub yesterday arvo. Don't see how he's gonna push a lawnmower any time soon.'

'Is that so,' Hamish said. 'That's a shame.'

'Ain't it. Esme's grass needs mowing again. Grows at about the same rate as mine.' Laurie reached for another biscuit to dunk in his tea.

'Funny about that,' Hamish said. 'You can tell her I'll come by tomorrow and cut it, if that suits her.'

Laurie nodded. 'The garden shed'll be unlocked. Just grab what you need.'

Hamish was totally aware of what was happening here, but found that he didn't mind at all. Cutlers Bay was growing on him. The longer he lived here, the more he liked the gentle ebb and flow of his days. He was even thinking seriously about joining the golf club. But he'd bide his time; wait and see what happened with Rosie's Cafe and Ruth before he committed himself further to the town and its community.

★ ★ ★

One Saturday evening towards the end of April, Hamish was at Ruth's place. They ate together most evenings—if he wasn't there, she was at his place. They sat at the kitchen table sharing takeaway fish and chips from Peg's. He'd have been happy to eat them out of the paper but Ruth had produced plates and cutlery, along with leftover coleslaw from the cafe. Ruth hadn't eaten much, had mostly rearranged the food on her plate. But the glass of wine he'd poured her was almost gone. He'd learned that if he was patient and if she wanted him to know, she'd eventually tell him whatever was on her mind.

'I don't think Elliot's ever going to come to Cutlers Bay for a visit,' she said, giving up on any pretence of eating and pushing away her plate. She picked up her wine and finished it off. 'Robert's death has really aged him. Taken away a lot of his confidence. I sometimes wonder if he's merely marking time, you know, until he meets his maker. He refuses to talk about any of it, so I've stopped asking.'

'But that hasn't stopped you from worrying.'

'No. Do you think I should say something to Stacey? I'd swear he's lost weight and I'm no health professional, but I think he's depressed. I'd never forgive myself if something happened and I hadn't said anything to her.'

'You've just answered your own question,' Hamish said. 'When I think back on my own situation, perhaps if someone had sat me down and told me a few home truths about the reality of my parents' circumstances, I'd like to think I would have stepped in and helped. Even if it was only with financial help. But I kept my distance, never asked questions and no-one ever volunteered information. Basically, I buried my head in the sand. I don't think Nat even realised how poorly they were coping and she visited them much more often than I did.'

'Sometimes we only see what we want to see, not what's actually there. On the other hand, your father struck me as an intensely private person. I never met your mother. There's every chance no-one knew what was really going on because they *chose* not to share or access any support services. All I've ever heard about them is that they kept to themselves.'

'That's about all I've gleaned from the few conversations I've had with the neighbours.' He stacked the empty plates and carried them to the sink. 'But back to your niece. I think you should confide your concerns to her, then it's up to her what she does with the information.'

'Leave the dishes,' Ruth said. But he'd already put the plug into the sink.

He turned on the hot water and squirted in detergent. 'You wash enough dishes in the cafe,' he said.

Ruth plucked a tea towel off the rail and he washed and she dried and put away. When they'd finished, they went through to the living room. Ruth plonked down onto the sofa.

'That was a big sigh,' Hamish said and sat down beside her.

'I feel as if I'm in this awful limbo. I just want to get on with it but my hands are tied until the business sells. And that could take months or even *years*. Can you imagine that? To think that, as well as everything else, I'll have to keep listening to bloody Audrey Franco rabbit on about things she knows nothing about. It's doing my head in and it's only been a month.' She leaned into him and he slipped his arm around her shoulders.

'What does Bryan say?'

'Nothing! He comes in every morning for his coffee and all he talks about is the weather.'

'Ask him.'

'You think I haven't?' She levered herself away, far enough to be able to glare at him. 'He says he'll tell me when he has something solid, that he won't give me false hope.'

'That sounds fair enough.'

She gave a frustrated groan and fell back against him. He pulled her close and kissed the top of her head. They sat that way until he felt the tension go out of her and she snuggled closer into him. He liked the way it felt; the feel of her beside him, her warmth, her strength. He liked that he'd been able to offer her something, even if it was only to listen.

'I need to share something with you,' he said. 'I wasn't going to tell you just yet, for no reason other than you have enough of your own stuff happening, or not happening, however you want to look at it.'

'Go on,' she prompted when he paused a beat too long.

'You know those appointments I've been having in Adelaide?'

'Uh-huh.'

'I've been seeing a psychologist.'

She shuffled around until she was facing him. 'That's very courageous of you. Are you okay with how it's going?'

'I think so. Someone I met on a job referred me to this bloke. It took me five years to work up enough guts to ring him. The irony of it all was Lenard could only see me because one of his other clients died suddenly. Took his own life.'

Ruth gasped. 'And he told you that? And you're still seeing him? Not a very good advert for what he does.'

'That's what I thought and he guessed that's what I'd think because he said it was an occupational hazard that made him try even harder with all his other clients.'

'I get it, like a cardiologist not being surprised when one of his patients dies of a heart attack. But you're okay, aren't you? Not likely to become an occupational hazard?' she said.

'Yes, I'm very okay. My life is good and getting better by the day. Maybe it's because of that I've been able to drum up the courage required to go back and rake over Jonathon's death and the impact it had on me and especially my relationship with Dad. It's a start.'

'More than that,' Ruth said. 'You are a good man, Hamish Adams, the real thing.'

He wrapped his arms around her, pulled her close. Her phone screeched impatiently from the bench in the kitchen. 'Don't answer it,' he whispered against her lips, but then drew back. 'Don't listen to me. It might be important.'

She disentangled herself and stood, her expression serious. 'You're here and no-one else rings on a Saturday night, not unless there's a problem.'

Hamish rested back, closed his eyes and listened to the murmur of Ruth's voice in the kitchen.

When she came back she had her phone in her hand and looked thunderstruck. 'That was Bryan,' she said. 'He has someone who wants to look through the cafe and the flat and everything. He said they're genuine, definitely not a tyre kicker. They're not local but they've been staying in Cutlers Bay and have eaten at Rosie's several times and now want to have a closer look. I wonder who it is? It's school holidays and there's always people around who I don't recognise. I'm to make myself scarce at ten on Monday morning.' She perched on the sofa beside Hamish, clutching her phone. 'I've imagined this happening for so long and now it has I can hardly believe it is.'

'Sometimes the best offer is the first one you get. What'll you do if this is it and everything sells?' he said, his heart thudding while he waited for her answer.

'I don't know,' she said. 'I wasn't expecting it to happen so soon.' She turned to face him and her voice trembled when she said, 'Tell me what you think I should do.'

49

Ruth

Before Hamish had a chance to open his mouth to answer my question, the phone rang again. Thinking it'd be Bryan, that he'd forgotten to relay an important detail, I didn't so much as glance at the caller ID before answering.

Silly me, because it wasn't Bryan, it was Lana.

'Oh, no,' I said when I recognised her voice. 'What's he been up to now?'

'He's in hospital, Ruth, having tests and a scan. They think he might have had a stroke.'

'Oh my goodness,' I said, pulse roaring in my ears. 'What happened?'

'Apparently, he was talking to his neighbour when he began acting peculiar, slurring his words, taking gibberish, and she had the wherewithal to dial triple zero for an ambulance.'

'Is he conscious? Should I come now?' The roaring in my ears was enough to almost deafen me. Hamish held my gaze, his frown deepening.

'Would you? Come now?' She sounded at the end of her tether.

'Of course I'll come now. Which hospital?'

'Same as Robert. I'm sorry,' she said and her distress made complete sense. 'I won't leave until you arrive, Ruth. He shouldn't be here on his own, although I haven't been allowed in to see him yet.'

'Hold tight, I'll be there as soon as I can.'

The phone went dead. I imagined Lana pacing the polished corridors in her high heels, waiting for news, any news, good or bad.

'They think Elliot's had a stroke,' I said to Hamish. 'I must go, now.'

'I'll take you,' he said, already on his feet. 'Put together whatever you'll need for an overnight stay.'

'My car's good to go, I have a full tank of petrol. Aren't you playing golf tomorrow?'

'Not tomorrow and your car might be good to go, but you're tired, you've had two glasses of wine, Elliot is your brother and this has come as a shock.'

I couldn't argue with him—I didn't have the energy or the desire. My hands were shaking and I felt like I could throw up any moment. What if Elliot died? Surely life would not be so cruel as to take him so soon after Robert? There'd only be me left.

'I must ring Stacey,' I said, searching for the phone I was holding in my hand.

'Do it in the car on the way. Now, collect what you need and we'll go.'

'What will I need?' I stood there as if I were frozen, unable to move. What should I pack for? Another funeral? I'd had my funeral dress dry-cleaned and it was ready to go again.

Hamish gripped my arms, looked me in the eye and said, 'Focus, Ruth. Where's your overnight bag?'

We were on our way twenty minutes later after a quick stop at Hamish's place to collect what he'd need. Stacey didn't answer so I left a voice message but hadn't heard back. At Port Wakefield, Hamish bought coffee and I called Lana.

'How is he?'

'Stable. They're not saying much to me. Stacey's on her way.'

'Did they ring her first?'

'No, they rang me. Elliot's electronic health record has Robert as his next of kin. When Robert was alive we shared the same mobile phone.'

'I'm sorry it had to be you,' I said. 'Thanks for getting in touch with Stacey. How was she?'

'Shocked. She'd talked to her dad only last night. Said they'd had a good old chinwag. She thought he'd sounded more like his old self.'

I didn't mention to Lana how worried I'd been.

'He's only a decade older than me,' I said to Hamish. We hadn't talked much the whole trip but I was so grateful I wasn't on my own. We passed the Gepps Cross Hotel; not much further to go. 'If it is a stroke, I wonder how bad it is? Will he recover enough to manage on his own?'

'Don't get ahead of yourself, Ruth. Not until you have more information.'

He was right but it was impossible not to get ahead of myself. If this left Elliot unable to look after himself, who would care for him? Stacey had her own family thousands of kilometres away. That left me. Or a care facility.

Hamish reached for my hands, limp in my lap, and gave them a squeeze.

When we arrived at the hospital he pulled into the drop-off bay at the well-lit entrance. 'I'll find a park and come in,' he said.

'Why don't you wait in the car? The waiting room chairs are uncomfortable and the vending machine coffee is awful.'

'You might need someone to lean on, Ruth, and I'm offering to be that person.'

Tears welled in my eyes. 'I would appreciate that. I know some people loathe hospitals … I can't say I like them much myself and I didn't want to presume. He's in the stroke unit. Message me if you can't find it.'

I shivered when I climbed out of the ute's cosy cab. It was cool, already after eleven, and several ambulances were lined up outside of accident and emergency. Lana had given me instructions on where to find the stroke unit. When she spotted me walking towards her in the corridor, her relief was palpable. Her eyes were shadowed, her hair messy and she wore sweats and sneakers. It's the first time I'd ever seen her without makeup and high heels.

'They let me go in briefly. He's awake and doing all right,' she said. 'Very pale and tired. The doctor wants you to let the nursing staff know you're here and she'll come and talk to you. Elliot knows you're on your way. Stacey's plane is somewhere between here and Cairns.' The facts were delivered in a monotone.

We hugged stiffly, I thanked her and she left, powering off down the corridor as if something was after her. She couldn't wait to get out of the place and I fully understood. The last time I'd been here was when my other brother had died. Before that, Mum. If given a choice, I would have stayed in the car.

★ ★ ★

Two hours later, Hamish and I walked out into the night. He'd waited without comment in the uncomfortable chairs, drunk the awful coffee and held me when I'd stumbled. 'Where to?' he said, studying me in the bright artificial light of the entrance way.

'Elliot's place. He said for us to stay there. I know where the spare key is.'

We didn't talk much on the way, except for me giving a few directions. I felt pummelled, as if I'd done several rounds in a boxing ring.

It wasn't until we were sitting down with hot drinks that Hamish asked, 'How was he?'

'He's had a mild stroke. The doctor said there's evidence of other small strokes in the past. They'll keep him in a day or two for more tests and then he can come home, under the care of his GP. Stacey's on her way or I'd have had to shut the cafe because he's not meant to be on his own. Hopefully she can stay a few days.'

'If she can't, I'll stay with him,' Hamish said. 'So you can be where you need to be the most right now.'

I gaped at him. My tired brain wouldn't process anything more.

He chuckled. 'Day at a time, Ruth, that's the most any of us can hope for.'

Sharing the queen-sized bed in the spare room seemed the most natural thing for us to do. We'd never shared a bed before but I was too exhausted to feel nervous. After hot showers, we crawled between the cool sheets. Hamish held me and I slept.

★ ★ ★

By the end of the week, Stacey had flown home again. Elliot was ensconced in a private rehabilitation facility for a month (Why not? He could afford it.) and I'd had a firm offer for the business, including the building and the flat. Bryan was confident the business would sell, but not as assured the building and the flat would go with it. 'The buyer's eager, but I don't think her bank will come at it with the same enthusiasm,' he said.

I signed wherever he instructed me to, told myself over and over that I was doing the right thing and began trawling realestate.com.au. It was so depressing. Units, townhouses, apartments—anything in reasonable proximity to Elliot were all over and above what I'd be able to afford. And what bank would lend money to a sixty-two-year-old woman without a job?

After the contracts were signed, I had no choice other than to tell the staff. Reactions were mixed. Mia was miserable; Suzie couldn't have cared less and Erin accepted that she was the last on and likely to be the first off. Gayle was the most apprehensive: when my idea of swapping Erin's shifts had flopped, she had taken on the extra hours because her partner's shifts had been cut. Lorna, who'd taken on Gayle's lunchtime shift alternate Thursday and Fridays, had merely raised her eyebrows at the news. Out of everyone, Liz was the only one who came across as smug. When I asked what it was she knew that I didn't, she tapped the side of her nose with a forefinger and said, 'I reckon I've already worked out who my new boss is.'

'Really?' I said, but probed no further. By this time, I knew the prospective buyer's name and had my own suspicions about who she was. A process of elimination really. Cutlers Bay wasn't exactly a metropolis and not every resident patronised the cafe, so when a new face popped up again and again …

Bryan said the buyer had been around since before Christmas caring for her elderly mother, who'd since gone into care. She liked the town and wanted to stay to be near her mum, but she needed a job. She'd had experience working in cafes. 'A bit different from owning one,' was all I said.

With the contract signed, I found myself in a different kind of limbo: did I start packing up the flat or not? Look for somewhere temporary to store my things? That I could be without an income and a home in the not-so-distant future was a constant source of consternation. Every time I worked my way through the situation I'd end up at exactly the same spot: there was never going to be an easier way to go about this.

One evening after I'd closed the cafe, I was on the phone off-loading to Elliot. He had a week left in rehab before discharge. The occupational therapist was satisfied. Elliot was bored with the food and the view from his room, but I could tell he was apprehensive about going home. On his own, twenty-four-seven.

'Come and stay with me,' he said. 'Until you find somewhere of your own. You can put all your gear into storage.'

'If the flat's sold, I might have to do that,' I said, unable to inject enthusiasm into my reply.

'Don't worry, old chook, it'll be fun.'

I wasn't as convinced. I had this awful vision of us pottering around his townhouse like a couple of old farts. Beyond depressing.

We said our goodbyes not long after that and I kicked off my sneakers and lifted my feet onto the sofa. It was almost dark. My stomach rumbled but I couldn't muster the energy to scrounge for food. Imagine a life living with my older brother? That's what a dried-up old spinster would do.

The thought made me shudder. I pushed it aside and dozed.

The slam of a car door woke me. Then the rap of knuckles on the sliding door. I wondered what time it was.

The door rumbled along its track and the kitchen light came on. 'Ruth?'

Hamish. I blinked into the glare, stood up yawning and walked through to the kitchen. 'I was talking to Elliot. Must have dropped off.' I felt fragile, as if I might shatter. 'How was golf?'

'Excellent. I've joined the golf club.'

'You have?'

'Yep.' He went to the fridge, grabbed a beer. 'And I was talking to a couple of the blokes afterwards, that's why I'm so late. I ran the idea past them.'

'What idea?' Had I missed something? Something major?

'Starting a home gardening and handyman business.'

I stared at him, mouth open. Then I burst into tears. Eyes squeezed shut, shoulders shaking, I hugged myself tightly as I blubbered like a child.

'What's happened, Ruth? Is Elliot all right?'

'I want my mum,' I wailed among the tears and the snot. Mum would know what I should do. She'd always known. I just hadn't always listened. I would listen now, if only she were still here. Hamish came close. Familiar, but not.

He didn't touch me, rather proffered a handful of tissues.

I took them, mopped at the mess on my face and hiccoughed loudly. 'Sorry,' I whispered, mortified by my outburst.

'Here,' he said and pressed a glass of water into my hand. 'Drink it.'

I meekly did as I was told. He pulled out a kitchen chair and I sat but couldn't quite work up the courage to look at him. The scrape of another chair on the vinyl floor; the tired complaint of the table as he sat down and rested his forearms on its surface.

'Now, are you going to tell me what's going on?' he said, his voice gentle, coaxing.

I sniffled, flicked my gaze to his and then away again. 'I don't know where to start,' I said.

'At the beginning?'

My lips twitched, remembering a time not so long ago when I'd said the same to him. 'You surprised me, that's all. On top of everything else, I suppose I'm feeling a bit swamped by it all. Here I am on the verge of having to leave Cutlers Bay and here you are joining the golf club and starting a business.'

'Who said you have to leave? There'll be life after Rosie's, Ruth. When you step out from behind that counter permanently you'll see the town and the community through a different lens, I guarantee it. The longer I stay, the more at home I feel. It's as if I'm becoming who I'm meant to be now, not just the bloke who used to be a diesel mechanic, or the son of that poor bastard who topped himself in his own car. You have so much to offer this town and community, and if you stay here I know it won't take you long to work exactly what that might be.'

'What about Elliot? He's anxious about going home, being on his own. He offered for me to come and stay with him, if the flat's sold, until I find a place of my own.'

Hamish eased back in the chair, his expression impossible to interpret. 'Is that what you want?'

'No, the very idea horrifies me. It's what I'd been thinking about before I dozed off. That I have a certain … obligation where he's concerned.'

'Personally, my belief is that he doesn't expect anything of you or from you.'

'Easy to say that, but hard to sit on my hands and not do anything when he's struggling.'

'But you are doing plenty already. You visit him as often as you can, you've offered to have him stay here whenever he wants. You've stacked his freezer with meals so he doesn't have to bother when he gets home. Time for you to concentrate on yourself for a bit, Ruth, don't you think?'

I sniffed, blinking away more ready tears. 'What about us?'

'As far as I'm concerned there is no *what about*. There is only an *us*. You and me, together. Or have I got that wrong?'

I shook my head, too overwhelmed to speak.

He stood, came around the table and pulled me to my feet. Linking his fingers with mine, he said, 'Ruth, if you decide your place is with your brother, that's your decision and I'll support it.'

'But it wouldn't be much of a life, would it? Let's face it, I'd end up being nothing more than his live-in housekeeper. And I've been away from Adelaide for a long time … It's hard to make new friends or breathe new life into old friendships. When I came back from overseas the last time, I caught up with one of my oldest and dearest friends. We'd been at primary school together and I thought we'd just pick up where we'd left off. Not so for her. She said, "Why would I bother, Ruth? You'll only up and leave again." She was right. I moved here and we haven't connected since.'

'Cutlers Bay is not so far away that we couldn't spend as much time together as we wanted to. But just so there's no misunderstanding, Ruth, that would not be my first preference. I want to be with you every day.' He tugged on my hands, pulled me towards him.

I slipped my arms around his middle. 'That would be my first preference too, and I think Selina might have been right: I have made a lot of friends here. And you know what? You might be considering starting your own business, well, I might just have a few ideas of my own.'

'Yeah? Like what?'

'A community wardrobe.'

'A what?'

'Remember what I told you about Angie, Zach's wife? What she said to me once, as a throwaway line when a friend of hers borrowed some of my clothes? Well, I've thought about it a lot since and I reckon I could make something like that work.'

'Go on. But first, if you don't mind, have you eaten? Because I'm ravenous.'

Right on cue, my stomach grumbled again. 'There are leftovers from the cafe.' I'd shoved them into the fridge before I'd called Elliot. It took ten minutes for me to set out a simple meal for us. While we ate, I outlined my idea to Hamish.

'It would work something like this: I would invite local women of all shapes and sizes to be a part of it. Every woman has clothes in her wardrobe that she's never worn, or worn only once or twice but they're too good to chuck. They'd choose what clothes they'd be willing to loan to others. I'd list it all online, maybe with photos, and then when someone came to me and said, I've been invited to a wedding and I've got nothing wear, I'd find something in the community wardrobe for them to wear based on their size, what'd suit them and so on. They wouldn't be out of pocket and I guarantee they'd feel like a million dollars when I'd finished with them. I can sew. I can do repairs, alterations, that sort of thing. What do you think?'

'Where would all these clothes be kept?'

'With the person who owns them. In the register I'd document that Mrs So-and-So is a size eighteen and has a pink-and-grey mother-of-the-bride outfit she'll never wear again but doesn't want to part with and would be happy to loan to someone in need.'

'You have given it some thought. But what about men? Women aren't the only ones who, on occasion, have nothing to wear. And you'd need some rules, wouldn't you?'

'Sure, about damage and dry-cleaning and the risks associated with loaning out your clothes. Simple. No reason it couldn't work for men or anyone. Tons of perfectly good clothes end up in landfill and yet we never have anything to wear.'

He pinched a fold of his faded cotton shirt. 'Most of my clothes end up in the ragbag. That's about all they're good for by the time I'm done with them.'

After we'd finished eating, Hamish rested his elbows on the table and said, 'So how do you feel now? Headache?'

'Much better, thanks. No headache. I still feel a bit fragile but I've had a lot to take in during the past few months. And it's not over yet.'

'We'll get there, you'll see. Day at a time, Ruth.' He stacked our plates in what was becoming a familiar ritual. 'Dishes first and then a movie. What do you say? It's Friday night and tomorrow's not a really early start.'

So that's what we did. And he stayed, all night. The first of many— or so I hoped.

Epilogue

Clothes were strewn everywhere: the bed, the floor, hanging on door handles and on the backs of chairs. I was finally packing, not to move house but because I was going on a holiday. Yes, I was going on a holiday! For a month. Two weeks in Cairns with Stacey and co, followed by a fortnight at a Port Douglas resort and spa with Hamish. I was as excited as a six-year-old in the lead-up to Christmas. So was he.

After the holiday I'd return to the flat, but only until Patricia—the owner/operator of Patricia's Teahouse, formerly Rosie's Cafe—sold her city unit and the sale of the shop and flat went through. As per Bryan's prediction, the bank hadn't been enthusiastic about lending Patricia the money to buy the business *and* the buildings outright. Initially, she'd been reluctant to sell her unit in Adelaide and that had dragged things out interminably, especially my patience. For a while there, I'd thought I was going to be stuck with the shop and the flat for the foreseeable future. But it was all resolved now and her unit was on the market.

Hamish had asked me to move into East Terrace with him when the flat was no longer mine. There was no pressure, but I liked the idea of Allie and Mia being neighbours. And Hamish and I spent most of our free time together already.

Elliot was doing fine on his own. He had cleaned up his act. The stroke had given him a scare and he'd realised he wasn't ready to follow Robert just yet. He was taking his medications and had joined a walking group. So had I. Imagine that!

Rosie's Cafe had closed mid-August, with great fanfare and a few tears, and Patricia's Teahouse had opened on the first day of spring. Yesterday. Tomorrow, I'd fly off to sunny Queensland for a month. Patricia had kept on all the staff except Liz, and Lorna had resigned. I'd heard on the grapevine, from Mia actually, that Erin had agreed to extend her hours to cover the lunch shifts on Thursdays and Fridays. Mia thought Patricia might be an okay boss, but not as awesome as me. That girl would go far.

Much quicker than I'd ever imagined, Rosie's Cafe became a thing of the past. If Patricia had kept the name it might have lingered longer, but the moment the new signage went up, I moved on. And I hadn't had time to miss the routine because I had too many other things to do. Ruth from Rosie's Cafe was no more!

I'd never regret my time running Rosie's Cafe but I was thrilled to be rediscovering who I was and who I might become. I had friends and loved ones, I was passionate about many things, full of opinions that, from now on, I wouldn't be afraid to voice. I was delighted to be embarking on a future filled with countless possibilities. What else could any woman ask for?

Acknowledgements

Thank you again to the team at HQ: Suzanne O'Sullivan, Laurie Ormond, Annabel Blay and Sarana Behan. A special thanks to Louisa Maggio for another beautiful cover. And to all the folk at HarperCollins who've assisted me along the way: I am extremely grateful for your ongoing support. And to Kylie Mason, freelance editor, it is always a pleasure to work with you.

To Julie Paech, cafe owner/operator extraordinaire: my sincere appreciation. This story would not have been possible without the amazing insider knowledge you so generously shared. Also to Kath Owen, friend and former successful cafe owner/operator: thanks so much for answering my questions! Thanks to all the other helpful people along the way who've listened to my ideas, answered questions and pointed me in the right direction whenever I've veered off track, or simply haven't known. I am forever in your debt.

Thank you to my husband Ken, sister Sandra, and special friends Pat and Sue. Your love, support and encouragement has been tireless.

To you dear reader, thank you so much, and next time you pull up a chair in your favourite cafe, spare a thought for the effort that goes into preparing the coffee and cake you're there to enjoy.

talk about it

Let's talk about books.

Join the conversation:

f @harlequinaustralia

♪ @hqanz

◉ @harlequinaus

harpercollins.com.au/hq

If you love reading and want to know about our
authors and titles, then let's talk about it.